# SANITY & TALLULAH
## FIELD TRIP

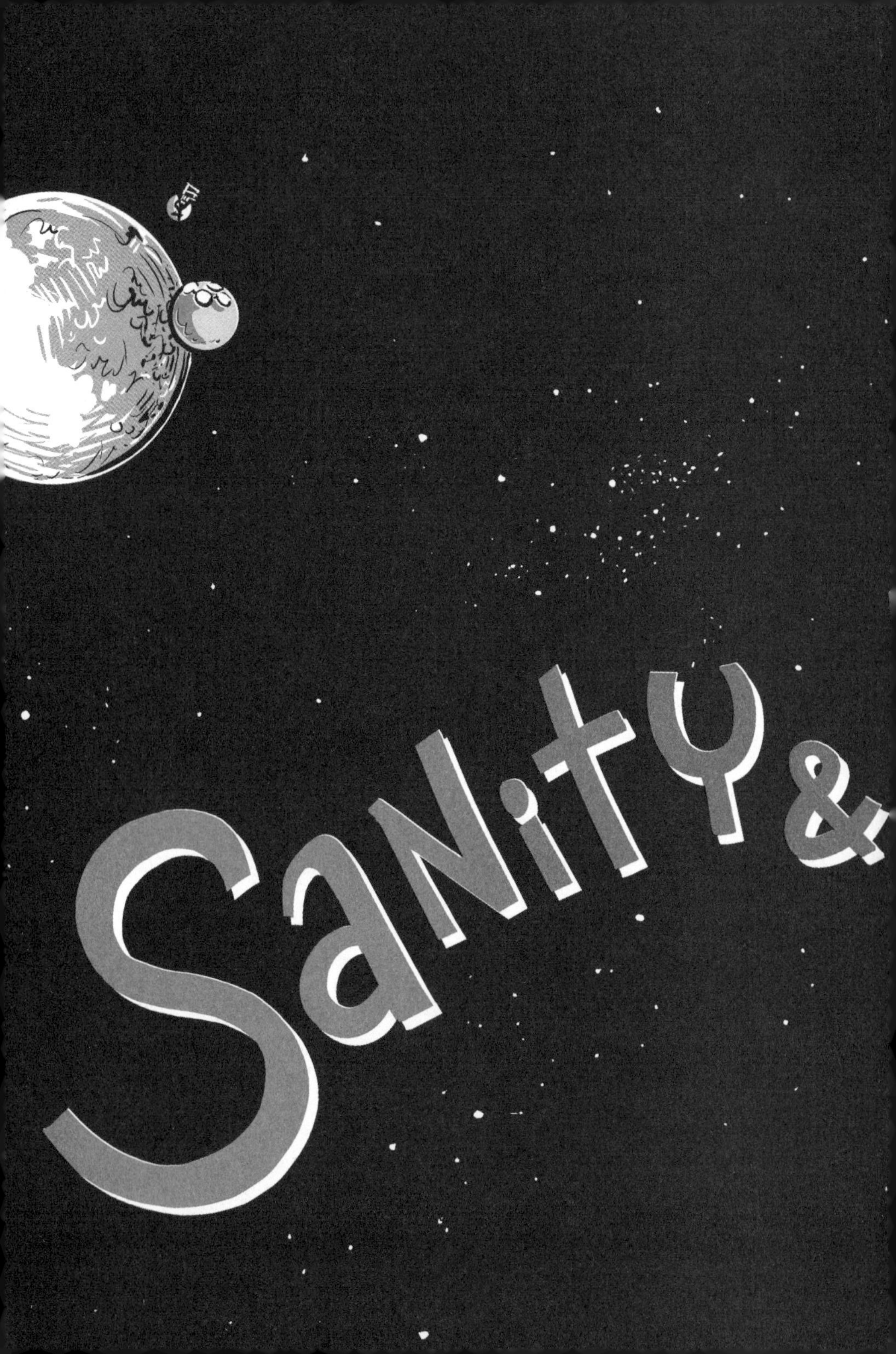
Sanity &

# TALLULAH
## FIELD TRIP

MOLLY BROOKS

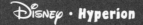

LOS ANGELES    NEW YORK

First Edition, October 2019

10 9 8 7 6 5 4 3 2 1

FAC-020093-19249

Printed in the United States of America


This book is set in 9-pt Gargle/Fontspring
Designed by Phil Buchanan


Library of Congress Cataloging-in-Publication Data

Names: Brooks, Molly (Molly Grayson), author, illustrator.
Title: Field trip / Molly Brooks.
Description: First edition. • Los Angeles ; New York : Disney-Hyperion, 2019 •
    Series: Sanity & Tallulah ; [2] • Summary: When Sanity and Tallulah are
    separated from their classmates during a disastrous field trip to a mining
    planet, they must rely on their creativity and problem-solving skills to
    save the day.
Identifiers: LCCN 2018057040 • ISBN 9781368009782 (hardcover) •
    ISBN 1368009786 (hardcover) • ISBN 9781368023771 (pbk.) • ISBN 1368023770 (pbk.)
Subjects: LCSH: Graphic novels. • CYAC: Graphic novels. • School field
    trips—Fiction. • Planets—Fiction. • Science fiction.
Classification: LCC PZ7.7.B765 Fie 2019 • DDC 741.5/973—dc23
LC record available at https://lccn.loc.gov/2018057040


Reinforced binding

Visit www.DisneyBooks.com

SUSTAINABLE FORESTRY INITIATIVE   Certified Sourcing
www.sfiprogram.org
SFI-00993
Logo Applies to Text Stock Only

for my brother, Eric.
I feel so lucky to be your friend. <3

# SANITY & TALLULAH
## FIELD TRIP

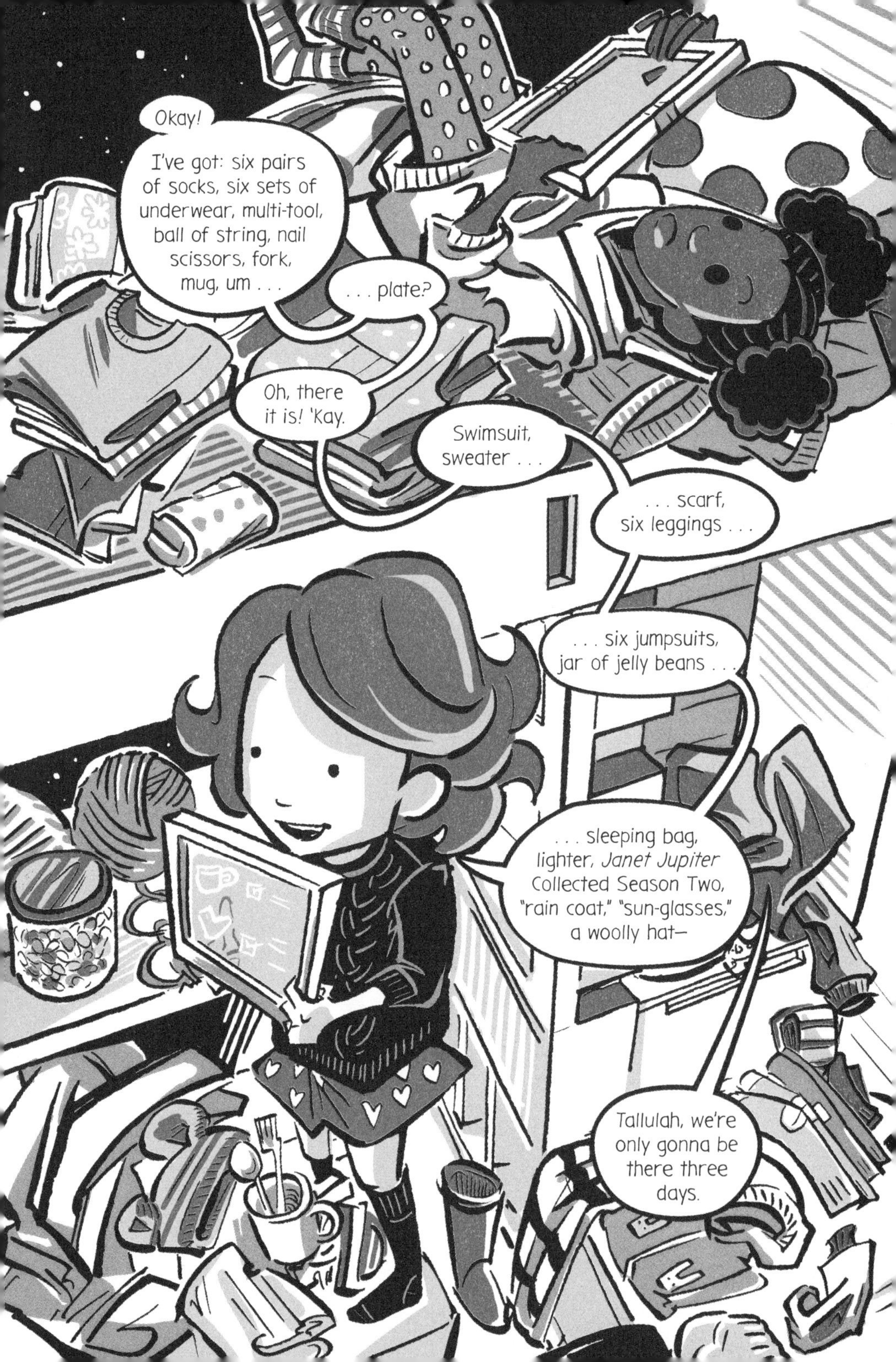
Okay!
I've got: six pairs of socks, six sets of underwear, multi-tool, ball of string, nail scissors, fork, mug, um . . .
. . . plate?
Oh, there it is! 'Kay.
Swimsuit, sweater . . .
. . . scarf, six leggings . . .
. . . six jumpsuits, jar of jelly beans . . .
. . . sleeping bag, lighter, *Janet Jupiter* Collected Season Two, "rain coat," "sun-glasses," a woolly hat—
Tallulah, we're only gonna be there three days.

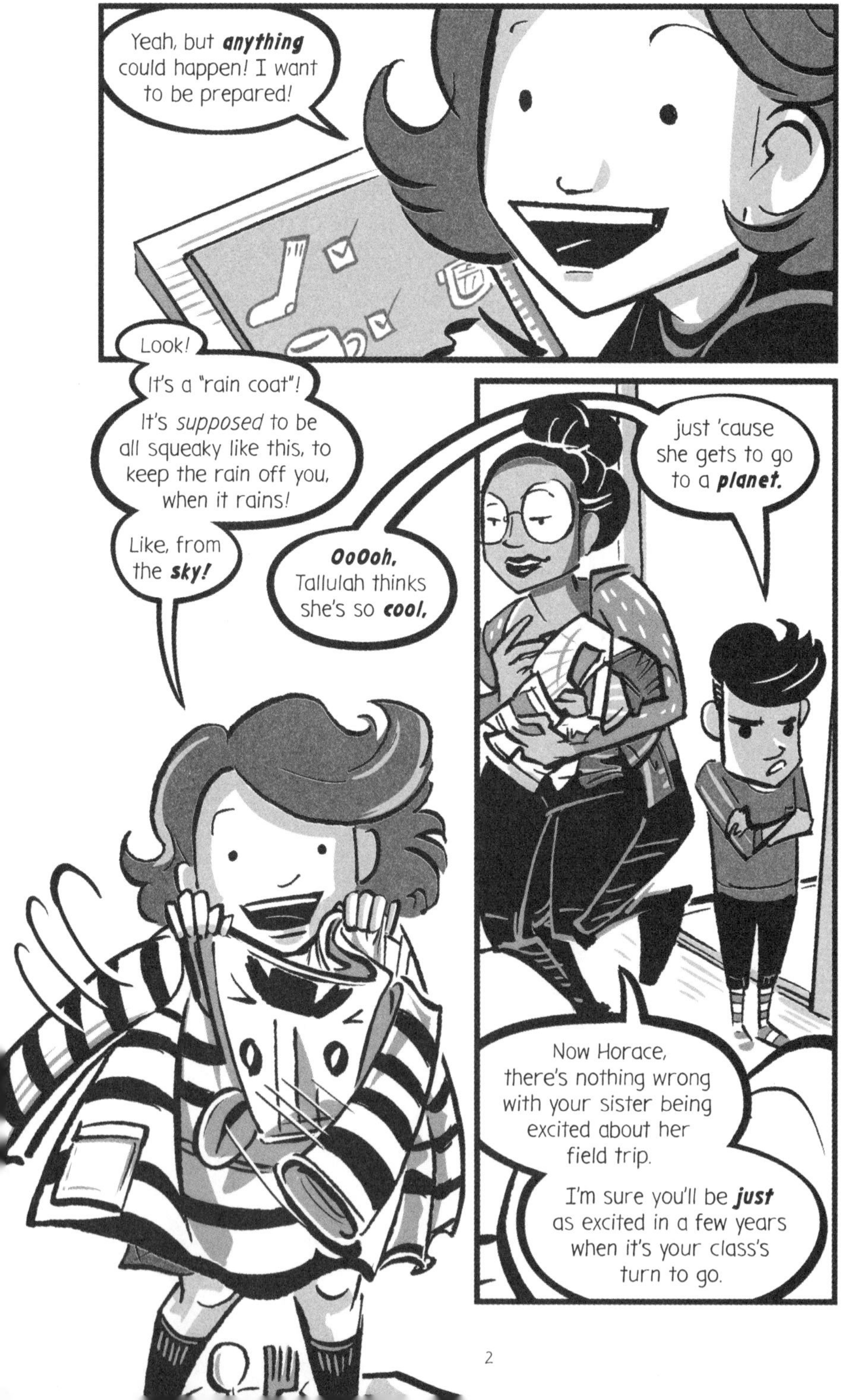

Yeah, but **anything** could happen! I want to be prepared!
Look!
It's a "rain coat"!
It's *supposed* to be all squeaky like this, to keep the rain off you, when it rains!
Like, from the **sky!**
**OoOoh,** Tallulah thinks she's so **cool,**
just 'cause she gets to go to a **planet.**
Now Horace, there's nothing wrong with your sister being excited about her field trip.
I'm sure you'll be **just** as excited in a few years when it's your class's turn to go.

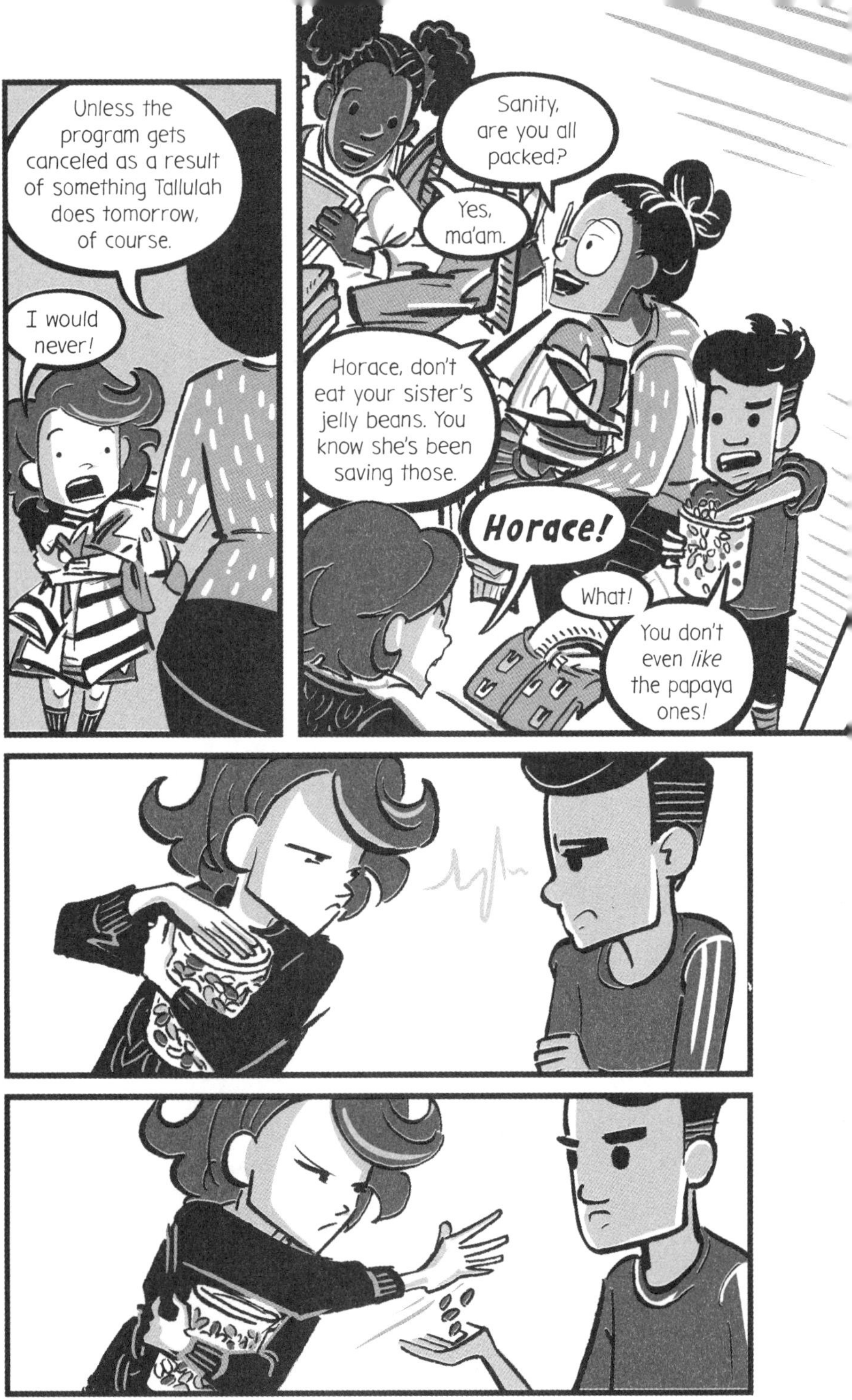
Unless the program gets canceled as a result of something Tallulah does tomorrow, of course.
I would never!
Sanity, are you all packed?
Yes, ma'am.
Horace, don't eat your sister's jelly beans. You know she's been saving those.
Horace!
What!
You don't even *like* the papaya ones!

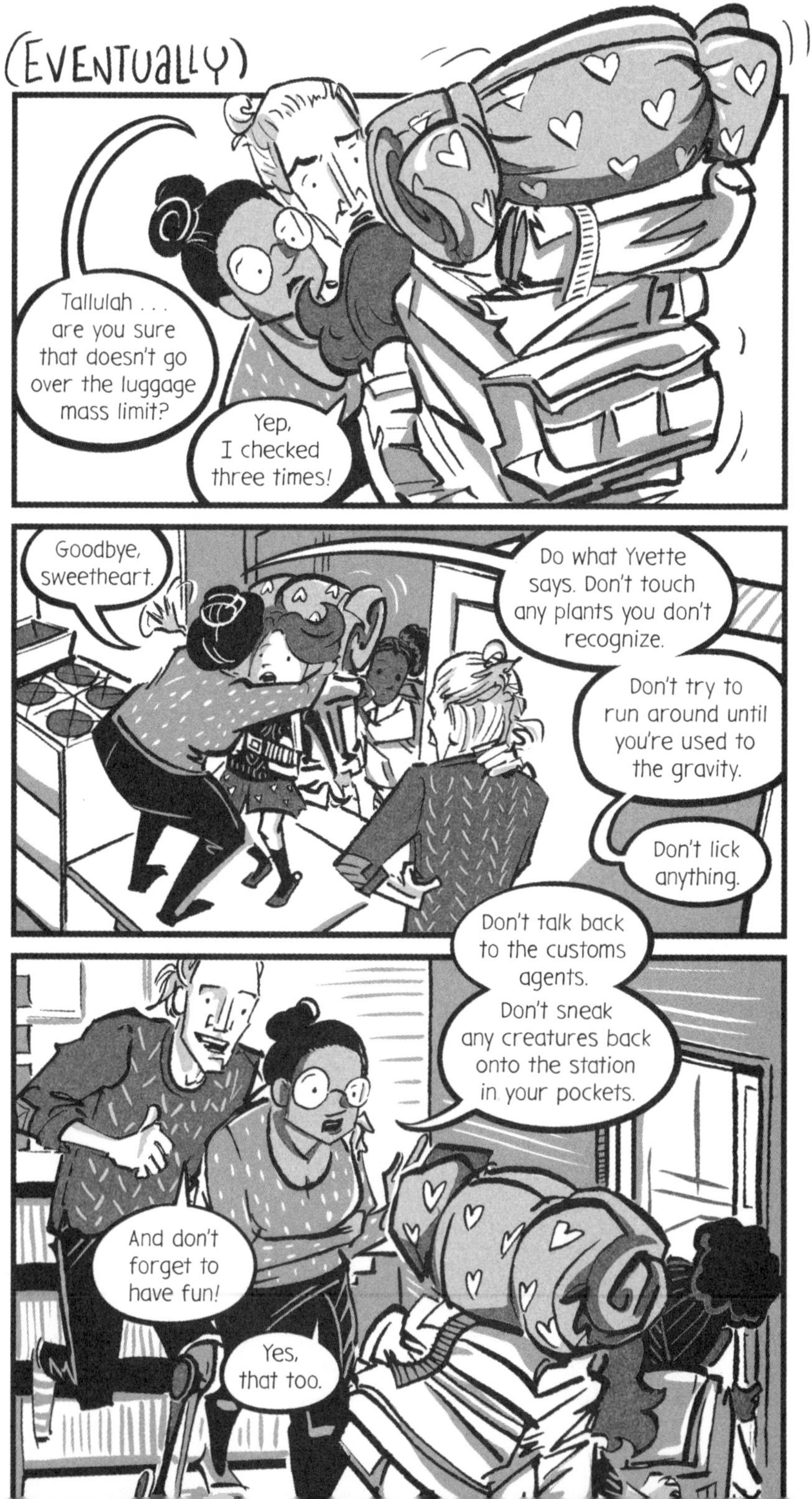
(EVENTUALLY)
Tallulah . . . are you sure that doesn't go over the luggage mass limit?
Yep, I checked three times!
Goodbye, sweetheart.
Do what Yvette says. Don't touch any plants you don't recognize.
Don't try to run around until you're used to the gravity.
Don't lick anything.
Don't talk back to the customs agents.
Don't sneak any creatures back onto the station in your pockets.
And don't forget to have fun!
Yes, that too.

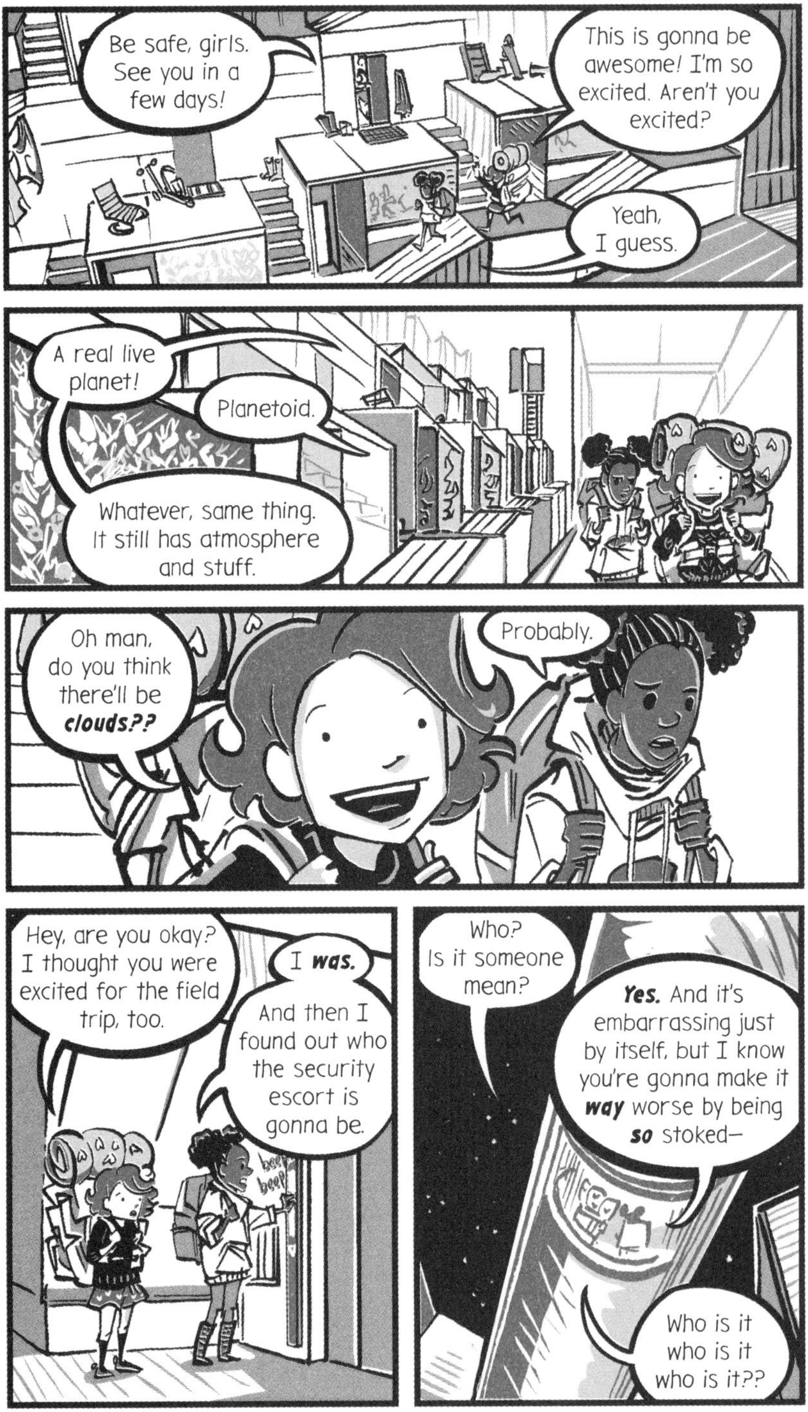
Be safe, girls. See you in a few days!
This is gonna be awesome! I'm so excited. Aren't you excited?
Yeah, I guess.
A real live planet!
Planetoid.
Whatever, same thing. It still has atmosphere and stuff.
Oh man, do you think there'll be **clouds??**
Probably.
Hey, are you okay? I thought you were excited for the field trip, too.
I **was.**
And then I found out who the security escort is gonna be.
beep beep
Who? Is it someone mean?
**Yes.** And it's embarrassing just by itself, but I know you're gonna make it **way** worse by being **so** stoked—
Who is it who is it who is it??

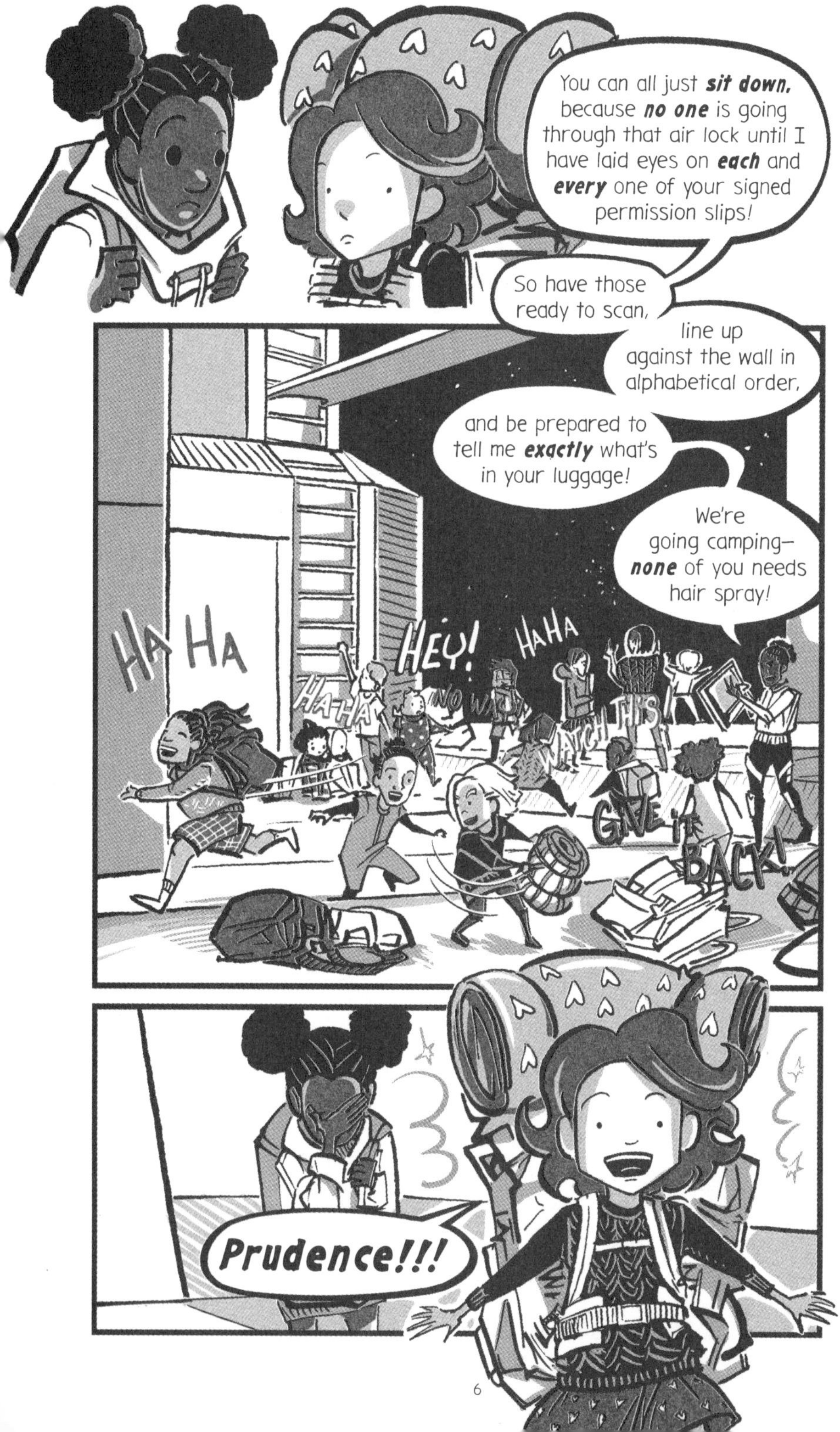
You can all just **sit down,** because **no one** is going through that air lock until I have laid eyes on **each** and **every** one of your signed permission slips!
So have those ready to scan,
line up against the wall in alphabetical order,
and be prepared to tell me **exactly** what's in your luggage!
We're going camping— **none** of you needs hair spray!
HA HA
HEY!
HA HA
HA HA
NO WAY
WATCH THIS
GIVE IT BACK!
**Prudence!!!**

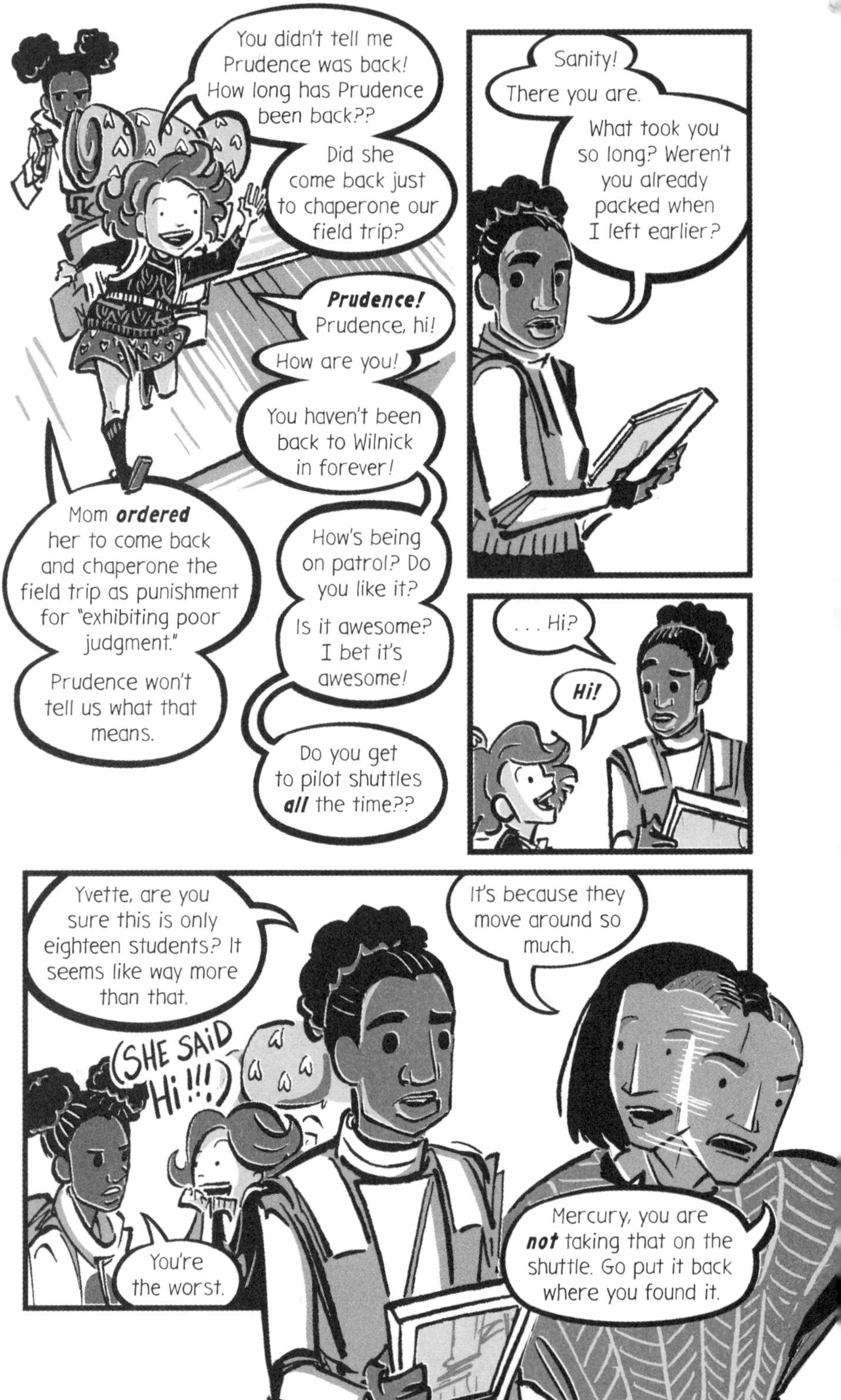
You didn't tell me Prudence was back! How long has Prudence been back??
Did she come back just to chaperone our field trip?
**Prudence!** Prudence, hi!
How are you!
You haven't been back to Wilnick in forever!
How's being on patrol? Do you like it?
Is it awesome? I bet it's awesome!
Do you get to pilot shuttles ***all*** the time??
Mom ***ordered*** her to come back and chaperone the field trip as punishment for "exhibiting poor judgment."
Prudence won't tell us what that means.
Sanity!
There you are.
What took you so long? Weren't you already packed when I left earlier?
. . . Hi?
***Hi!***
Yvette, are you sure this is only eighteen students? It seems like way more than that.
It's because they move around so much.
(SHE SAID Hi!!!)
You're the worst.
Mercury, you are ***not*** taking that on the shuttle. Go put it back where you found it.

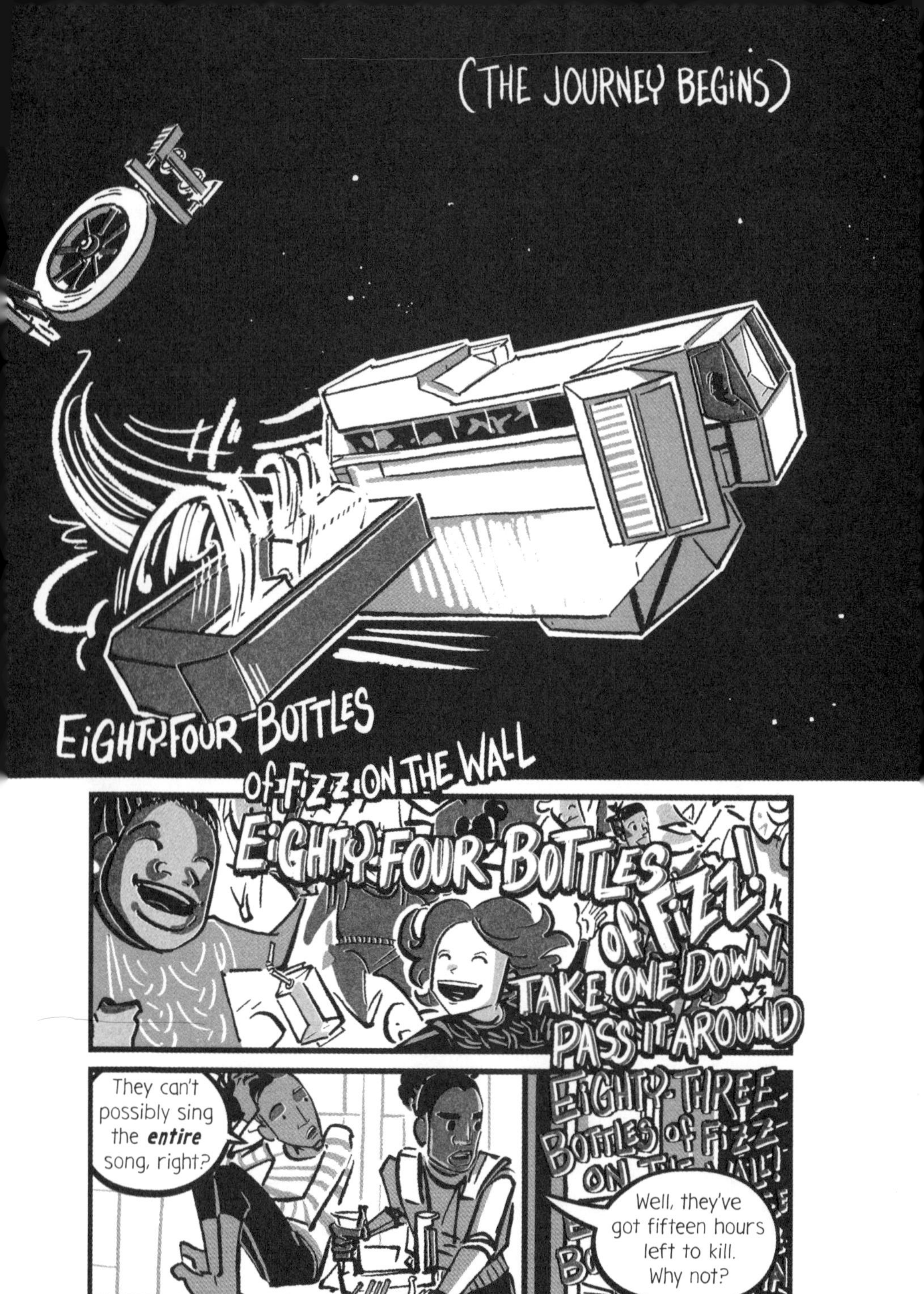
(THE JOURNEY BEGINS)
EIGHTY-FOUR BOTTLES
of FIZZ ON THE WALL
EIGHTY-FOUR BOTTLES
of FIZZ!
TAKE ONE DOWN,
PASS IT AROUND
EIGHTY-THREE
BOTTLES of FIZZ
They can't possibly sing the ***entire*** song, right?
Well, they've got fifteen hours left to kill. Why not?

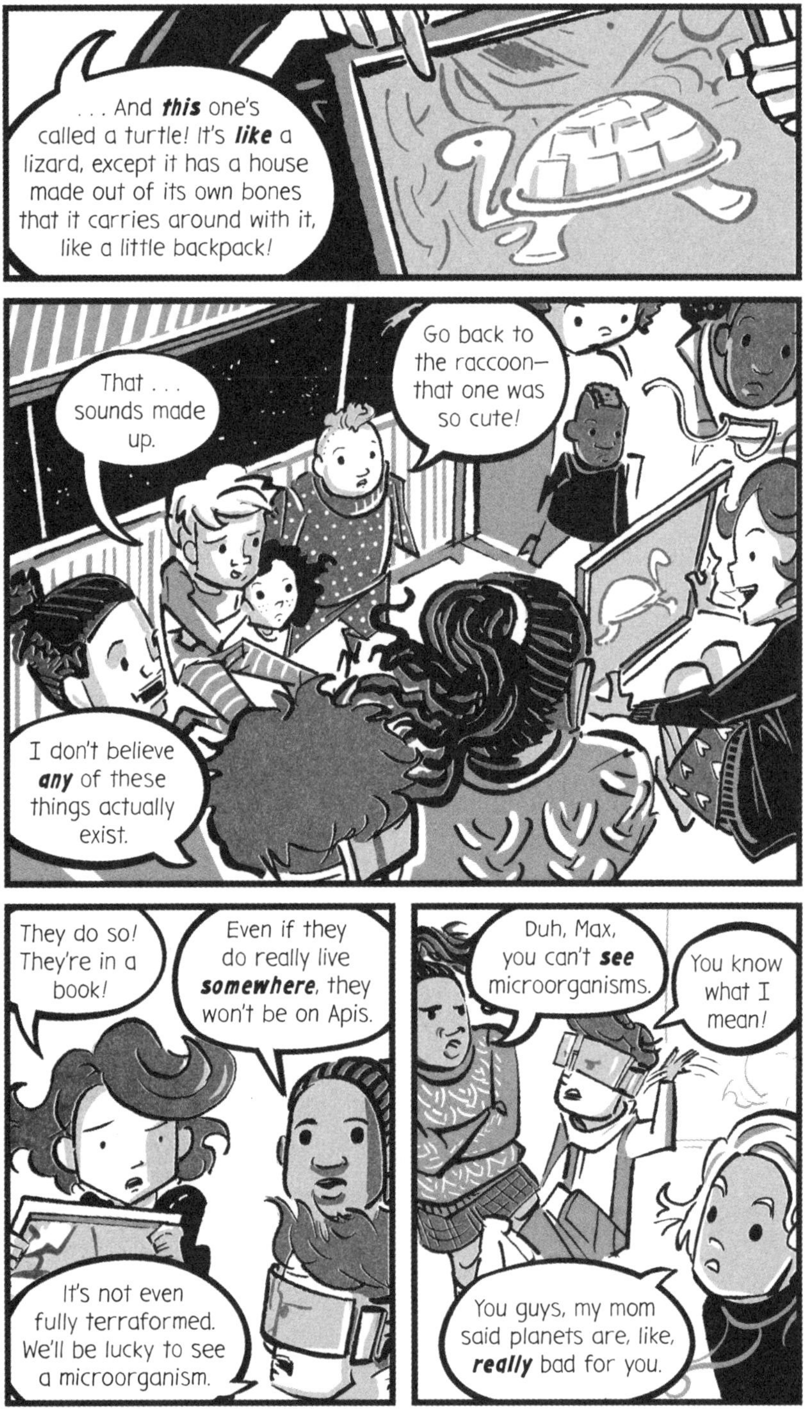
. . . And **this** one's called a turtle! It's **like** a lizard, except it has a house made out of its own bones that it carries around with it, like a little backpack!
That . . . sounds made up.
Go back to the raccoon—that one was so cute!
I don't believe **any** of these things actually exist.
They do so! They're in a book!
Even if they do really live **somewhere**, they won't be on Apis.
It's not even fully terraformed. We'll be lucky to see a microorganism.
Duh, Max, you can't **see** microorganisms.
You know what I mean!
You guys, my mom said planets are, like, **really** bad for you.

Atmospheres let in lots of ultraviolet radiation and stuff, like *way* more than window panels on-station.

So you're just walking around and it seems normal, but then suddenly you have, like, actual *burns* on your skin.

That's why landsiders are so weird. They don't have any skin left because it all *burned off.*

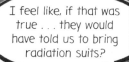

I feel like, if that was true . . . they would have told us to bring radiation suits?

And not just warm socks?

I'm not *lying!*

Sanity, your dad grew up on a planet, right? He seems pretty normal.

Wait, really? I didn't know that!

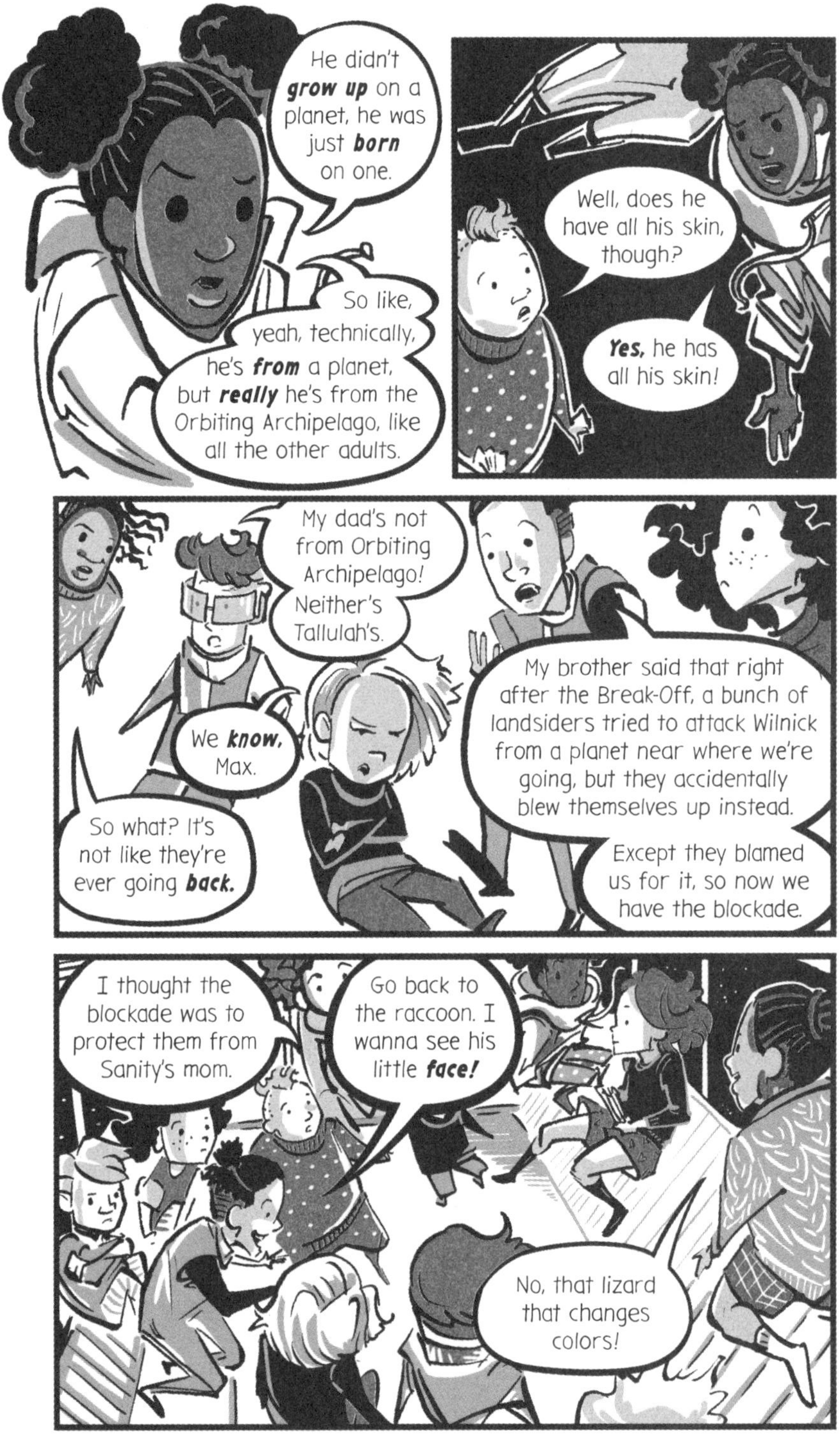
He didn't **grow up** on a planet, he was just **born** on one.
So like, yeah, technically, he's **from** a planet, but **really** he's from the Orbiting Archipelago, like all the other adults.
Well, does he have all his skin, though?
**Yes,** he has all his skin!
My dad's not from Orbiting Archipelago! Neither's Tallulah's.
We **know,** Max.
So what? It's not like they're ever going **back.**
My brother said that right after the Break-Off, a bunch of landsiders tried to attack Wilnick from a planet near where we're going, but they accidentally blew themselves up instead.
Except they blamed us for it, so now we have the blockade.
I thought the blockade was to protect them from Sanity's mom.
Go back to the raccoon. I wanna see his little **face!**
No, that lizard that changes colors!

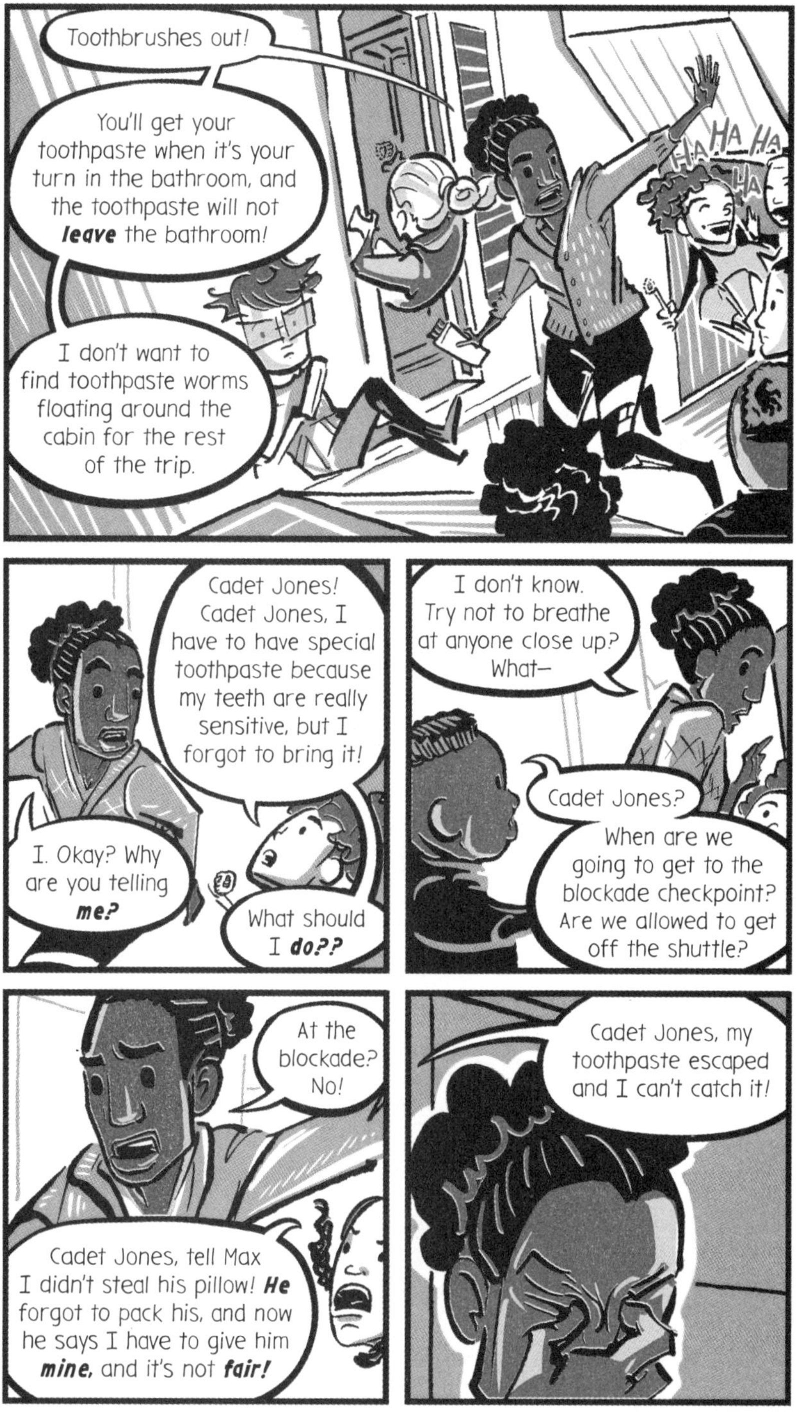
Toothbrushes out!
You'll get your toothpaste when it's your turn in the bathroom, and the toothpaste will not **leave** the bathroom!
I don't want to find toothpaste worms floating around the cabin for the rest of the trip.
HA HA HA HA HA
Cadet Jones! Cadet Jones, I have to have special toothpaste because my teeth are really sensitive, but I forgot to bring it!
I. Okay? Why are you telling **me?**
What should I **do??**
I don't know. Try not to breathe at anyone close up? What–
Cadet Jones?
When are we going to get to the blockade checkpoint? Are we allowed to get off the shuttle?
At the blockade? No!
Cadet Jones, tell Max I didn't steal his pillow! **He** forgot to pack his, and now he says I have to give him **mine**, and it's not **fair!**
Cadet Jones, my toothpaste escaped and I can't catch it!

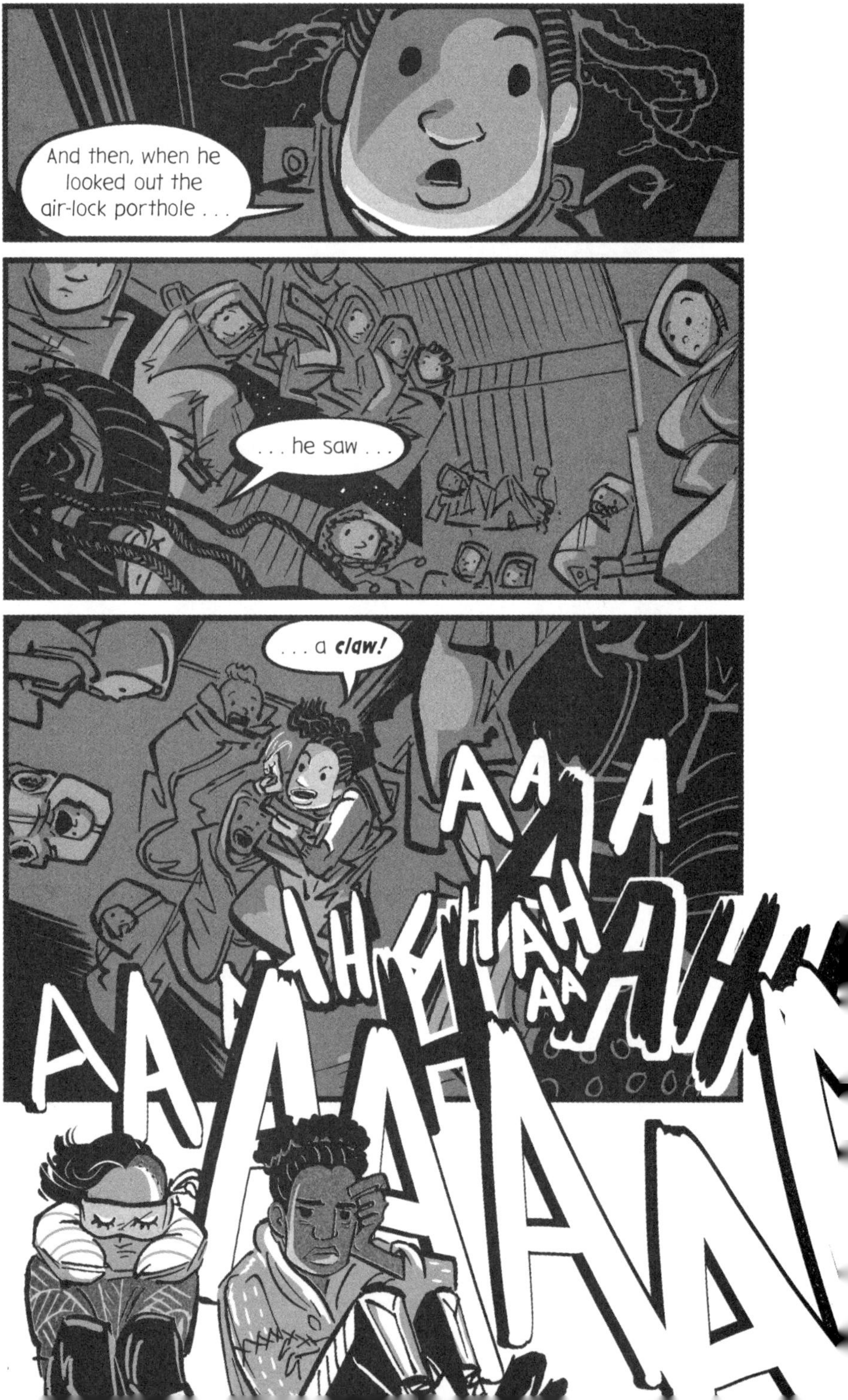
And then, when he looked out the air-lock porthole . . .
. . . he saw . . .
. . . a *claw!*

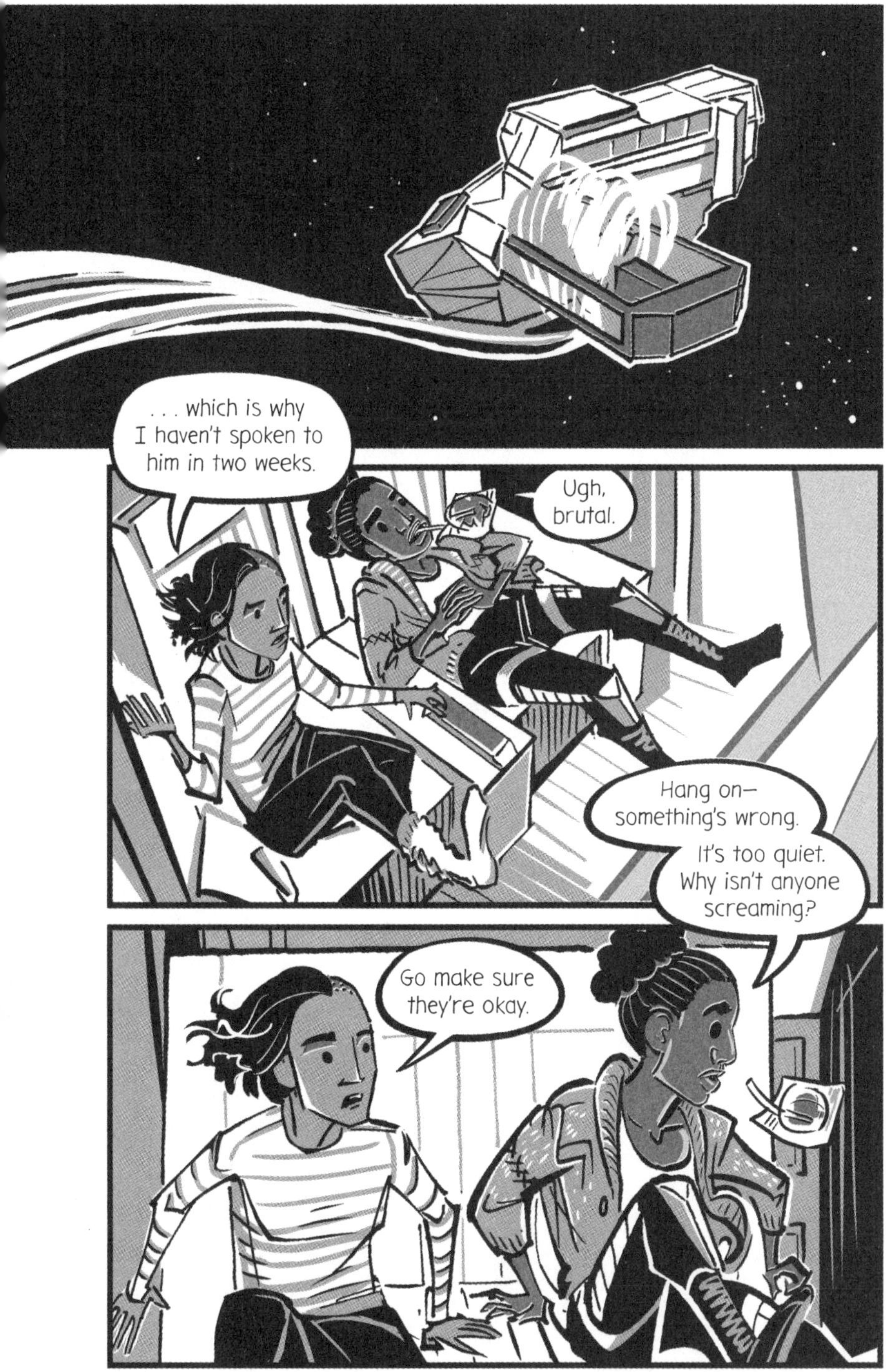
. . . which is why I haven't spoken to him in two weeks.
Ugh, brutal.
Hang on— something's wrong.
It's too quiet. Why isn't anyone screaming?
Go make sure they're okay.

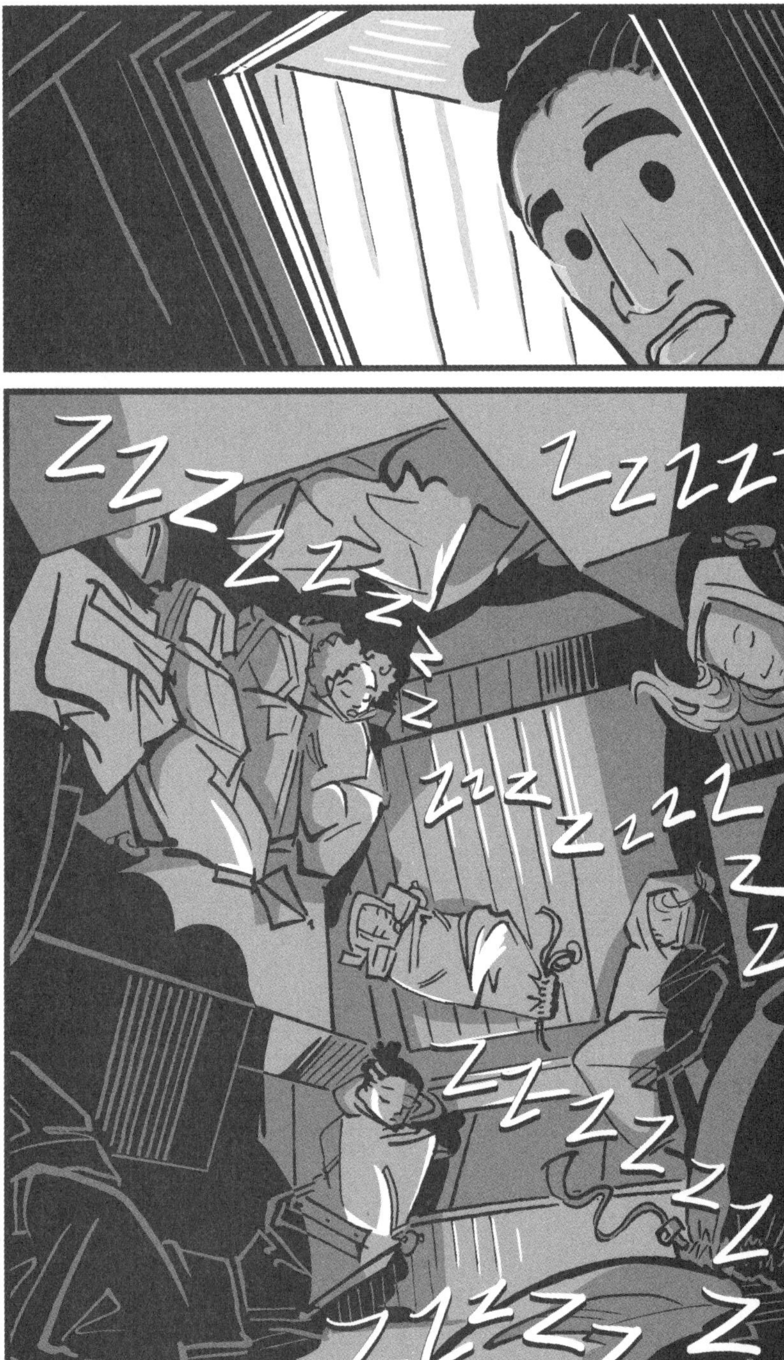
ZZZZZZZZZ
ZZZZZ
ZZZZZZZZZ
ZZZZZZZ
ZZZZZZZ

( APiS SYSTEM)
Hello, unidentified craft, you have entered airspace under commercial claim by the FootHold Corporation.
Please identify yourselves and state your business.

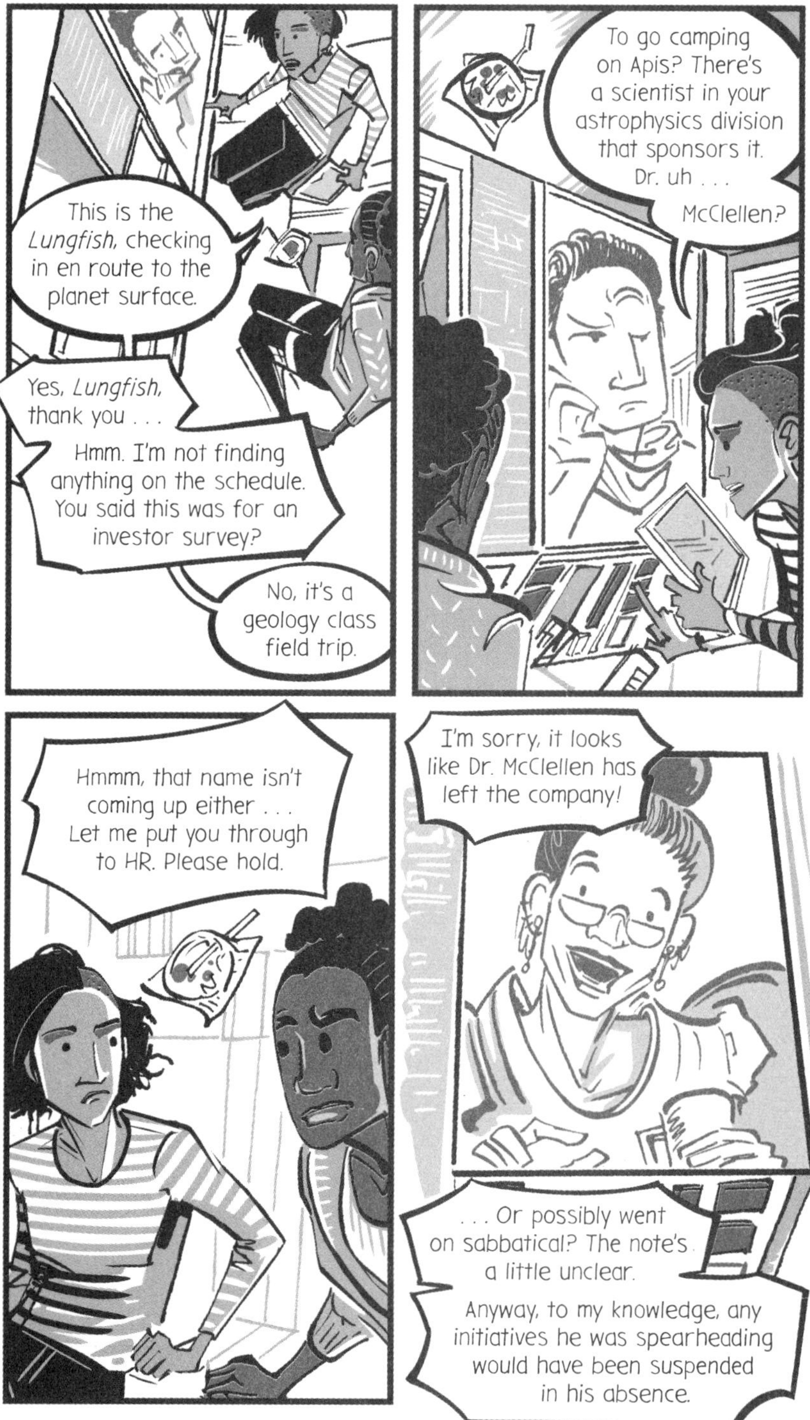
This is the *Lungfish,* checking in en route to the planet surface.
Yes, *Lungfish,* thank you . . .
Hmm. I'm not finding anything on the schedule. You said this was for an investor survey?
No, it's a geology class field trip.
To go camping on Apis? There's a scientist in your astrophysics division that sponsors it. Dr. uh . . .
McClellen?
Hmmm, that name isn't coming up either . . . Let me put you through to HR. Please hold.
I'm sorry, it looks like Dr. McClellen has left the company!
. . . Or possibly went on sabbatical? The note's a little unclear.
Anyway, to my knowledge, any initiatives he was spearheading would have been suspended in his absence.

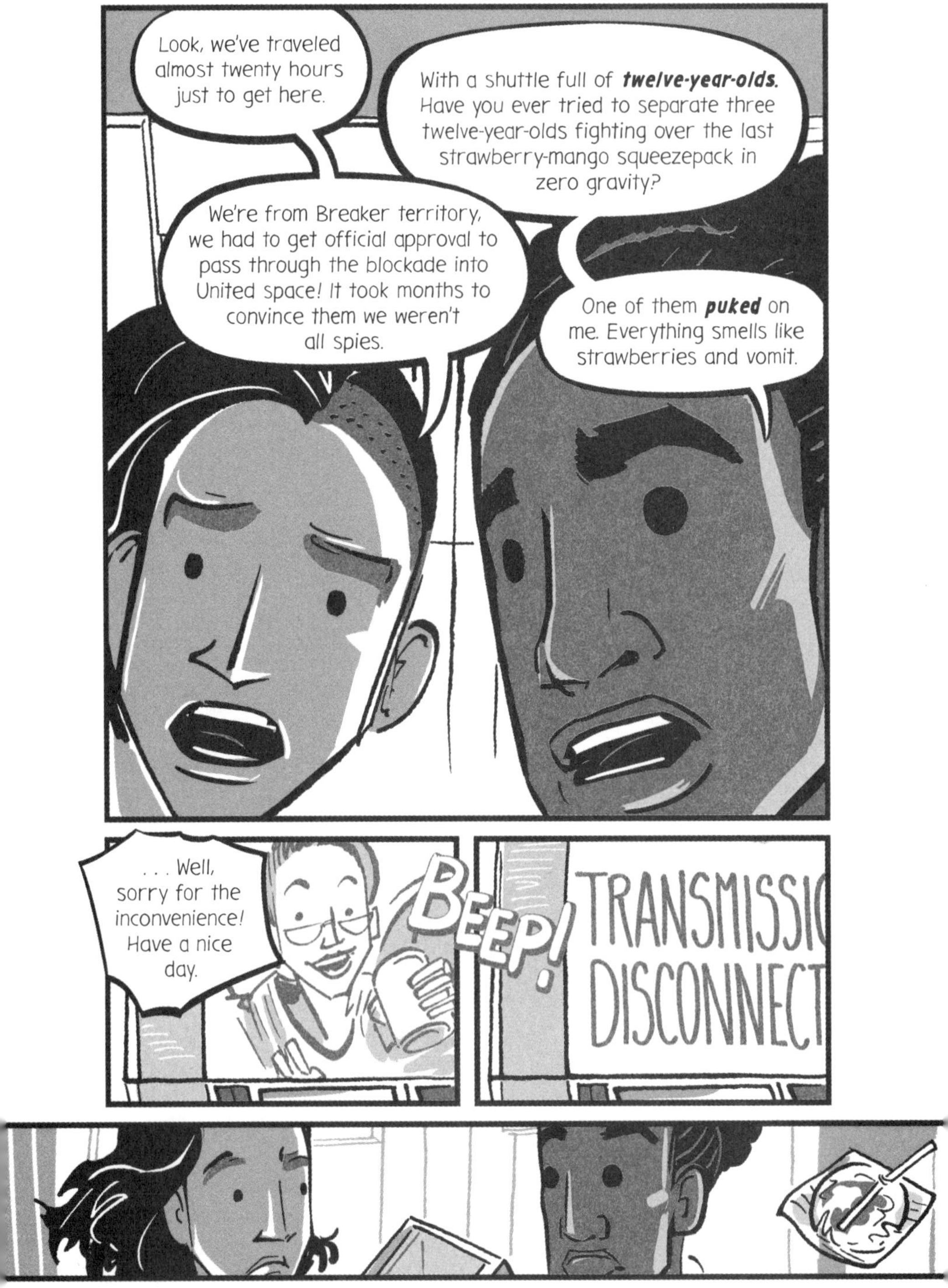

Look, we've traveled almost twenty hours just to get here.
With a shuttle full of **twelve-year-olds.** Have you ever tried to separate three twelve-year-olds fighting over the last strawberry-mango squeezepack in zero gravity?
We're from Breaker territory, we had to get official approval to pass through the blockade into United space! It took months to convince them we weren't all spies.
One of them **puked** on me. Everything smells like strawberries and vomit.
. . . Well, sorry for the inconvenience! Have a nice day.
BEEP!
TRANSMISSIO
DISCONNECT

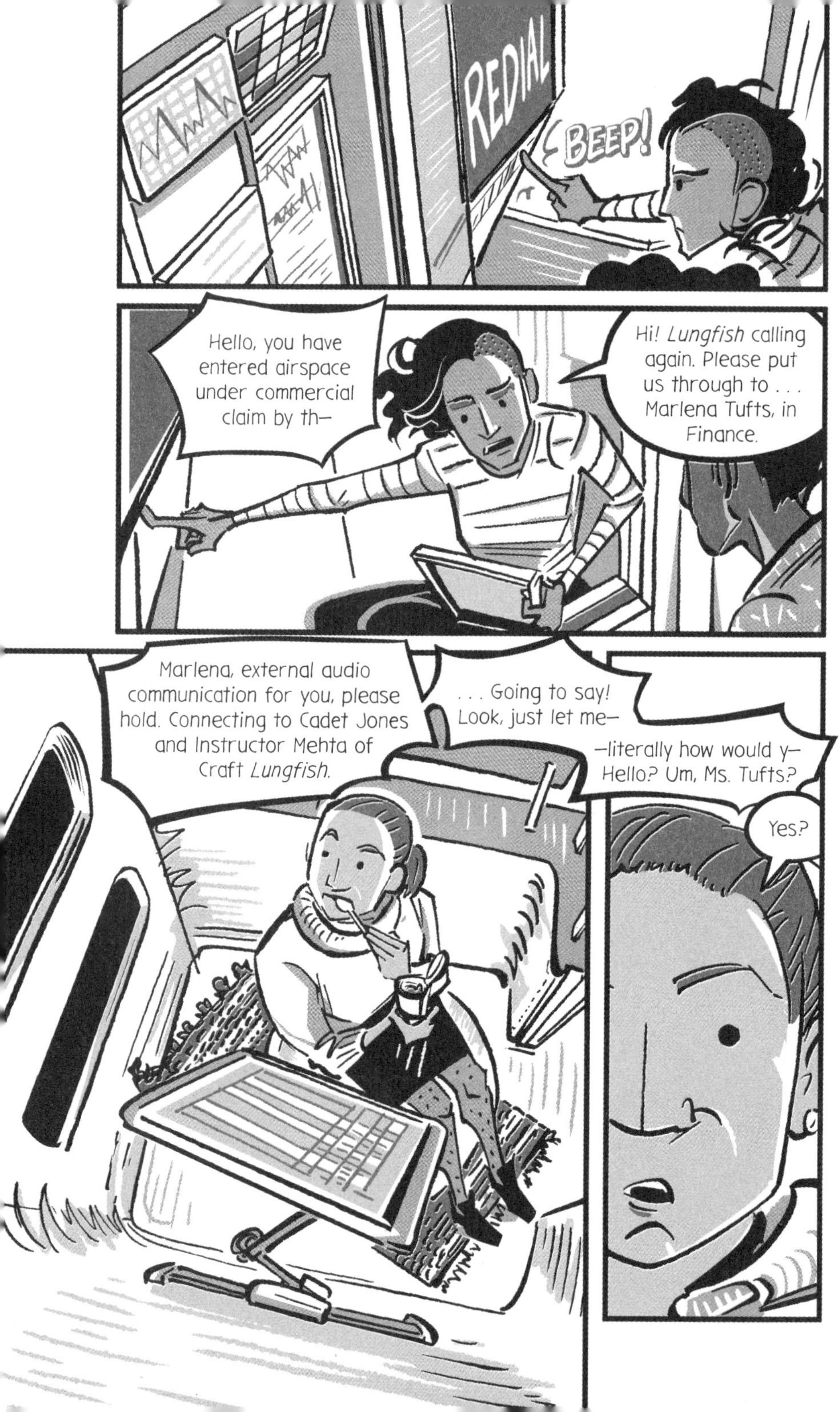
REDIAL
BEEP!
Hello, you have entered airspace under commercial claim by th—
Hi! *Lungfish* calling again. Please put us through to . . . Marlena Tufts, in Finance.
Marlena, external audio communication for you, please hold. Connecting to Cadet Jones and Instructor Mehta of Craft *Lungfish*.
. . . Going to say! Look, just let me—
—literally how would y— Hello? Um, Ms. Tufts?
Yes?

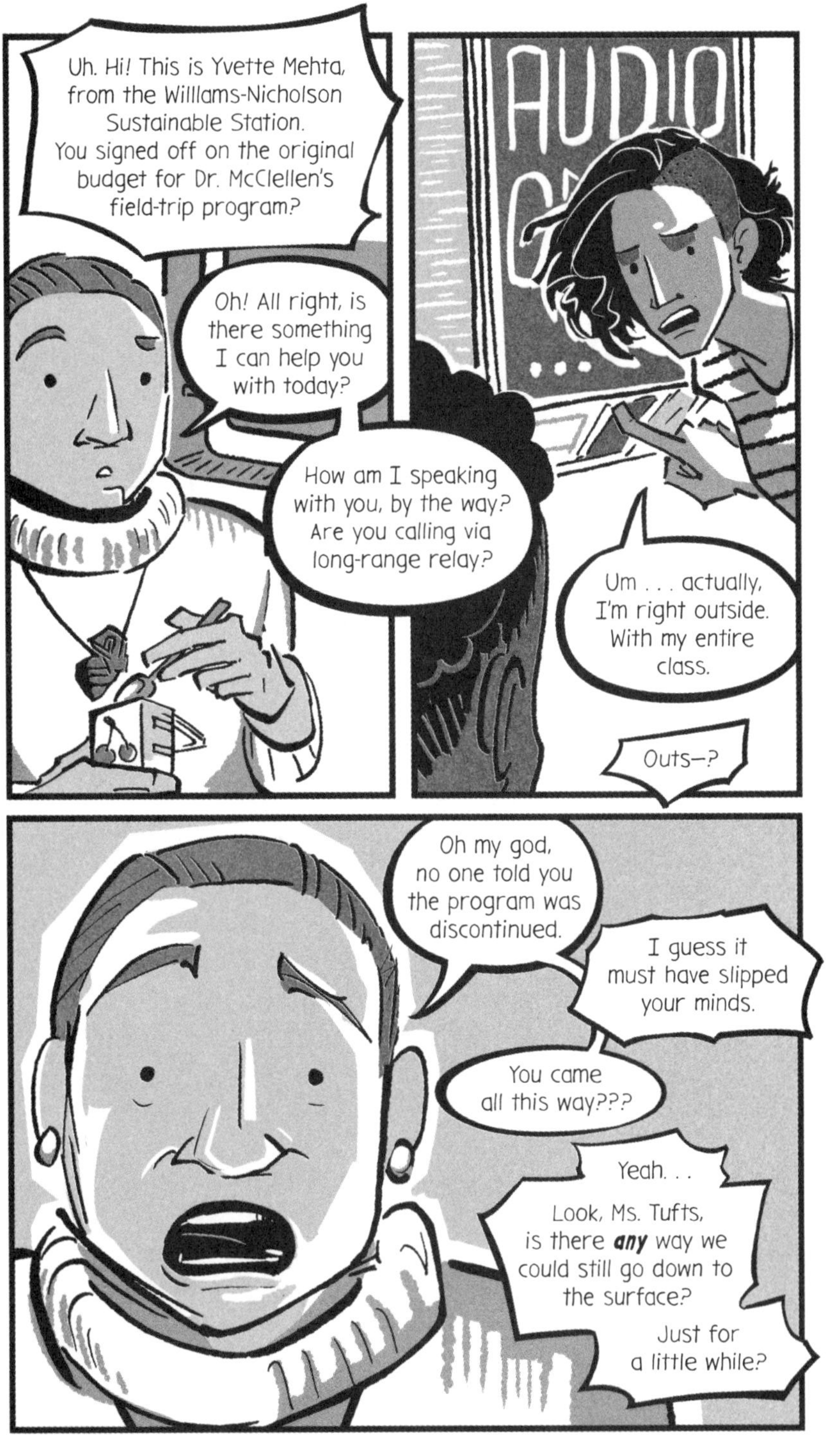
Uh. Hi! This is Yvette Mehta, from the Williams-Nicholson Sustainable Station. You signed off on the original budget for Dr. McClellen's field-trip program?
Oh! All right, is there something I can help you with today?
How am I speaking with you, by the way? Are you calling via long-range relay?
AUDIO
Um . . . actually, I'm right outside. With my entire class.
Outs—?
Oh my god, no one told you the program was discontinued.
I guess it must have slipped your minds.
You came all this way???
Yeah. . .
Look, Ms. Tufts, is there **any** way we could still go down to the surface?
Just for a little while?

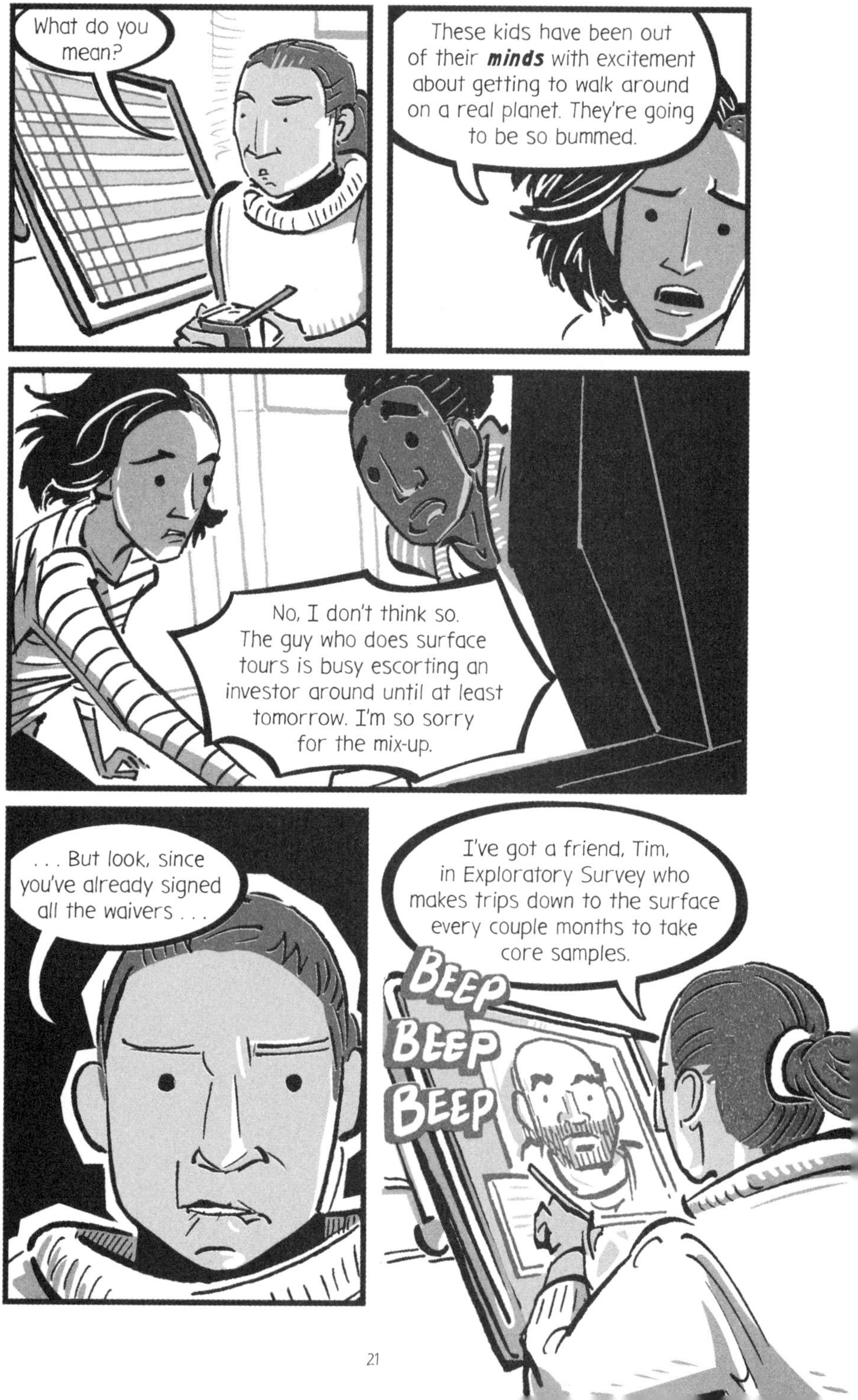
What do you mean?
These kids have been out of their **minds** with excitement about getting to walk around on a real planet. They're going to be so bummed.
No, I don't think so. The guy who does surface tours is busy escorting an investor around until at least tomorrow. I'm so sorry for the mix-up.
. . . But look, since you've already signed all the waivers . . .
I've got a friend, Tim, in Exploratory Survey who makes trips down to the surface every couple months to take core samples.
BEEP
BEEP
BEEP

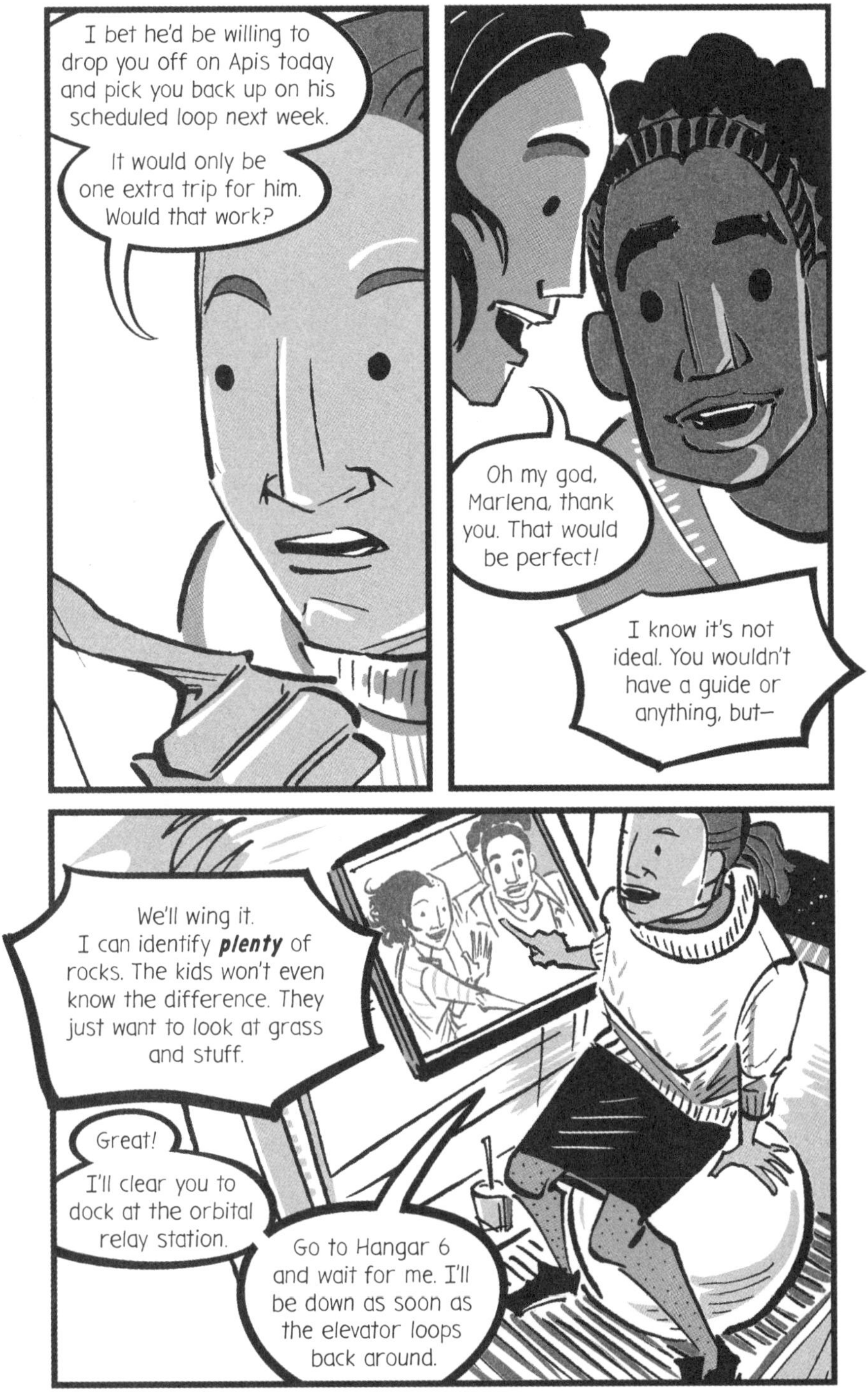
I bet he'd be willing to drop you off on Apis today and pick you back up on his scheduled loop next week.
It would only be one extra trip for him. Would that work?
Oh my god, Marlena, thank you. That would be perfect!
I know it's not ideal. You wouldn't have a guide or anything, but–
We'll wing it. I can identify **plenty** of rocks. The kids won't even know the difference. They just want to look at grass and stuff.
Great!
I'll clear you to dock at the orbital relay station.
Go to Hangar 6 and wait for me. I'll be down as soon as the elevator loops back around.

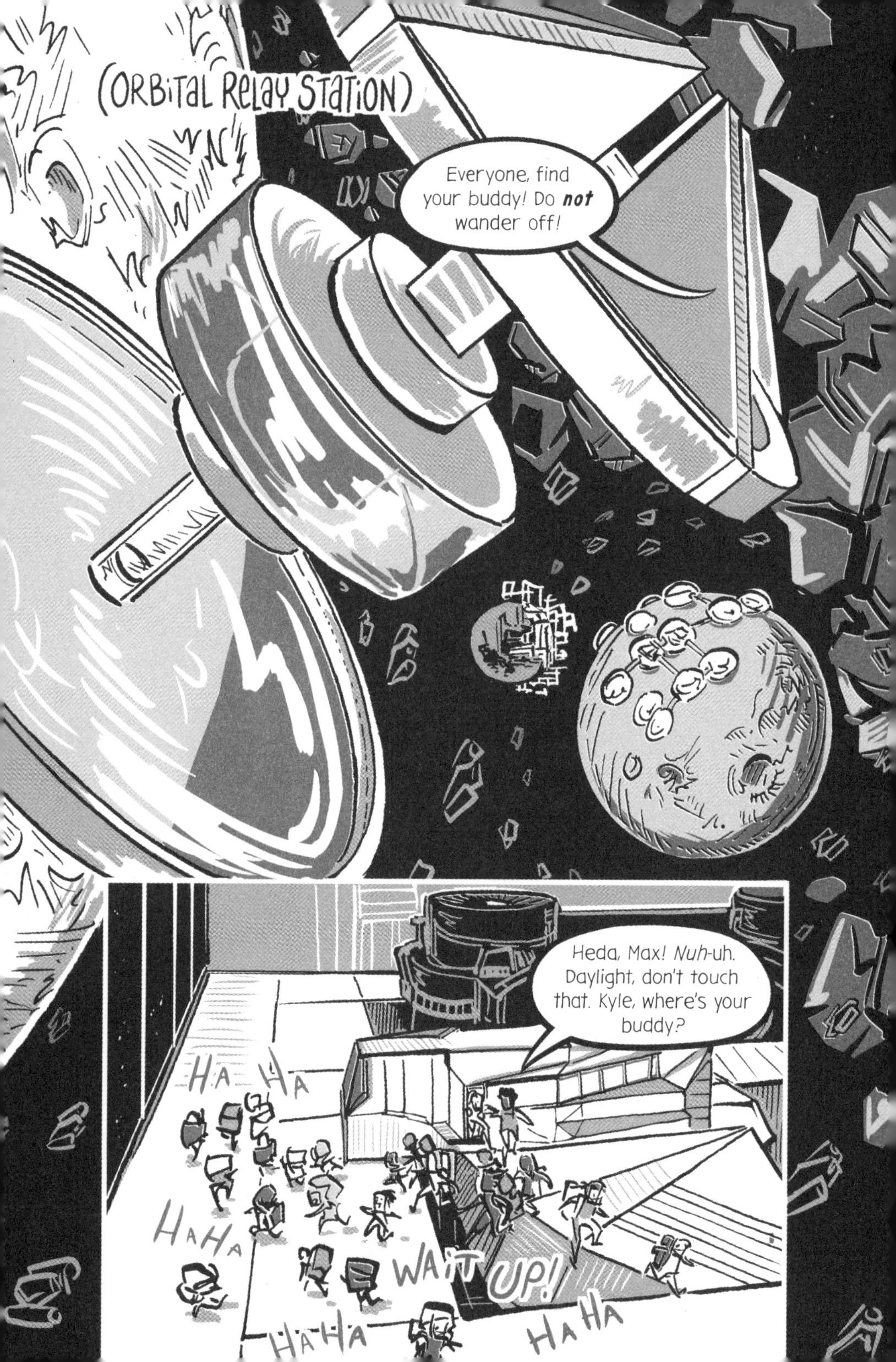
(ORBITAL RELAY STATION)
Everyone, find your buddy! Do **not** wander off!
Heda, Max! *Nuh*-uh. Daylight, don't touch that. Kyle, where's your buddy?
HA HA
HAHA
WAIT UP!
HAHA
HA HA

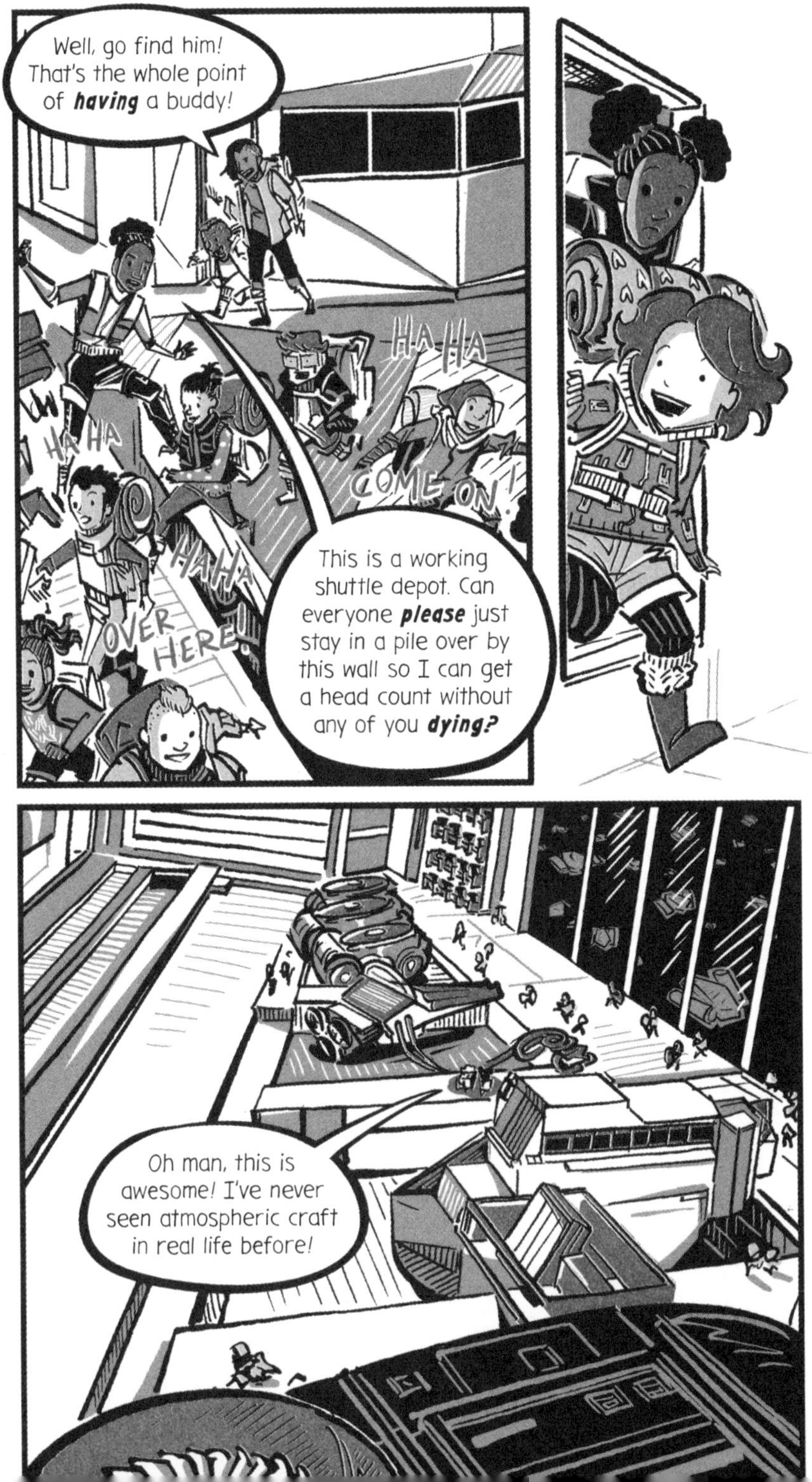
Well, go find him! That's the whole point of **having** a buddy!
HA HA
HA HA
COME ON!
HA HA
OVER HERE!
This is a working shuttle depot. Can everyone **please** just stay in a pile over by this wall so I can get a head count without any of you **dying?**
Oh man, this is awesome! I've never seen atmospheric craft in real life before!

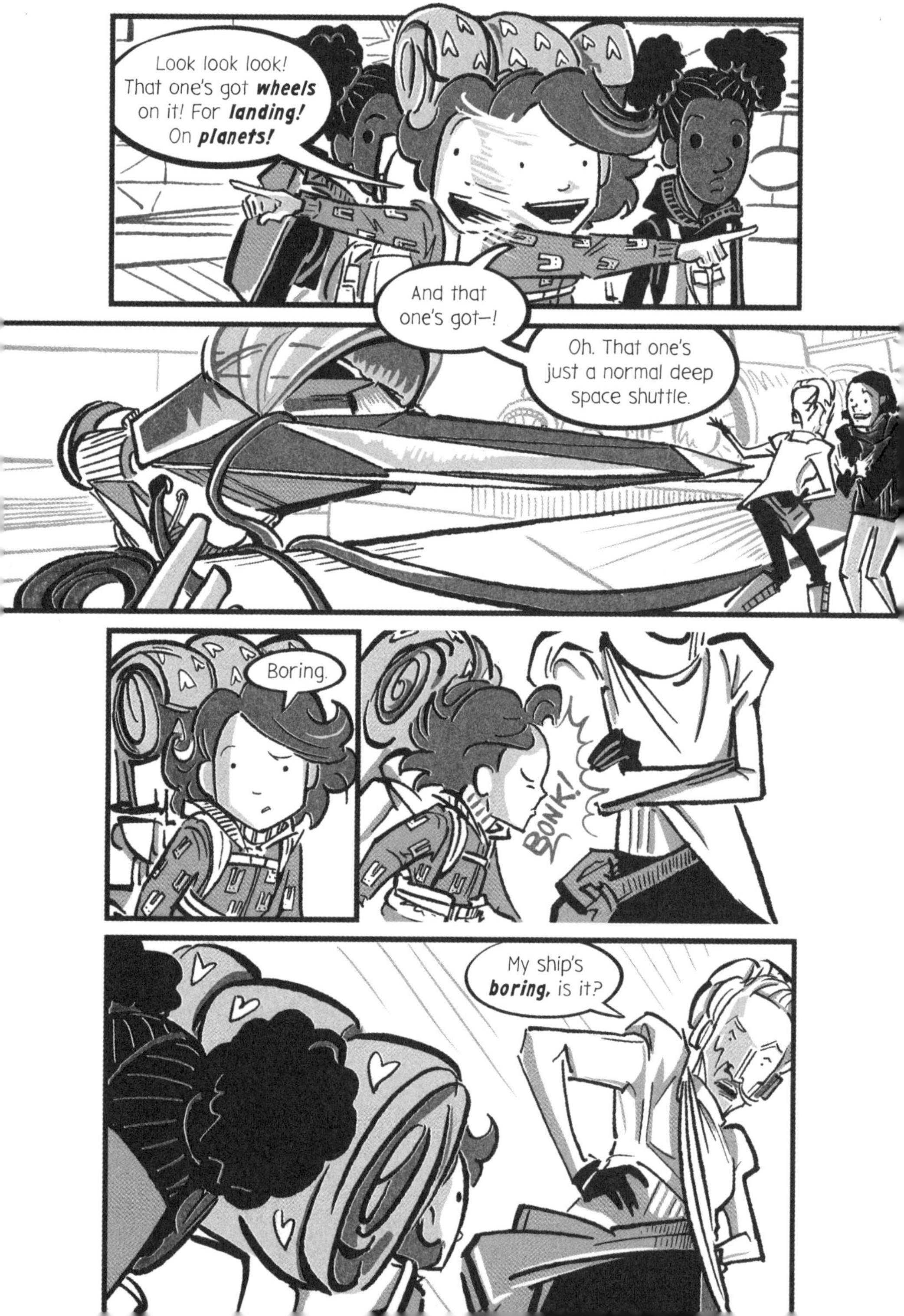
Look look look! That one's got **wheels** on it! For **landing!** On **planets!**
And that one's got—!
Oh. That one's just a normal deep space shuttle.
Boring.
BONK!
My ship's **boring**, is it?

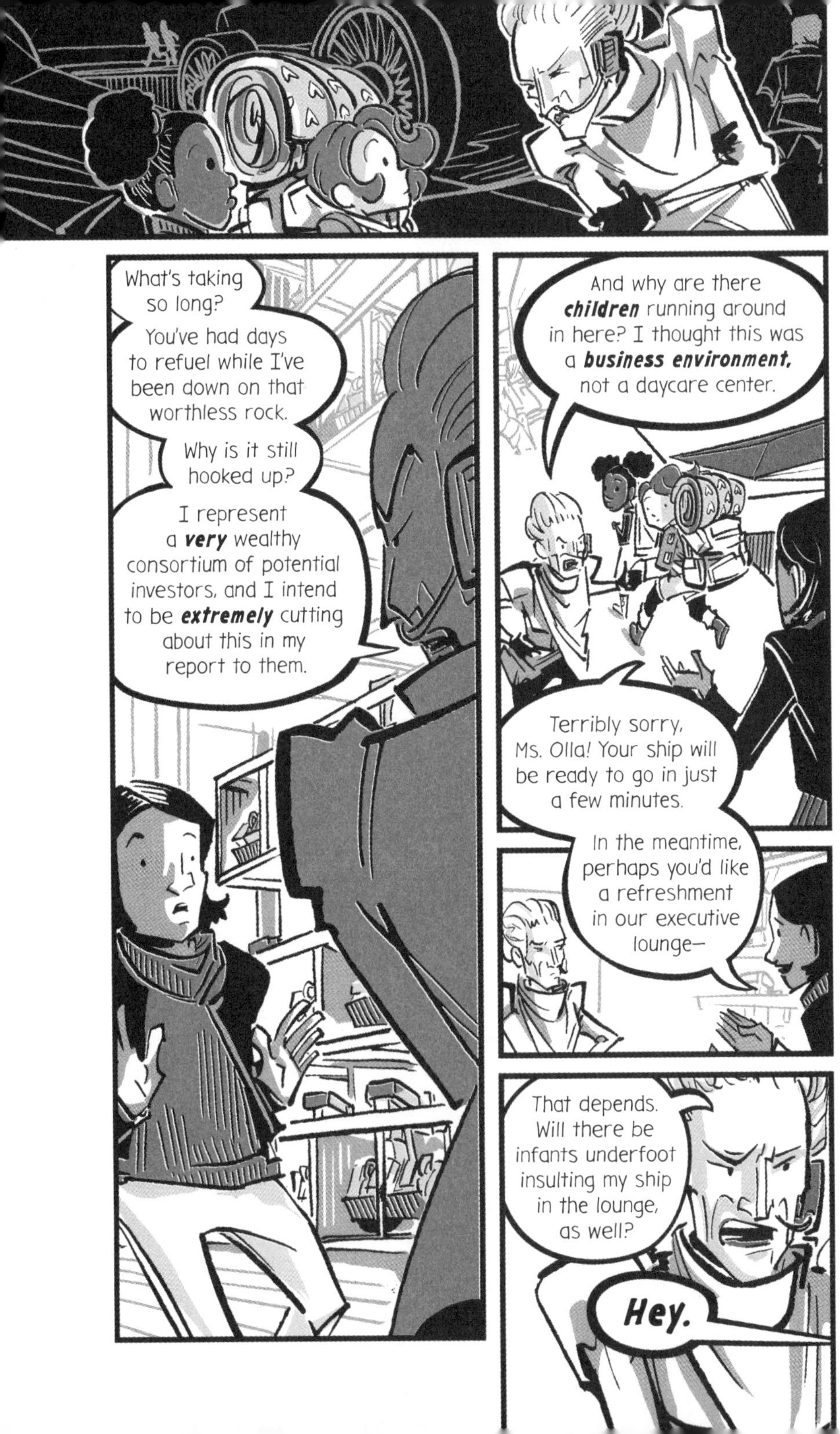
What's taking so long?
You've had days to refuel while I've been down on that worthless rock.
Why is it still hooked up?
I represent a **very** wealthy consortium of potential investors, and I intend to be **extremely** cutting about this in my report to them.
And why are there **children** running around in here? I thought this was a **business environment,** not a daycare center.
Terribly sorry, Ms. Olla! Your ship will be ready to go in just a few minutes.
In the meantime, perhaps you'd like a refreshment in our executive lounge—
That depends. Will there be infants underfoot insulting my ship in the lounge, as well?
**Hey.**

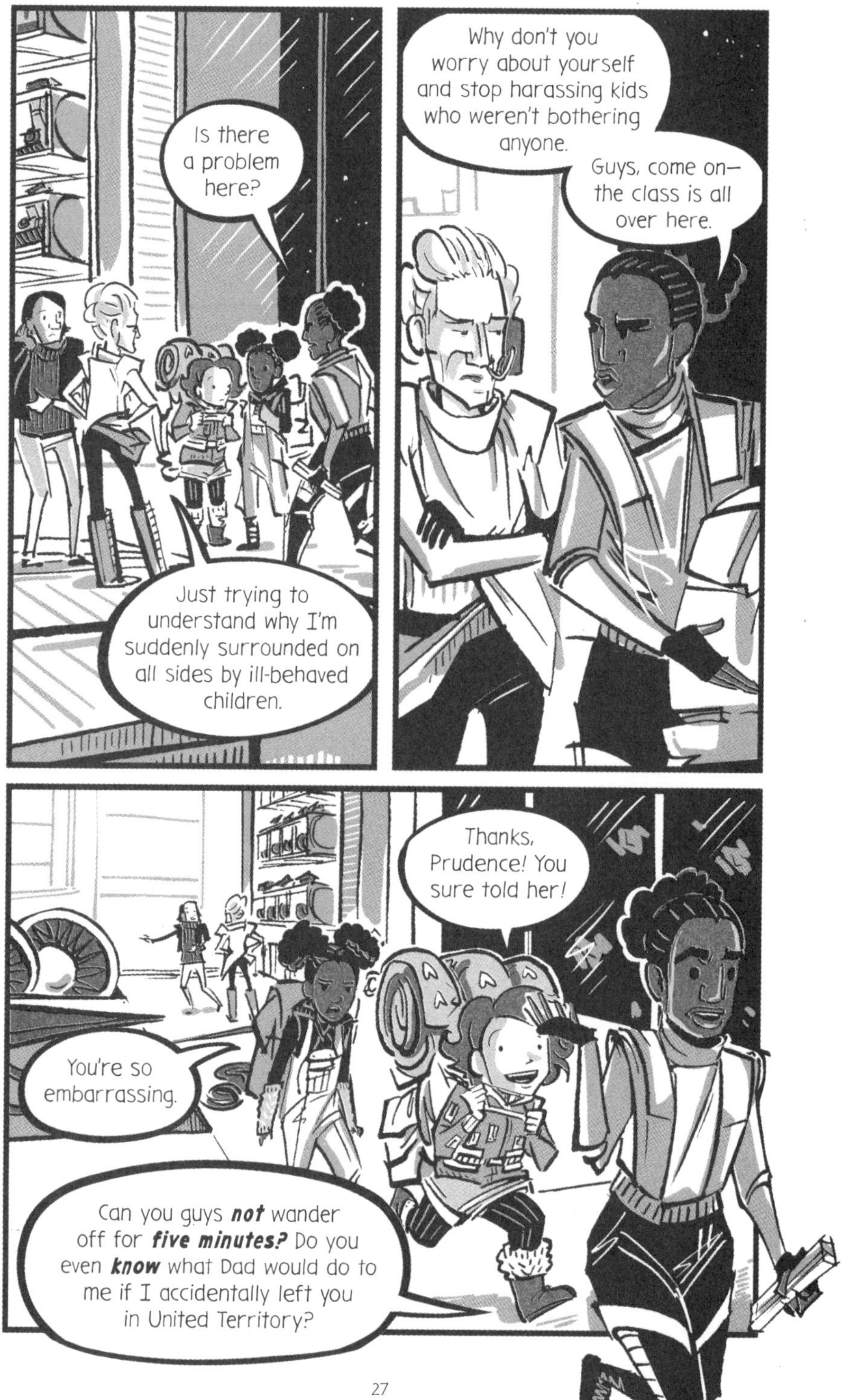
Is there a problem here?
Just trying to understand why I'm suddenly surrounded on all sides by ill-behaved children.
Why don't you worry about yourself and stop harassing kids who weren't bothering anyone.
Guys, come on—the class is all over here.
Thanks, Prudence! You sure told her!
You're so embarrassing.
Can you guys **not** wander off for **five minutes?** Do you even **know** what Dad would do to me if I accidentally left you in United Territory?

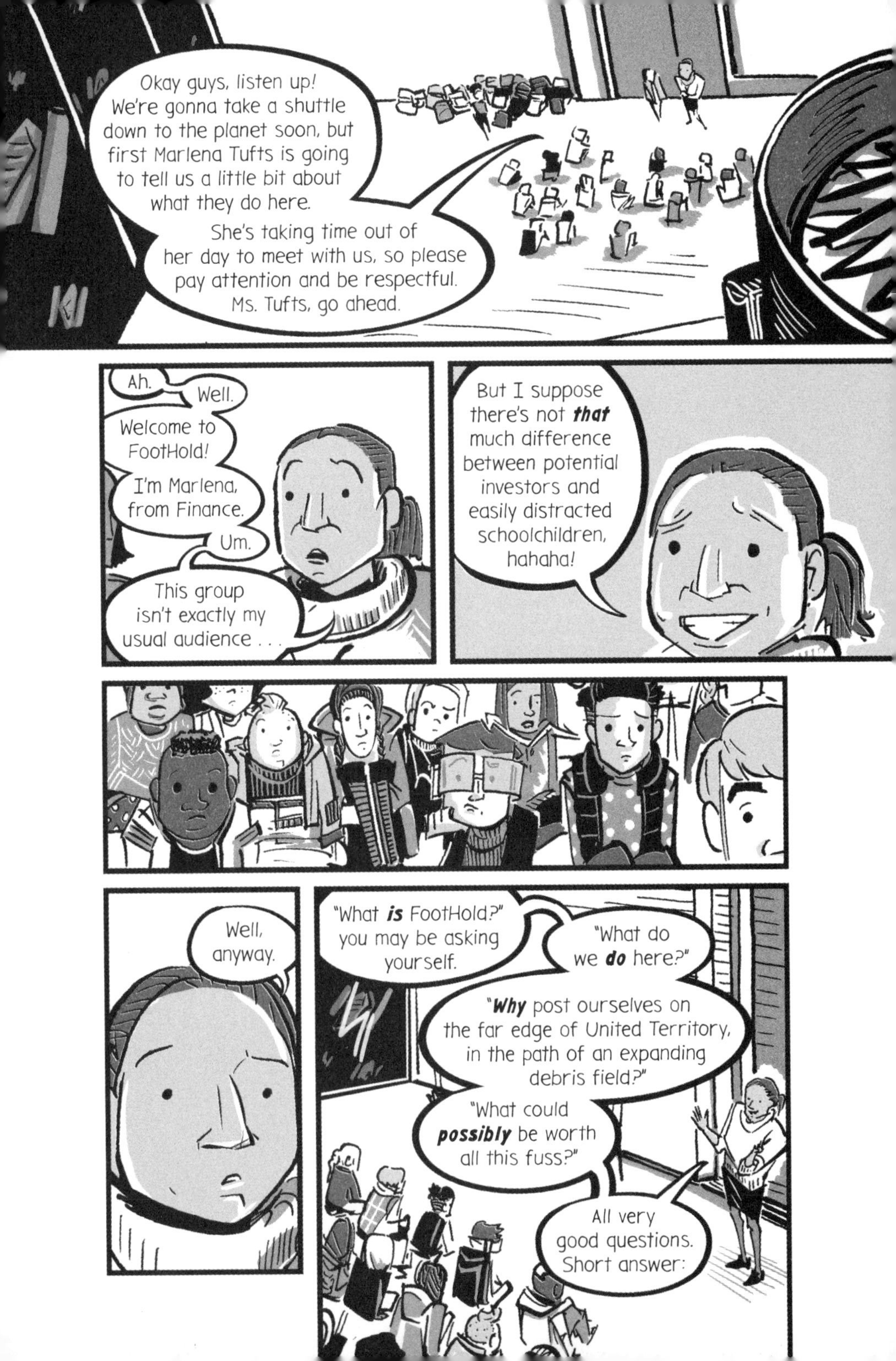
Okay guys, listen up! We're gonna take a shuttle down to the planet soon, but first Marlena Tufts is going to tell us a little bit about what they do here.
She's taking time out of her day to meet with us, so please pay attention and be respectful. Ms. Tufts, go ahead.
Ah.
Well.
Welcome to FootHold!
I'm Marlena, from Finance.
Um.
This group isn't exactly my usual audience . . .
But I suppose there's not **that** much difference between potential investors and easily distracted schoolchildren, hahaha!
Well, anyway.
"What **is** FootHold?" you may be asking yourself.
"What do we **do** here?"
"**Why** post ourselves on the far edge of United Territory, in the path of an expanding debris field?"
"What could **possibly** be worth all this fuss?"
All very good questions. Short answer:

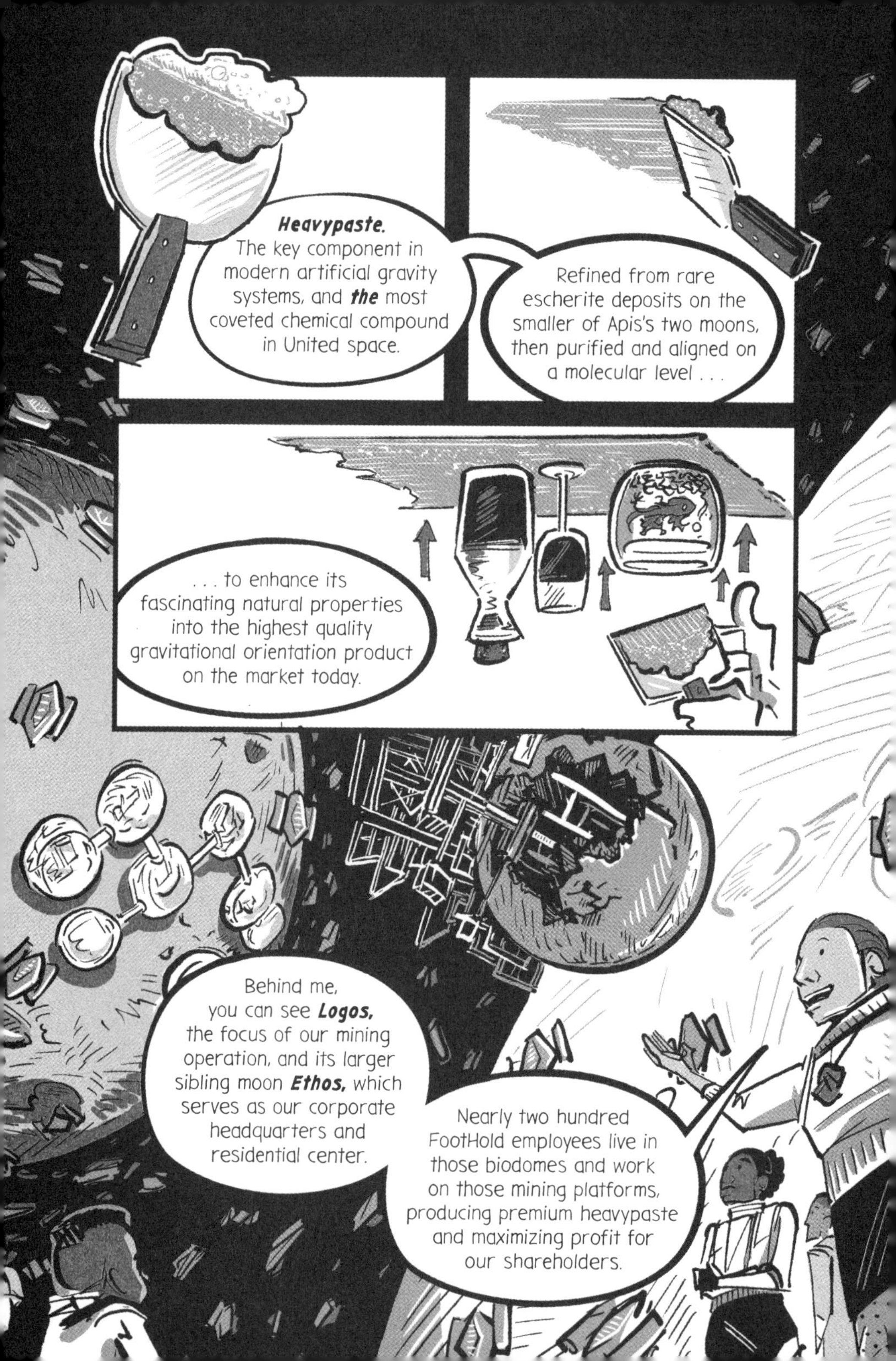
**Heavypaste.** The key component in modern artificial gravity systems, and ***the*** most coveted chemical compound in United space.
Refined from rare escherite deposits on the smaller of Apis's two moons, then purified and aligned on a molecular level . . .
. . . to enhance its fascinating natural properties into the highest quality gravitational orientation product on the market today.
Behind me, you can see ***Logos,*** the focus of our mining operation, and its larger sibling moon ***Ethos,*** which serves as our corporate headquarters and residential center.
Nearly two hundred FootHold employees live in those biodomes and work on those mining platforms, producing premium heavypaste and maximizing profit for our shareholders.

BEEP BEEP

Now you, like many investors— er, **visitors**—

might be concerned by our location inside the still-spreading Battlefield Debris Field.

And it's true—impacts from asteroids and other space debris are near-constant.

But thanks to our innovative satellite network developed entirely in-house, FootHold Corp has lost less than **one hundred** work hours to asteroid strikes!

ZAP!

These cost-effective devices use complex orbital models to intercept only objects on a collision course with our corporate property, and break them up into harmless pieces with a blast of sonic energy.

FootHold's orbital sonic satellite network is hyperaccurate and fully automated, needing only **one** salaried team member to stay on Apis monitoring the transmission control tower.

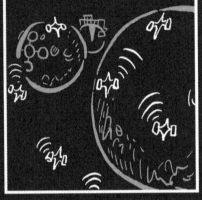

APIS

ETHOS

THE LOGOS

While most of the surface is uninhabitable, the small area dedicated to our planetary operations has been terraformed, and is protected by the sonic shield array. That's where Tim will drop you off in the lander, so you can spend the next four days doing . . . whatever educational activities you're here for.

ZAP!

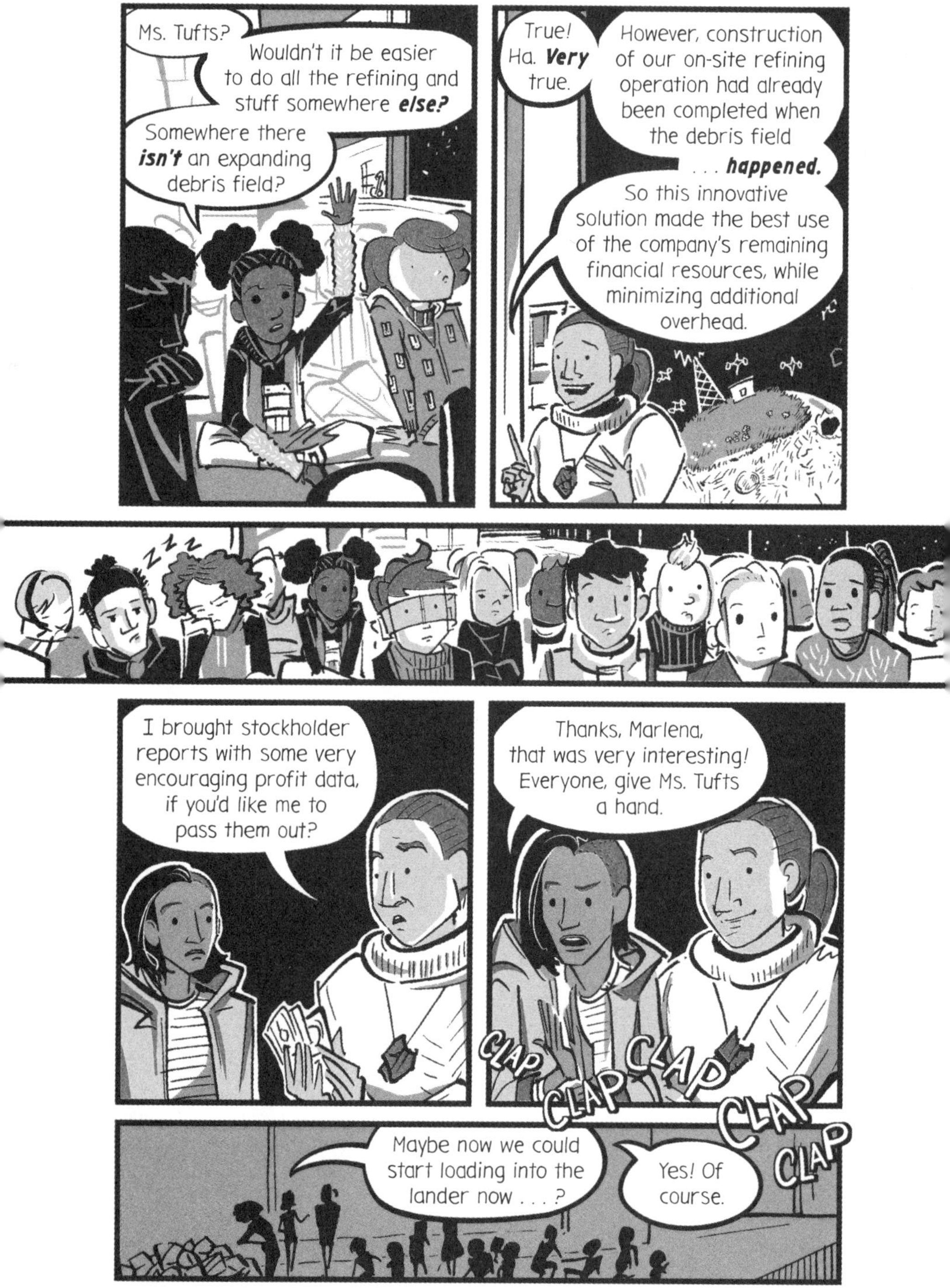

Ms. Tufts?
Wouldn't it be easier to do all the refining and stuff somewhere ***else?***
Somewhere there ***isn't*** an expanding debris field?
True! Ha. **Very** true.
However, construction of our on-site refining operation had already been completed when the debris field
. . . ***happened.***
So this innovative solution made the best use of the company's remaining financial resources, while minimizing additional overhead.
Z Z Z
I brought stockholder reports with some very encouraging profit data, if you'd like me to pass them out?
Thanks, Marlena, that was very interesting! Everyone, give Ms. Tufts a hand.
CLAP CLAP CLAP CLAP CLAP
Maybe now we could start loading into the lander now . . . ?
Yes! Of course.

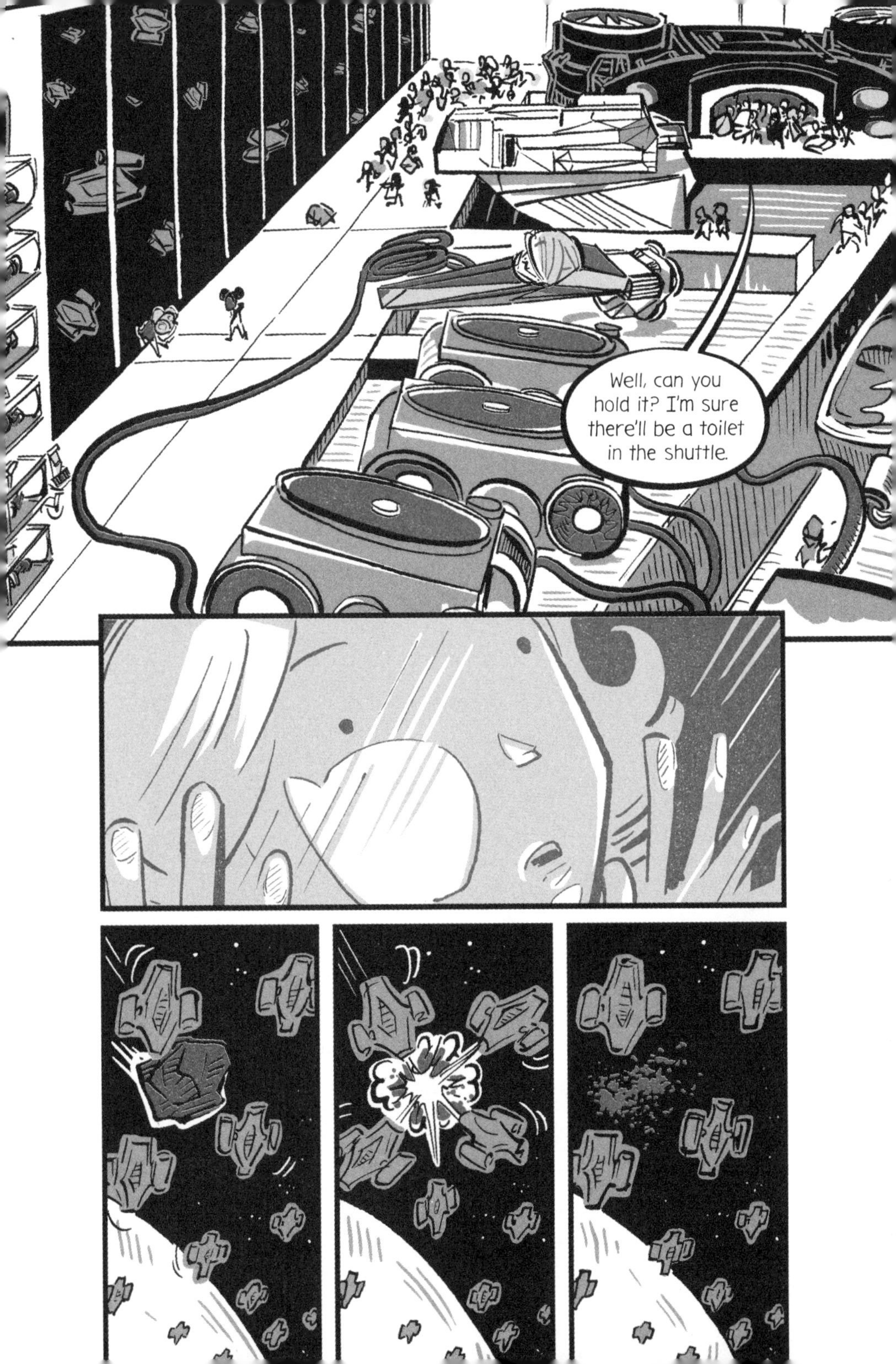
Well, can you hold it? I'm sure there'll be a toilet in the shuttle.

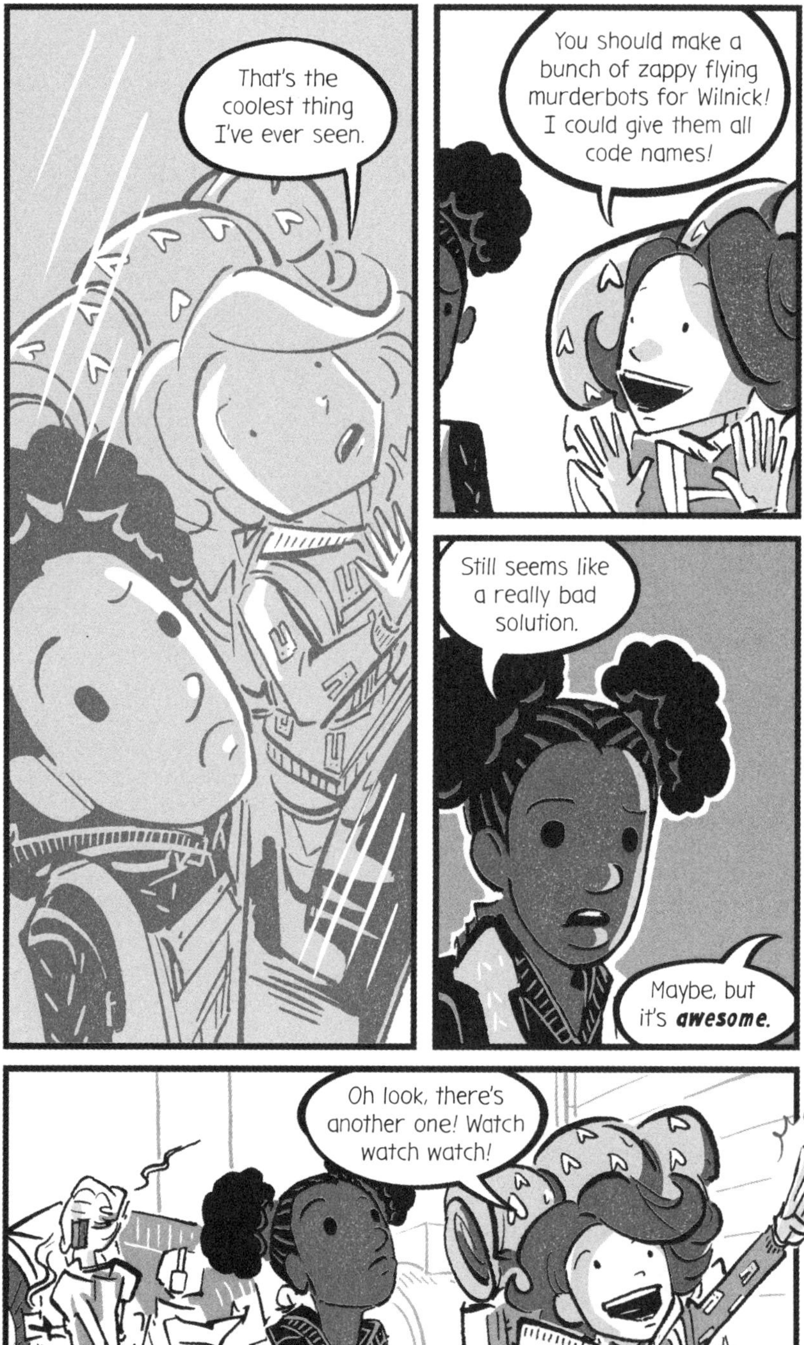
That's the coolest thing I've ever seen.
You should make a bunch of zappy flying murderbots for Wilnick! I could give them all code names!
Still seems like a really bad solution.
Maybe, but it's **awesome.**
Oh look, there's another one! Watch watch watch!

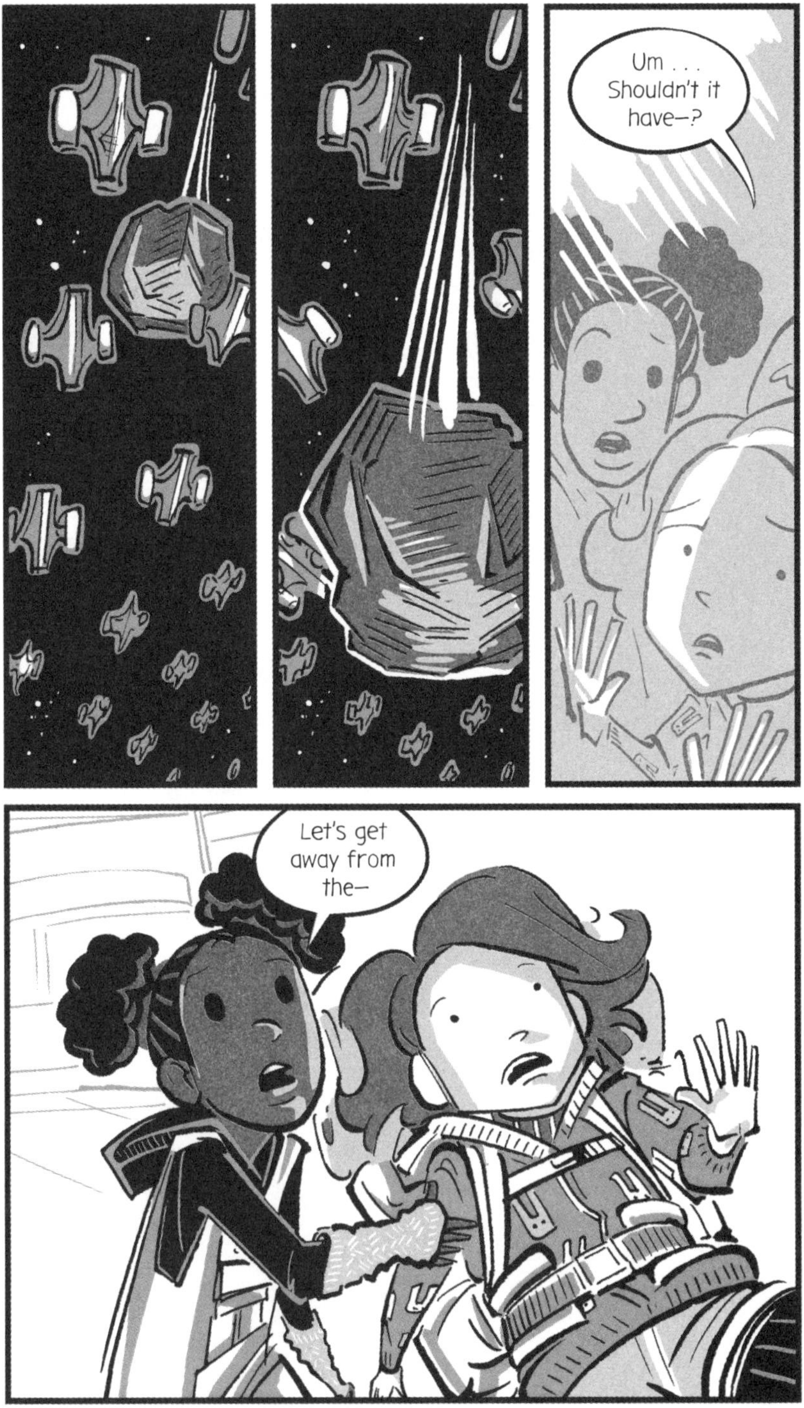
Um . . . Shouldn't it have—?
Let's get away from the—

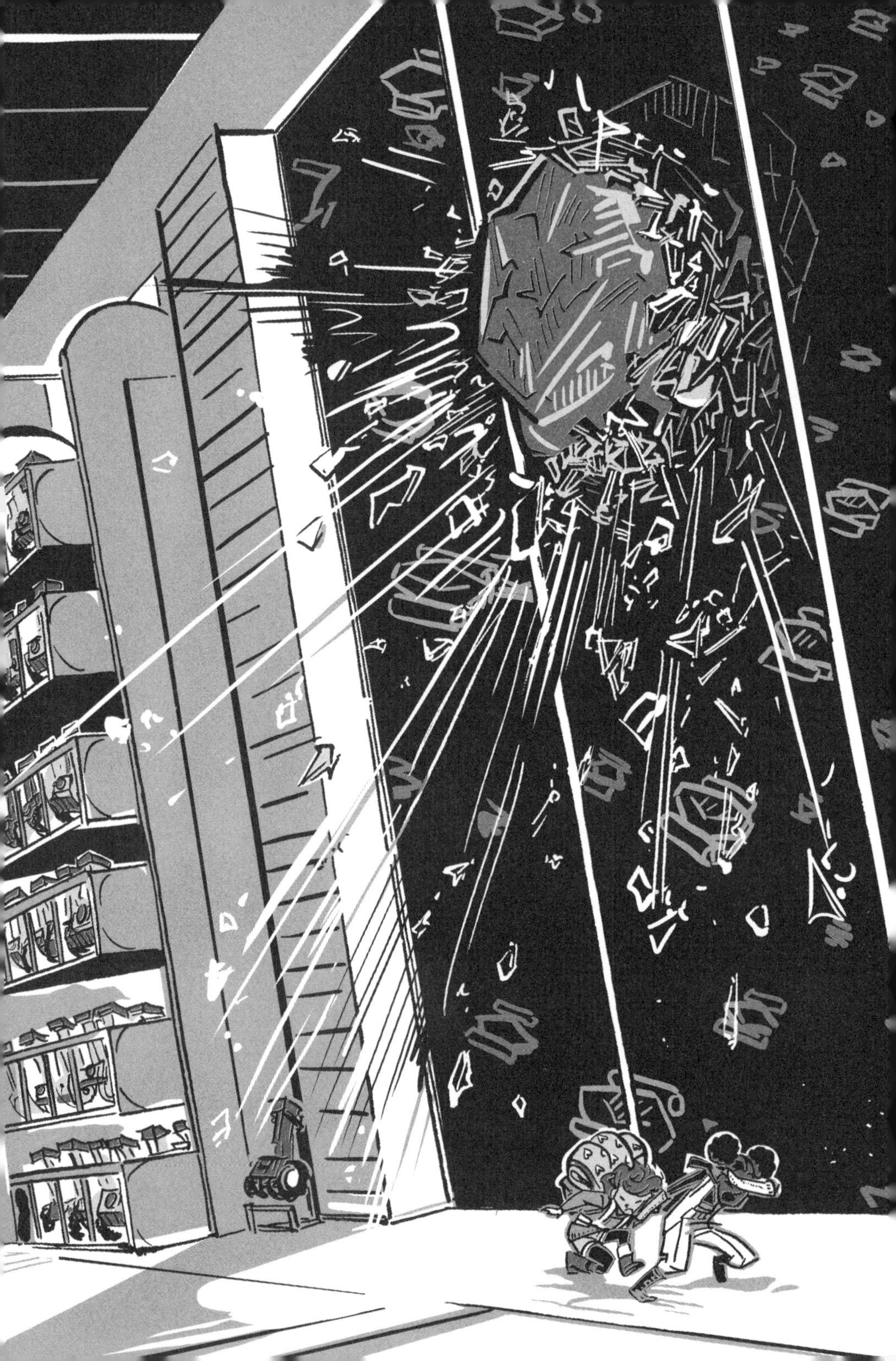

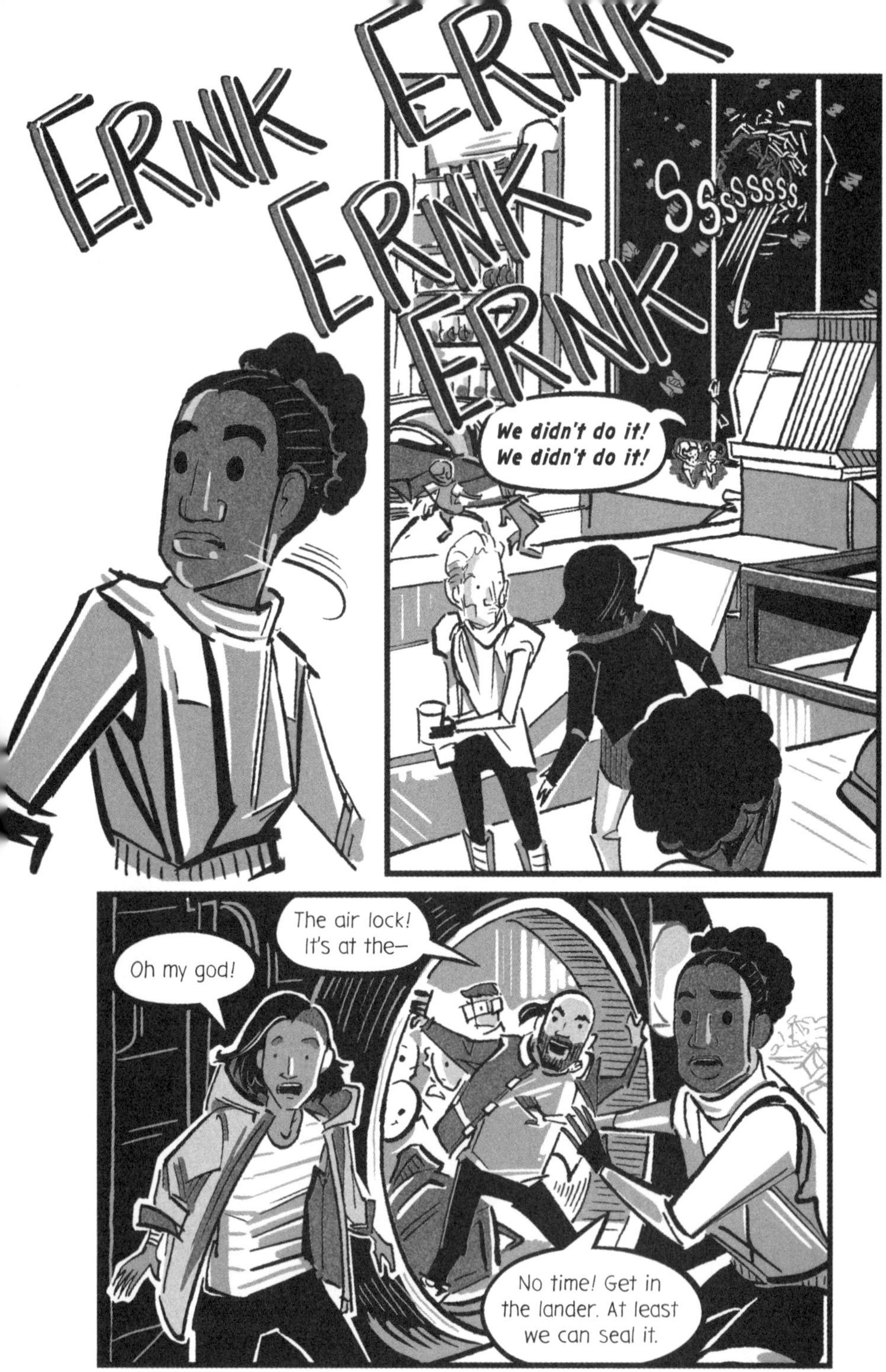
ERNK ERNK
ERNK
ERNK
Ssssssss
We didn't do it! We didn't do it!
Oh my god!
The air lock! It's at the–
No time! Get in the lander. At least we can seal it.

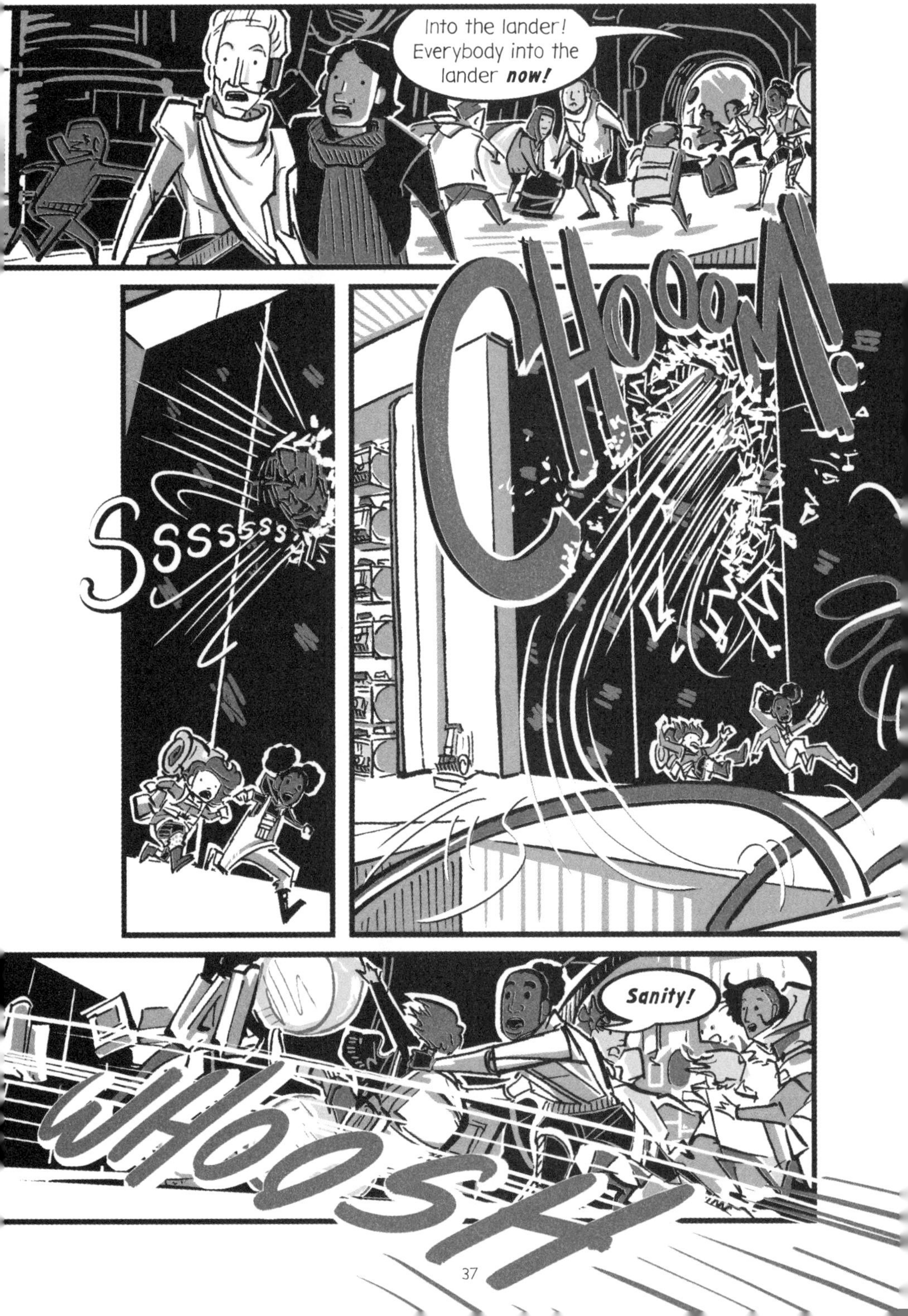
Into the lander! Everybody into the lander **now!**
SSSSSSS
CHOOOM!
Sanity!
WHOOSH

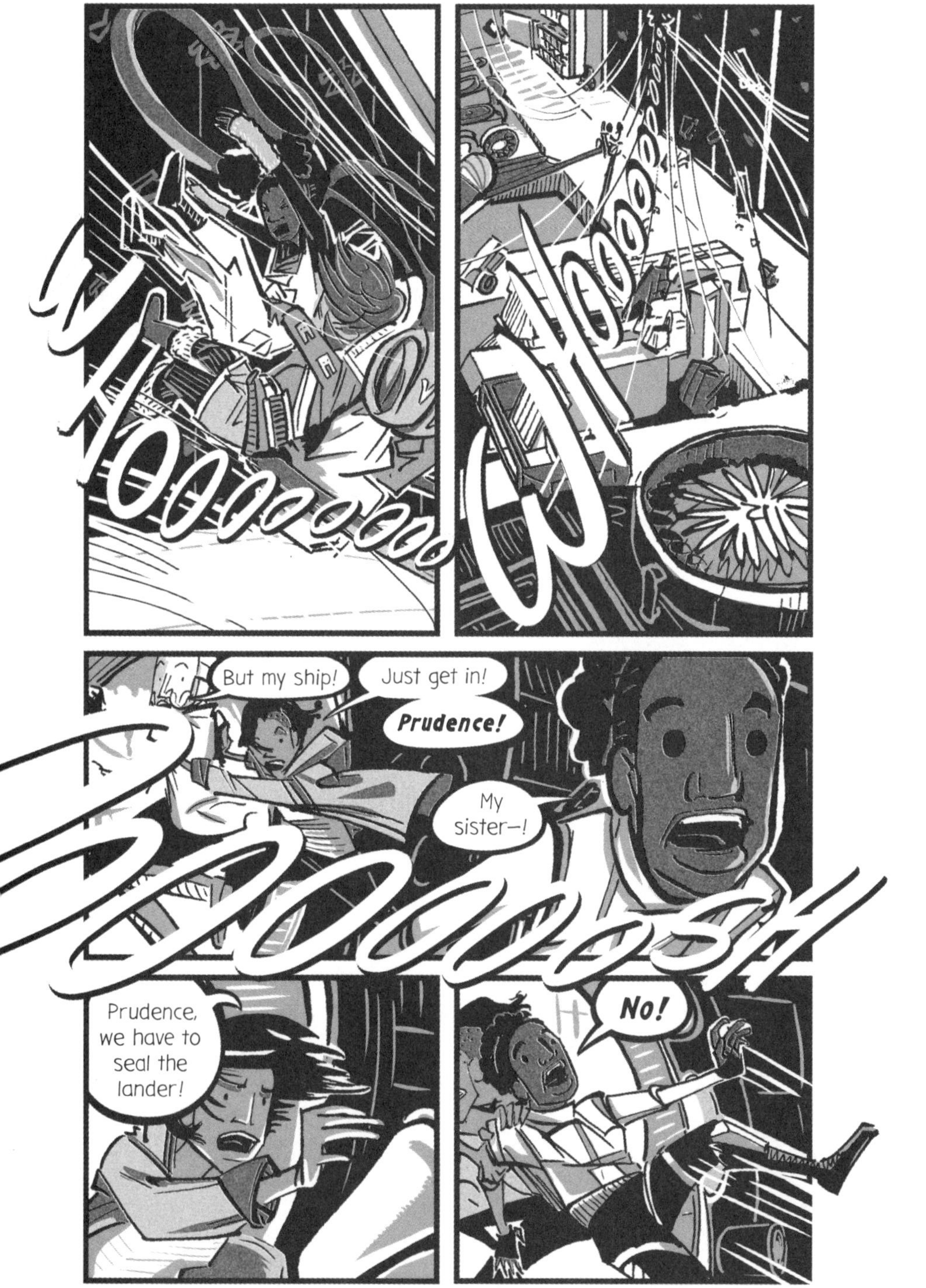

SHHOOOOOOOOOOOOOOM
But my ship!
Just get in!
Prudence!
My sister—!
BOOOOOSH
Prudence, we have to seal the lander!
No!

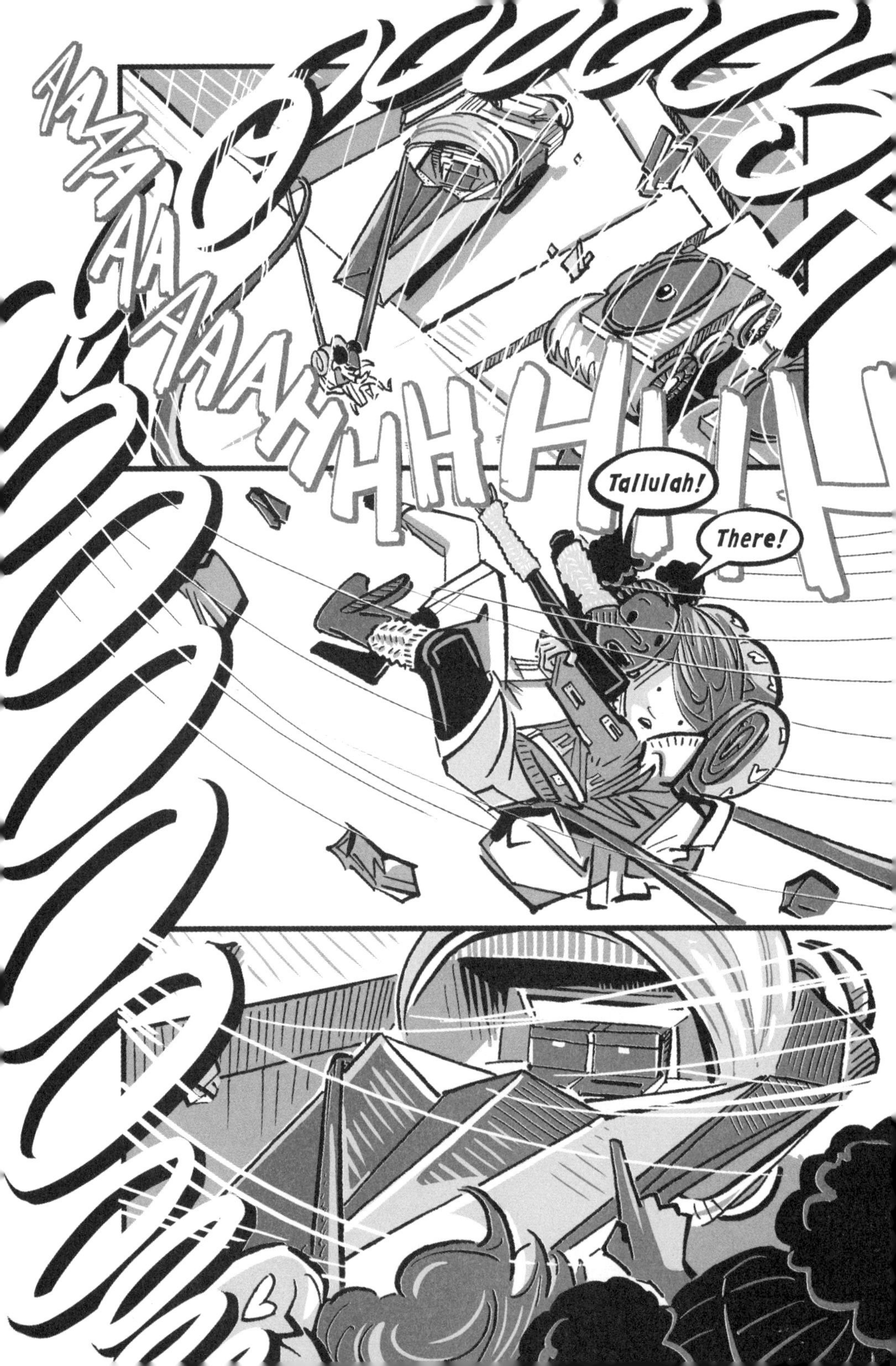
Tallulah!
There!

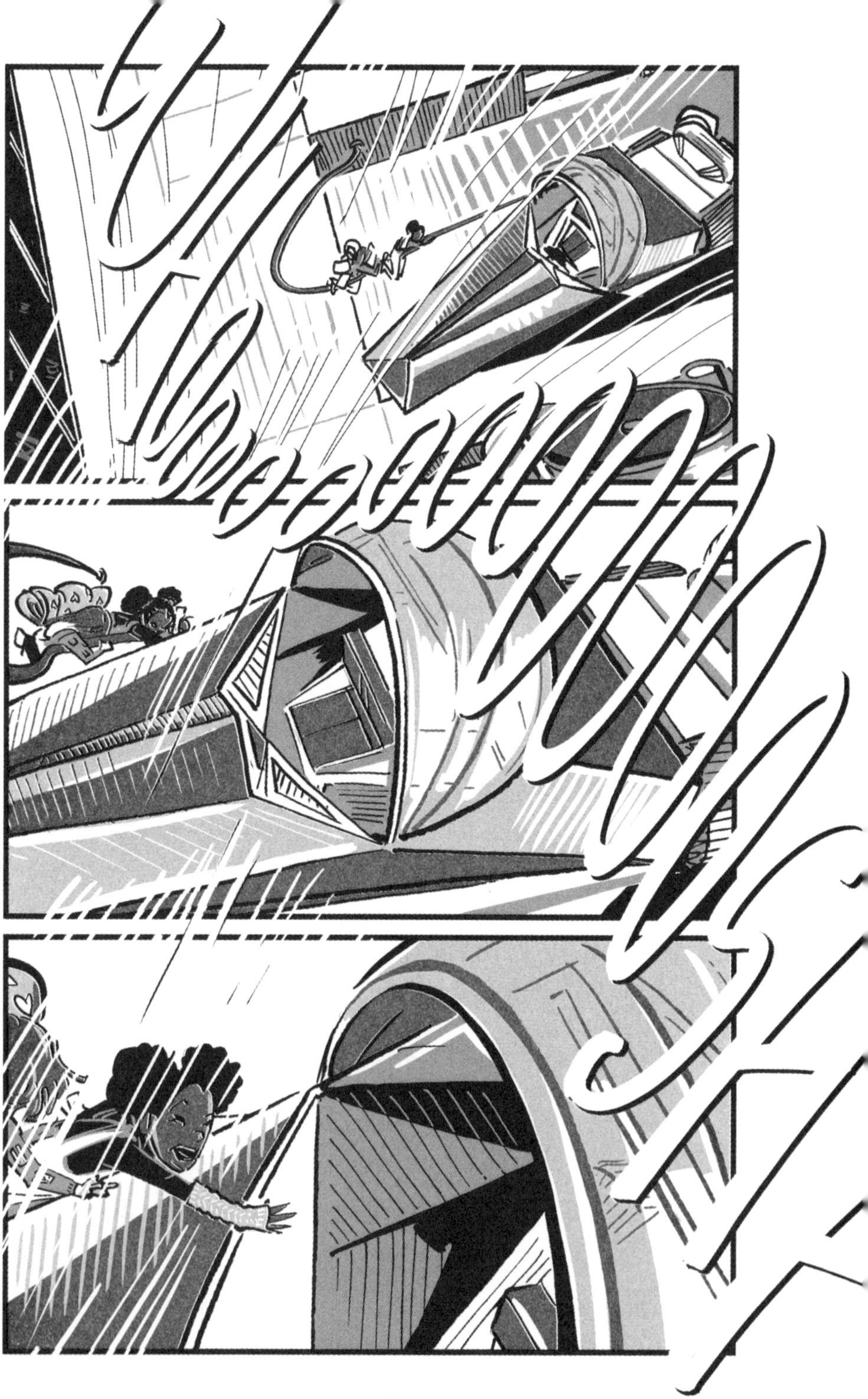
WHOOOOOOOOOOOOSH

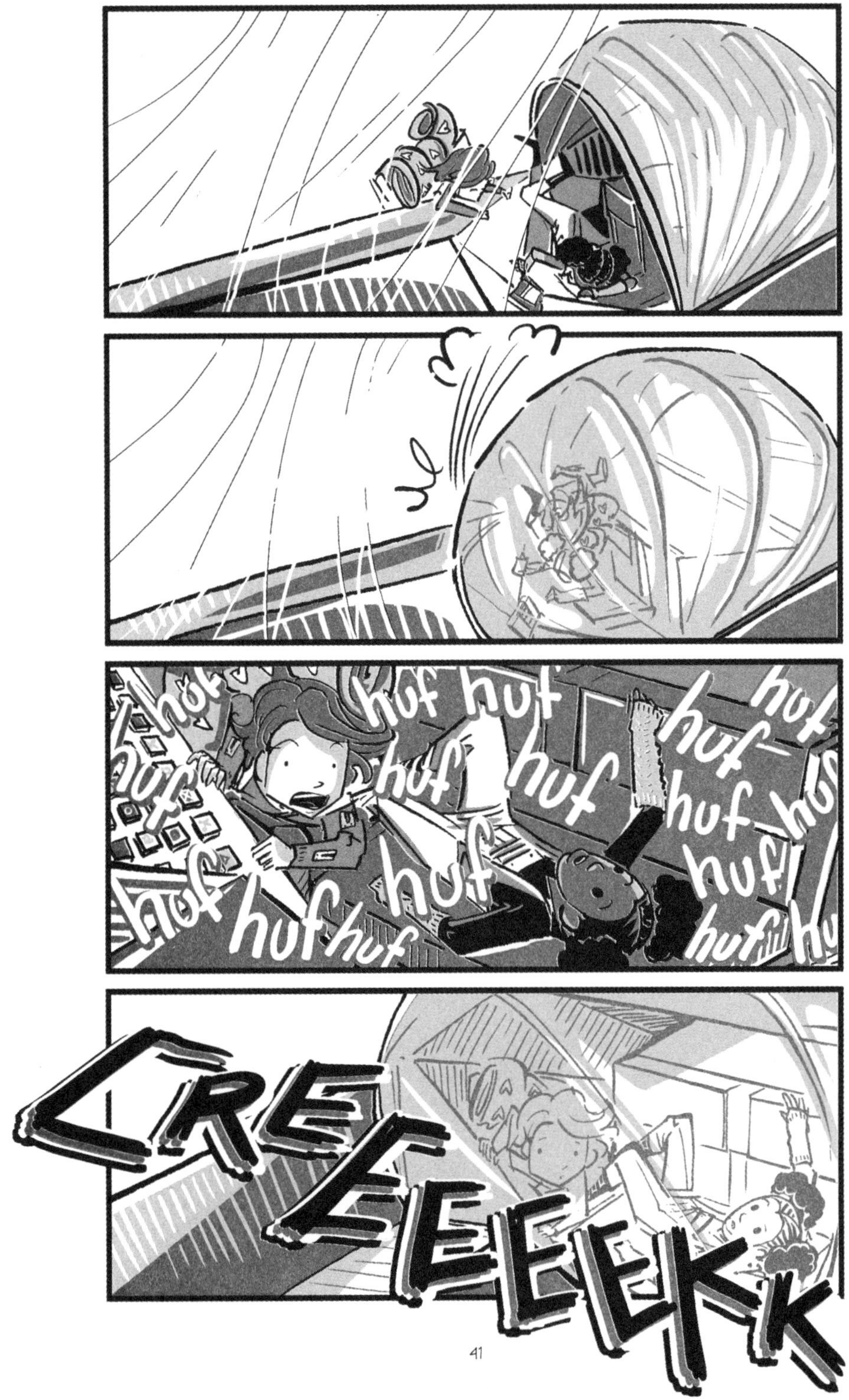
huf huf
huf
huf
huf
huf
huf
huf
huf
huf
huf
huf
huf huf
huf
huf
CREEEEEKK

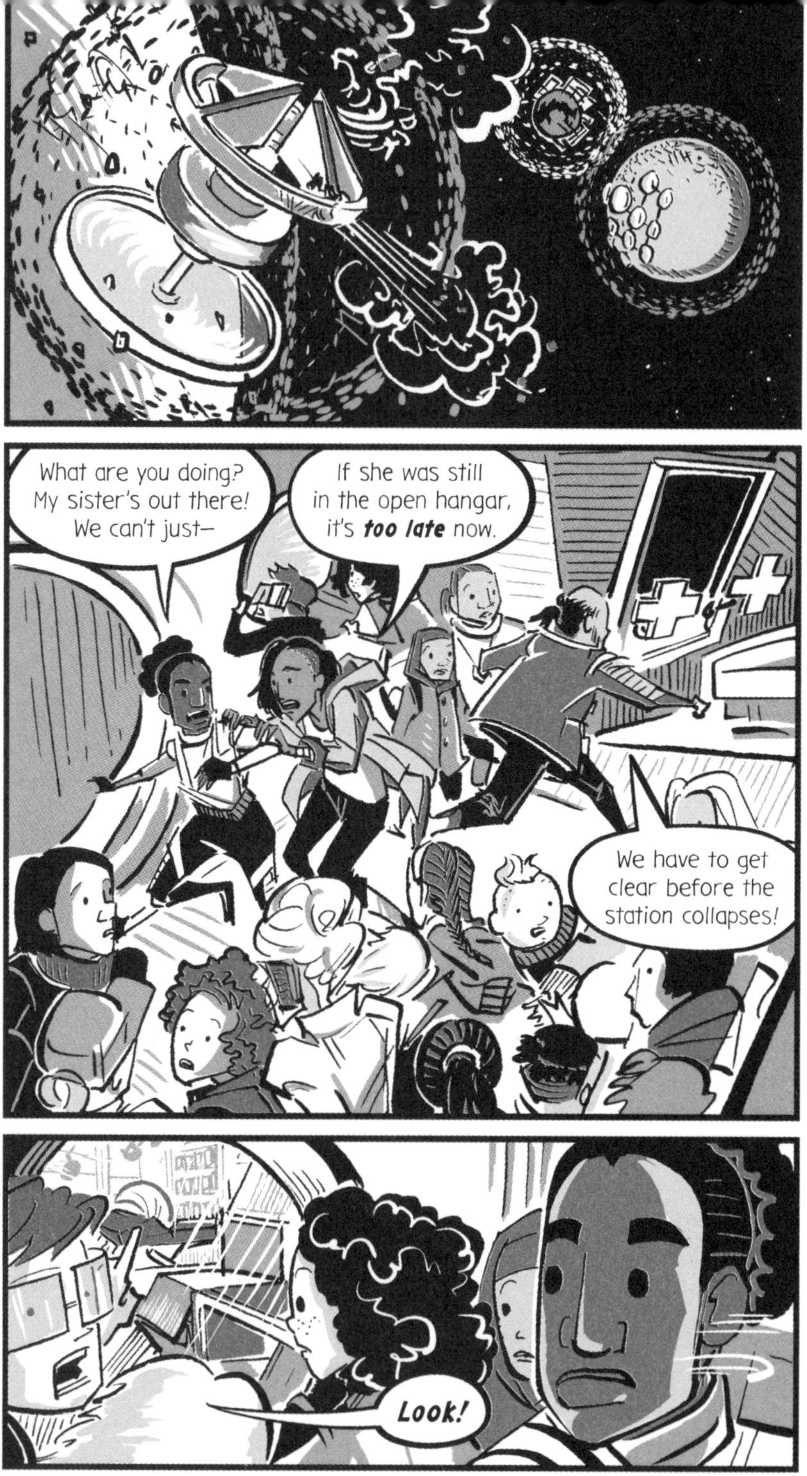
What are you doing? My sister's out there! We can't just—
If she was still in the open hangar, it's **too late** now.
We have to get clear before the station collapses!
Look!

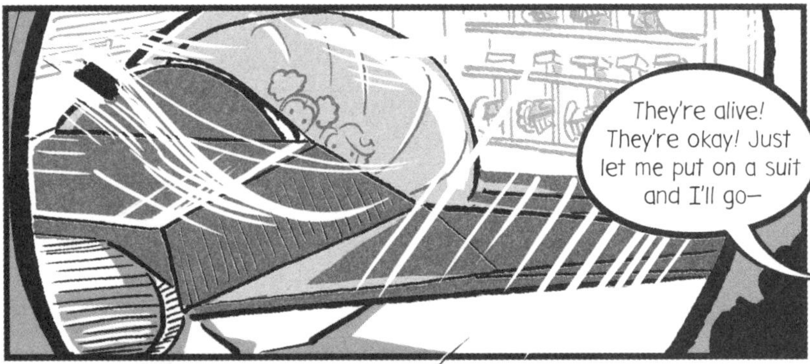
They're alive! They're okay! Just let me put on a suit and I'll go—

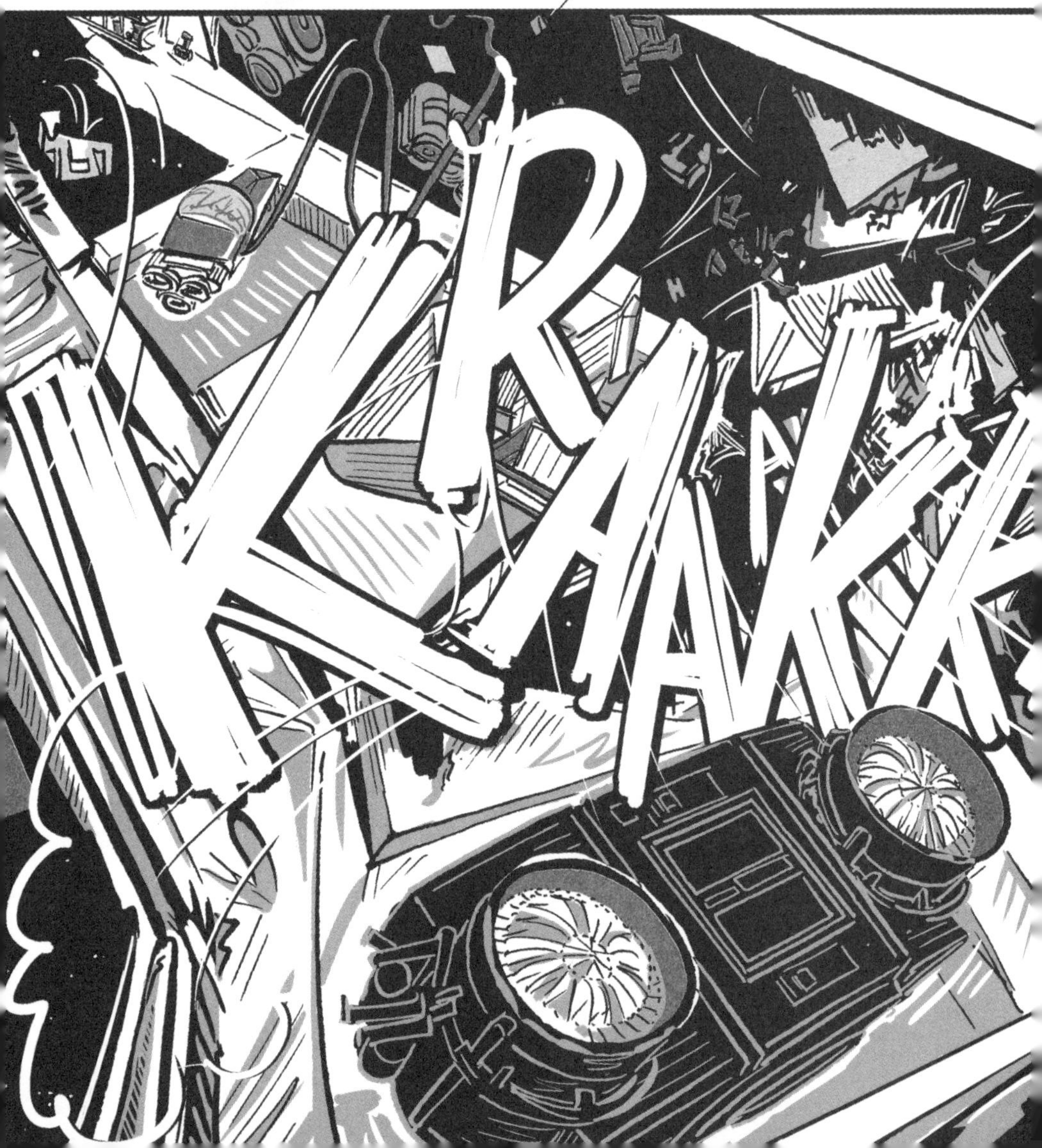
KRAKK

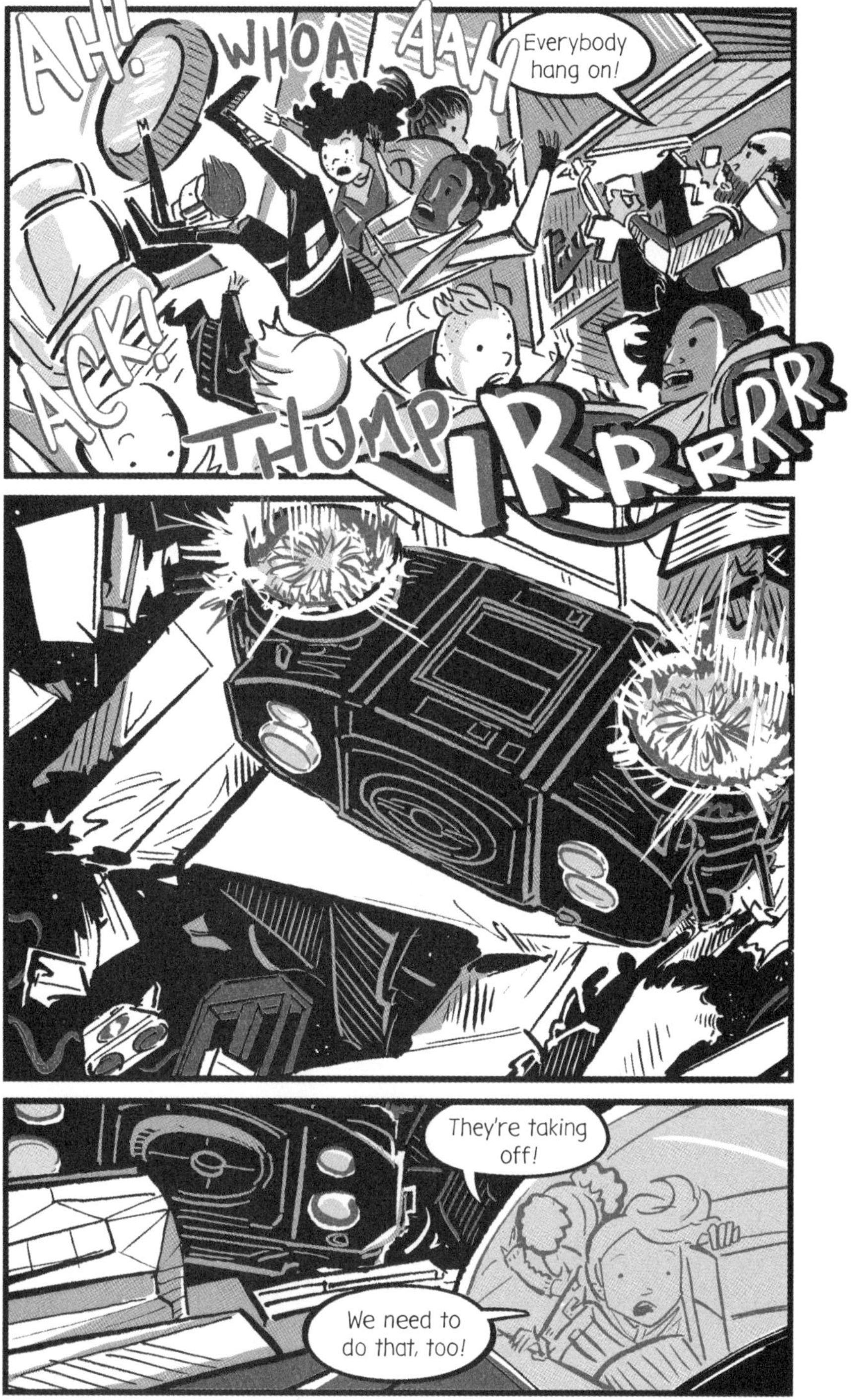
AH!
WHOA
AAH
Everybody hang on!
ACK!
THUMP
VRRRRR
They're taking off!
We need to do that, too!

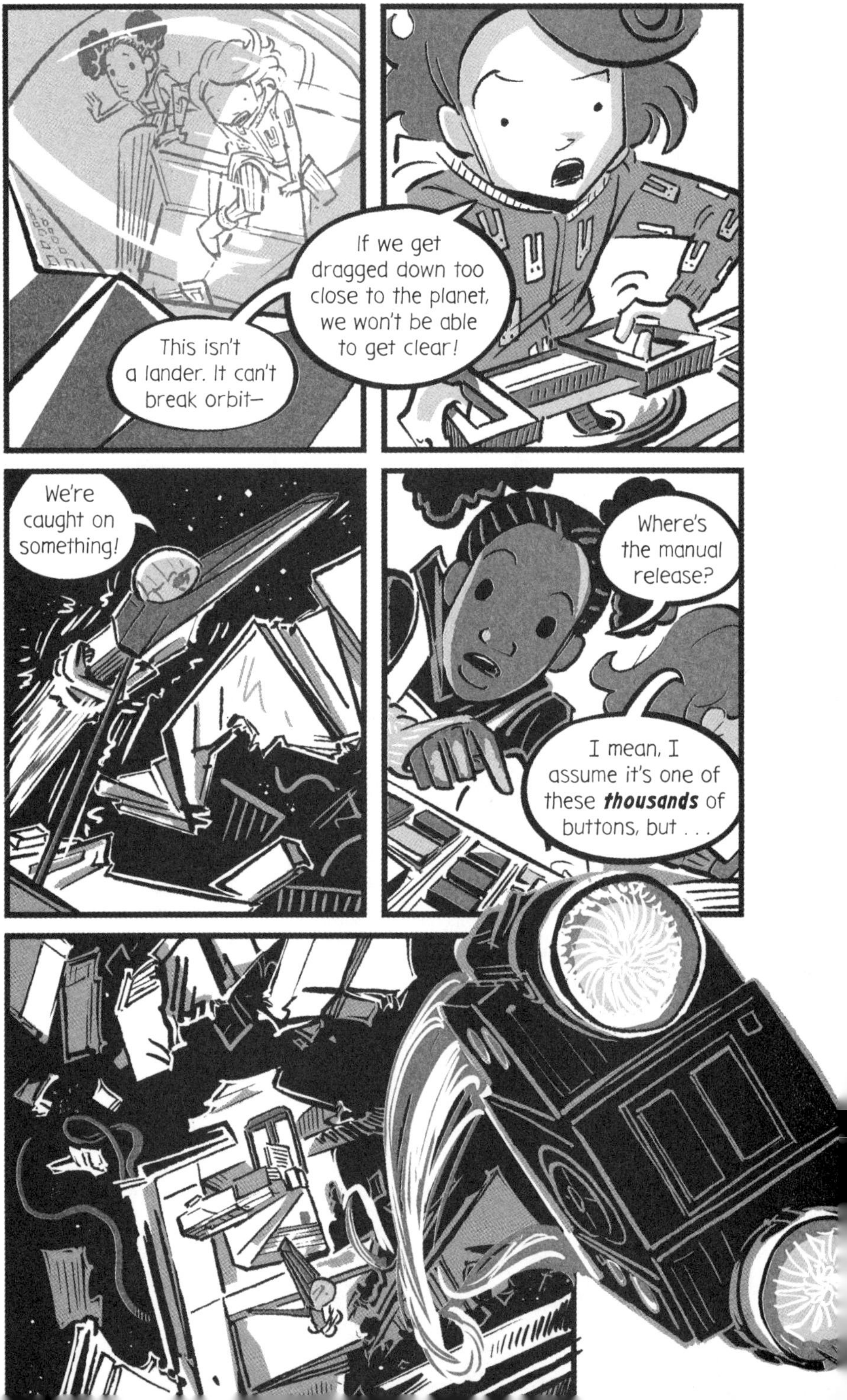
This isn't a lander. It can't break orbit–
If we get dragged down too close to the planet, we won't be able to get clear!
We're caught on something!
Where's the manual release?
I mean, I assume it's one of these ***thousands*** of buttons, but . . .

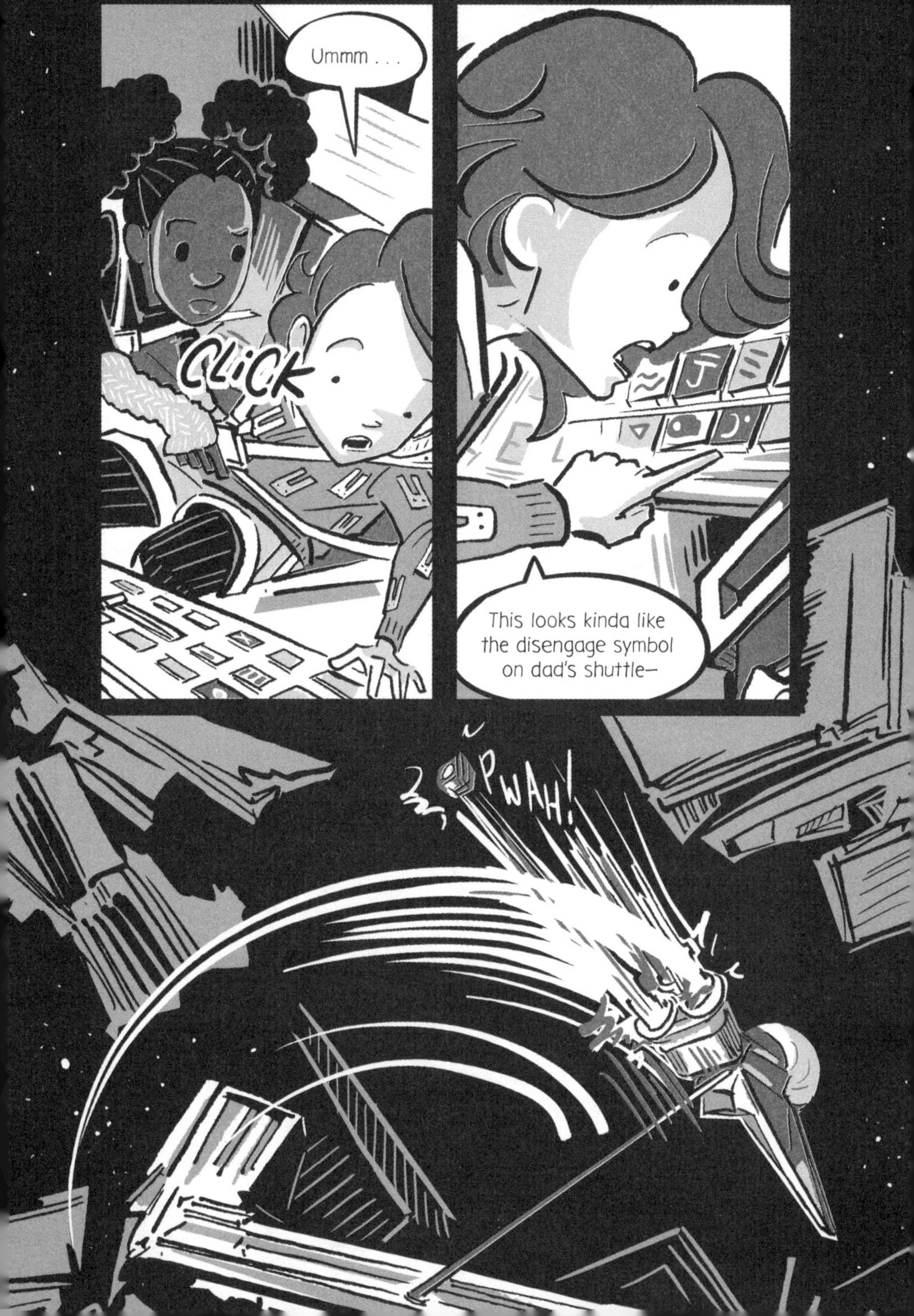
Ummm . . .
CLICK
This looks kinda like the disengage symbol on dad's shuttle–
PWAH!

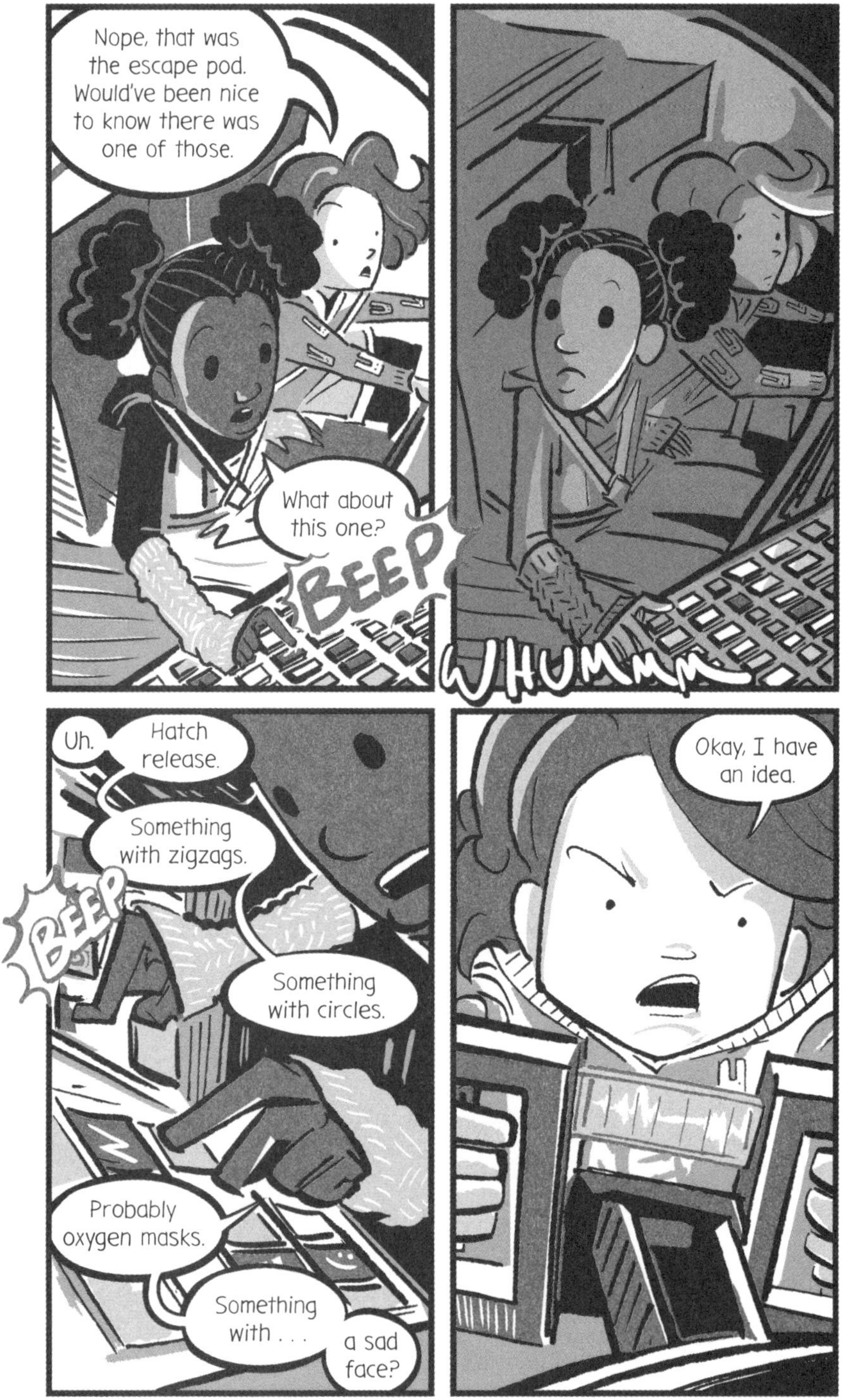
Nope, that was the escape pod. Would've been nice to know there was one of those.
What about this one?
BEEP
WHUMMM
Uh.
Hatch release.
Something with zigzags.
BEEP
Something with circles.
Probably oxygen masks.
Something with . . .
a sad face?
Okay, I have an idea.

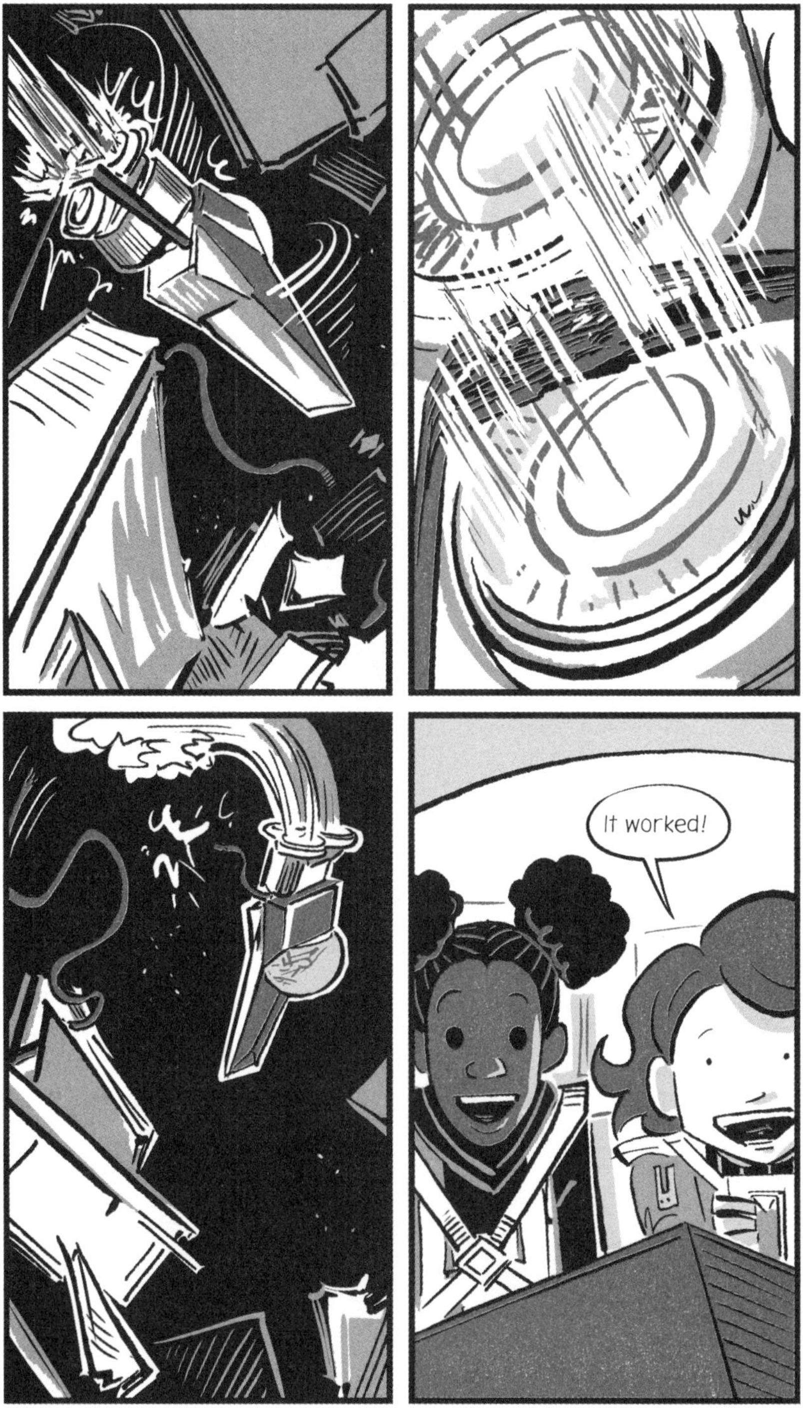
It worked!

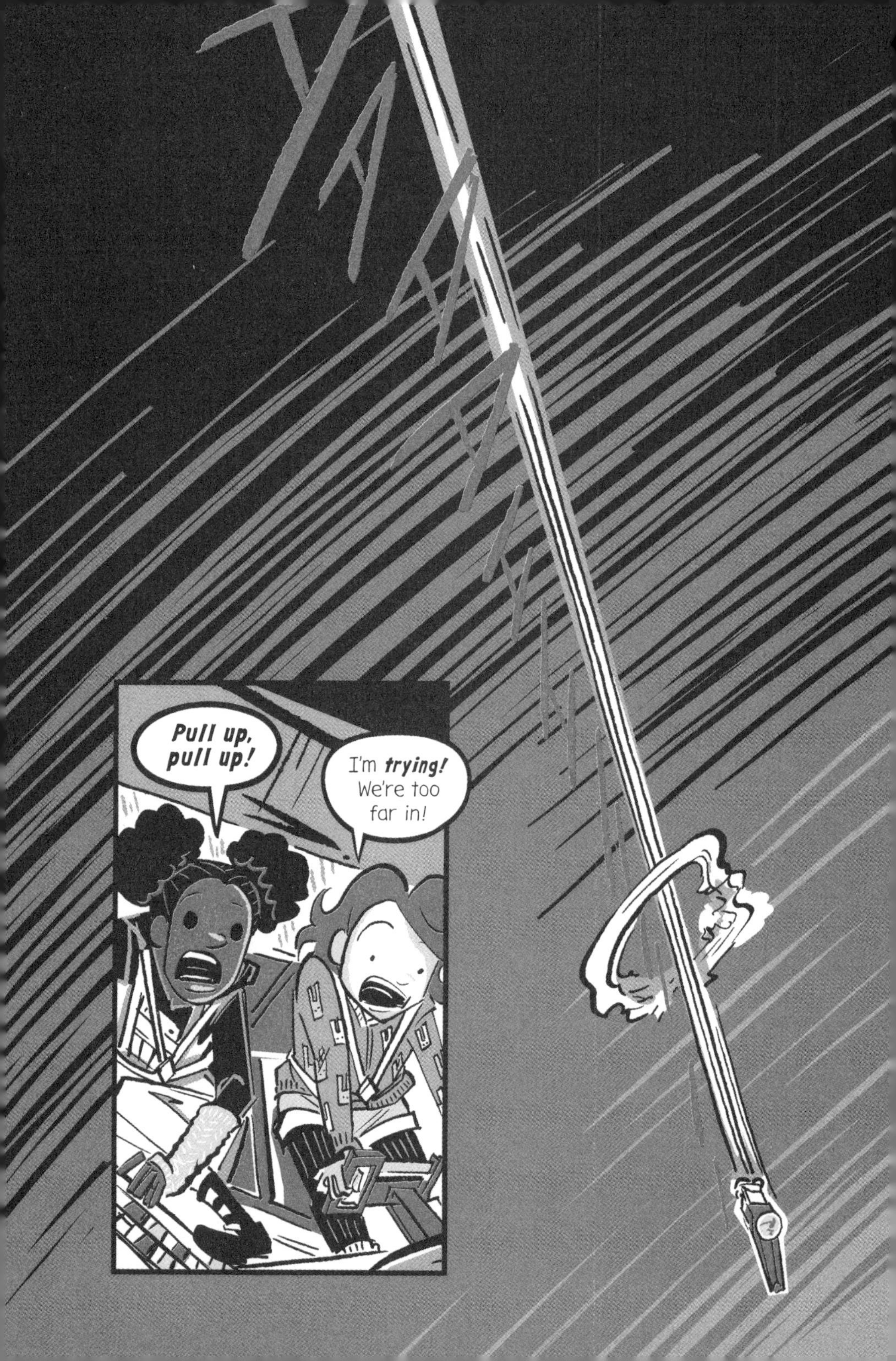
YAAAAAAAA
Pull up, pull up!
I'm trying! We're too far in!

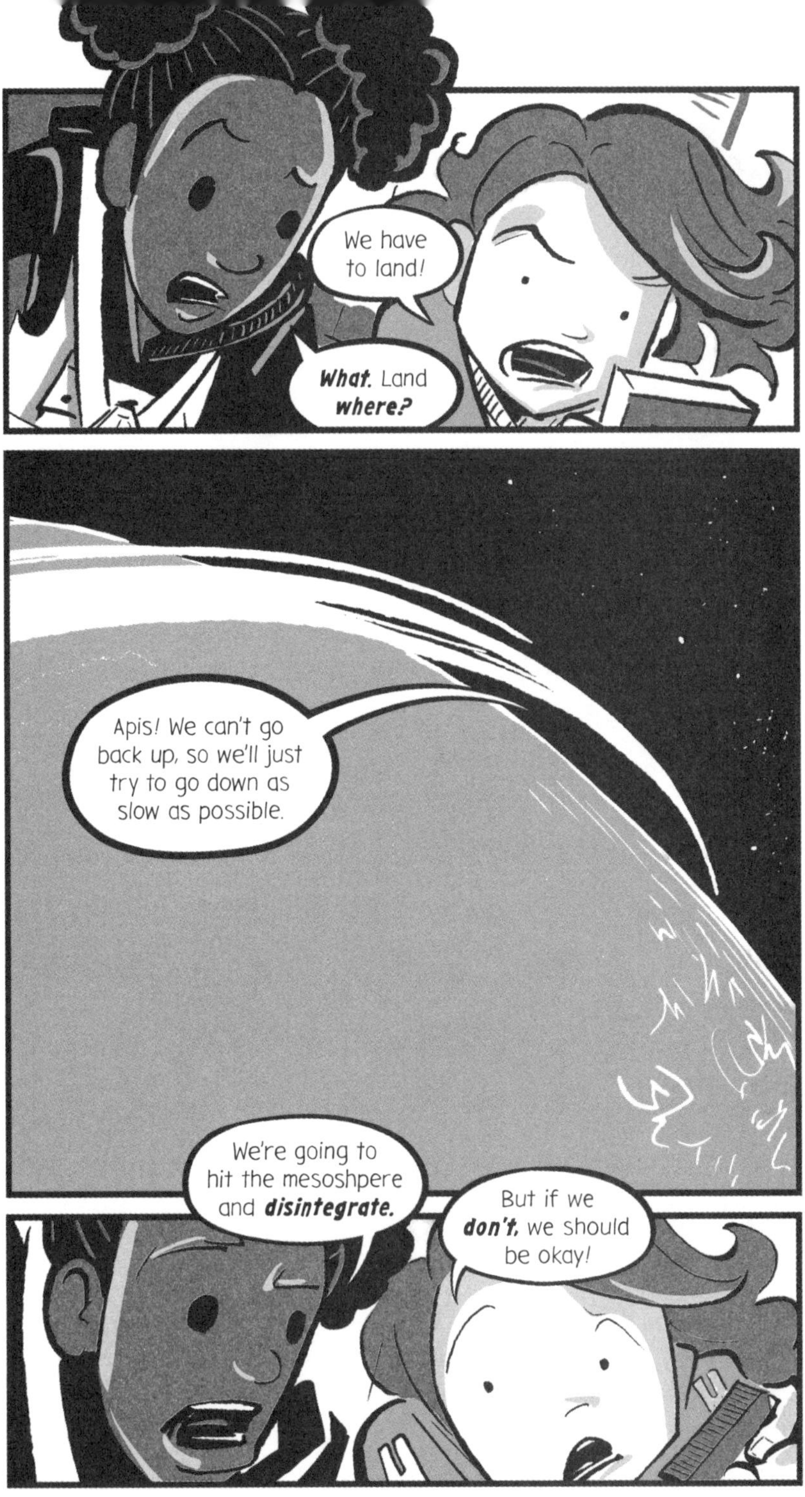
We have to land!
What. Land where?
Apis! We can't go back up, so we'll just try to go down as slow as possible.
We're going to hit the mesoshpere and disintegrate.
But if we don't, we should be okay!

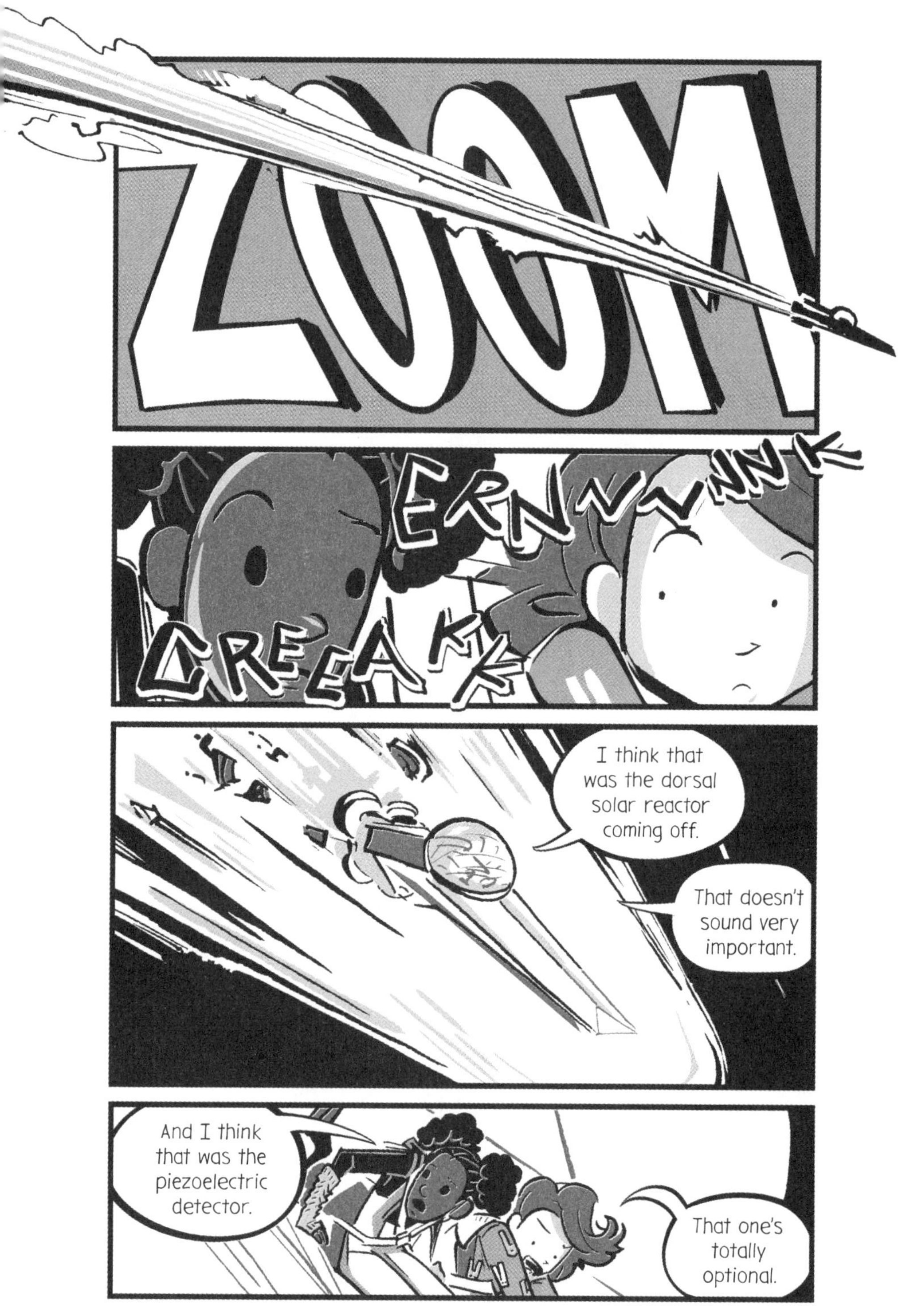
ZOOM
ERNNNNNK
CREEAKK
I think that was the dorsal solar reactor coming off.
That doesn't sound very important.
And I think that was the piezoelectric detector.
That one's totally optional.

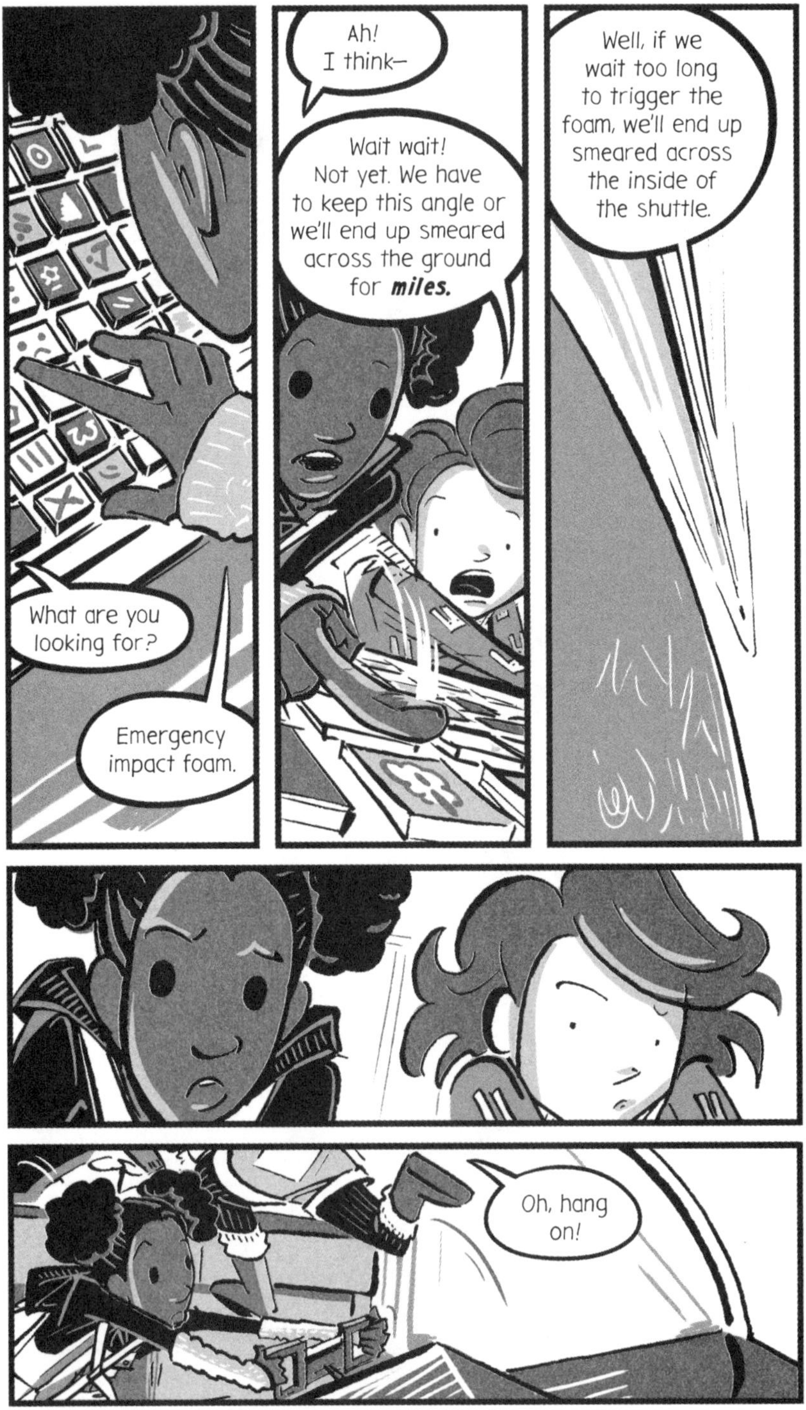
What are you looking for?
Emergency impact foam.
Ah! I think—
Wait wait! Not yet. We have to keep this angle or we'll end up smeared across the ground for **miles.**
Well, if we wait too long to trigger the foam, we'll end up smeared across the inside of the shuttle.
Oh, hang on!

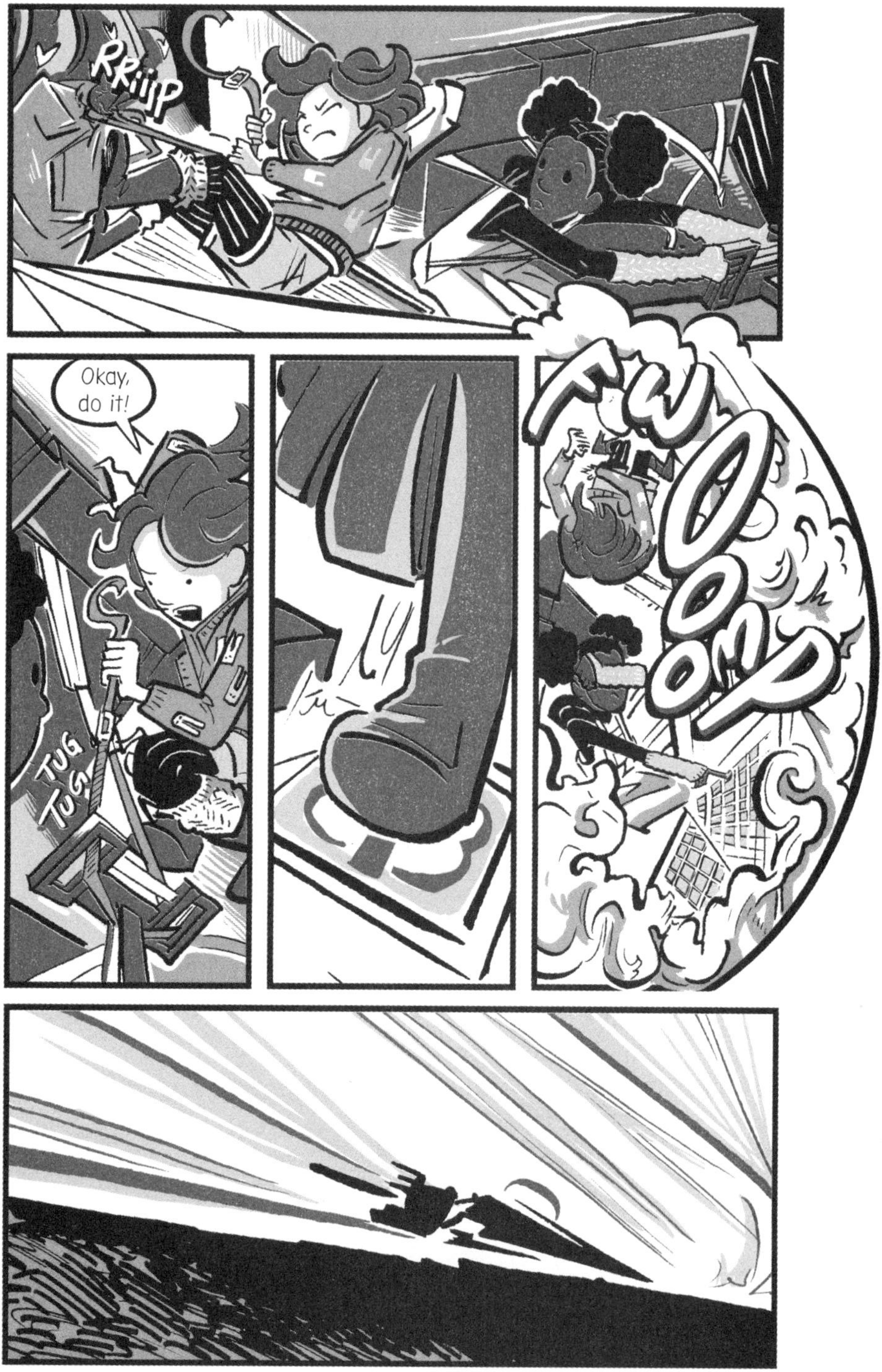
RRIIIP
Okay, do it!
TUG TUG
FWOOOOMP

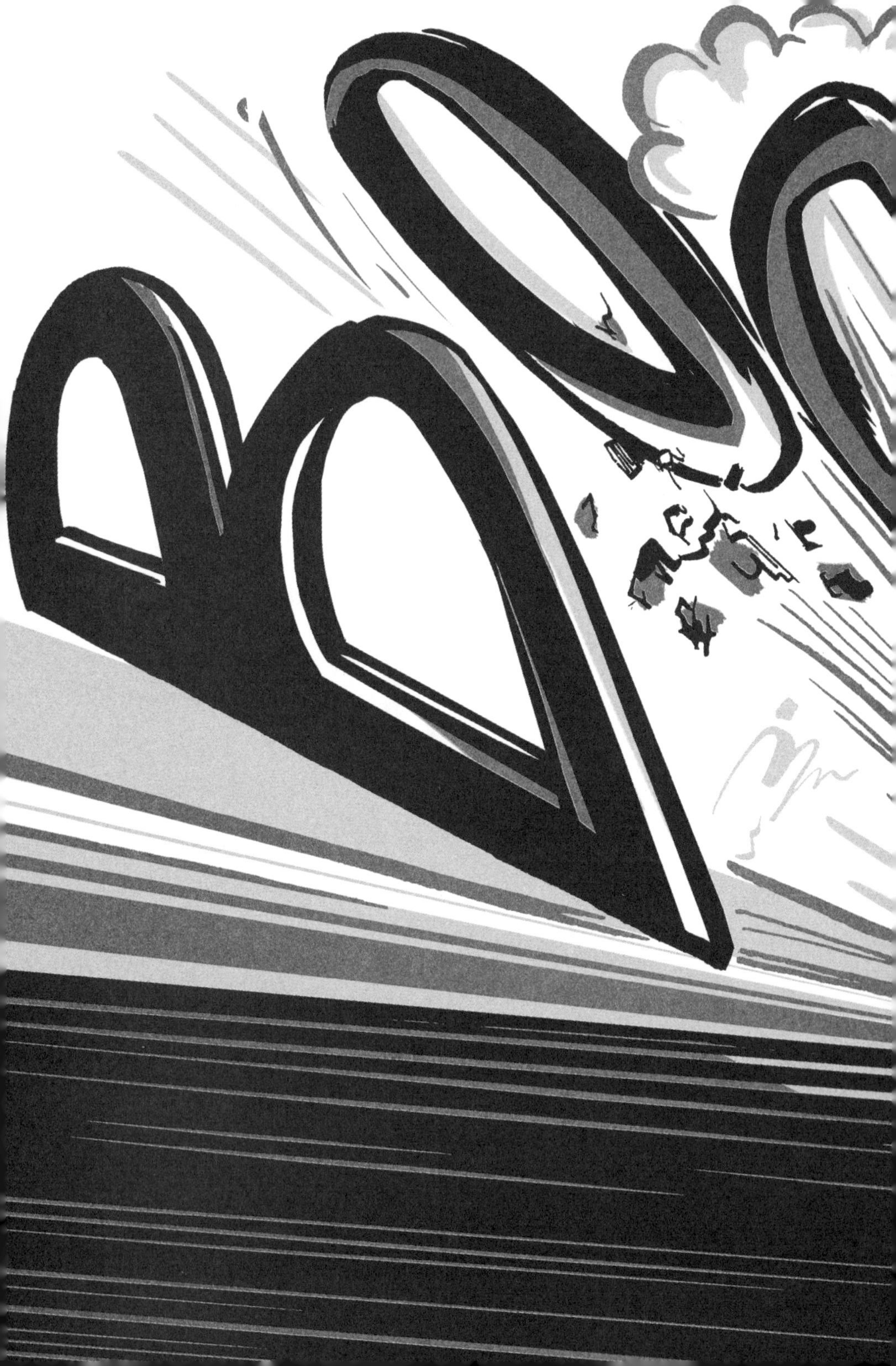
BOO

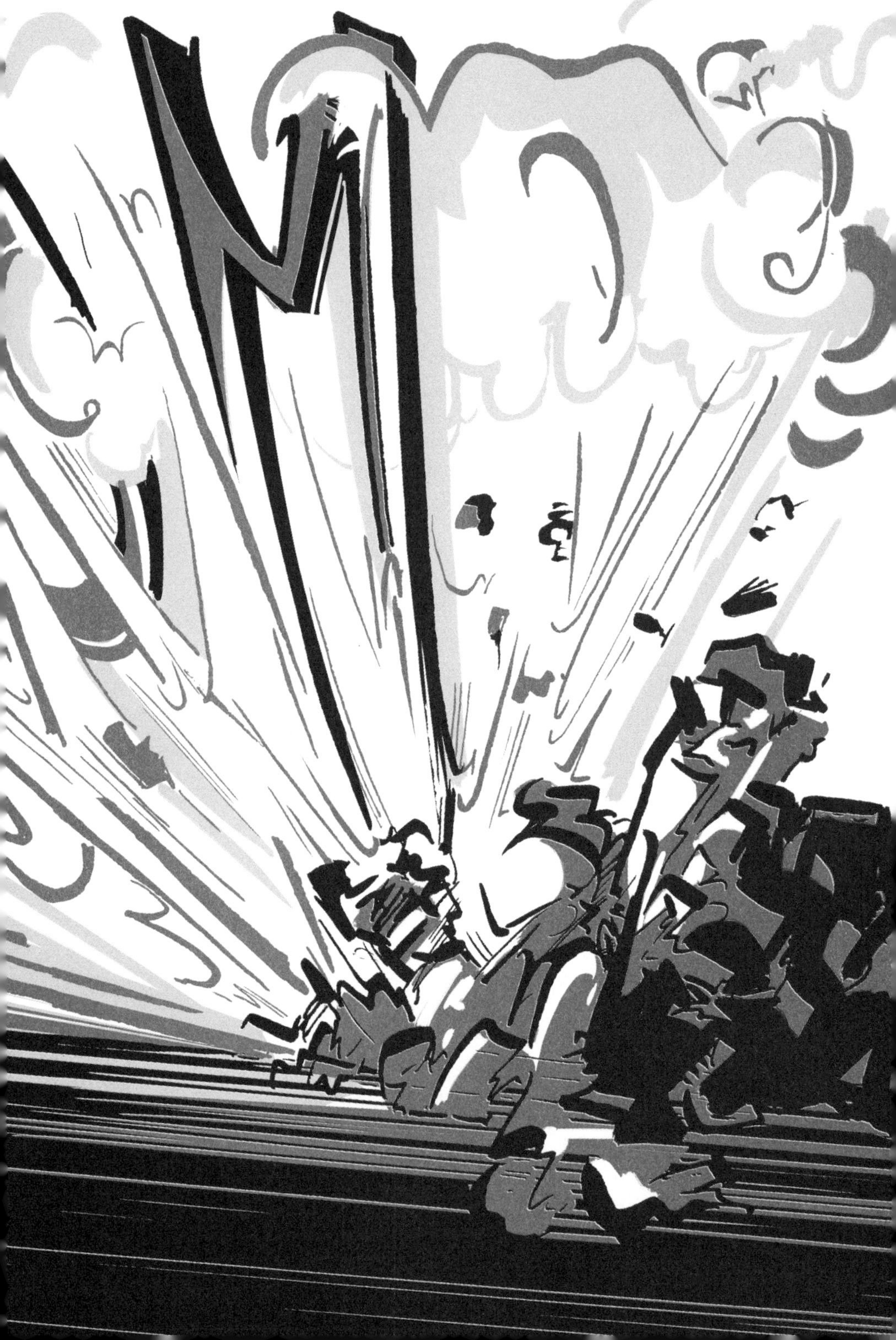

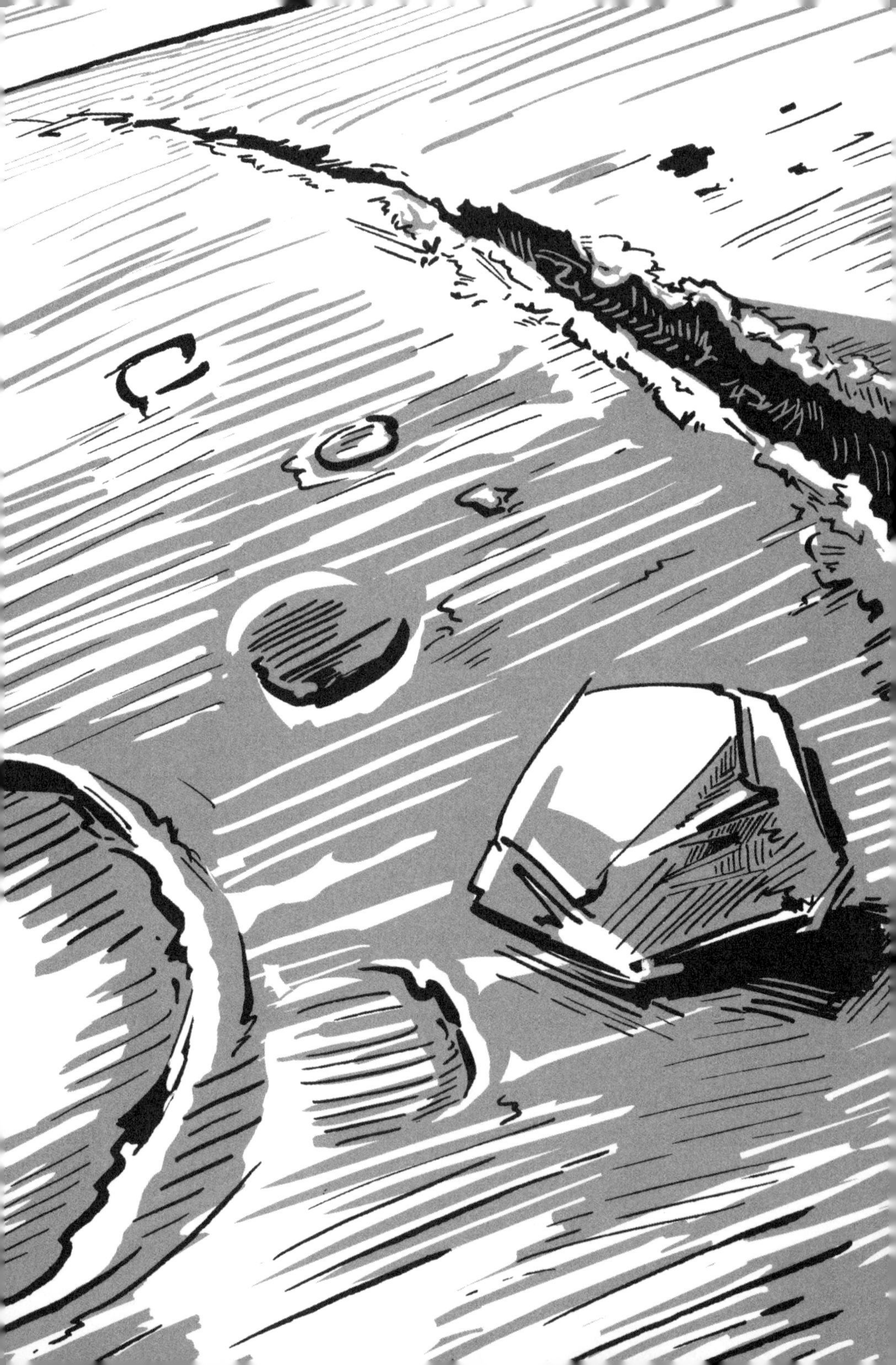

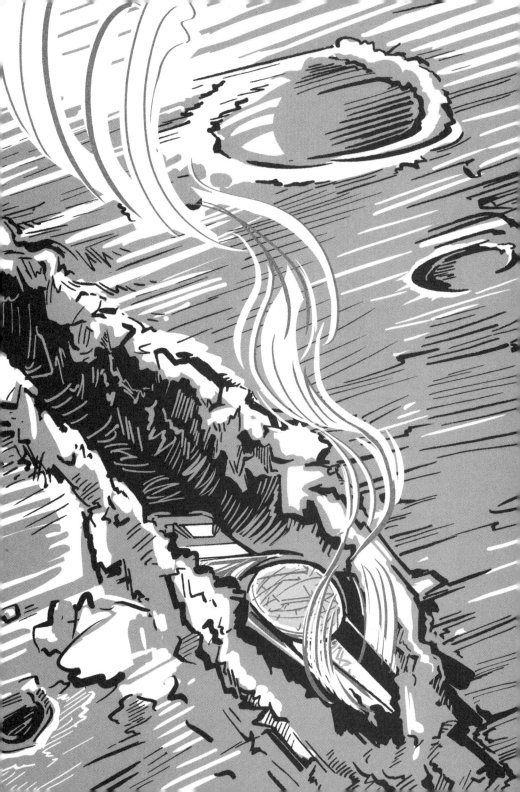

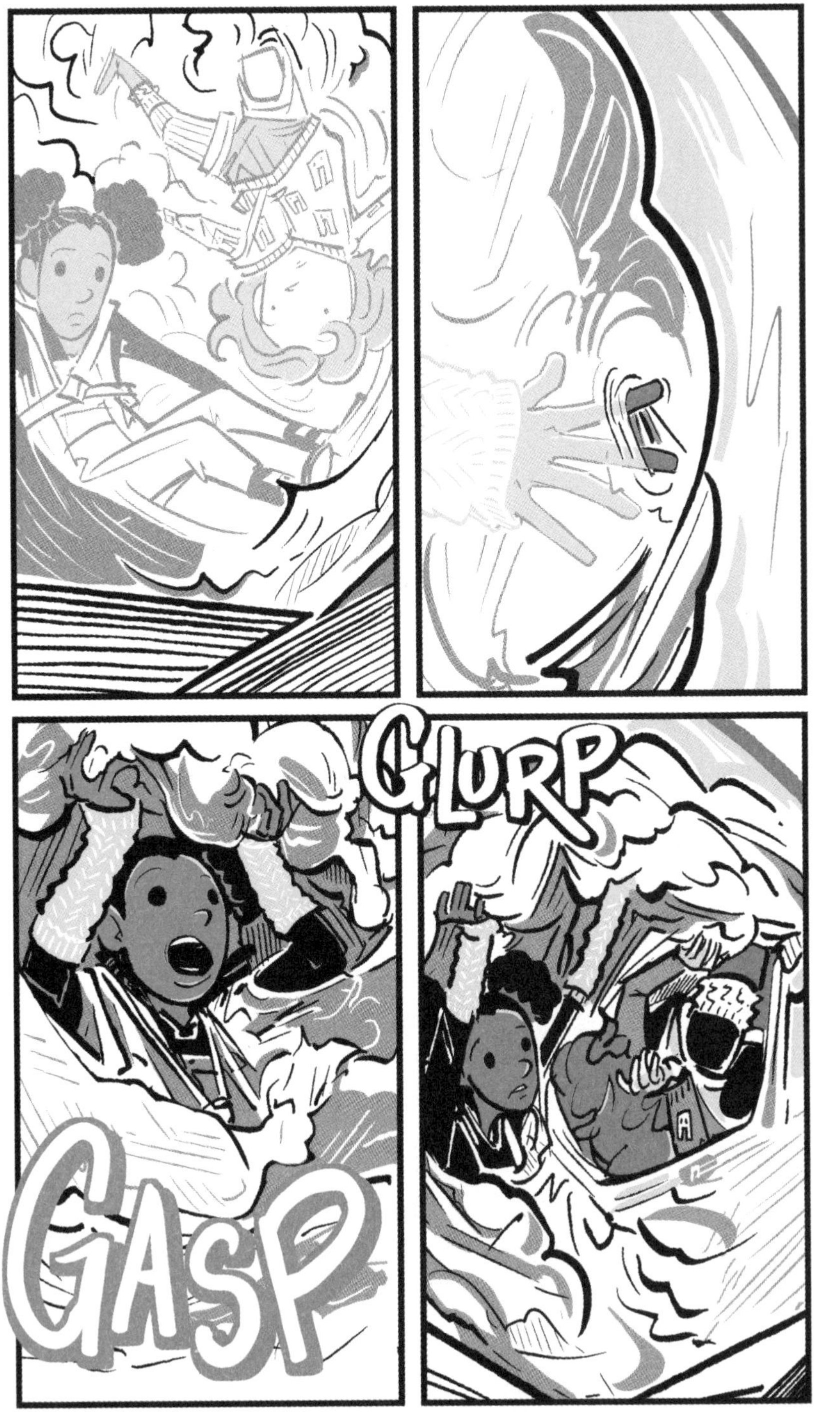
GLURP
GASP

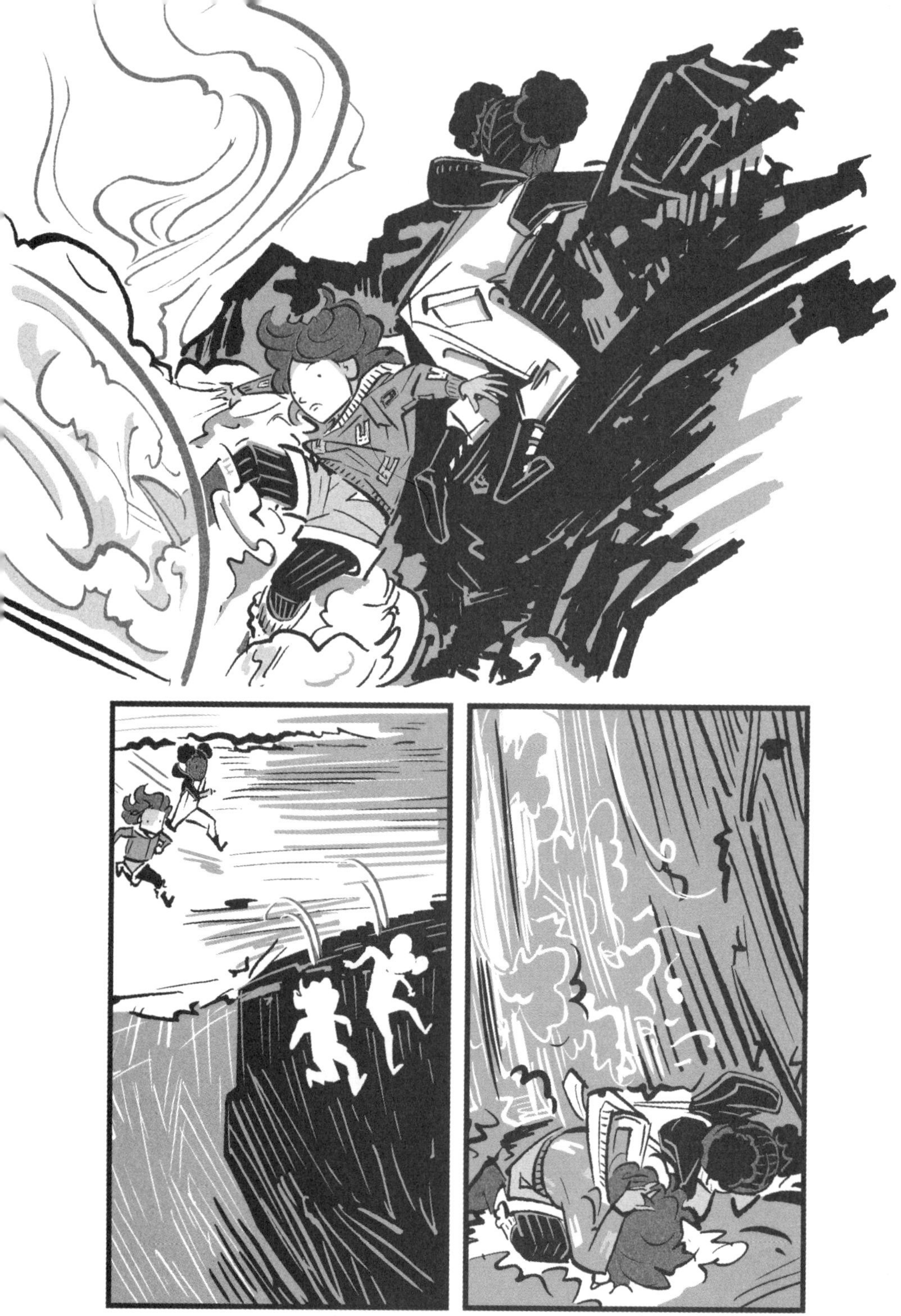

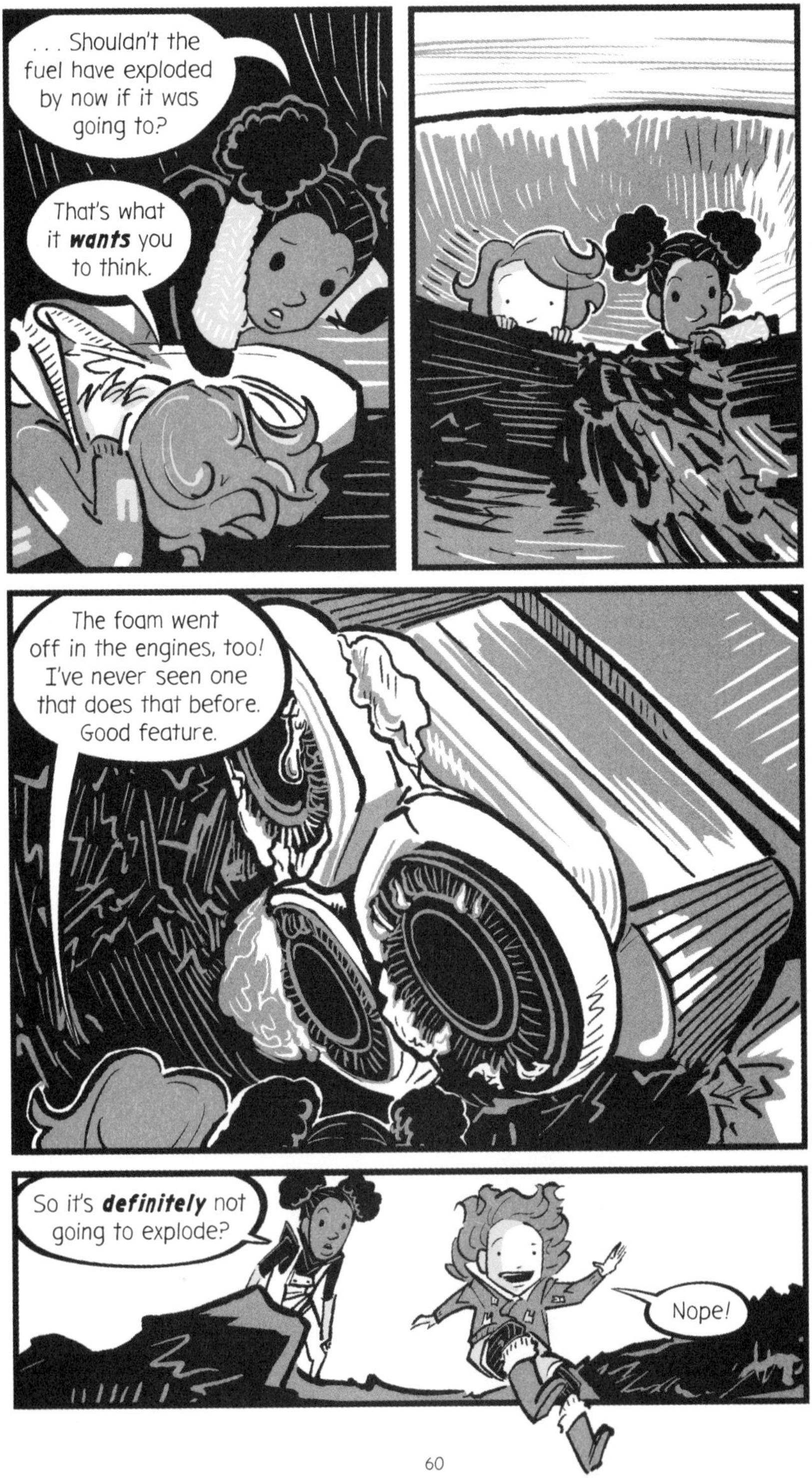
. . . Shouldn't the fuel have exploded by now if it was going to?
That's what it **wants** you to think.
The foam went off in the engines, too! I've never seen one that does that before. Good feature.
So it's **definitely** not going to explode?
Nope!

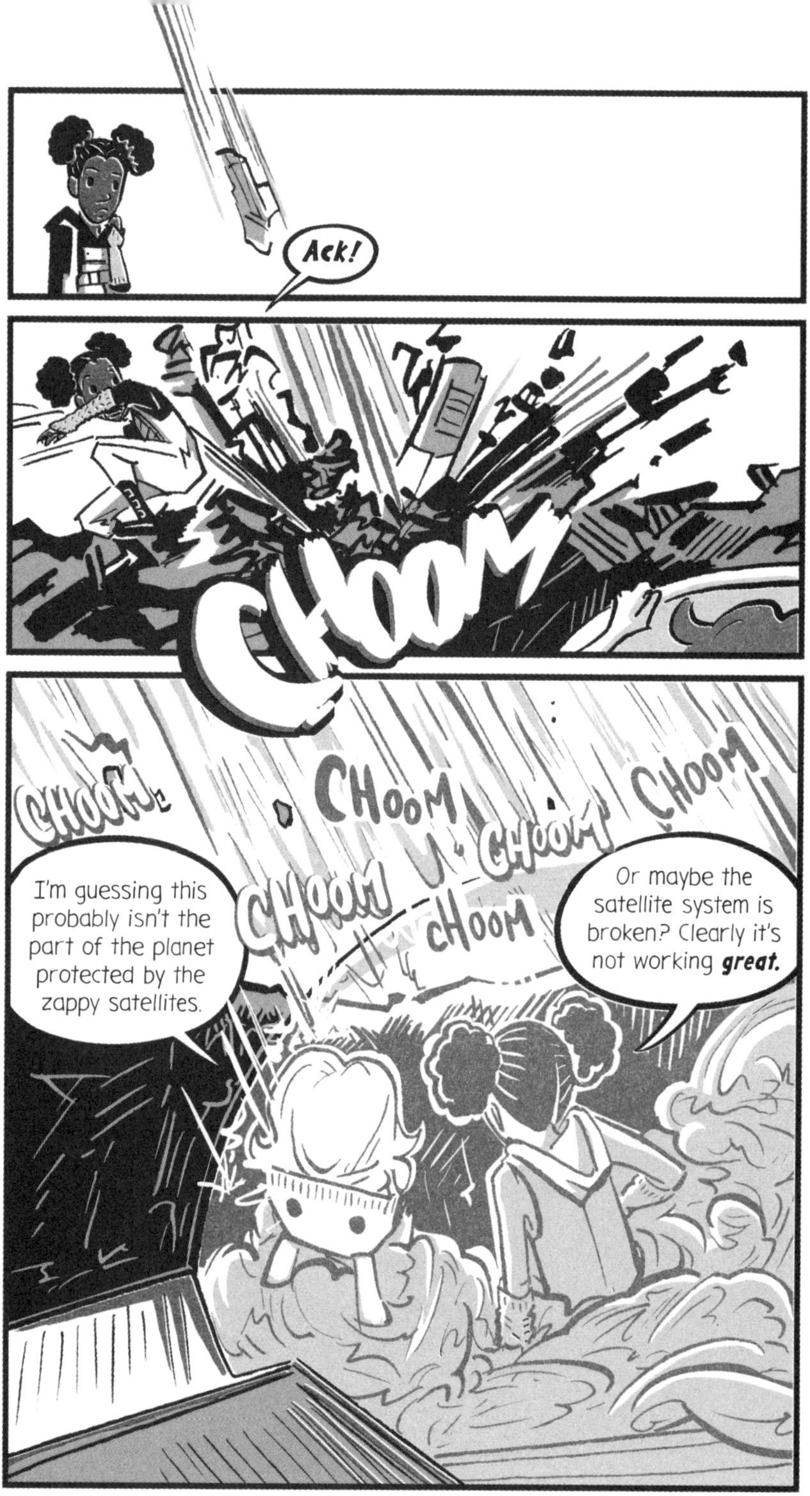
Ack!
CHOOM
CHOOM
CHOOM
CHOOM
CHOOM
CHOOM
CHOOM
I'm guessing this probably isn't the part of the planet protected by the zappy satellites.
Or maybe the satellite system is broken? Clearly it's not working **great.**

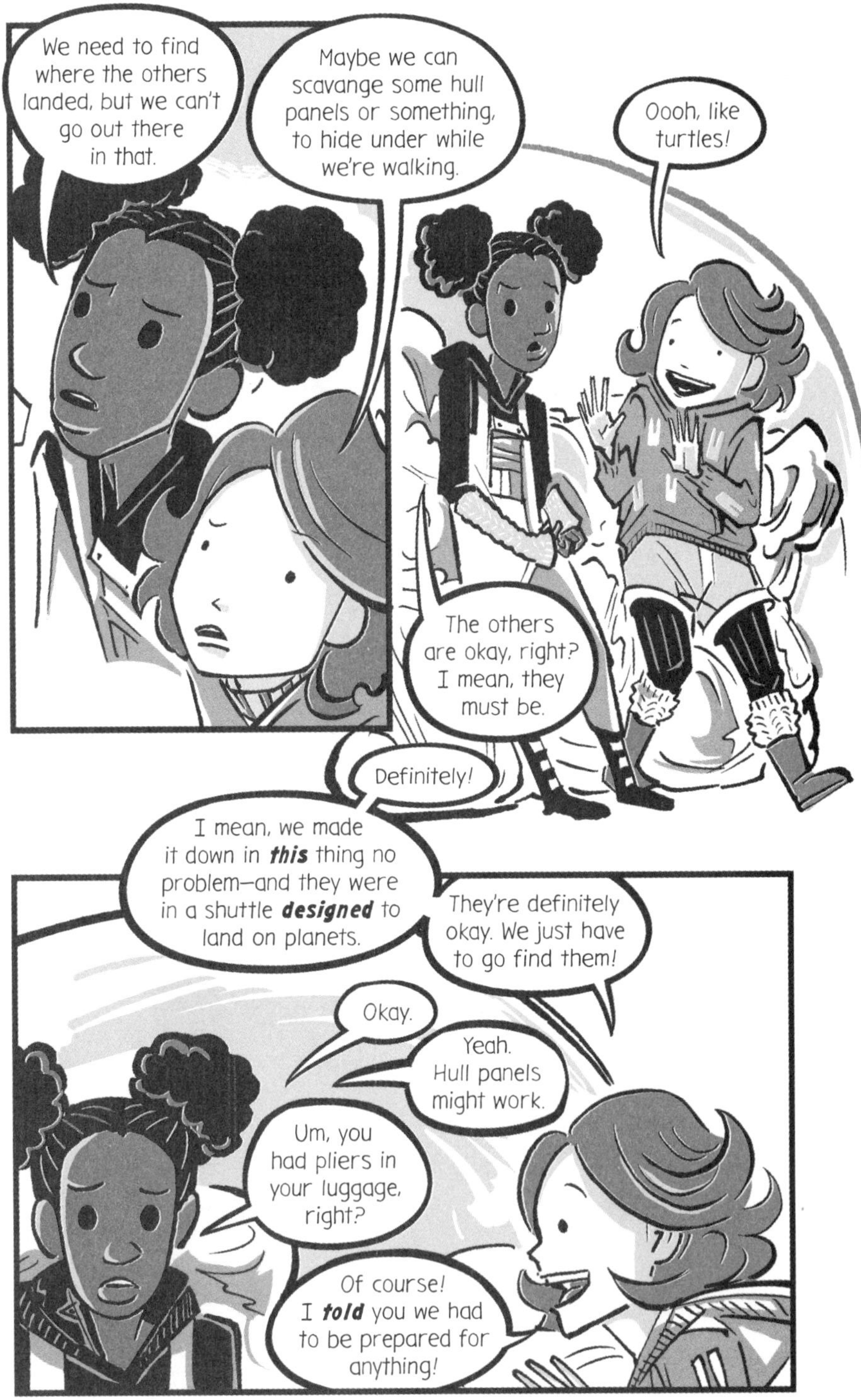
We need to find where the others landed, but we can't go out there in that.
Maybe we can scavange some hull panels or something, to hide under while we're walking.
Oooh, like turtles!
The others are okay, right? I mean, they must be.
Definitely!
I mean, we made it down in **this** thing no problem—and they were in a shuttle **designed** to land on planets.
They're definitely okay. We just have to go find them!
Okay.
Yeah. Hull panels might work.
Um, you had pliers in your luggage, right?
Of course! I **told** you we had to be prepared for anything!

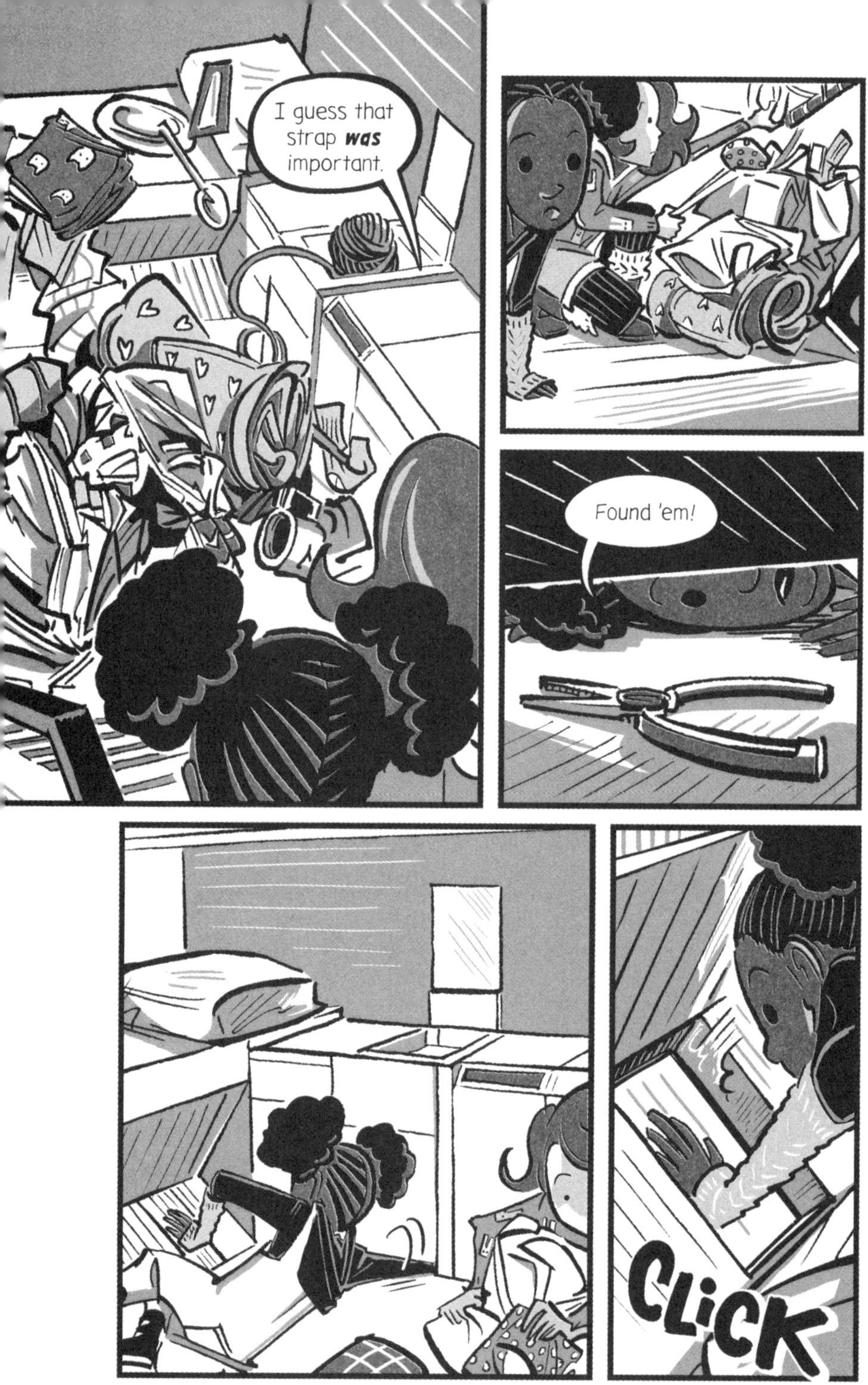
I guess that strap **was** important.
Found 'em!
CLICK

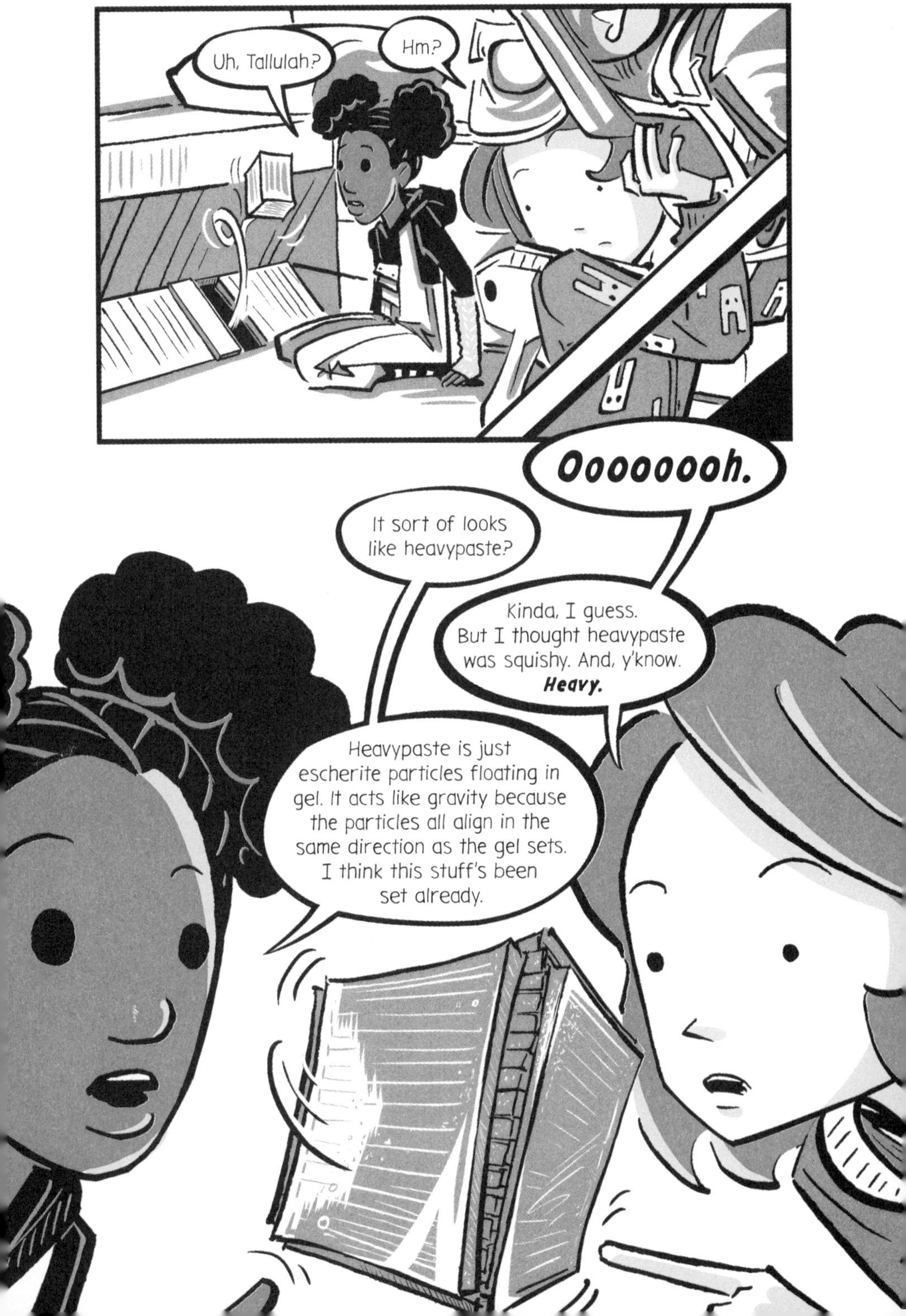
Uh, Tallulah?
Hm?
Oooooooh.
It sort of looks like heavypaste?
Kinda, I guess. But I thought heavypaste was squishy. And, y'know. **Heavy.**
Heavypaste is just escherite particles floating in gel. It acts like gravity because the particles all align in the same direction as the gel sets. I think this stuff's been set already.

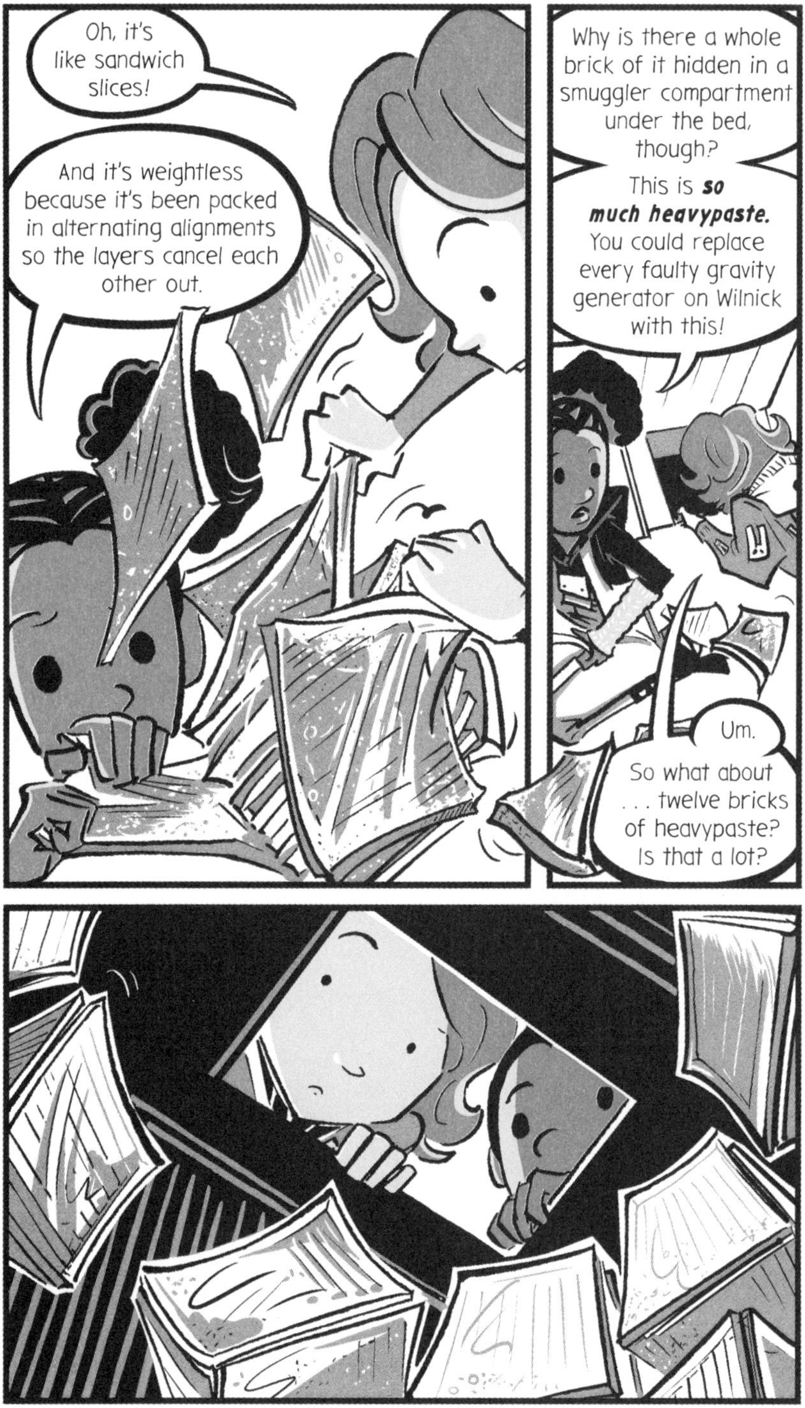
Oh, it's like sandwich slices!
And it's weightless because it's been packed in alternating alignments so the layers cancel each other out.
Why is there a whole brick of it hidden in a smuggler compartment under the bed, though?
This is **so much heavypaste.** You could replace every faulty gravity generator on Wilnick with this!
Um.
So what about . . . twelve bricks of heavypaste? Is that a lot?

(MEANWHILE, ON THE OTHER SIDE of the PLANET)

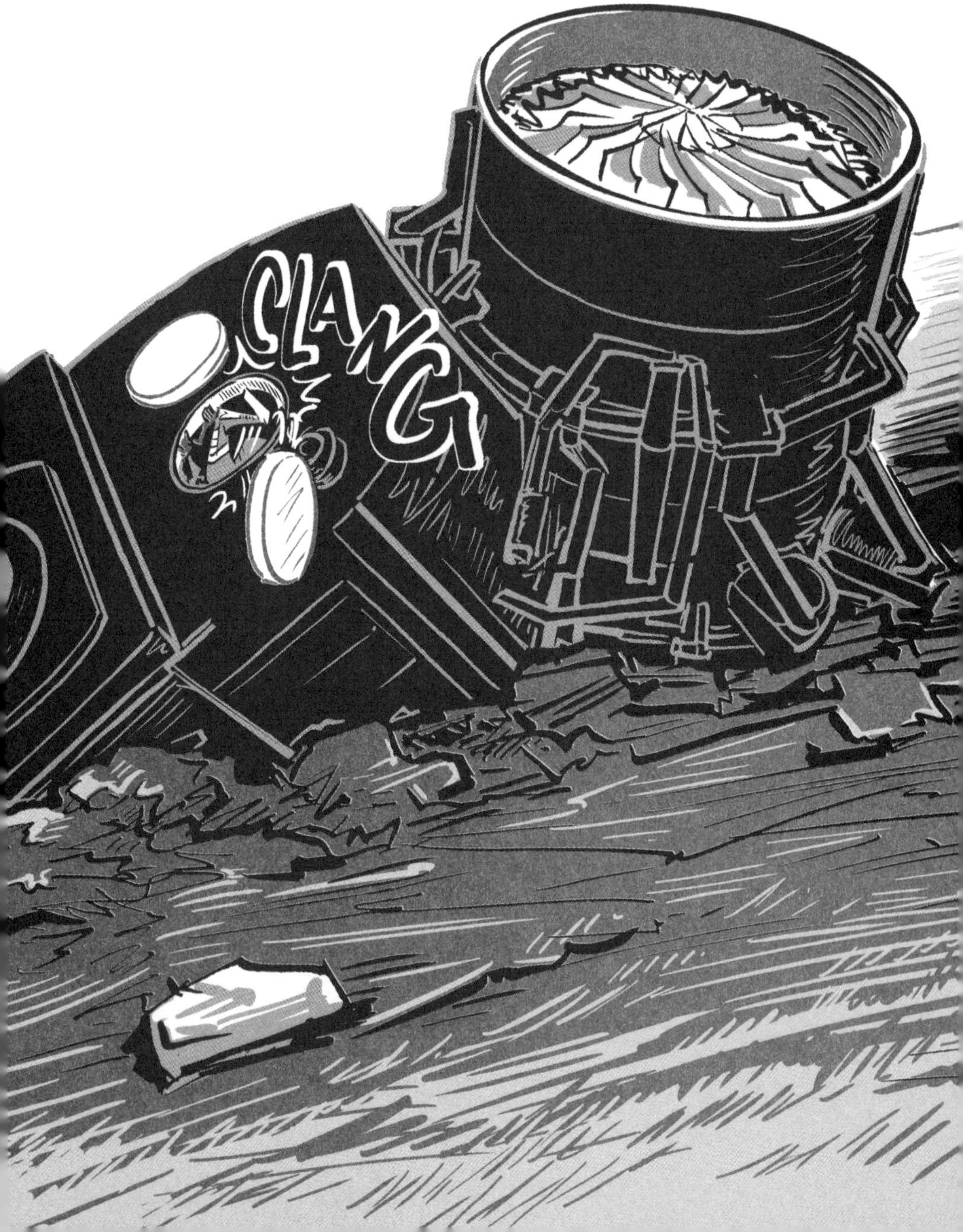
CLANG

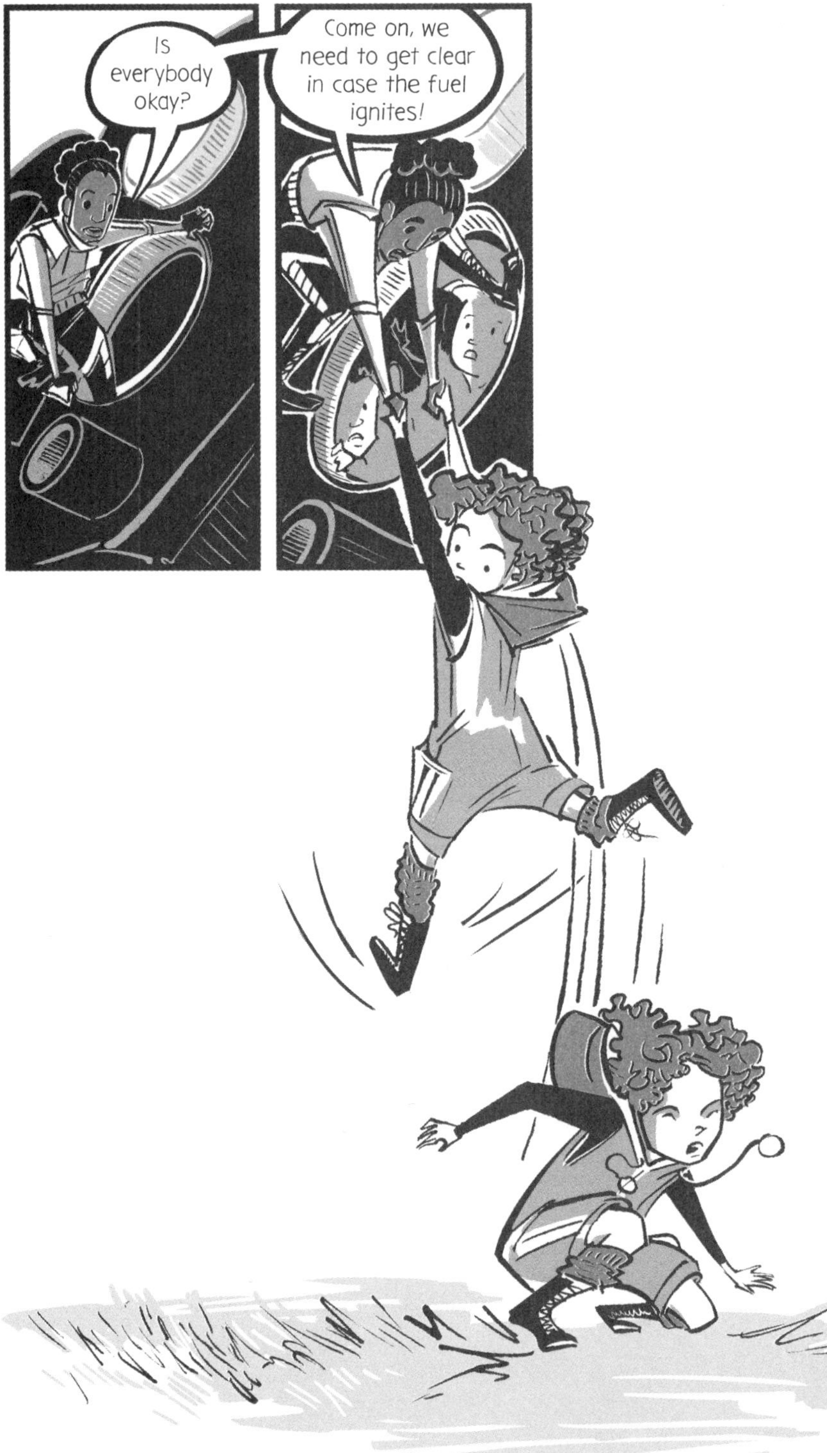
Is everybody okay?
Come on, we need to get clear in case the fuel ignites!

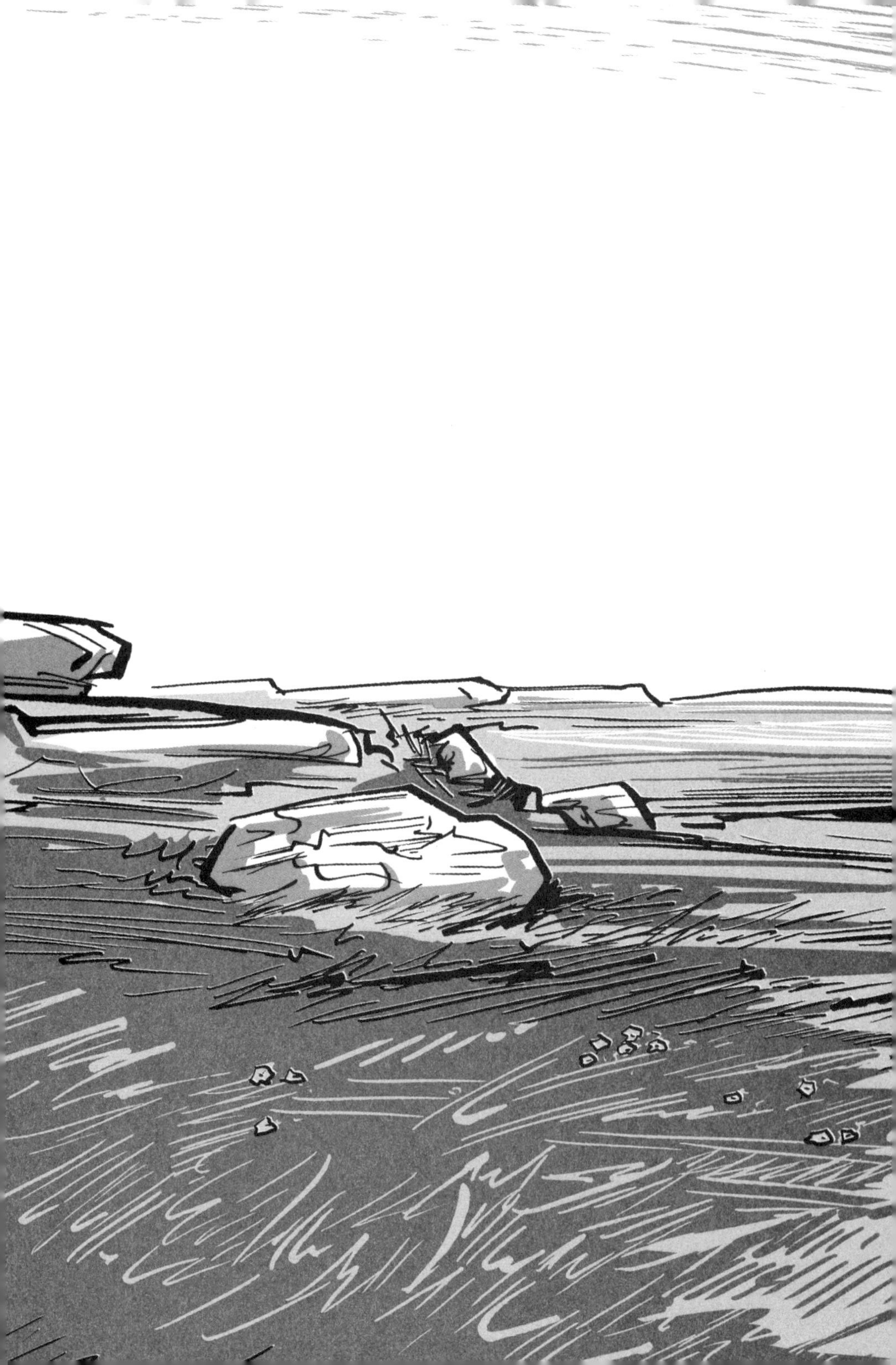

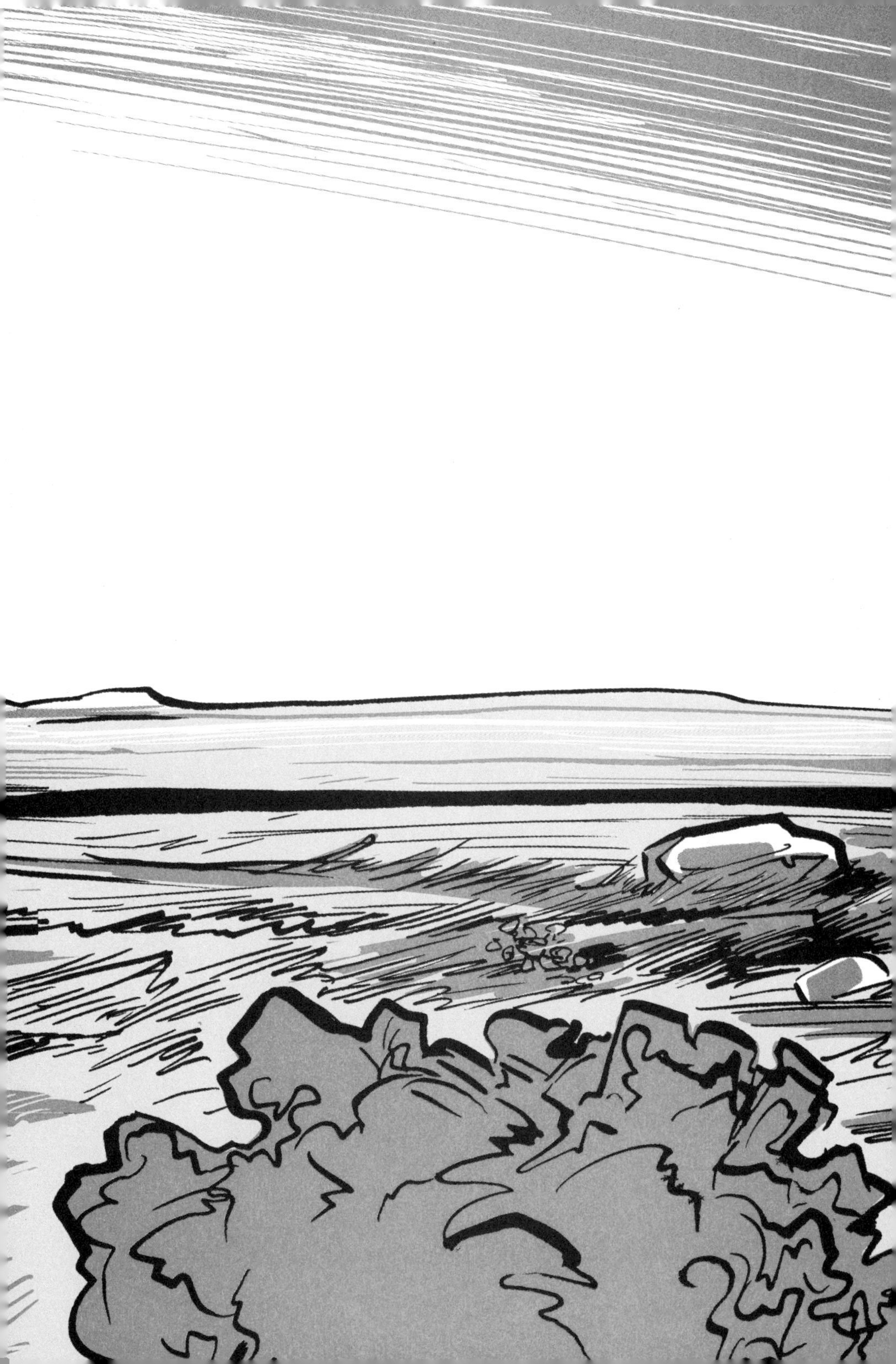

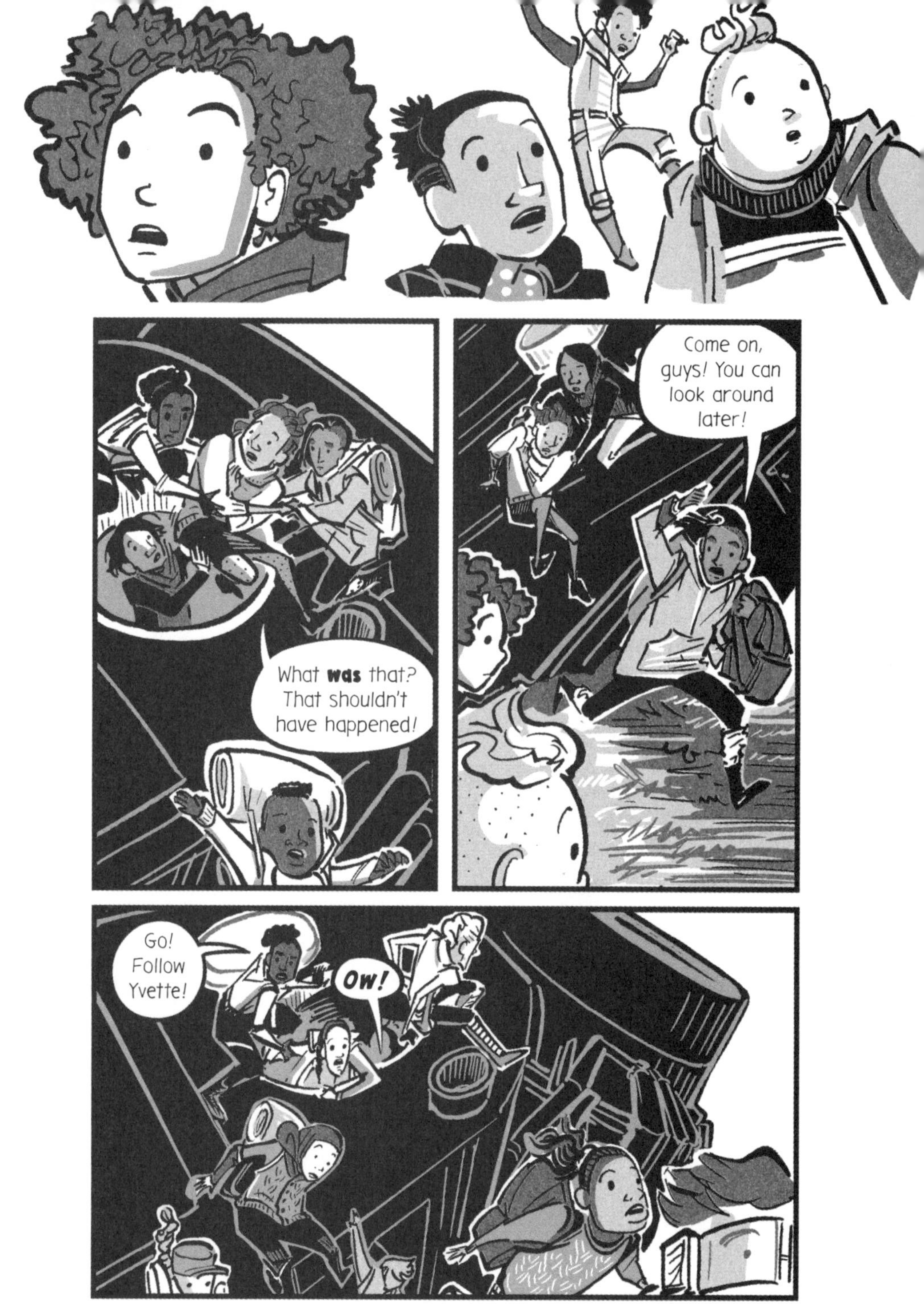
What **was** that? That shouldn't have happened!
Come on, guys! You can look around later!
Go! Follow Yvette!
Ow!

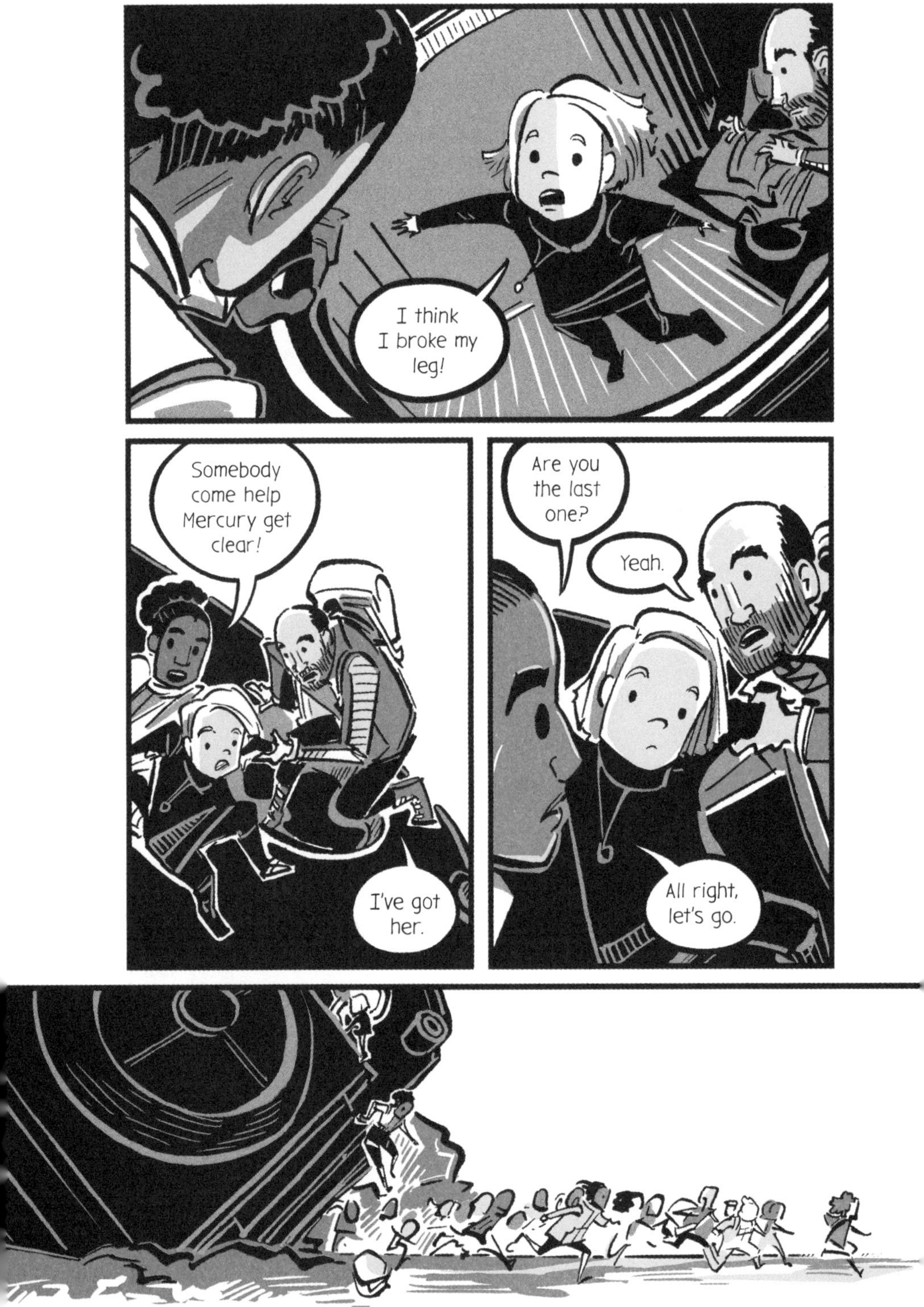
I think I broke my leg!
Somebody come help Mercury get clear!
I've got her.
Are you the last one?
Yeah.
All right, let's go.

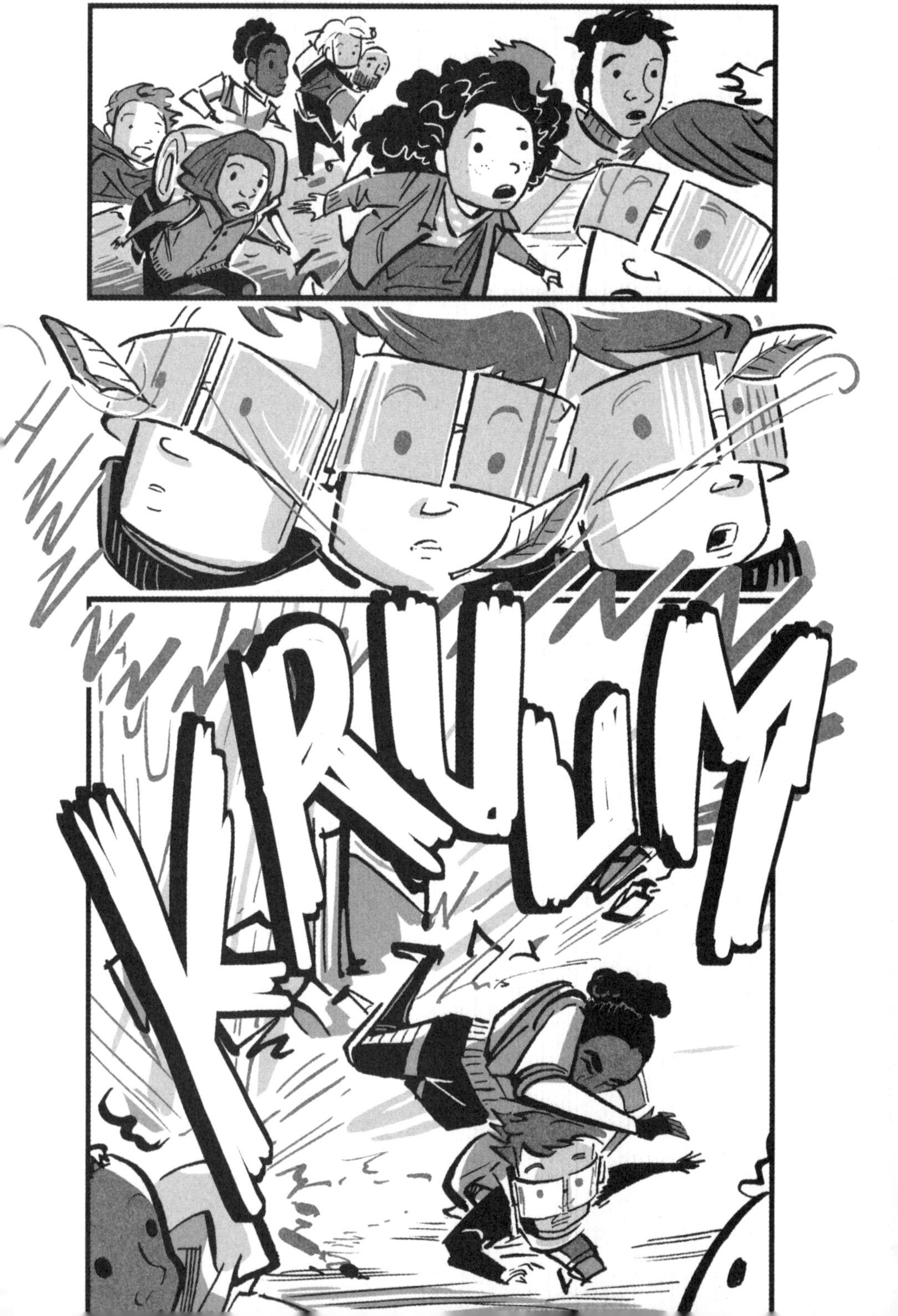
KRUUM

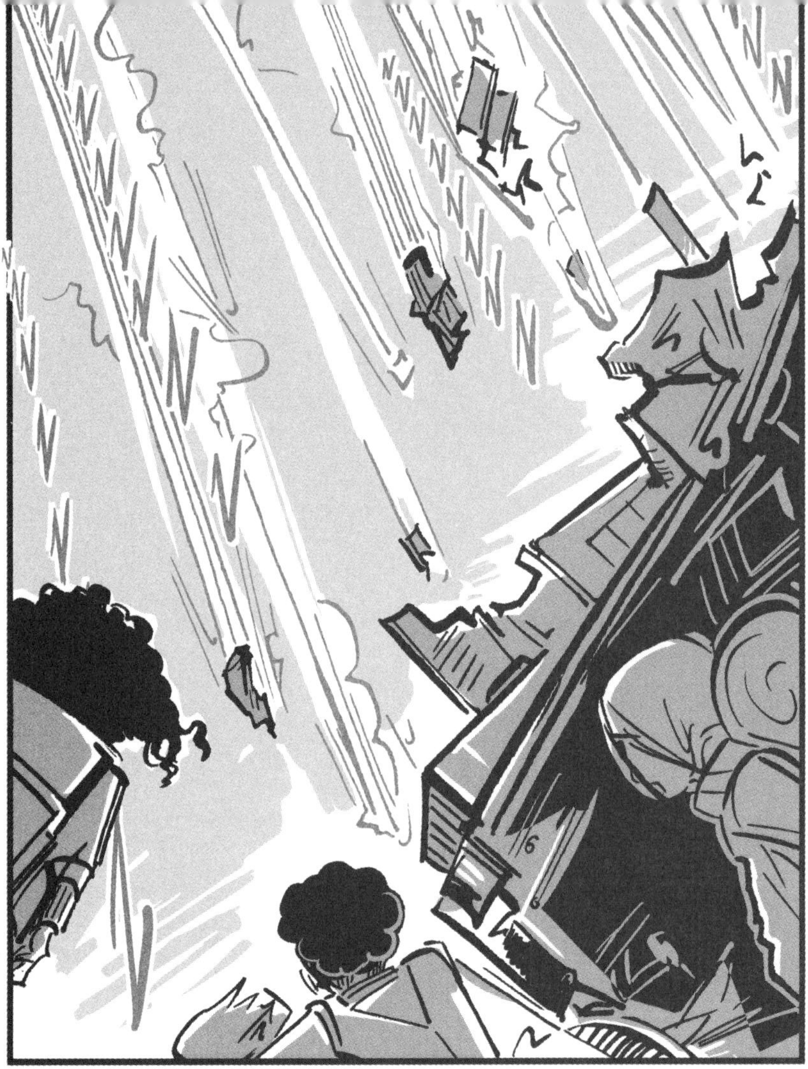

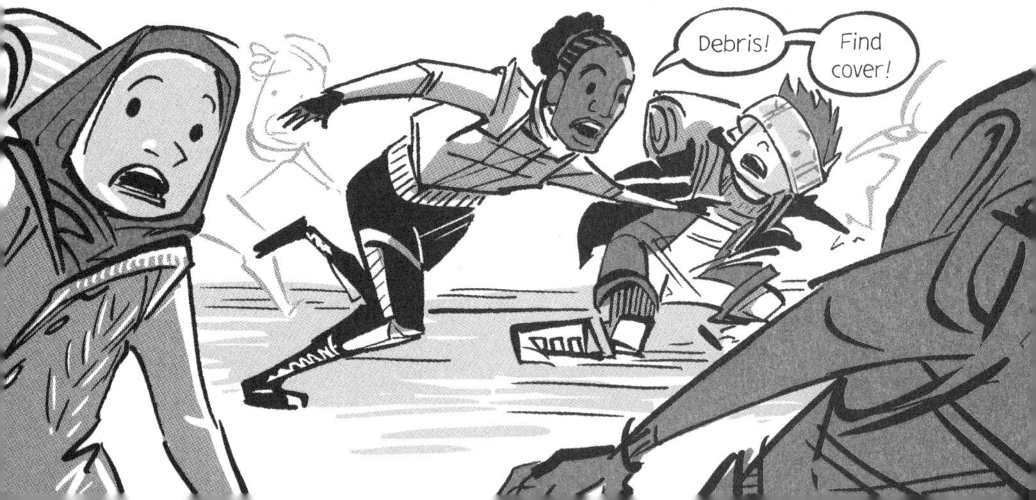
Debris!
Find cover!

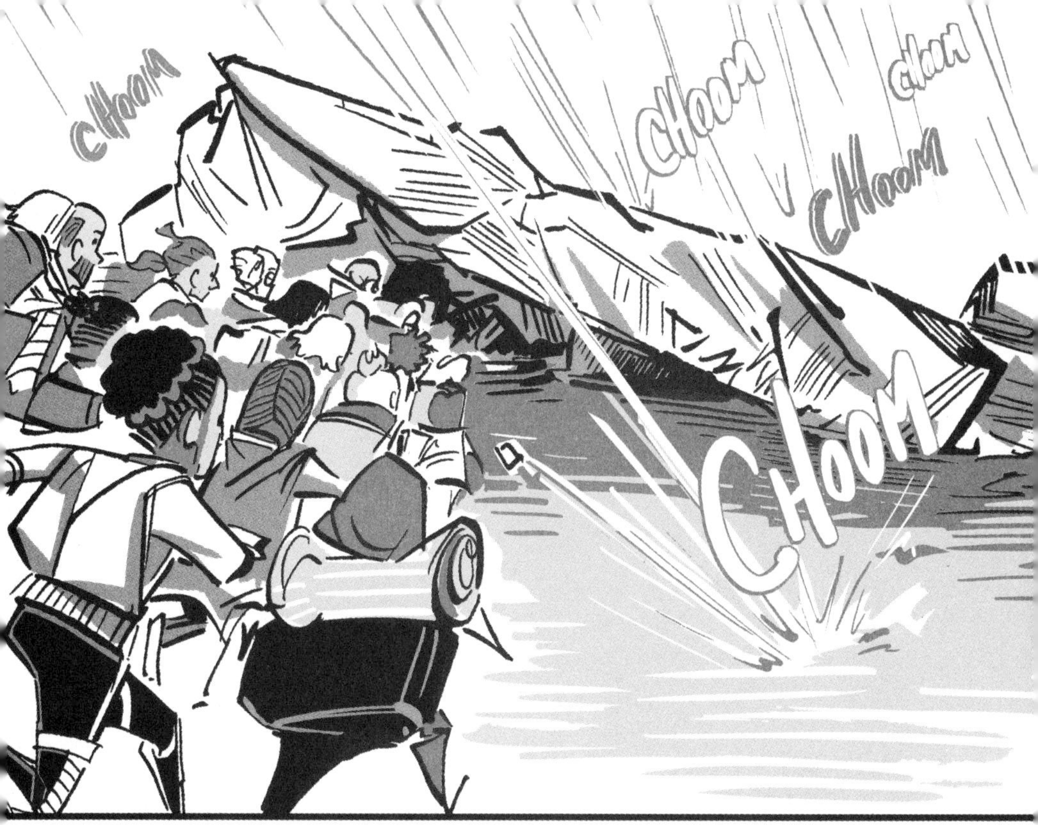
CHOOM
CHOOM
CHOOM
CHOOM
CHOOM

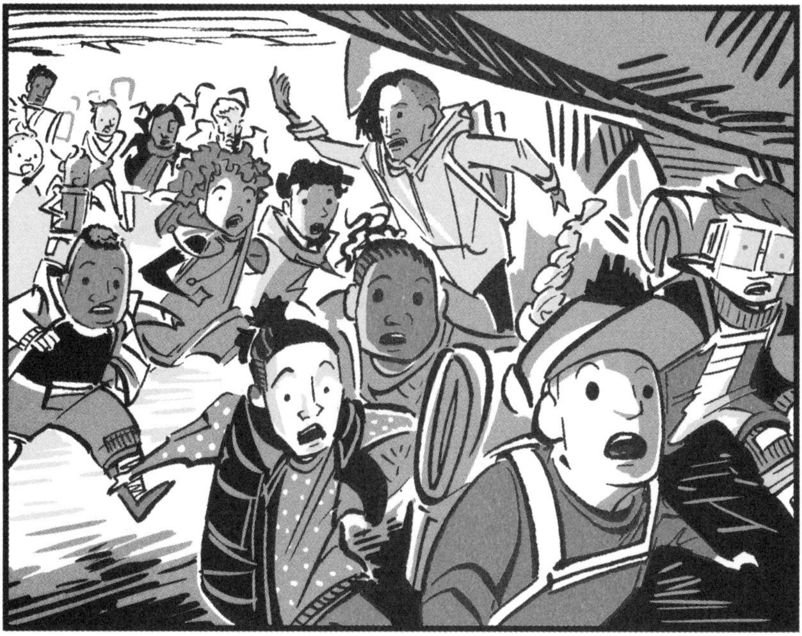

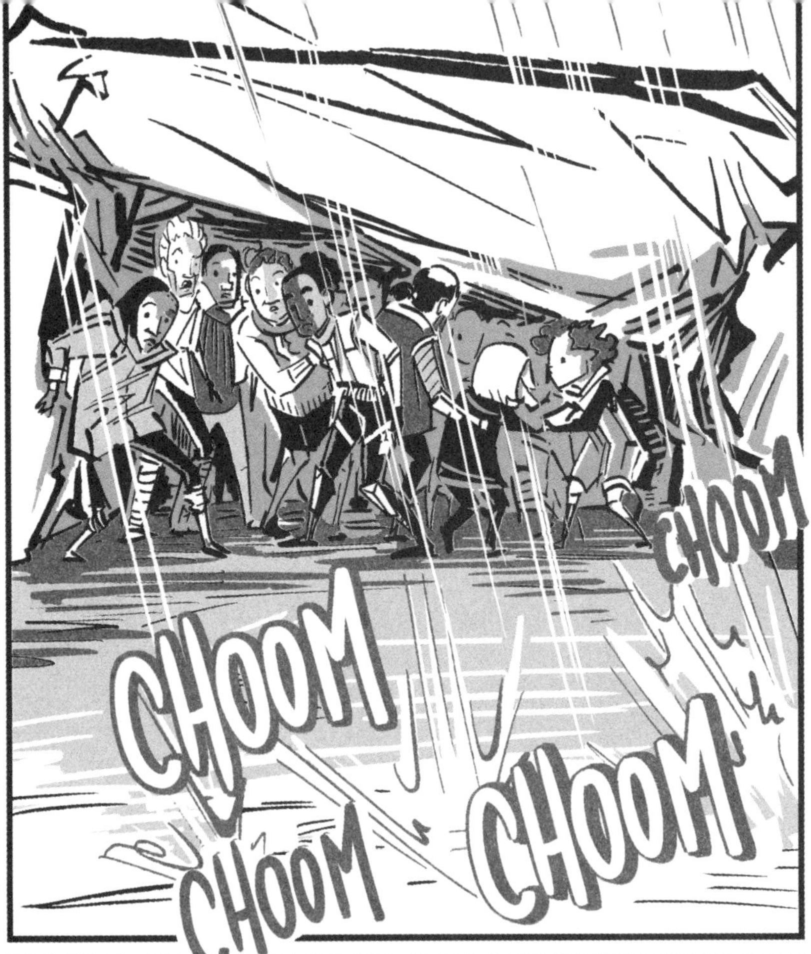
CHOOM
CHOOM
CHOOM
CHOOM

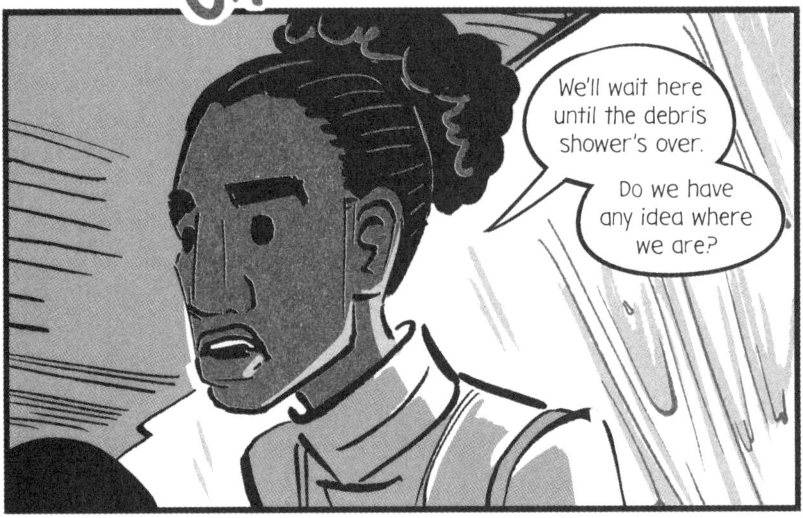
We'll wait here until the debris shower's over.
Do we have any idea where we are?

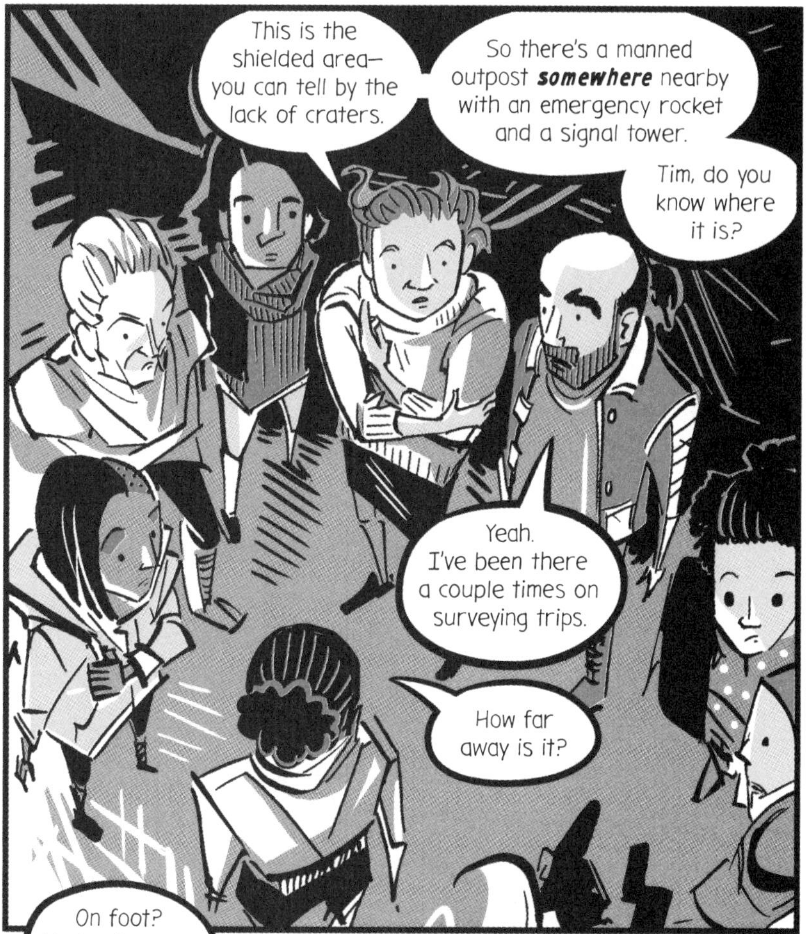
This is the shielded area—you can tell by the lack of craters.
So there's a manned outpost **somewhere** nearby with an emergency rocket and a signal tower.
Tim, do you know where it is?
Yeah. I've been there a couple times on surveying trips.
How far away is it?

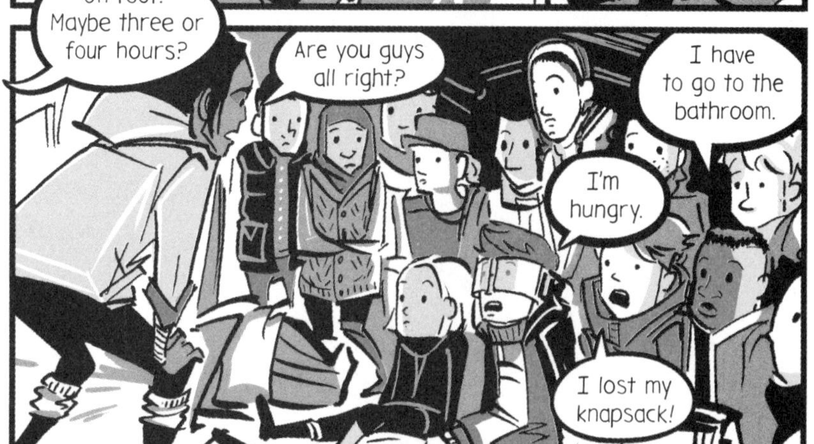
On foot? Maybe three or four hours?
Are you guys all right?
I have to go to the bathroom.
I'm hungry.
I lost my knapsack!

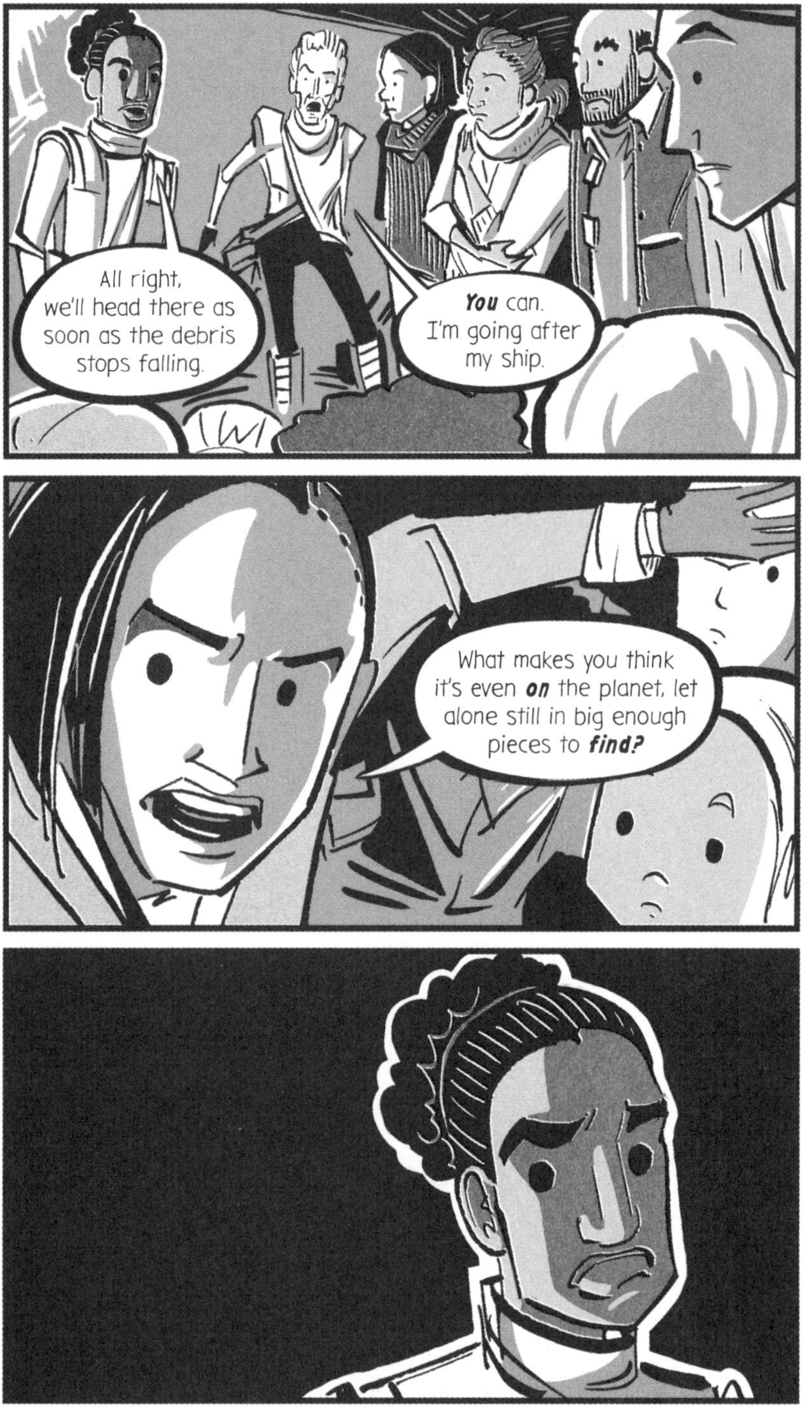
All right, we'll head there as soon as the debris stops falling.
***You*** can. I'm going after my ship.
What makes you think it's even ***on*** the planet, let alone still in big enough pieces to ***find?***

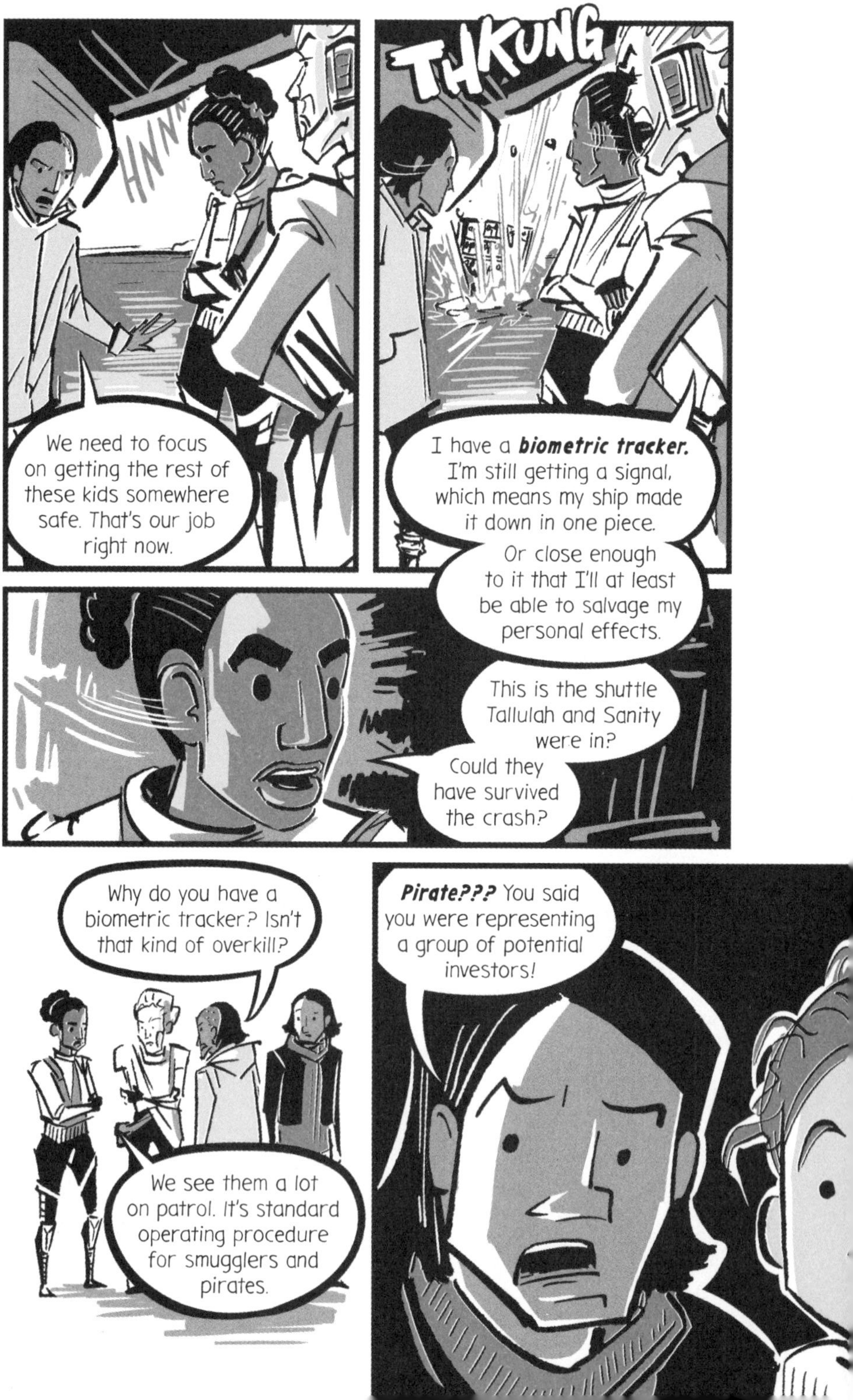
HNNN
We need to focus on getting the rest of these kids somewhere safe. That's our job right now.
THKUNG
I have a **biometric tracker.** I'm still getting a signal, which means my ship made it down in one piece.
Or close enough to it that I'll at least be able to salvage my personal effects.
This is the shuttle Tallulah and Sanity were in?
Could they have survived the crash?
Why do you have a biometric tracker? Isn't that kind of overkill?
We see them a lot on patrol. It's standard operating procedure for smugglers and pirates.
**Pirate???** You said you were representing a group of potential investors!

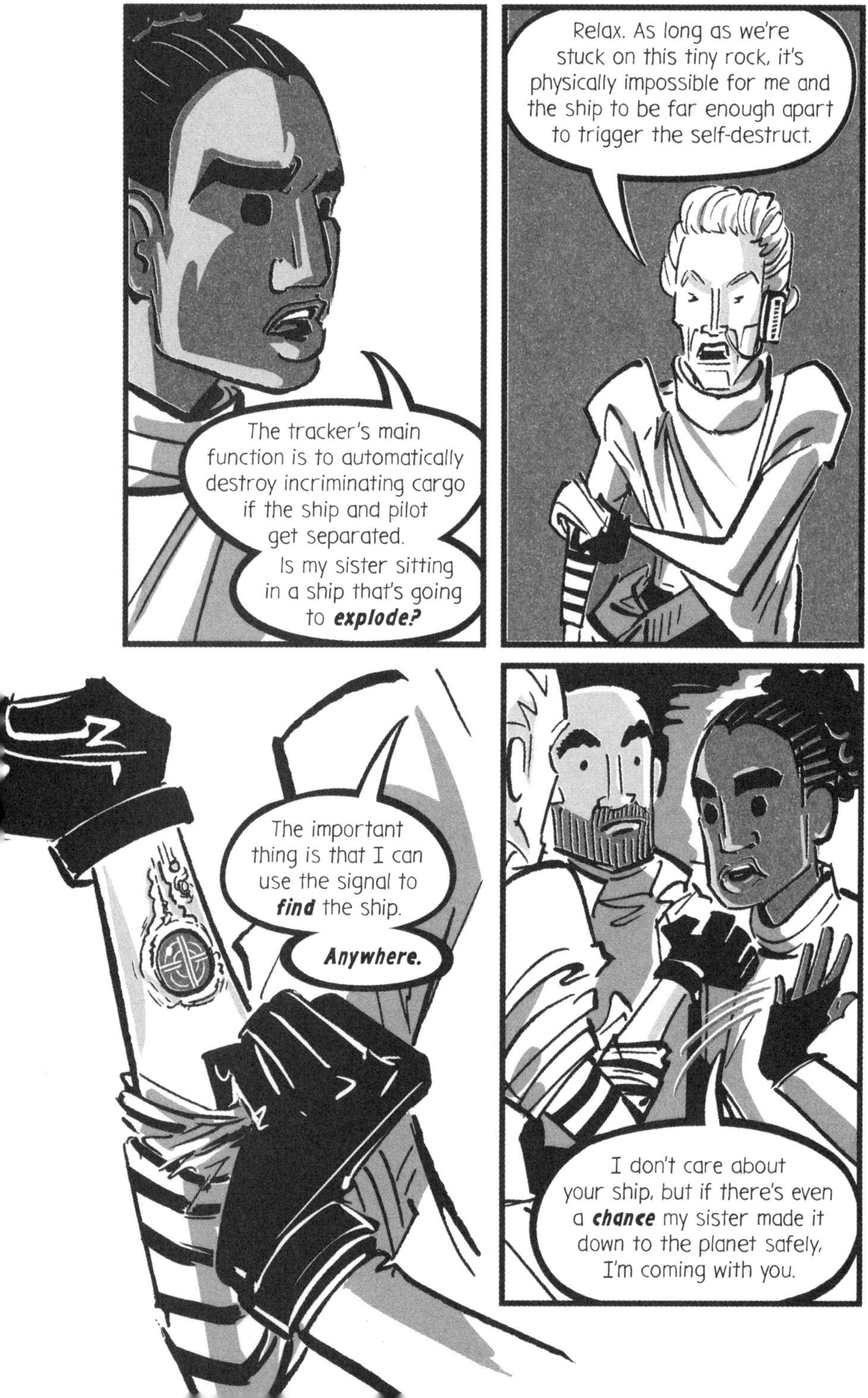

The tracker's main function is to automatically destroy incriminating cargo if the ship and pilot get separated.
Is my sister sitting in a ship that's going to ***explode?***
Relax. As long as we're stuck on this tiny rock, it's physically impossible for me and the ship to be far enough apart to trigger the self-destruct.
The important thing is that I can use the signal to ***find*** the ship.
***Anywhere.***
I don't care about your ship, but if there's even a ***chance*** my sister made it down to the planet safely, I'm coming with you.

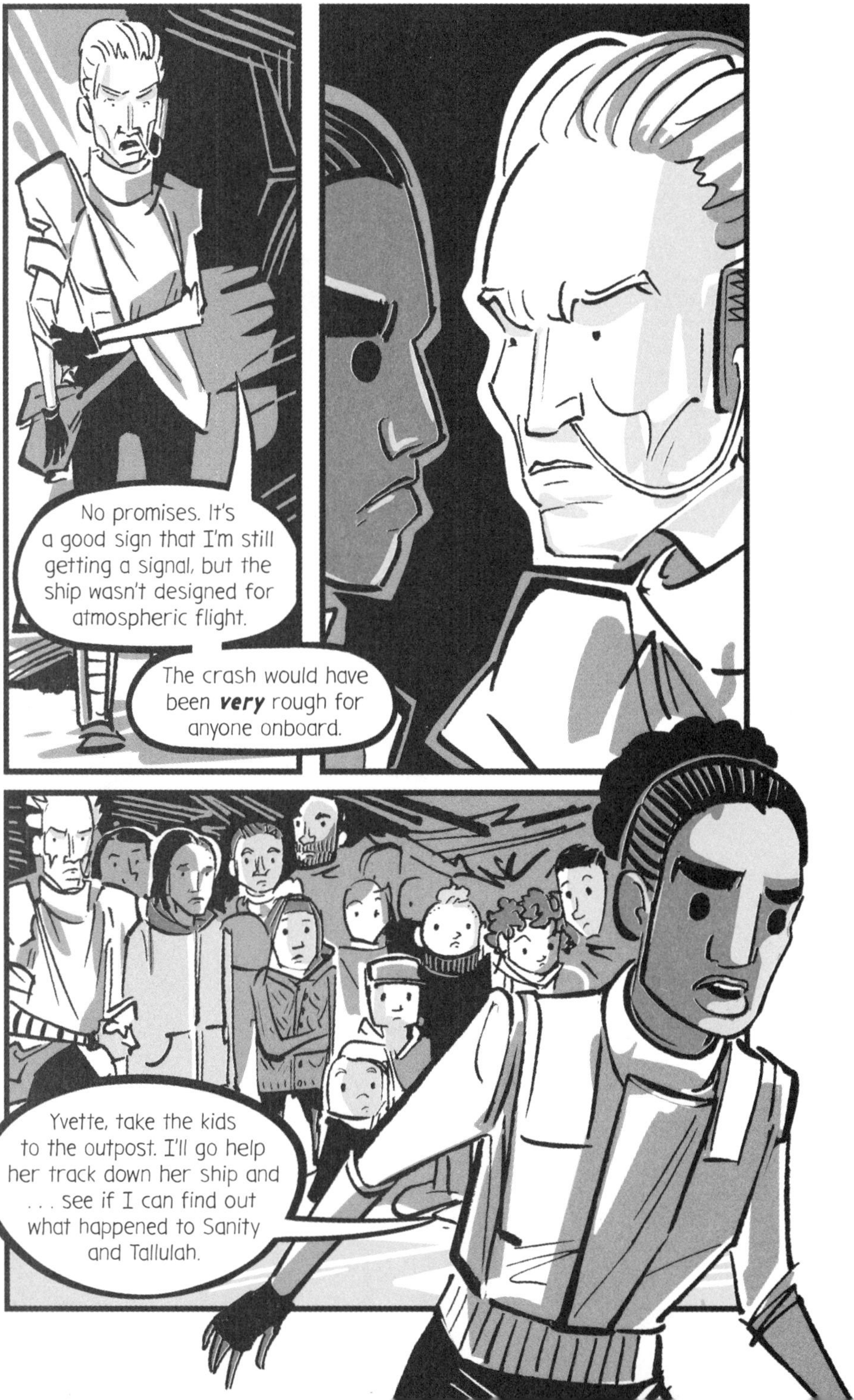
No promises. It's a good sign that I'm still getting a signal, but the ship wasn't designed for atmospheric flight.
The crash would have been ***very*** rough for anyone onboard.
Yvette, take the kids to the outpost. I'll go help her track down her ship and . . . see if I can find out what happened to Sanity and Tallulah.

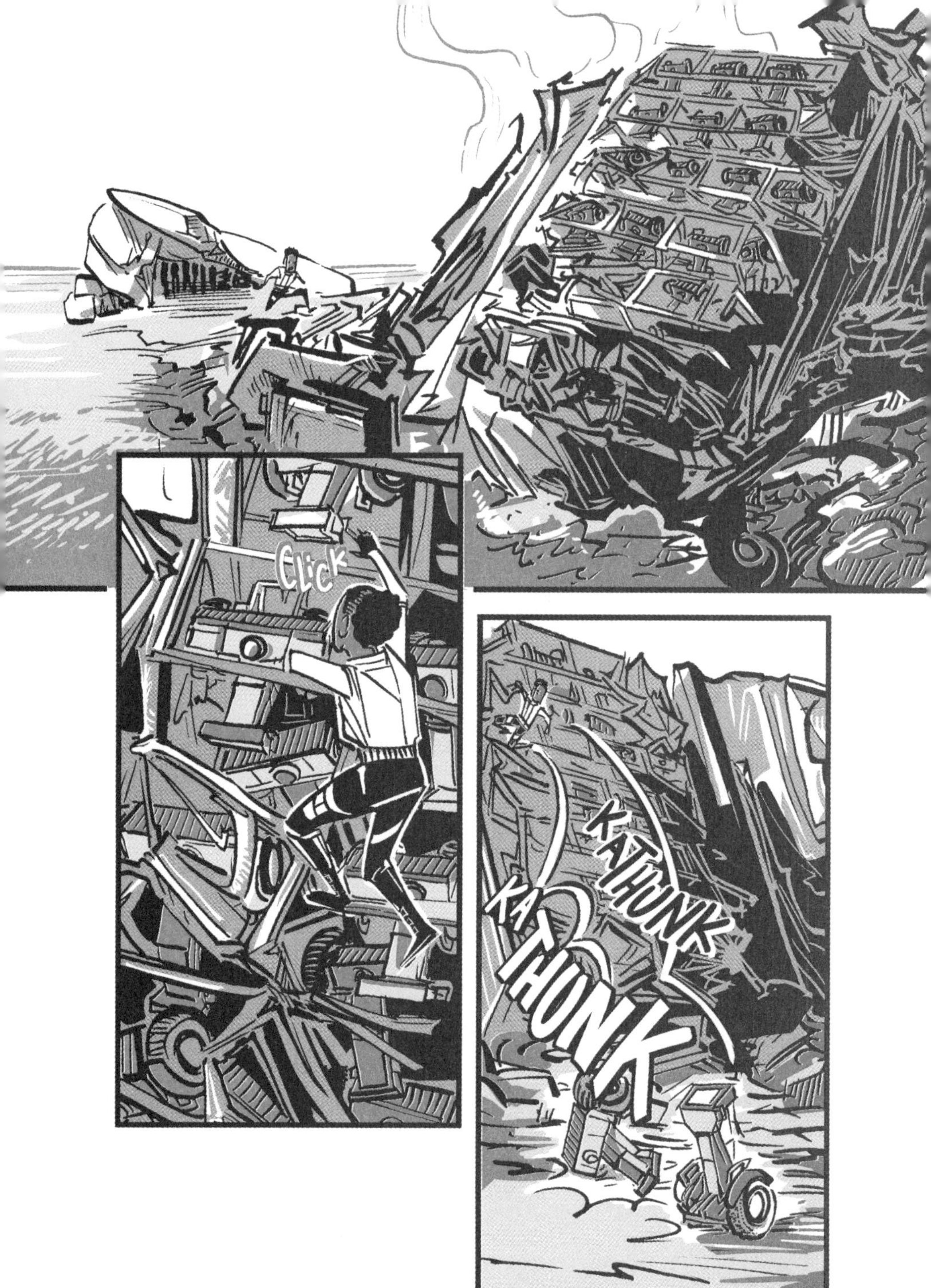
CLICK
KA-THUNK
KA-THUNK

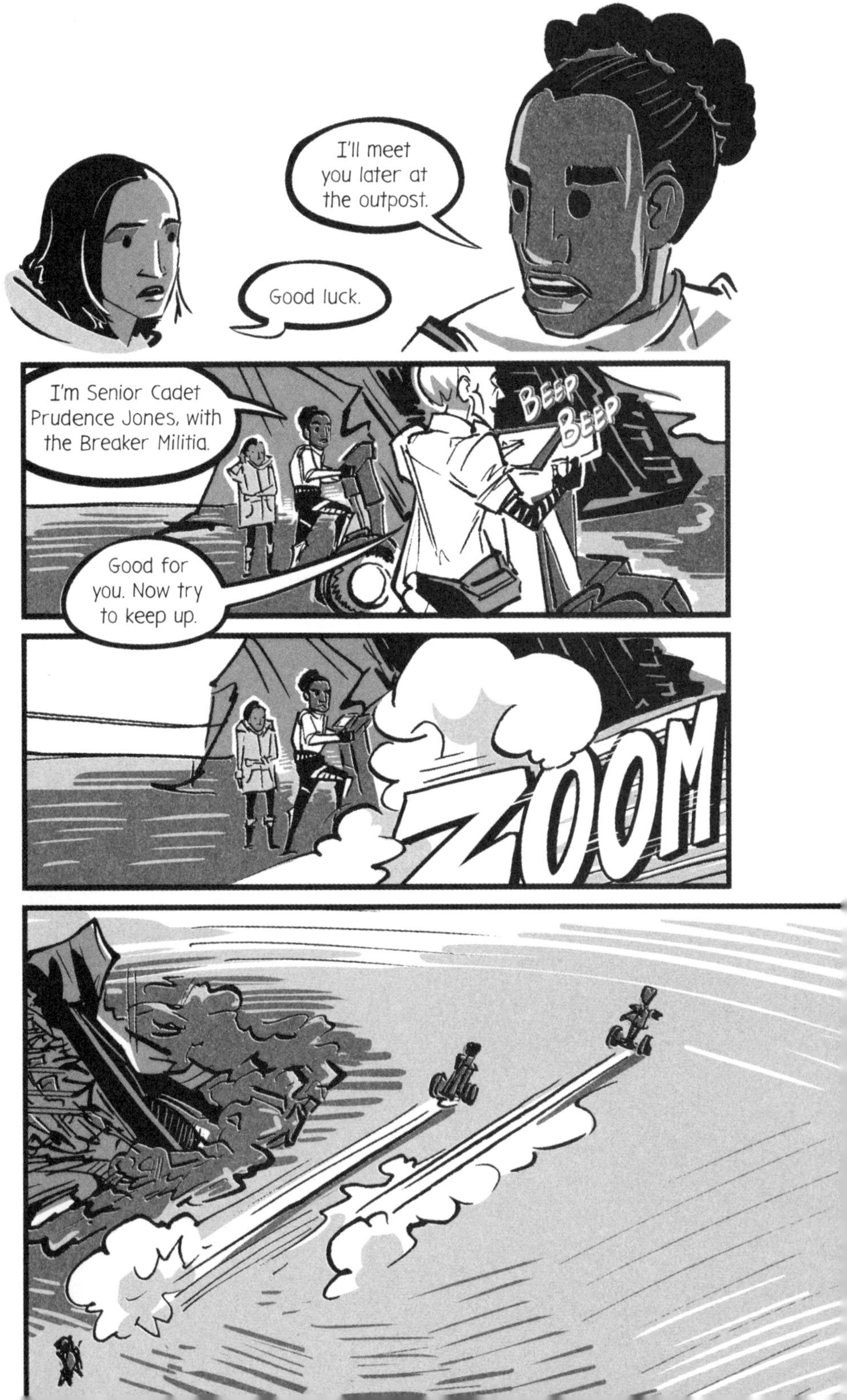
I'll meet you later at the outpost.
Good luck.
I'm Senior Cadet Prudence Jones, with the Breaker Militia.
BEEP BEEP
Good for you. Now try to keep up.
ZOOM

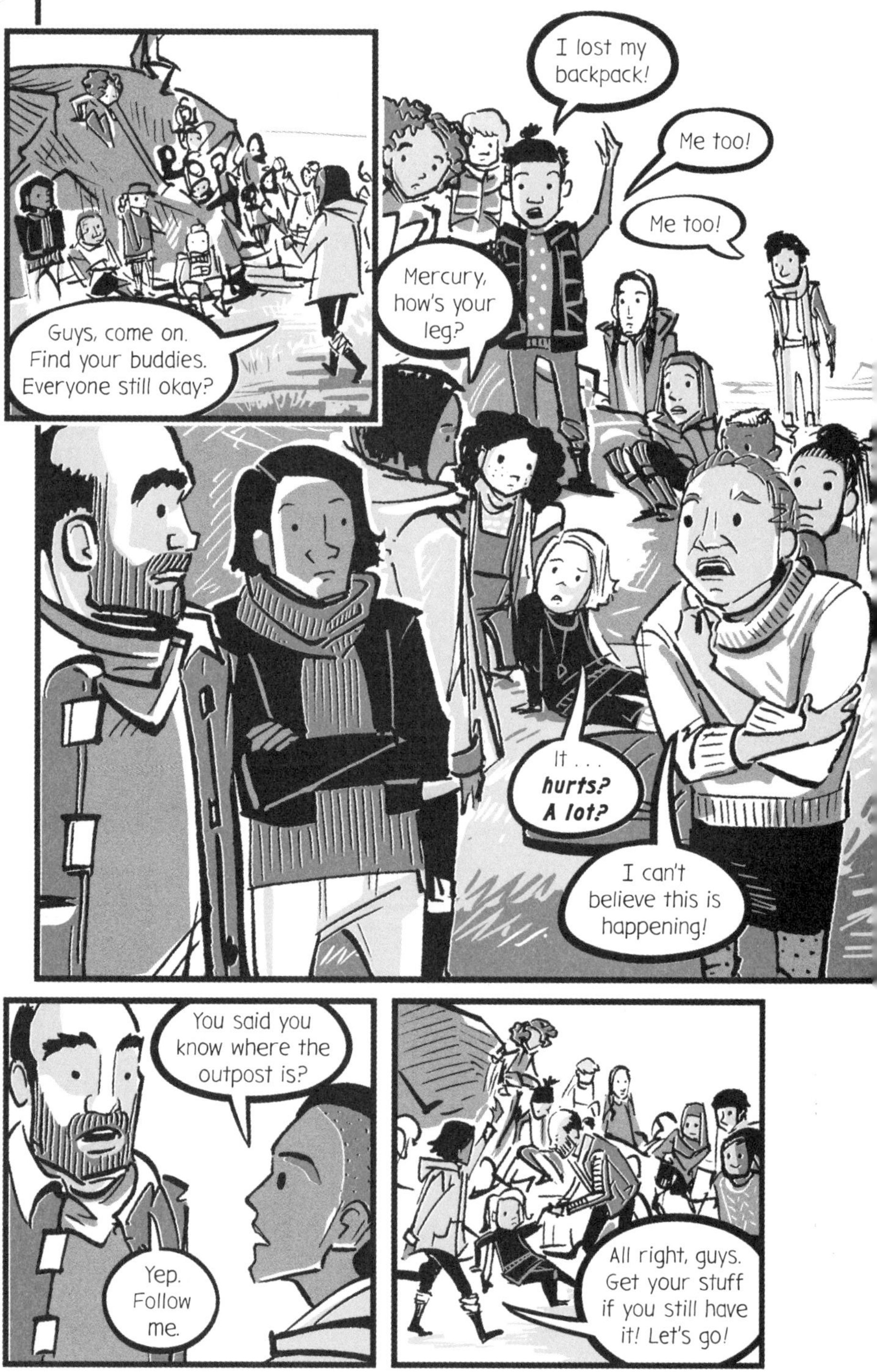
Guys, come on. Find your buddies. Everyone still okay?
I lost my backpack!
Me too!
Me too!
Mercury, how's your leg?
It . . . **hurts? A lot?**
I can't believe this is happening!
You said you know where the outpost is?
Yep. Follow me.
All right, guys. Get your stuff if you still have it! Let's go!

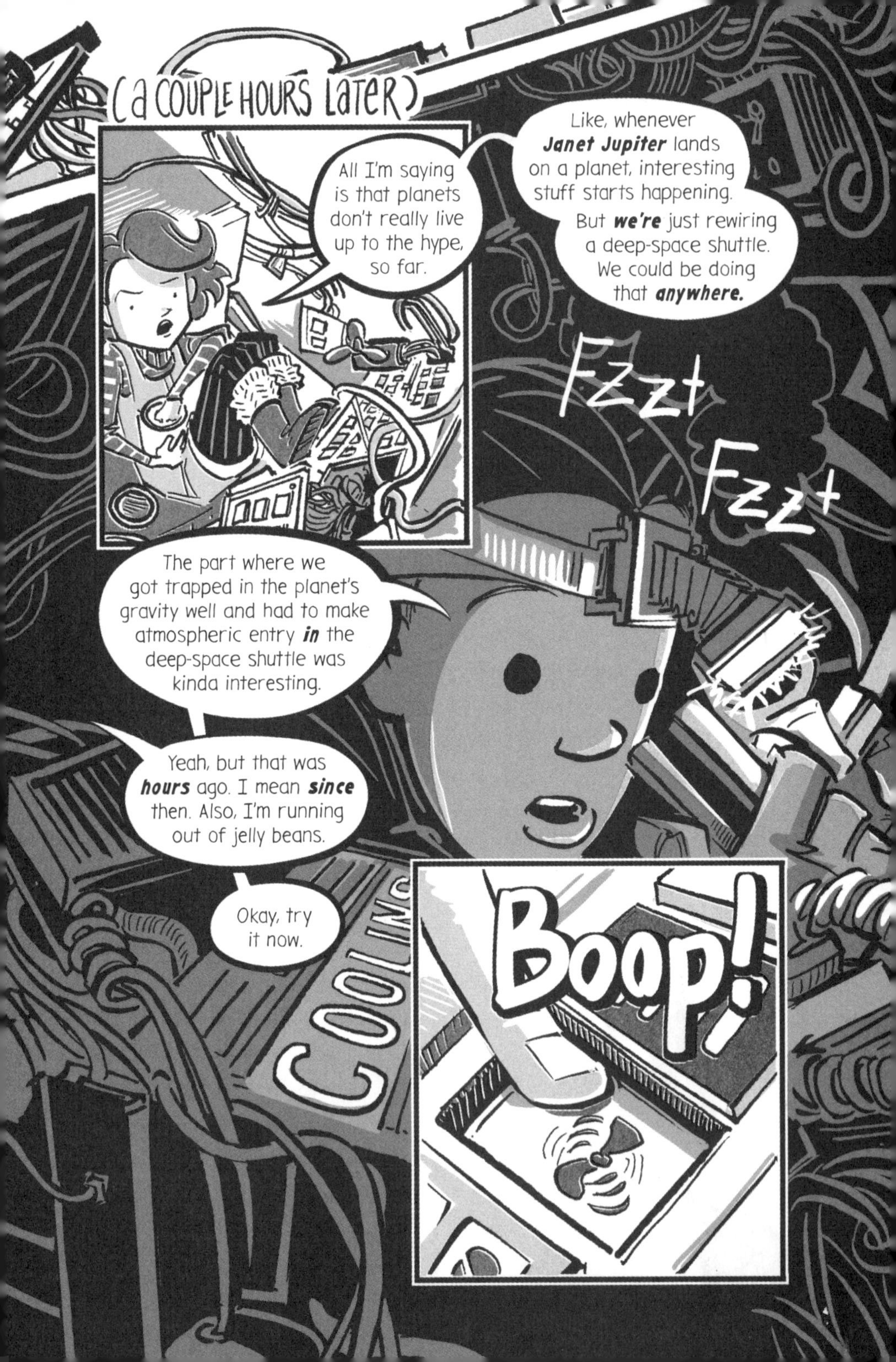
(a couple hours later)
All I'm saying is that planets don't really live up to the hype, so far.
Like, whenever **Janet Jupiter** lands on a planet, interesting stuff starts happening.
But **we're** just rewiring a deep-space shuttle. We could be doing that **anywhere.**
Fzzt
Fzzt
The part where we got trapped in the planet's gravity well and had to make atmospheric entry **in** the deep-space shuttle was kinda interesting.
Yeah, but that was **hours** ago. I mean **since** then. Also, I'm running out of jelly beans.
Okay, try it now.
COOLING
Boop!

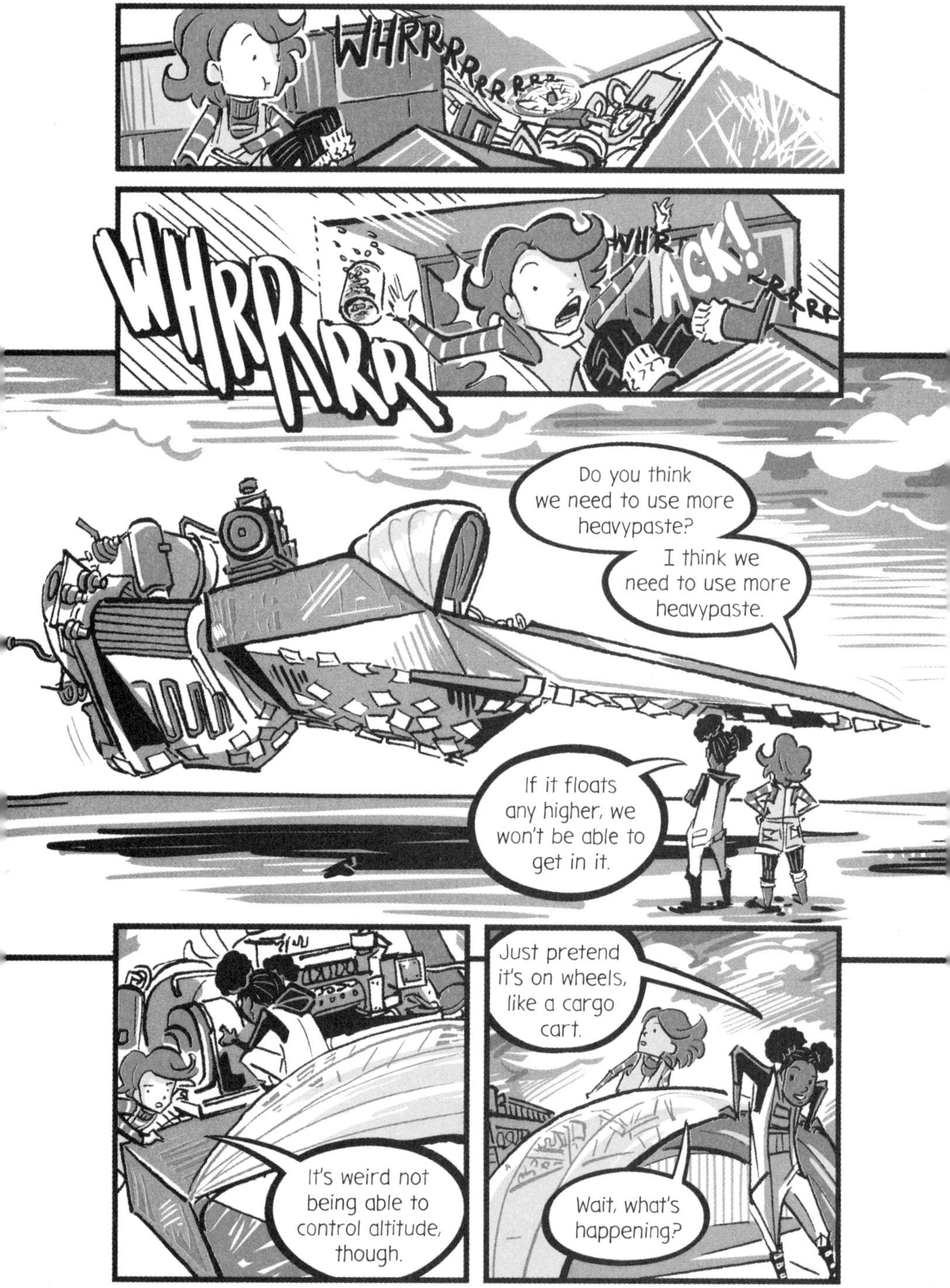
WHRRRRRRRRRR
WHRRRRR
WHR
ACK!
RRRR
Do you think we need to use more heavypaste?
I think we need to use more heavypaste.
If it floats any higher, we won't be able to get in it.
It's weird not being able to control altitude, though.
Just pretend it's on wheels, like a cargo cart.
Wait, what's happening?

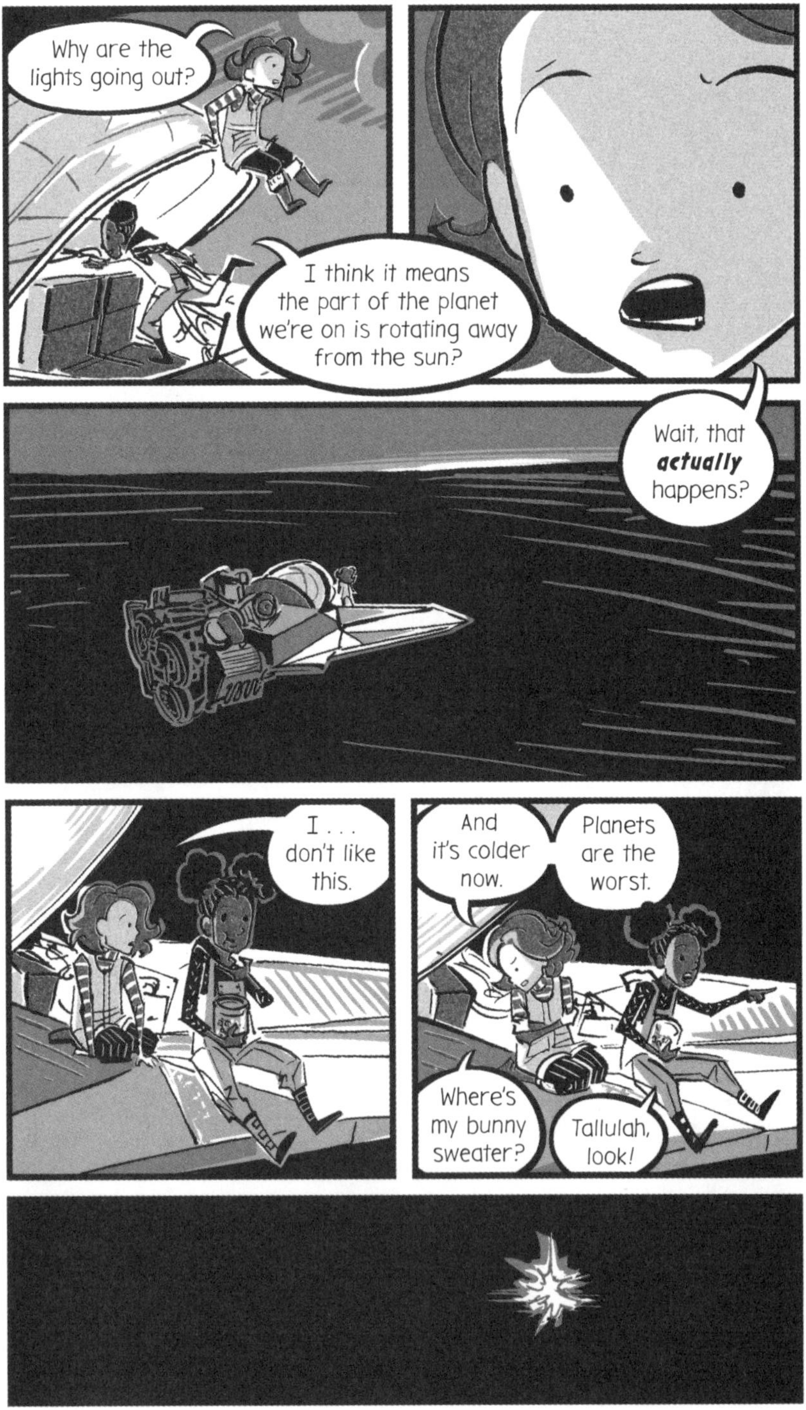

Why are the lights going out?
I think it means the part of the planet we're on is rotating away from the sun?
Wait, that **actually** happens?
I . . . don't like this.
And it's colder now.
Planets are the worst.
Where's my bunny sweater?
Tallulah, look!

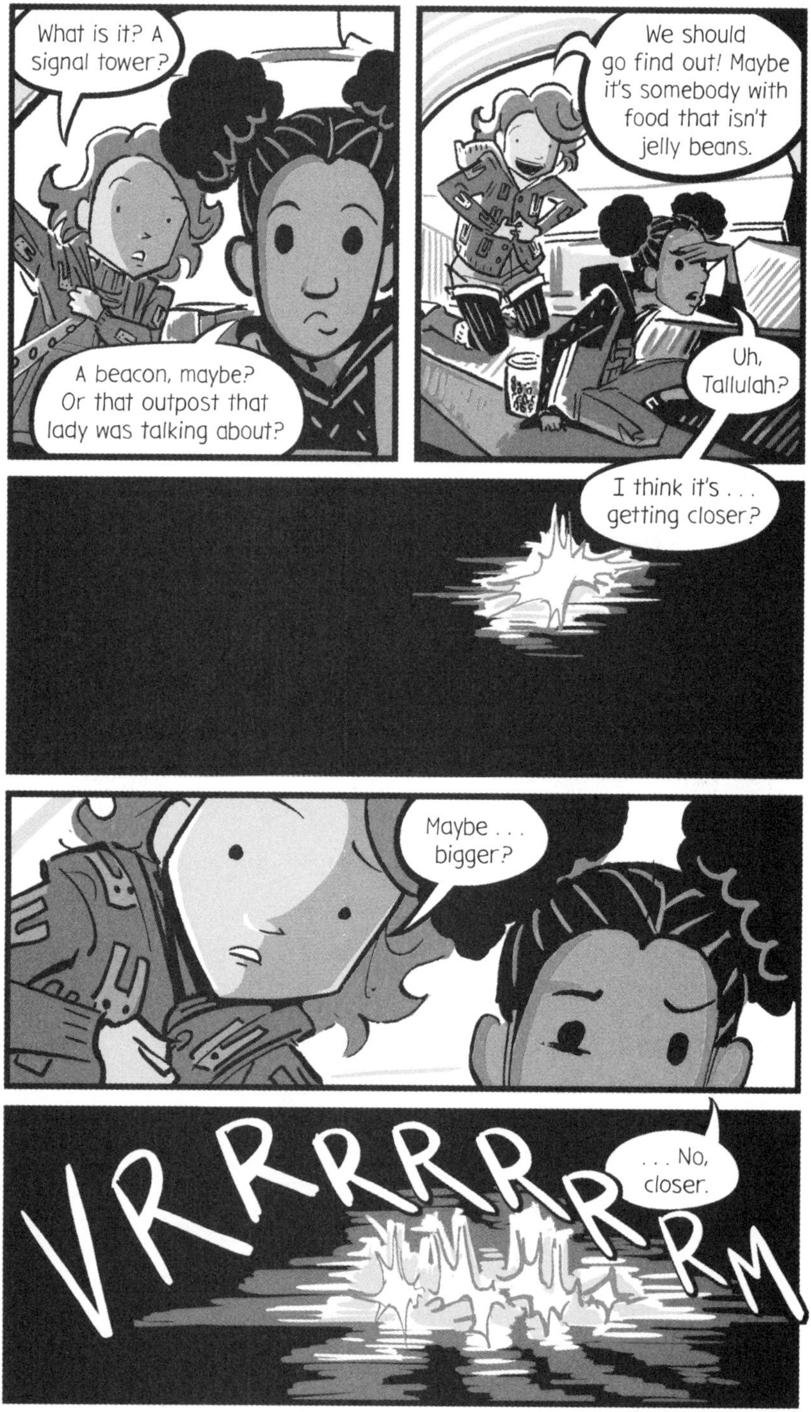
What is it? A signal tower?
A beacon, maybe? Or that outpost that lady was talking about?
We should go find out! Maybe it's somebody with food that isn't jelly beans.
Uh, Tallulah?
I think it's . . . getting closer?
Maybe . . . bigger?
VRRRRRRRM
. . . No, closer.

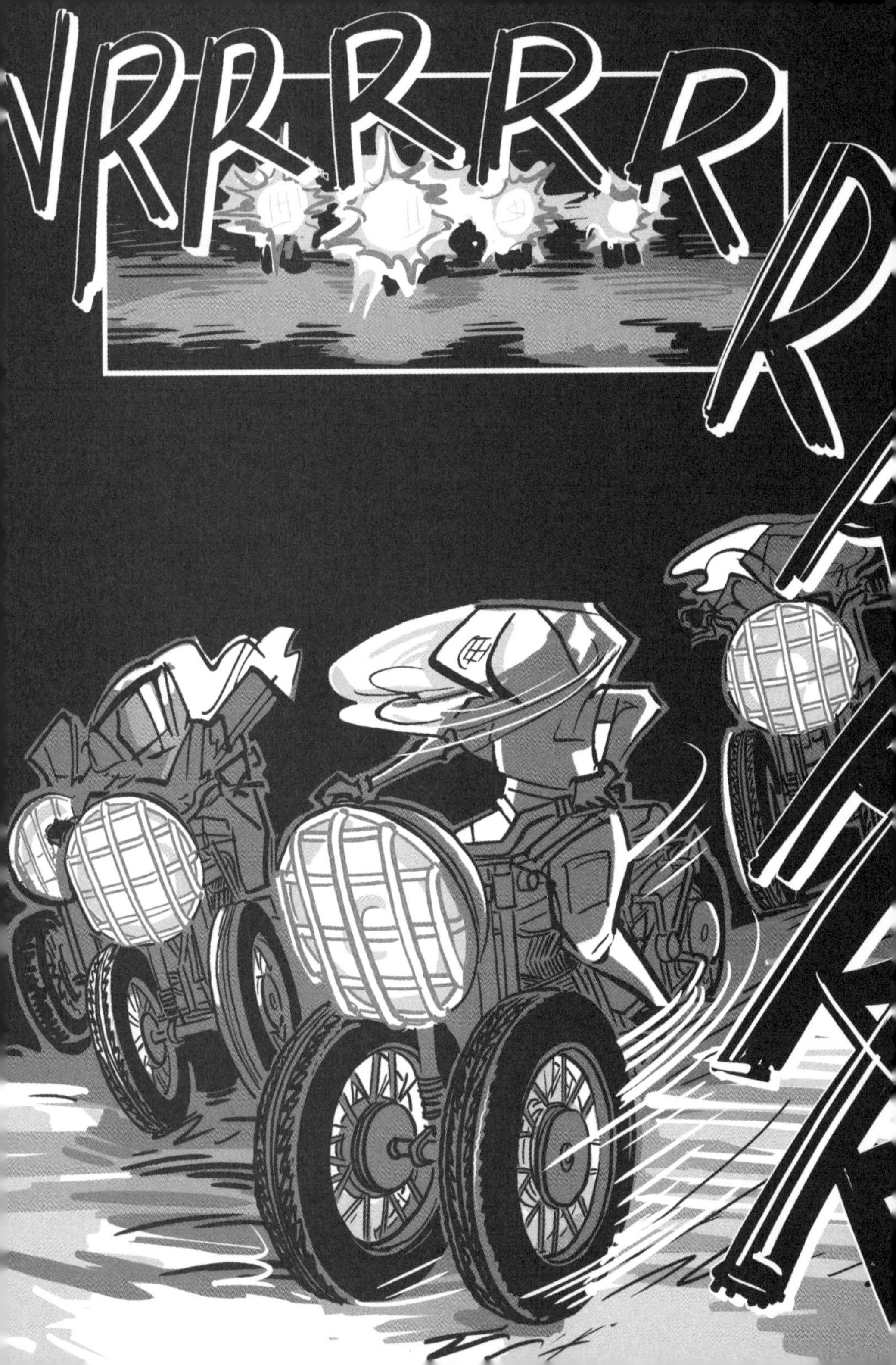
VRRRRRRRRRRRR

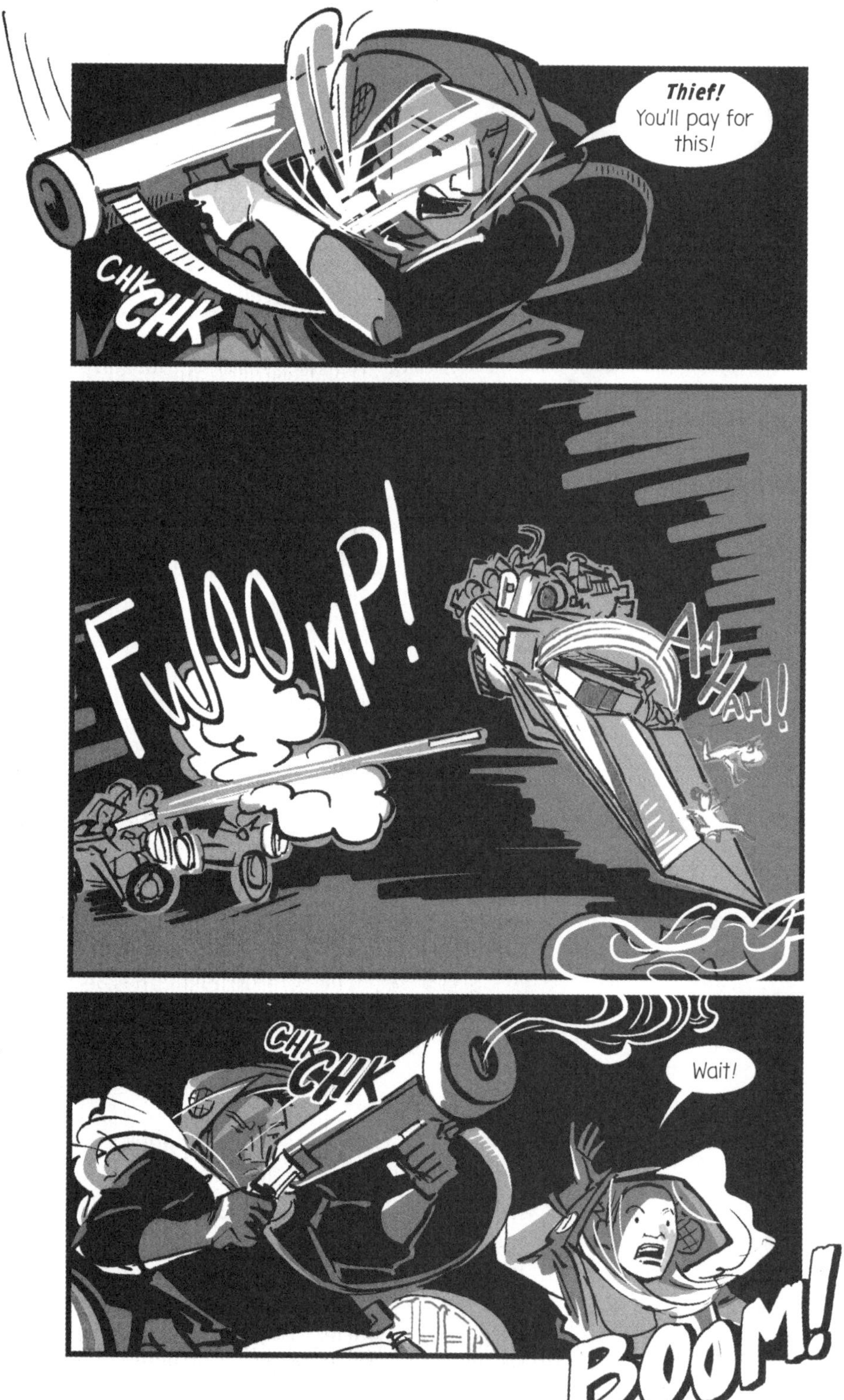
**Thief!**
You'll pay for this!
CHK CHK
FWOOMP!
AAHAH!
CHK CHK
Wait!
BOOM!

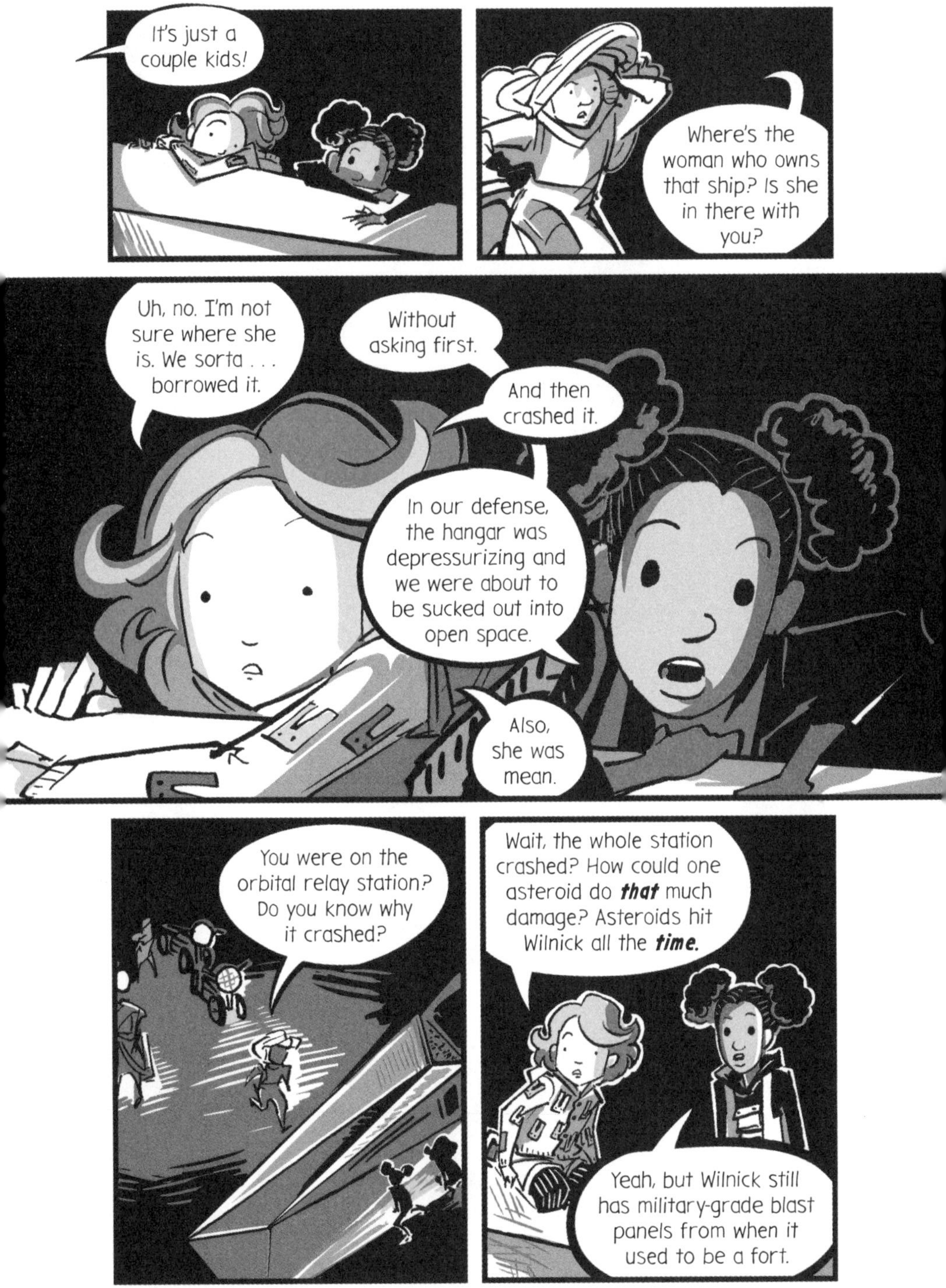
It's just a couple kids!
Where's the woman who owns that ship? Is she in there with you?
Uh, no. I'm not sure where she is. We sorta . . . borrowed it.
Without asking first.
And then crashed it.
In our defense, the hangar was depressurizing and we were about to be sucked out into open space.
Also, she was mean.
You were on the orbital relay station? Do you know why it crashed?
Wait, the whole station crashed? How could one asteroid do ***that*** much damage? Asteroids hit Wilnick all the ***time.***
Yeah, but Wilnick still has military-grade blast panels from when it used to be a fort.

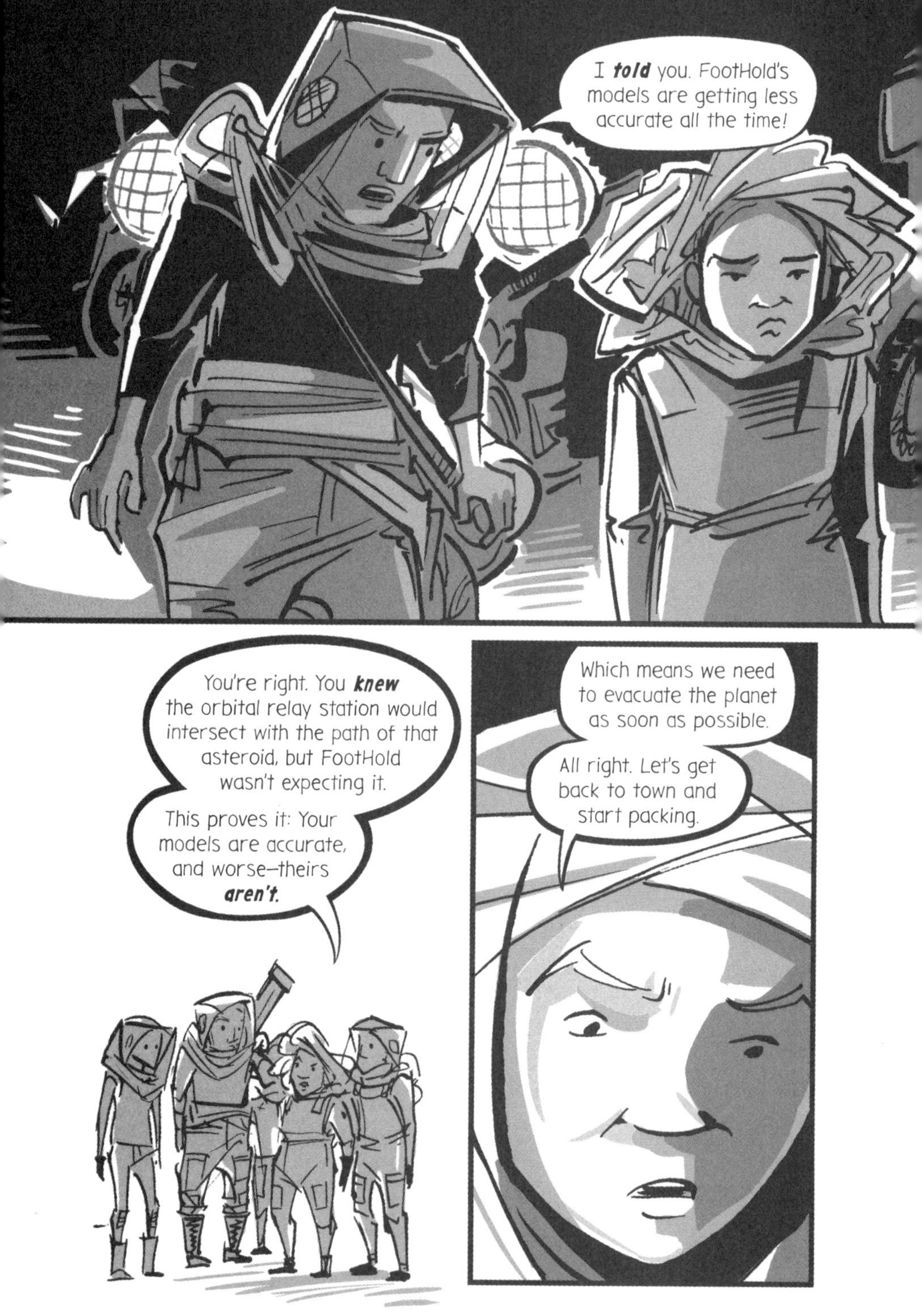
I **told** you. FootHold's models are getting less accurate all the time!
You're right. You **knew** the orbital relay station would intersect with the path of that asteroid, but FootHold wasn't expecting it.
This proves it: Your models are accurate, and worse—theirs **aren't.**
Which means we need to evacuate the planet as soon as possible.
All right. Let's get back to town and start packing.

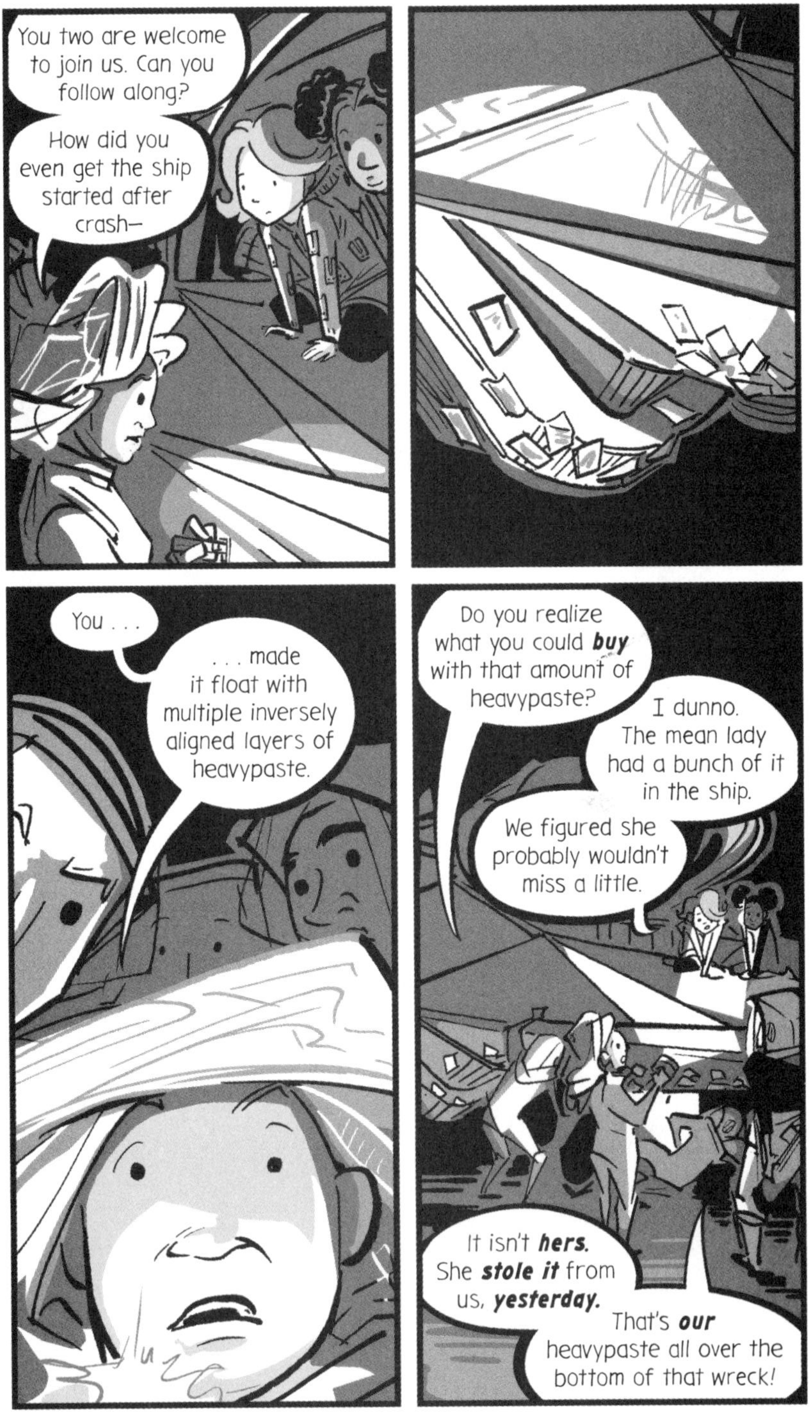
You two are welcome to join us. Can you follow along?
How did you even get the ship started after crash—
You . . .
. . . made it float with multiple inversely aligned layers of heavypaste.
Do you realize what you could **buy** with that amount of heavypaste?
I dunno. The mean lady had a bunch of it in the ship.
We figured she probably wouldn't miss a little.
It isn't **hers.** She **stole it** from us, **yesterday.**
That's **our** heavypaste all over the bottom of that wreck!

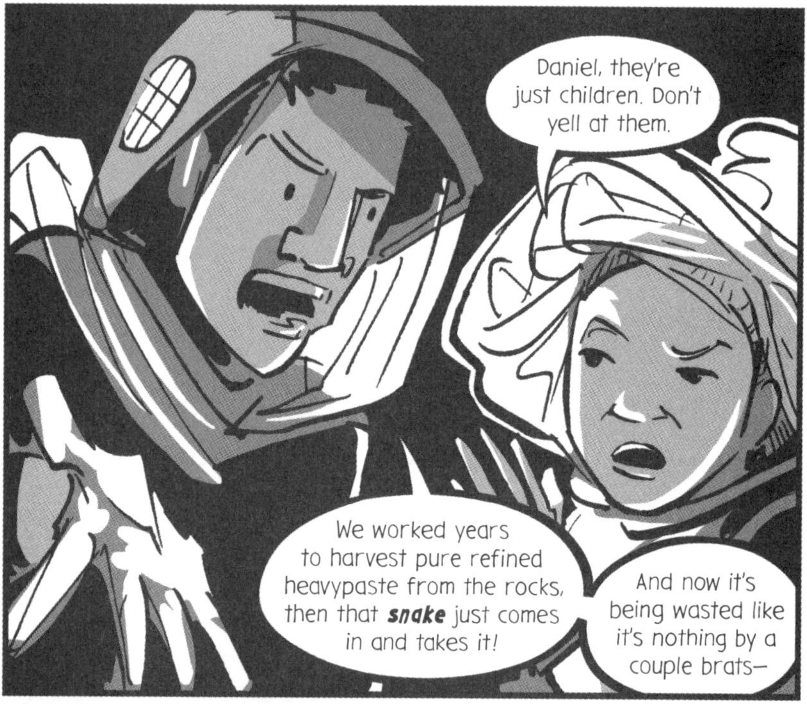
Daniel, they're just children. Don't yell at them.
We worked years to harvest pure refined heavypaste from the rocks, then that **snake** just comes in and takes it!
And now it's being wasted like it's nothing by a couple brats—

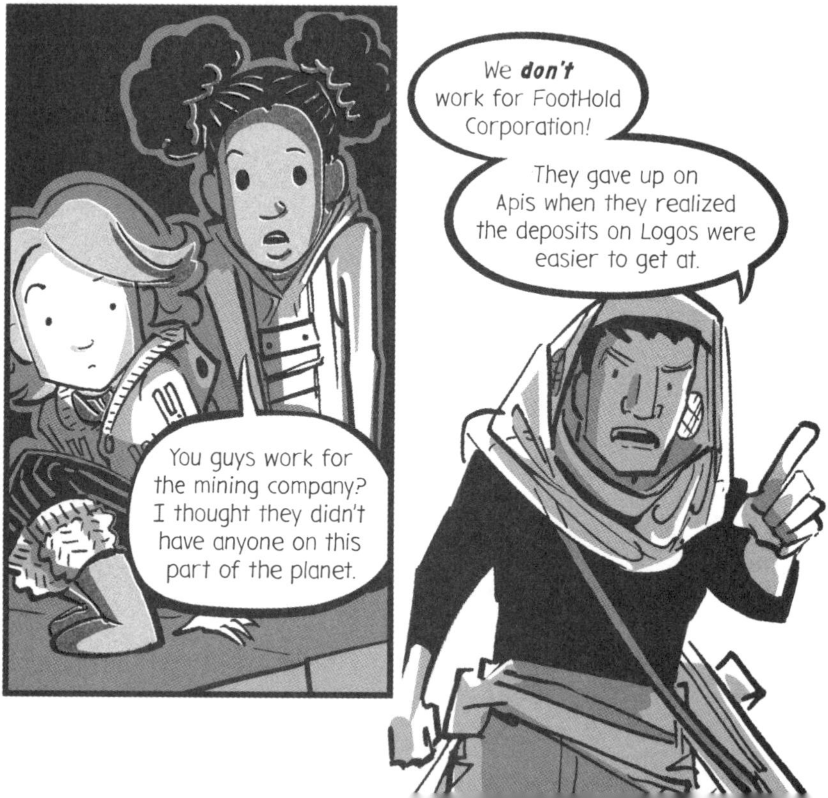
You guys work for the mining company? I thought they didn't have anyone on this part of the planet.
We **don't** work for FootHold Corporation!
They gave up on Apis when they realized the deposits on Logos were easier to get at.

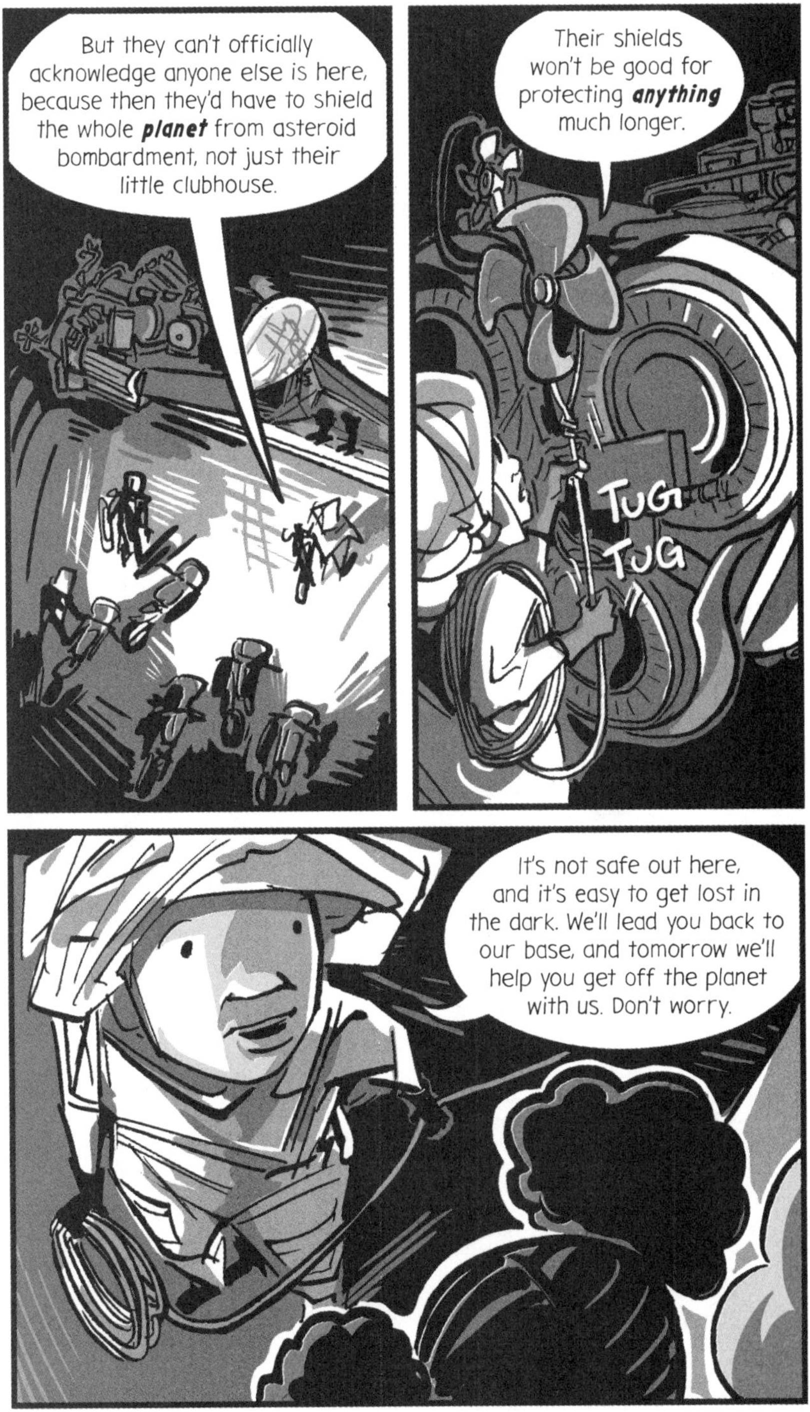

But they can't officially acknowledge anyone else is here, because then they'd have to shield the whole **planet** from asteroid bombardment, not just their little clubhouse.
Their shields won't be good for protecting **anything** much longer.
TUG TUG
It's not safe out here, and it's easy to get lost in the dark. We'll lead you back to our base, and tomorrow we'll help you get off the planet with us. Don't worry.

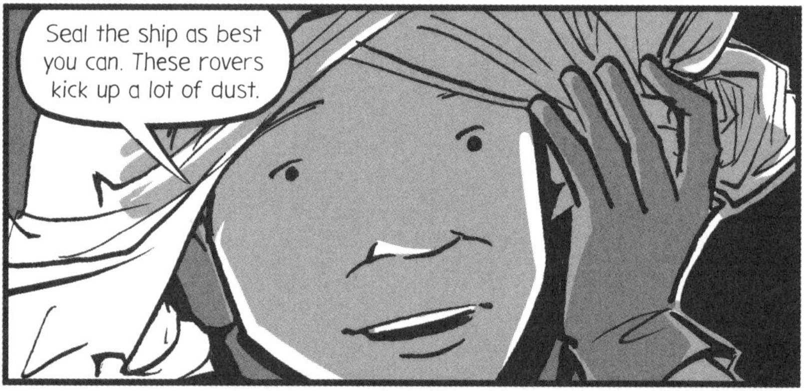
Seal the ship as best you can. These rovers kick up a lot of dust.

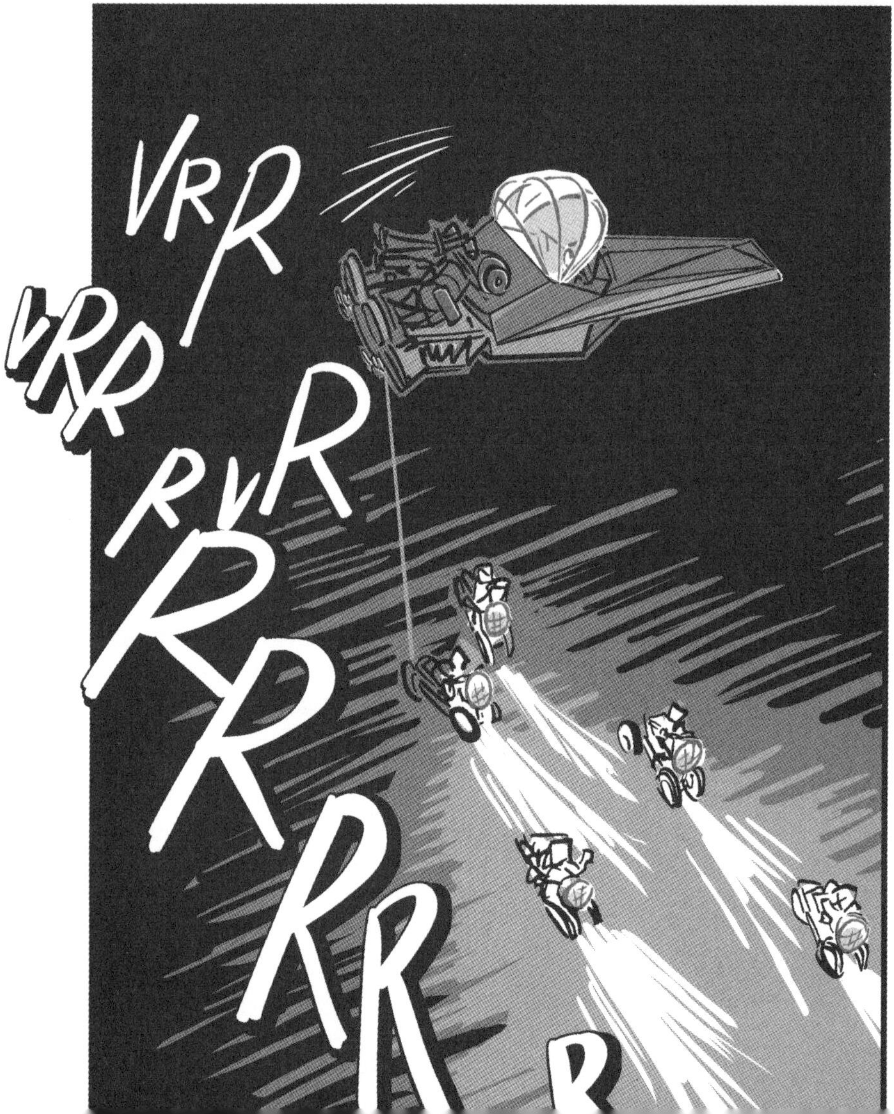
VRR
VRR
RVR
RRRR

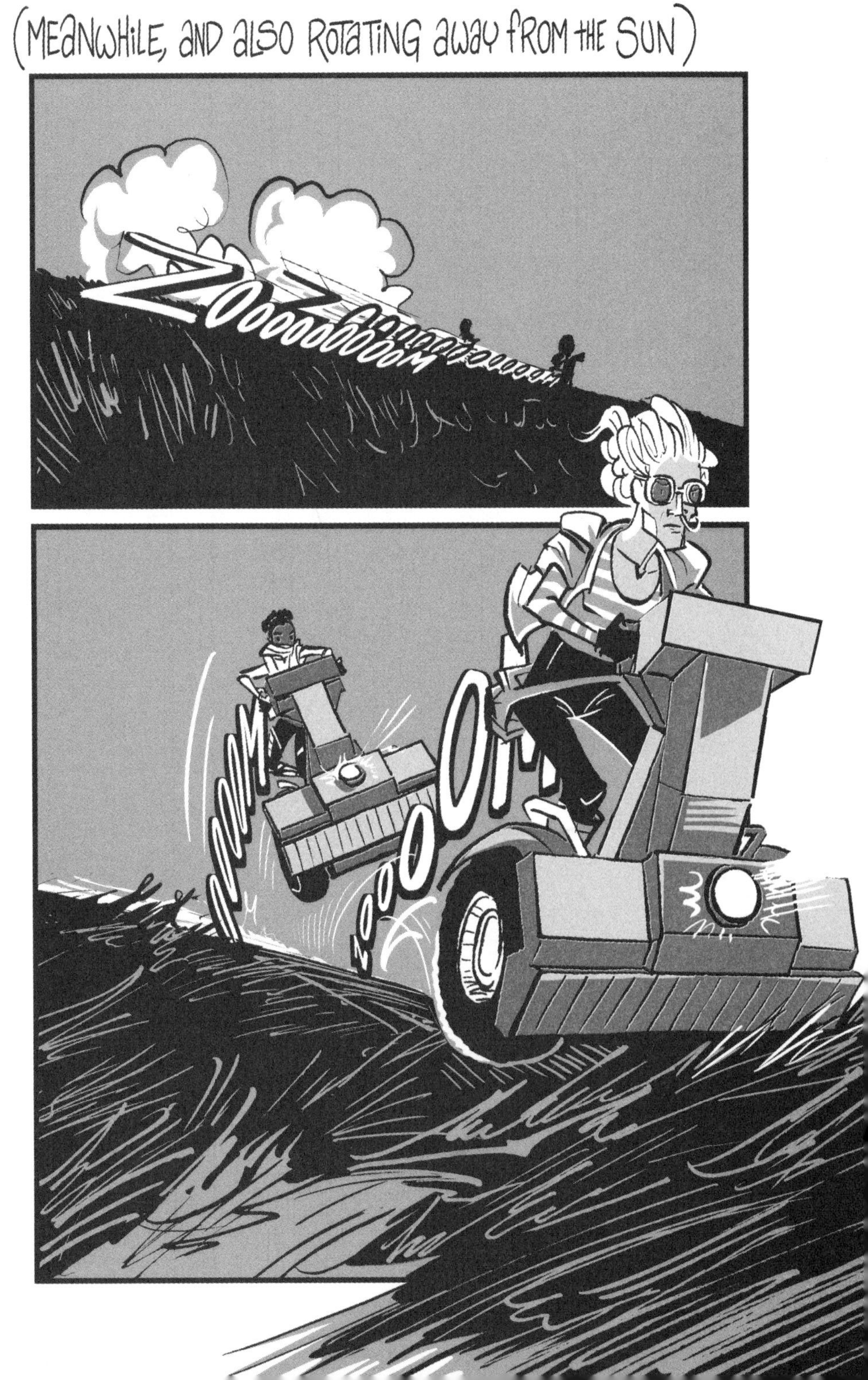
(MEANWHILE, AND ALSO ROTATING AWAY FROM THE SUN)

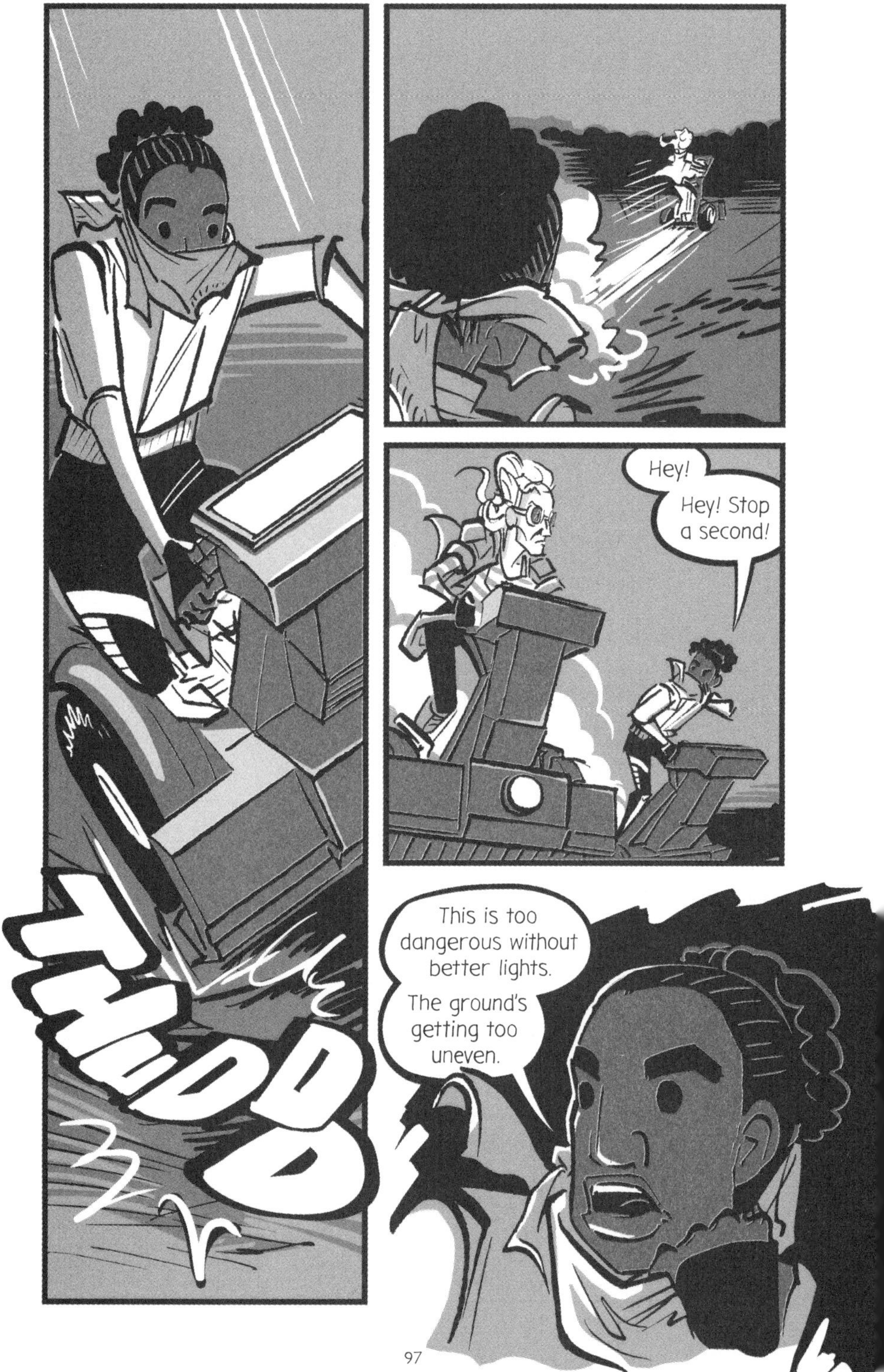

Hey!
Hey! Stop a second!
THUDD
This is too dangerous without better lights.
The ground's getting too uneven.

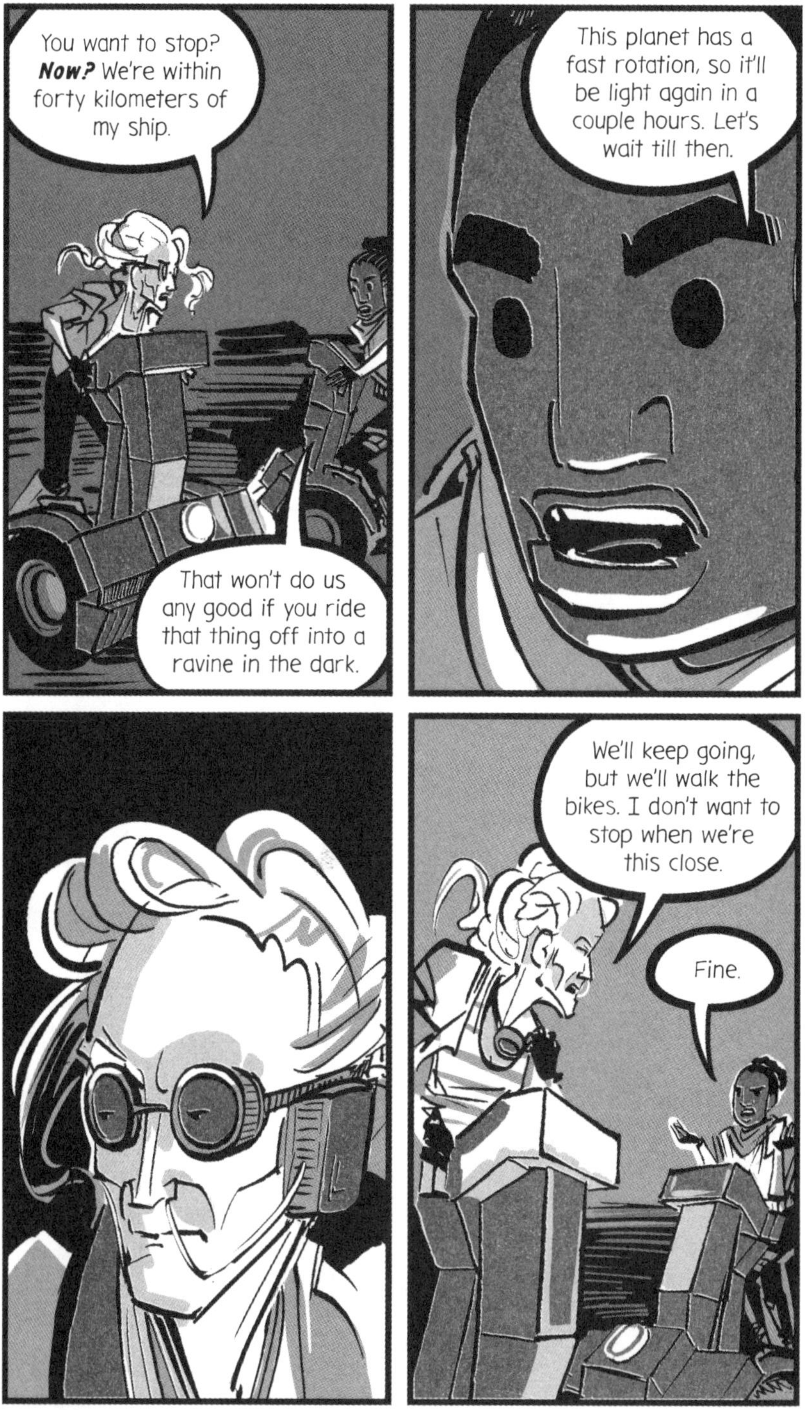
You want to stop? **Now?** We're within forty kilometers of my ship.
That won't do us any good if you ride that thing off into a ravine in the dark.
This planet has a fast rotation, so it'll be light again in a couple hours. Let's wait till then.
We'll keep going, but we'll walk the bikes. I don't want to stop when we're this close.
Fine.

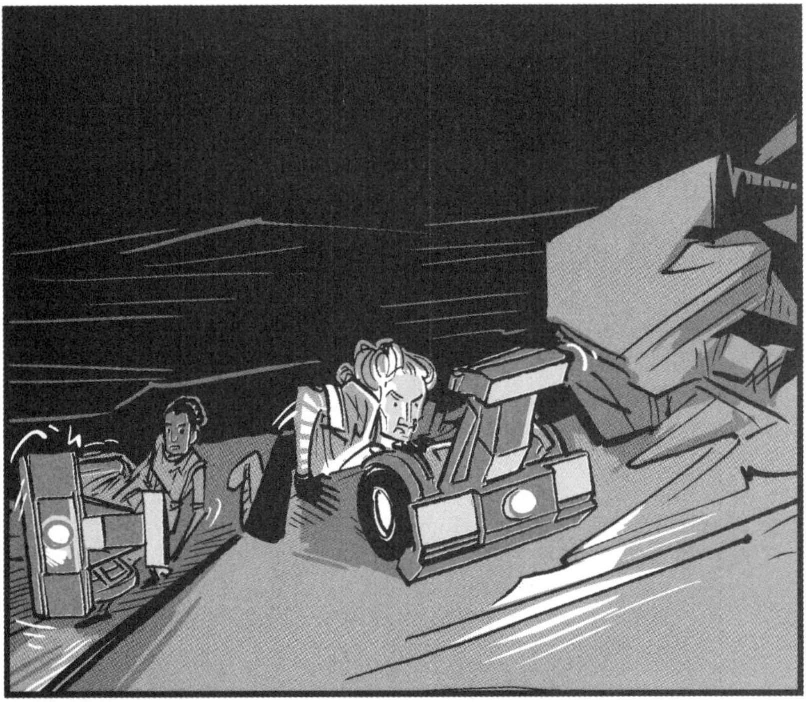

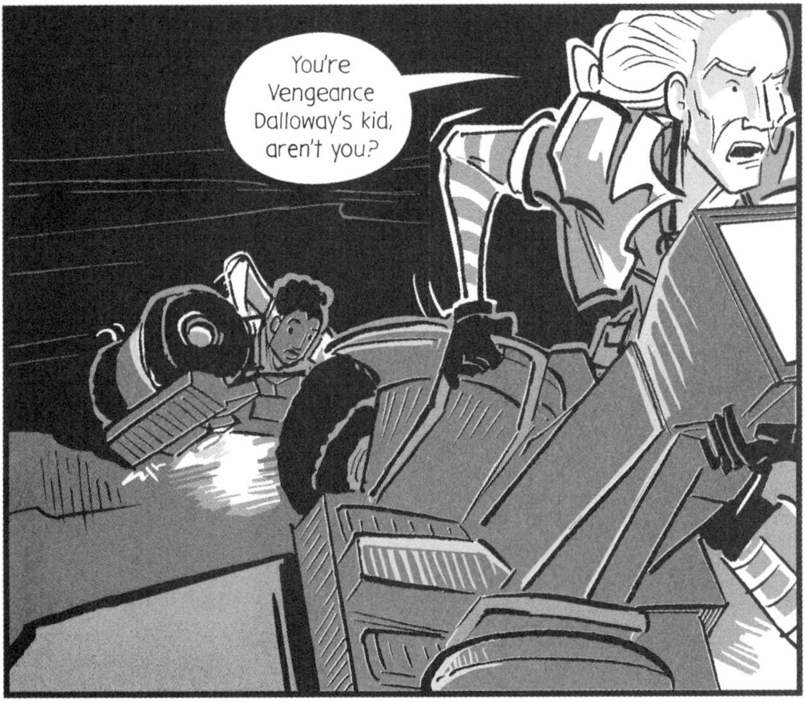
You're Vengeance Dalloway's kid, aren't you?

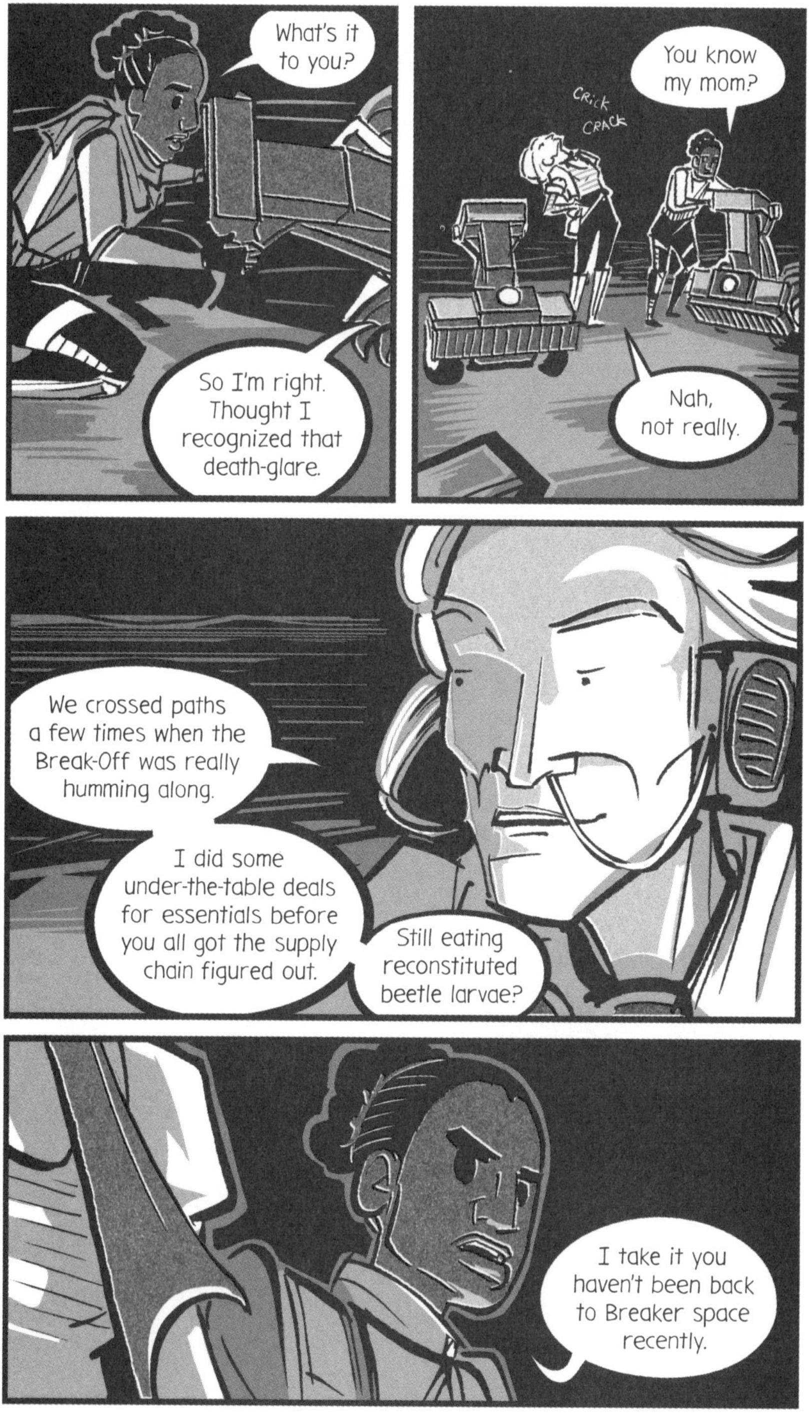
What's it to you?
So I'm right. Thought I recognized that death-glare.
You know my mom?
CRICK CRACK
Nah, not really.
We crossed paths a few times when the Break-Off was really humming along.
I did some under-the-table deals for essentials before you all got the supply chain figured out.
Still eating reconstituted beetle larvae?
I take it you haven't been back to Breaker space recently.

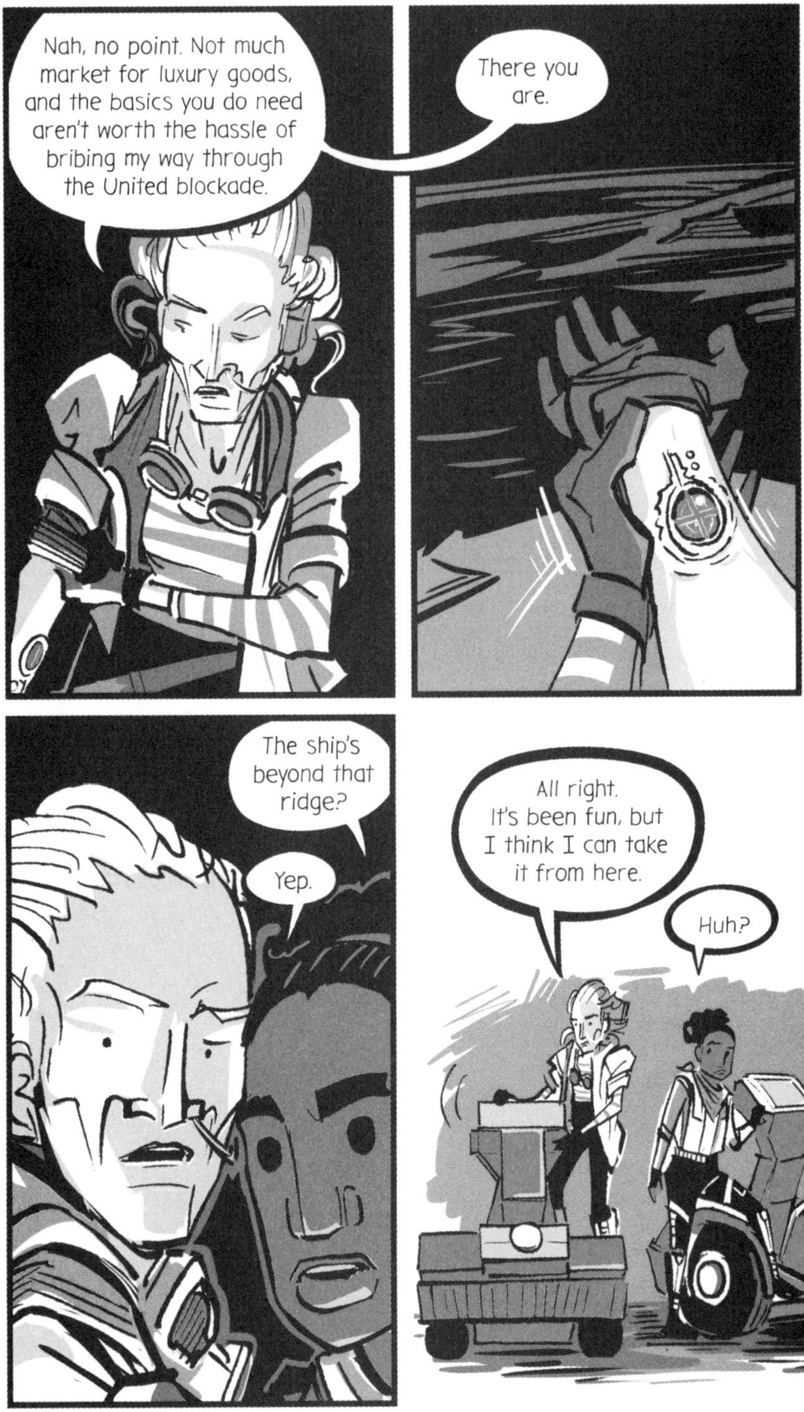
Nah, no point. Not much market for luxury goods, and the basics you do need aren't worth the hassle of bribing my way through the United blockade.
There you are.
The ship's beyond that ridge?
Yep.
All right. It's been fun, but I think I can take it from here.
Huh?

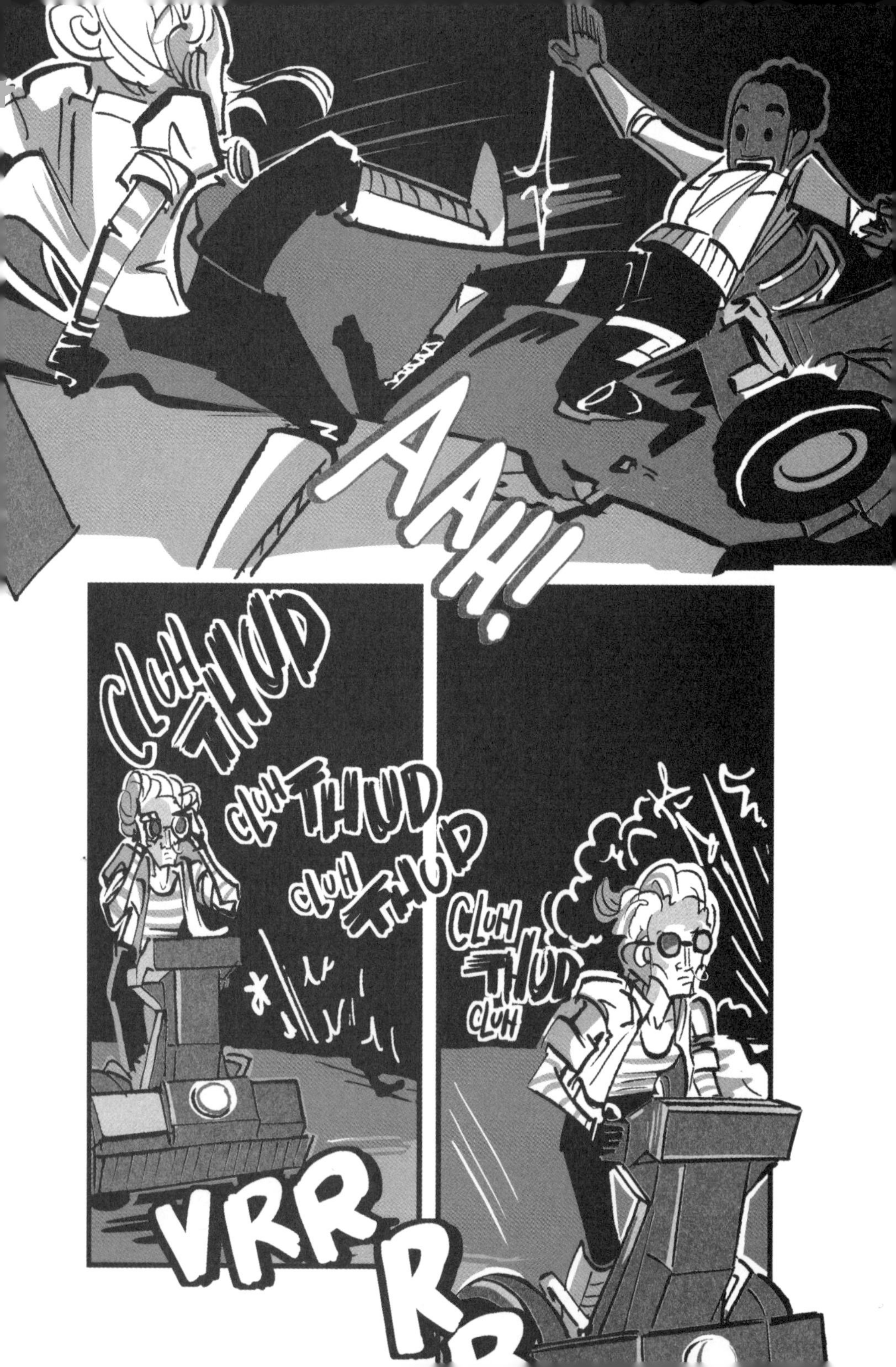
AAHH!
CLUH THUD
CLUH THUD
CLUH THUD
CLUH THUD CLUH
VRRRR

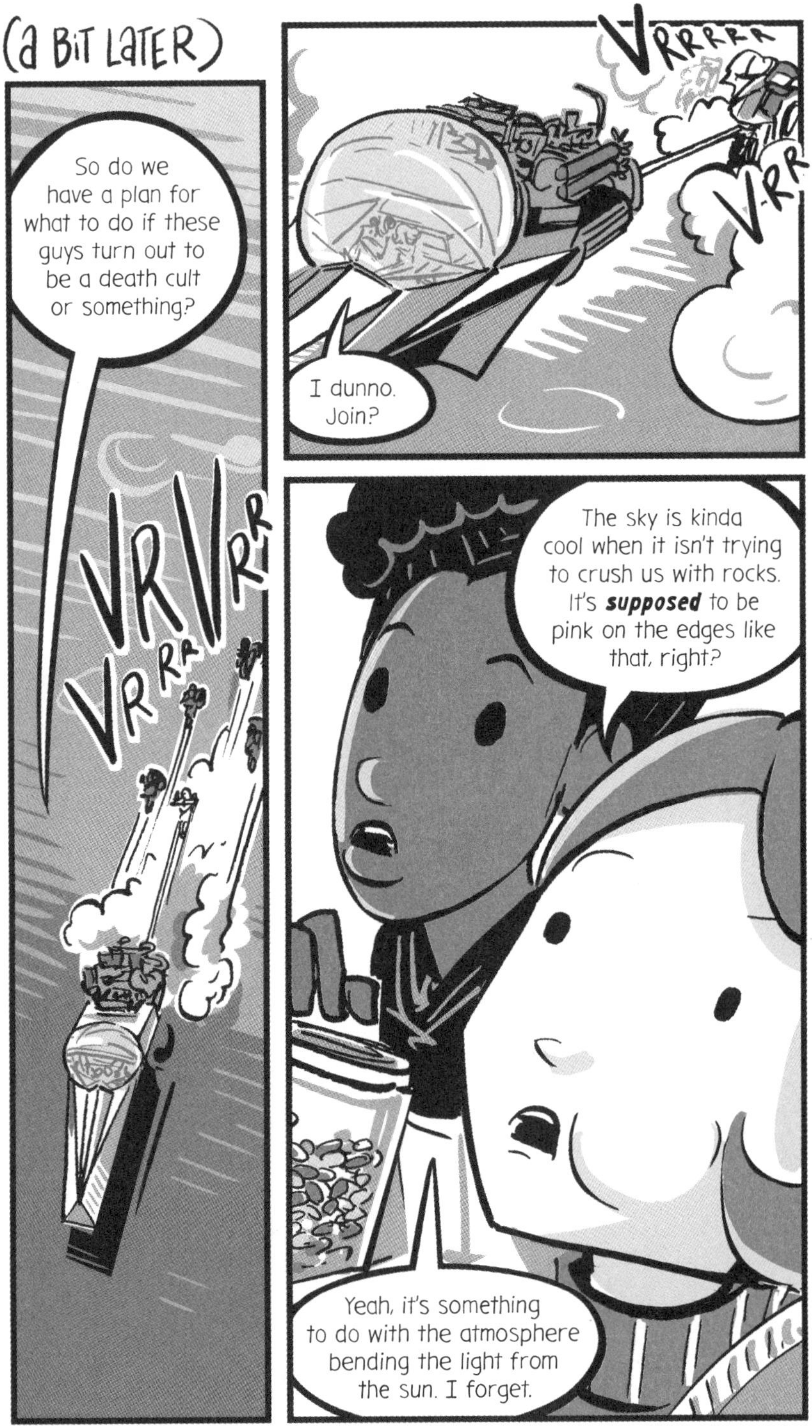
(a bit later)
So do we have a plan for what to do if these guys turn out to be a death cult or something?
VR VRRR VRR
VRRRRR VRR
I dunno. Join?
The sky is kinda cool when it isn't trying to crush us with rocks. It's **supposed** to be pink on the edges like that, right?
Yeah, it's something to do with the atmosphere bending the light from the sun. I forget.

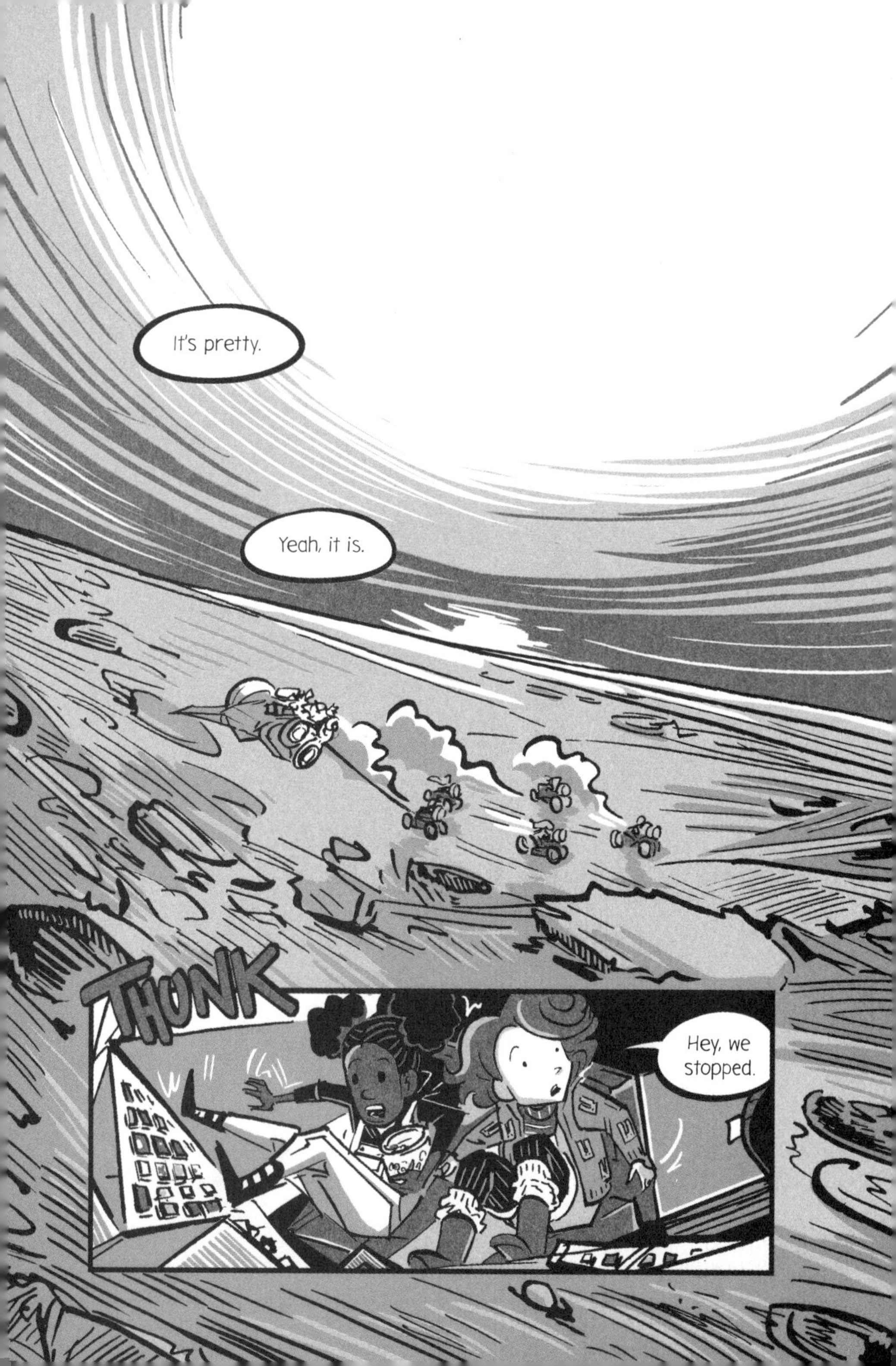
It's pretty.
Yeah, it is.
THONK
Hey, we stopped.

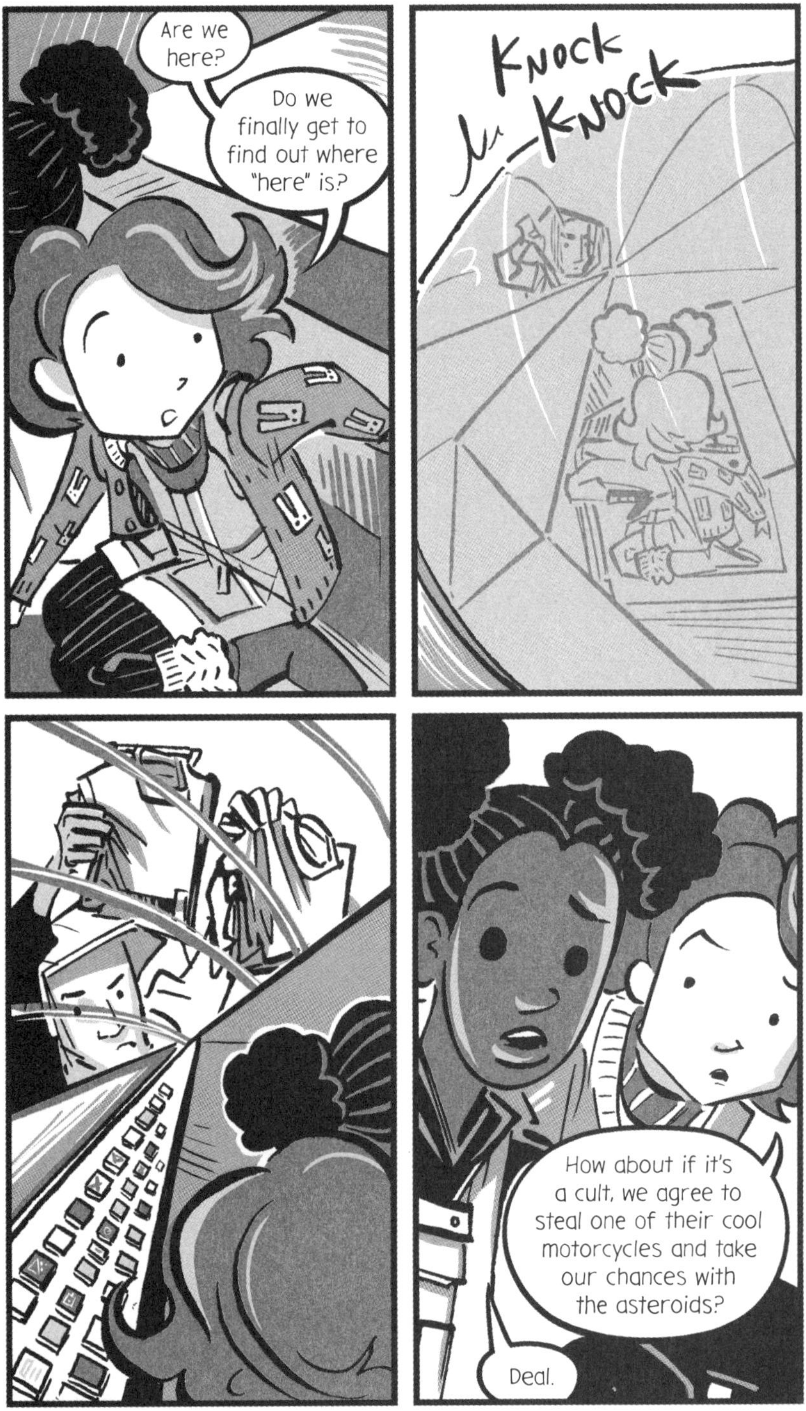
Are we here?
Do we finally get to find out where "here" is?
KNOCK KNOCK
How about if it's a cult, we agree to steal one of their cool motorcycles and take our chances with the asteroids?
Deal.

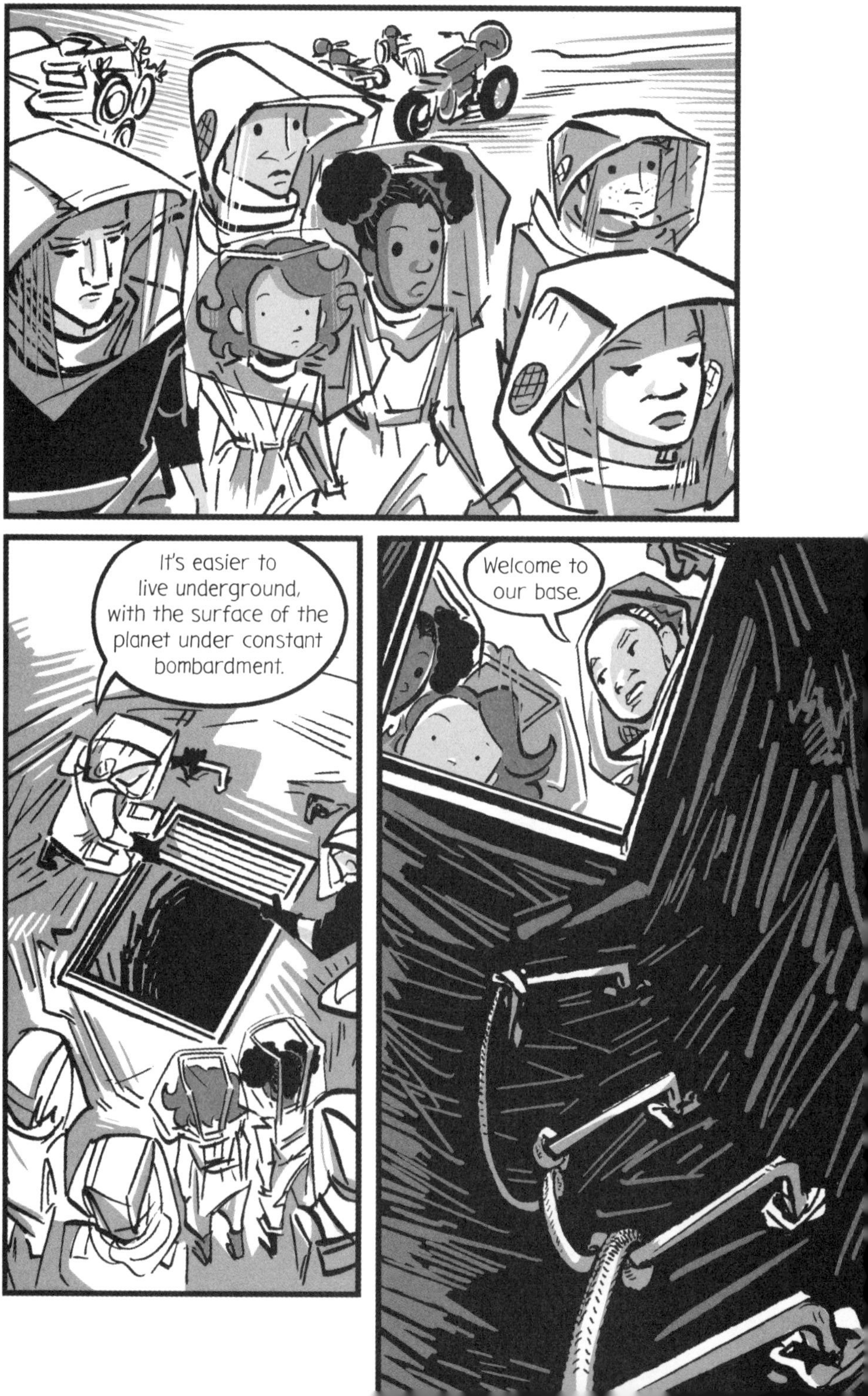
It's easier to live underground, with the surface of the planet under constant bombardment.
Welcome to our base.

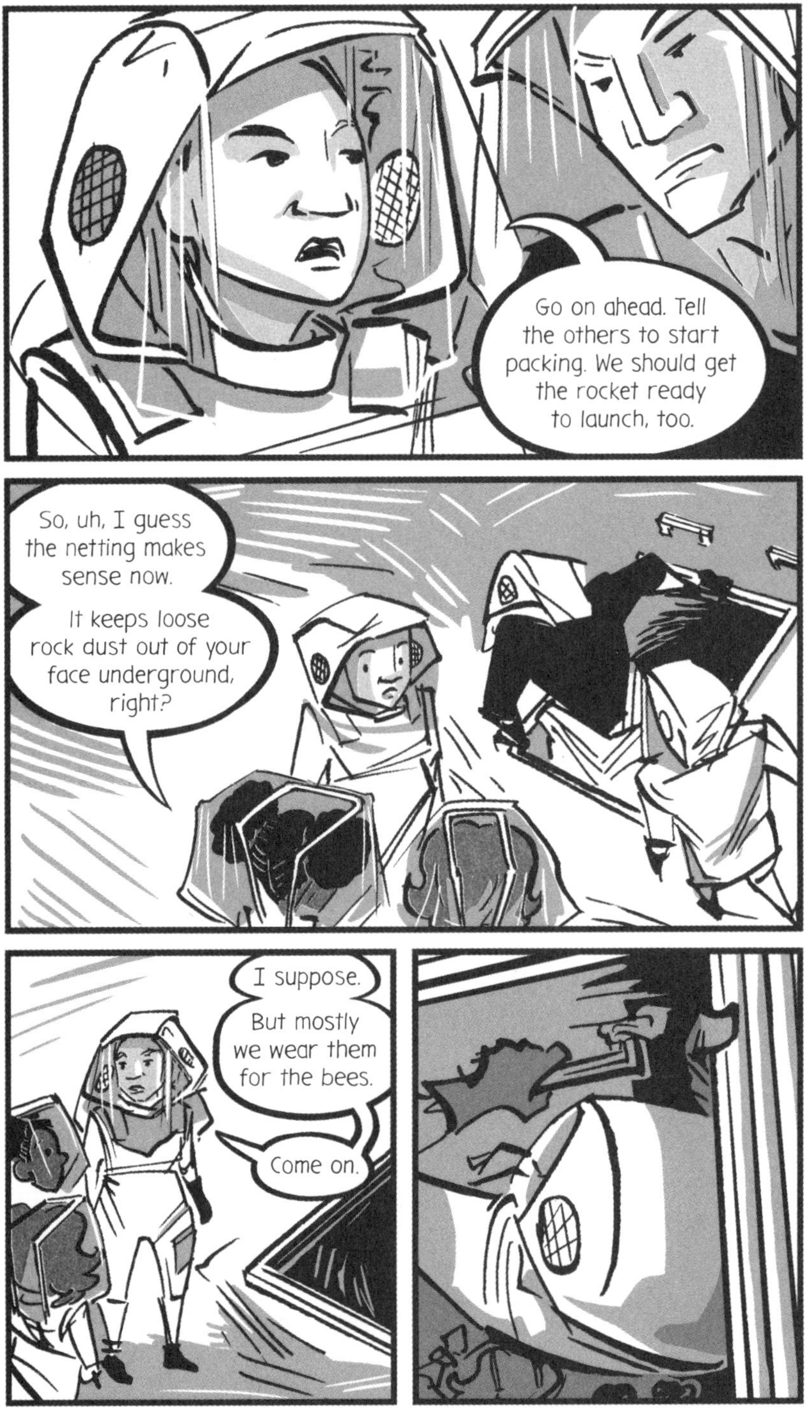
Go on ahead. Tell the others to start packing. We should get the rocket ready to launch, too.
So, uh, I guess the netting makes sense now.
It keeps loose rock dust out of your face underground, right?
I suppose.
But mostly we wear them for the bees.
Come on.

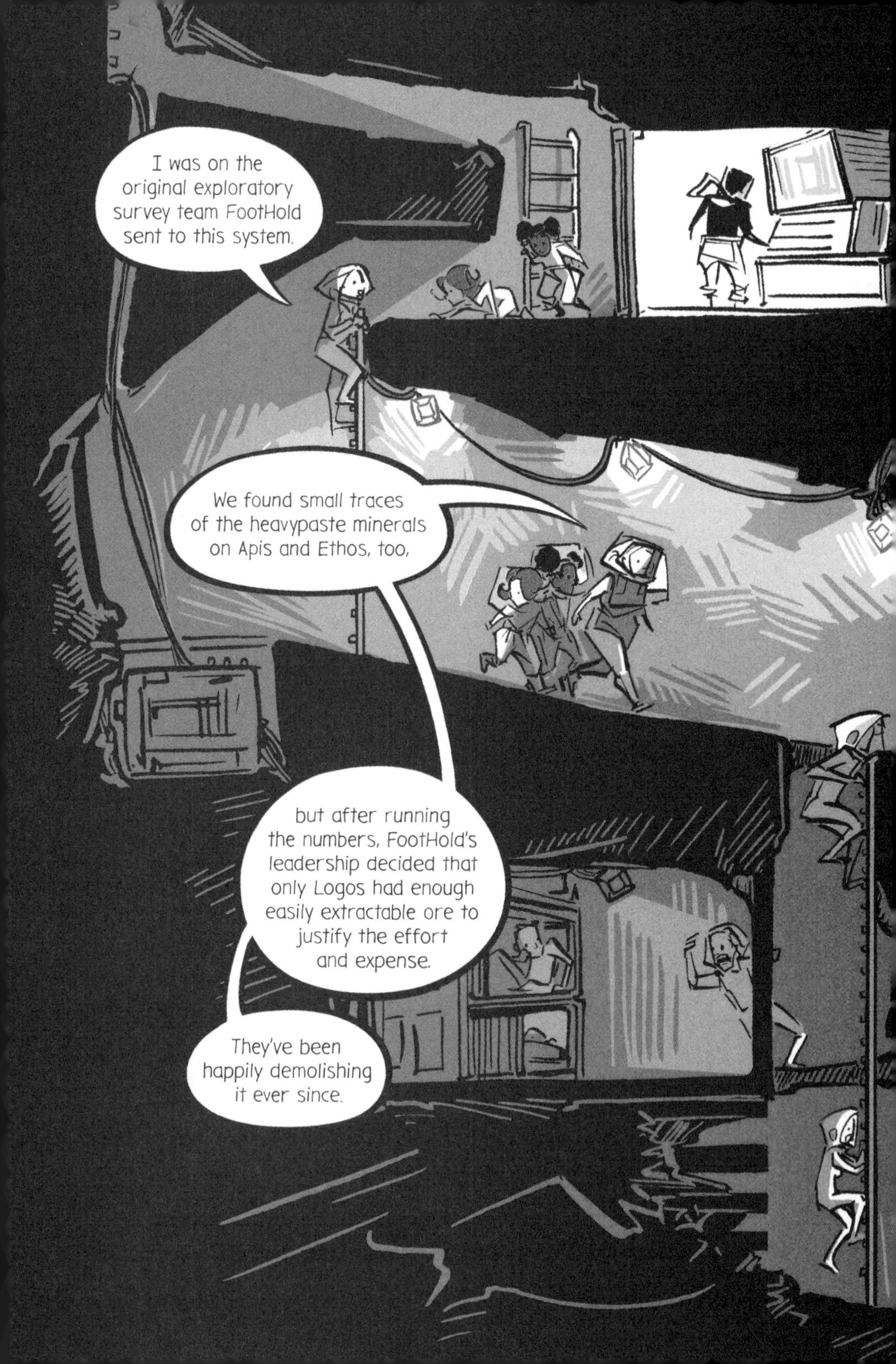
I was on the original exploratory survey team FootHold sent to this system.
We found small traces of the heavypaste minerals on Apis and Ethos, too,
but after running the numbers, FootHold's leadership decided that only Logos had enough easily extractable ore to justify the effort and expense.
They've been happily demolishing it ever since.

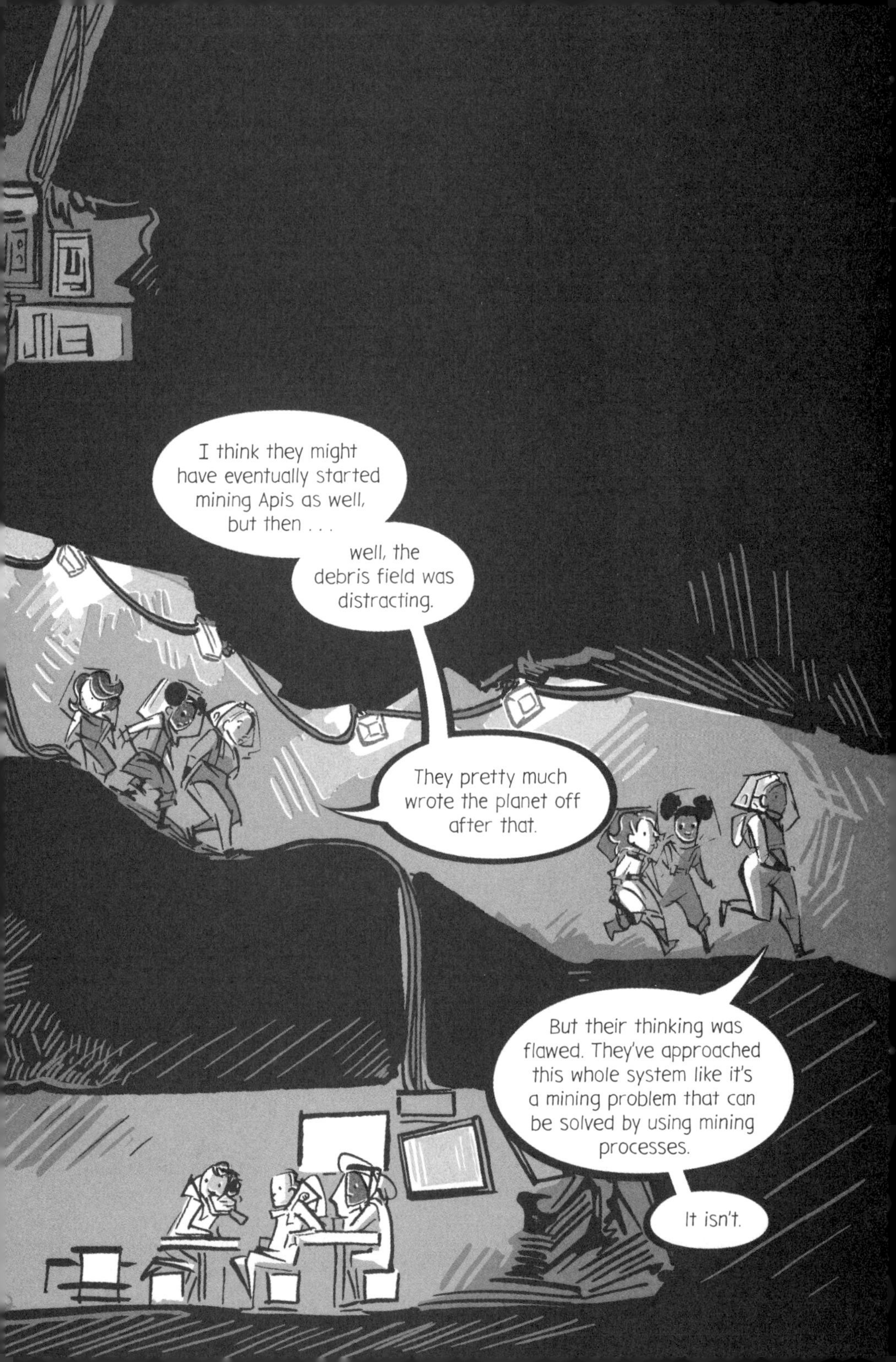
I think they might have eventually started mining Apis as well, but then . . .
well, the debris field was distracting.
They pretty much wrote the planet off after that.
But their thinking was flawed. They've approached this whole system like it's a mining problem that can be solved by using mining processes.
It isn't.

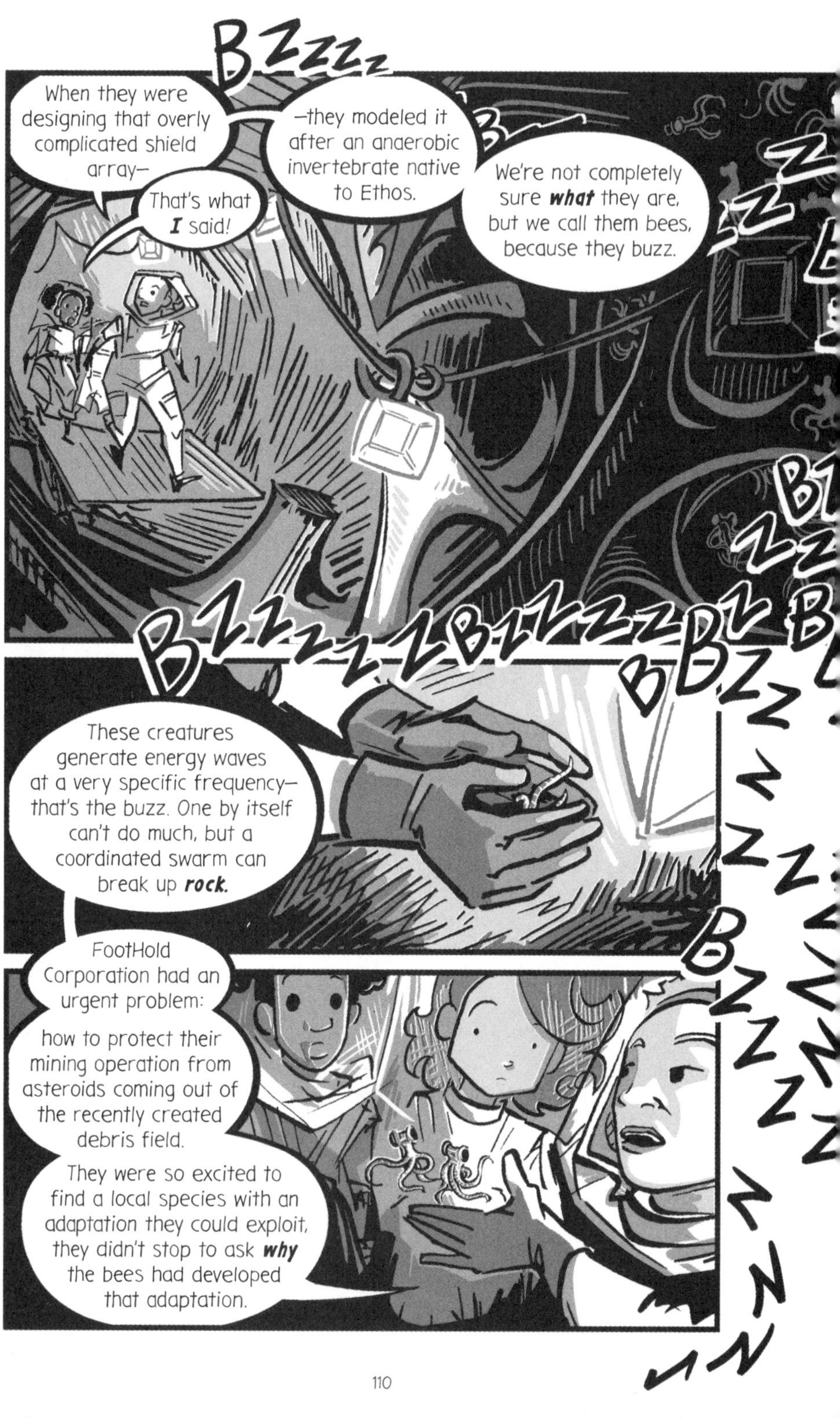
BZZZZ
When they were designing that overly complicated shield array—
That's what **I** said!
—they modeled it after an anaerobic invertebrate native to Ethos.
We're not completely sure **what** they are, but we call them bees, because they buzz.
BZZZZZZBZZZZZZZBBZ
These creatures generate energy waves at a very specific frequency—that's the buzz. One by itself can't do much, but a coordinated swarm can break up **rock**.
FootHold Corporation had an urgent problem:
how to protect their mining operation from asteroids coming out of the recently created debris field.
They were so excited to find a local species with an adaptation they could exploit, they didn't stop to ask **why** the bees had developed that adaptation.

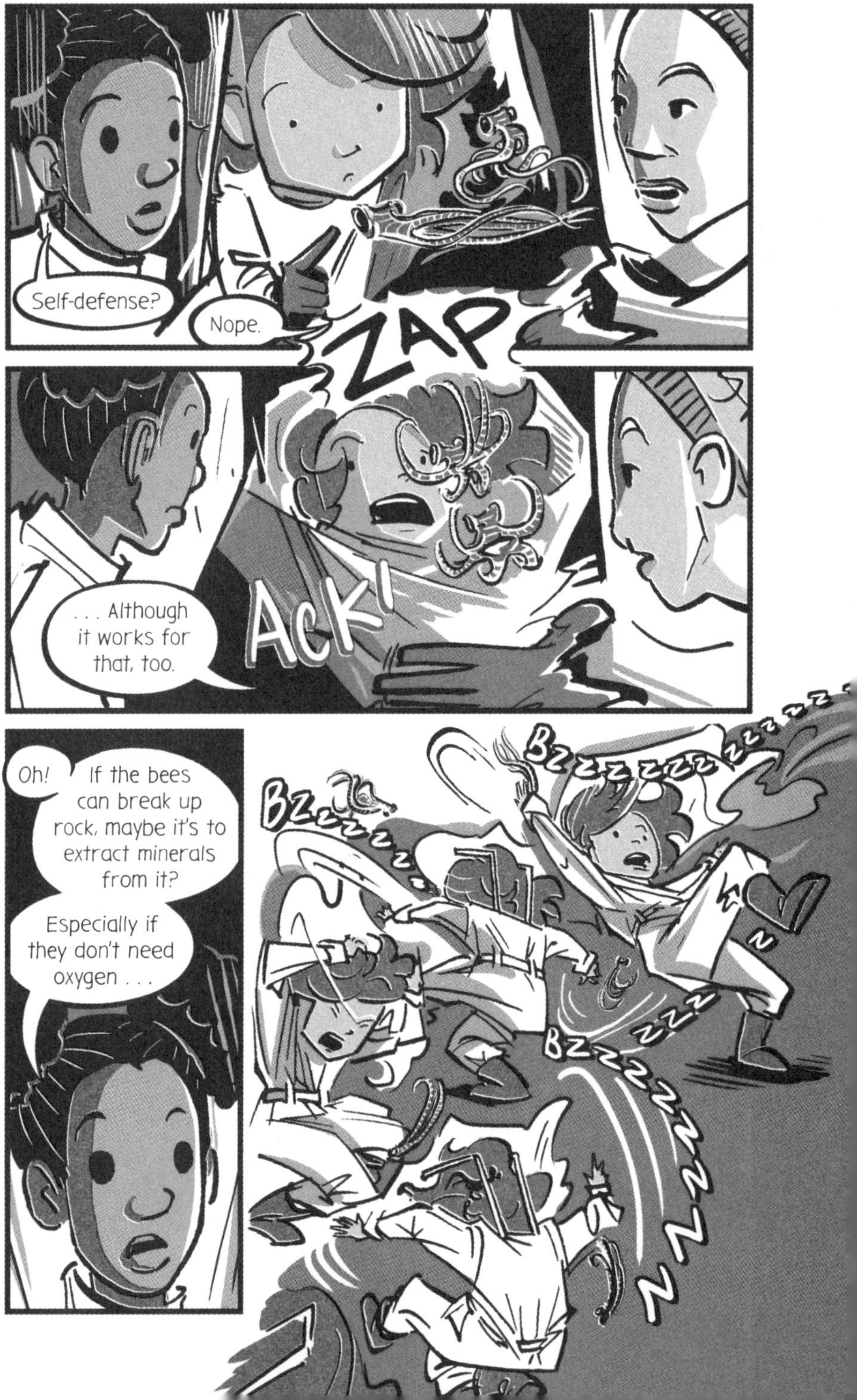
Self-defense?
Nope.
ZAP
. . . Although it works for that, too.
ACK!
Oh!
If the bees can break up rock, maybe it's to extract minerals from it?
Especially if they don't need oxygen . . .
Bzzzzzz
Bzzzzzzzzzzzzzzzz
Bzzzzzzzzzzzzzz

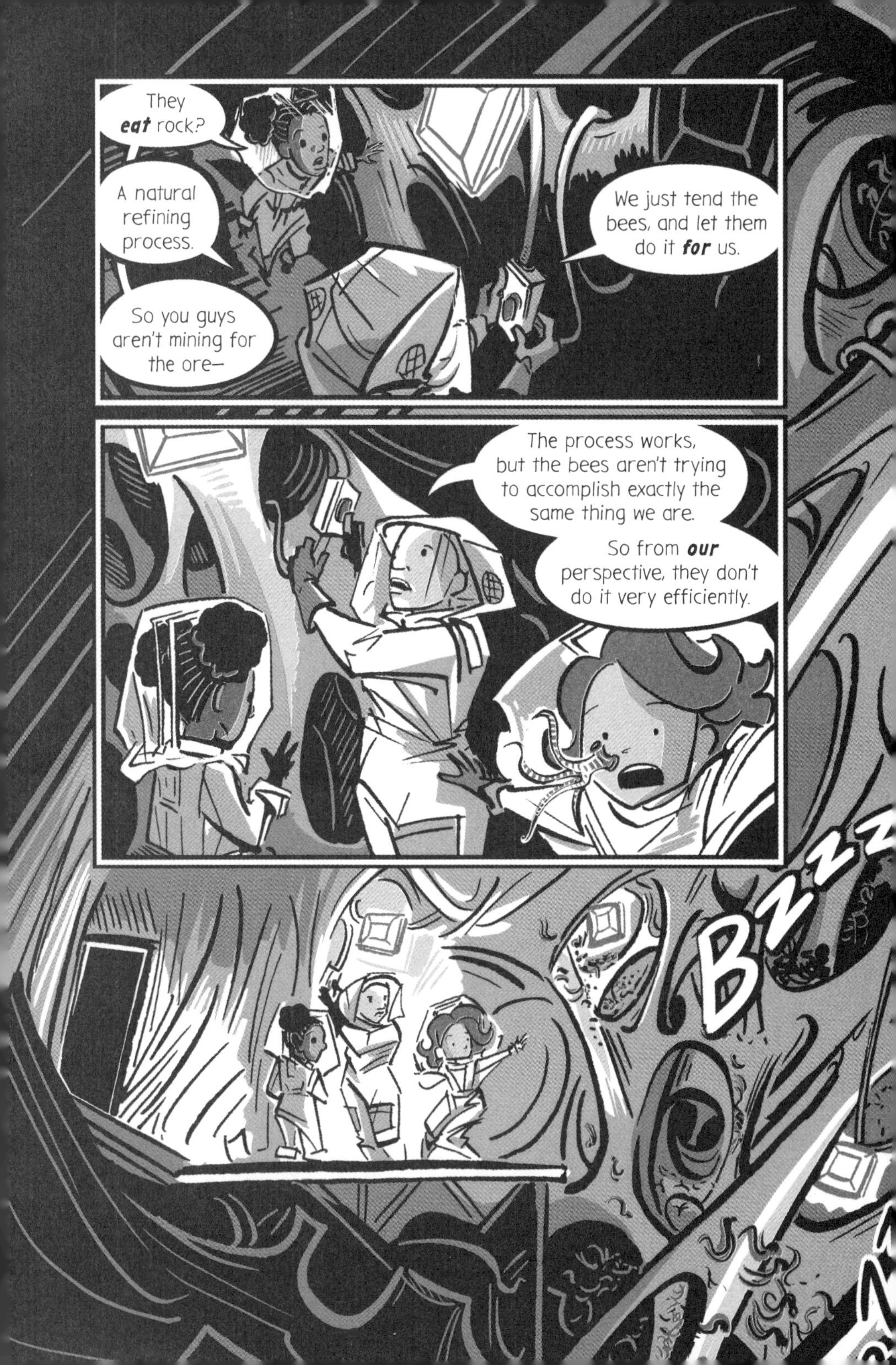
They **eat** rock?
A natural refining process.
We just tend the bees, and let them do it **for** us.
So you guys aren't mining for the ore—
The process works, but the bees aren't trying to accomplish exactly the same thing we are.
So from **our** perspective, they don't do it very efficiently.
BZZZ

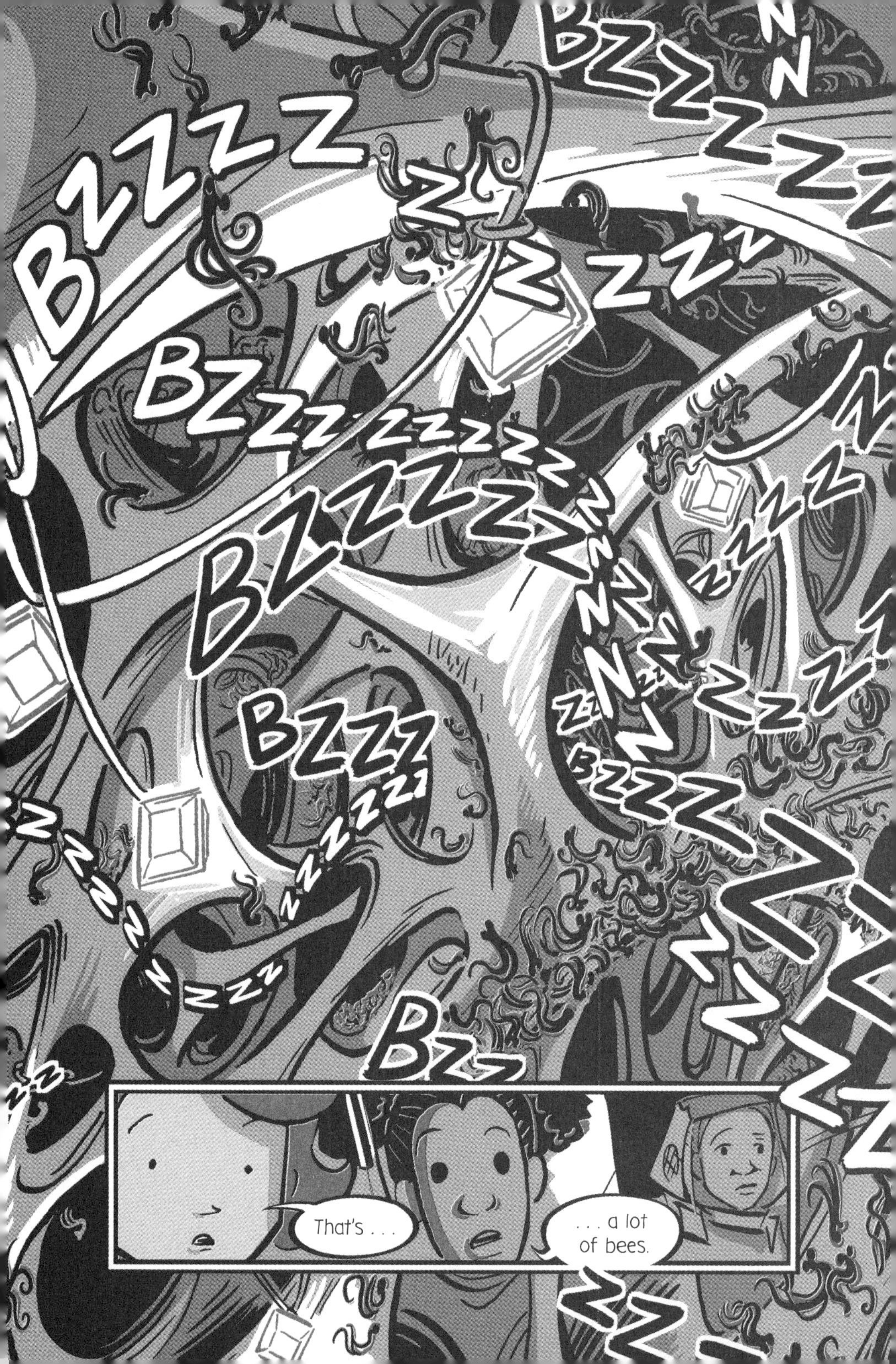

That's . . .
. . . a lot of bees.

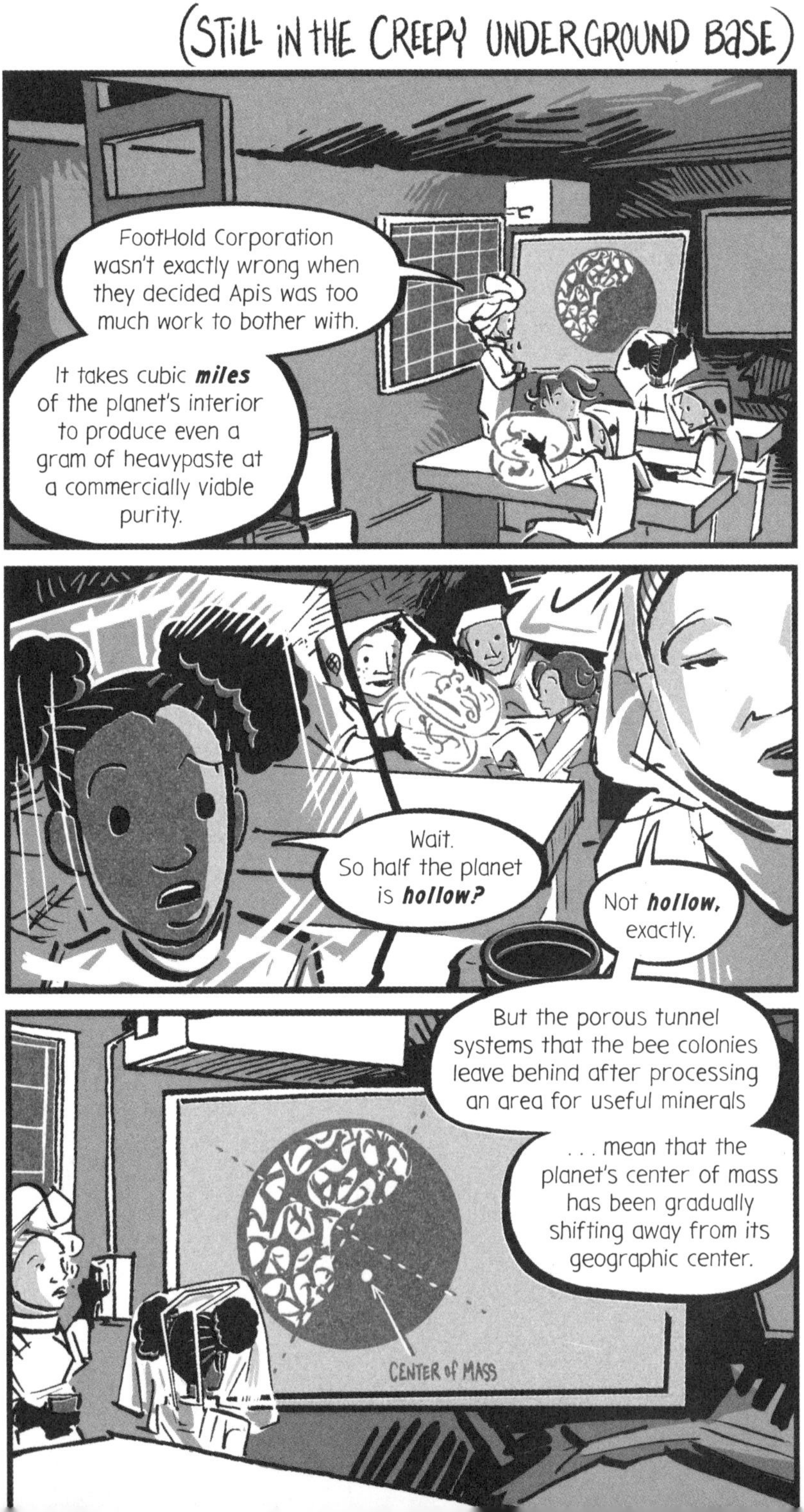
(STILL IN THE CREEPY UNDERGROUND BASE)
FootHold Corporation wasn't exactly wrong when they decided Apis was too much work to bother with.
It takes cubic ***miles*** of the planet's interior to produce even a gram of heavypaste at a commercially viable purity.
Wait. So half the planet is ***hollow?***
Not ***hollow,*** exactly.
But the porous tunnel systems that the bee colonies leave behind after processing an area for useful minerals
. . . mean that the planet's center of mass has been gradually shifting away from its geographic center.
CENTER OF MASS

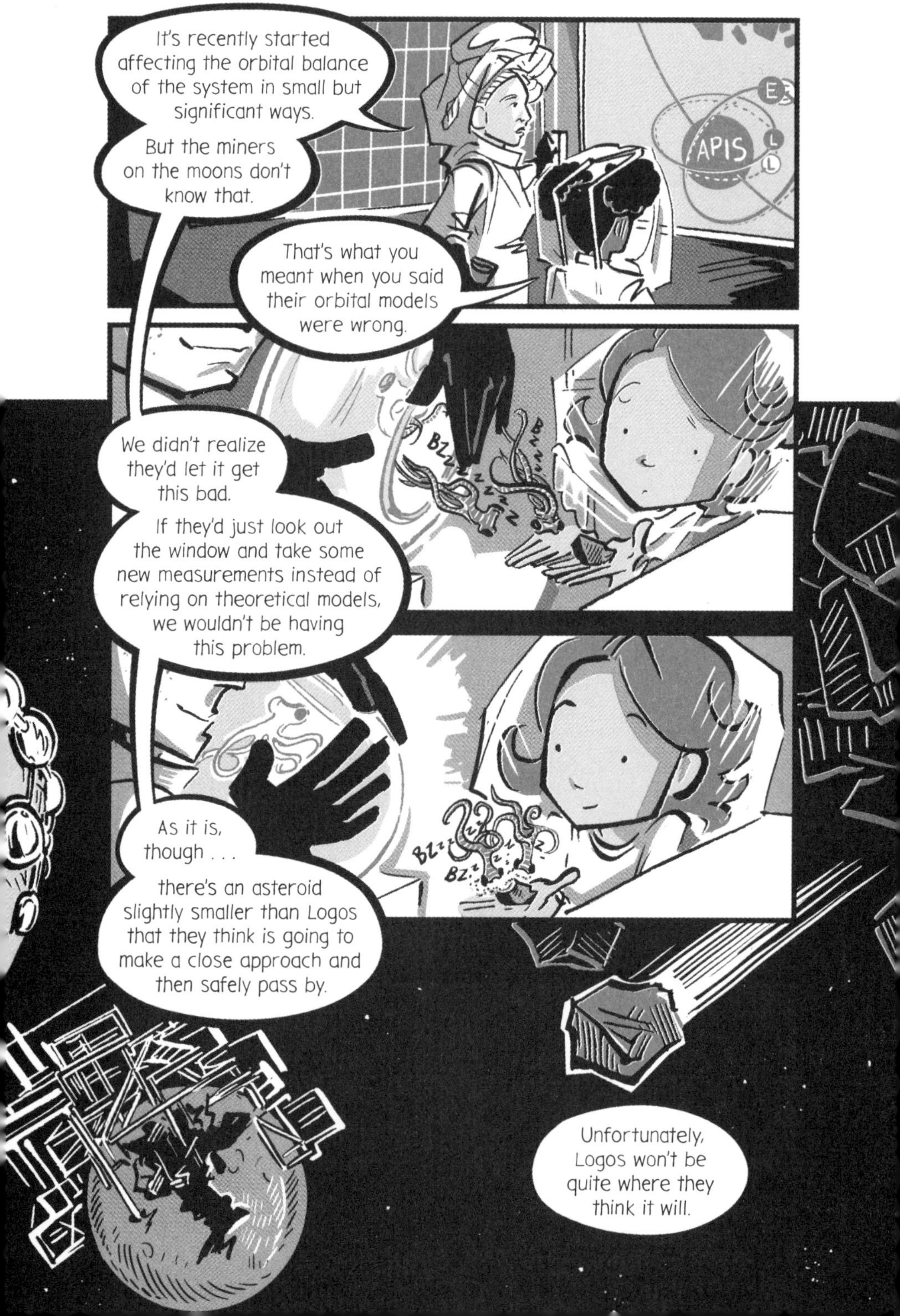
It's recently started affecting the orbital balance of the system in small but significant ways.
But the miners on the moons don't know that.
E
APIS
L
L
That's what you meant when you said their orbital models were wrong.
We didn't realize they'd let it get this bad.
If they'd just look out the window and take some new measurements instead of relying on theoretical models, we wouldn't be having this problem.
BZZZ
As it is, though . . .
there's an asteroid slightly smaller than Logos that they think is going to make a close approach and then safely pass by.
BZ
BZ
Unfortunately, Logos won't be quite where they think it will.

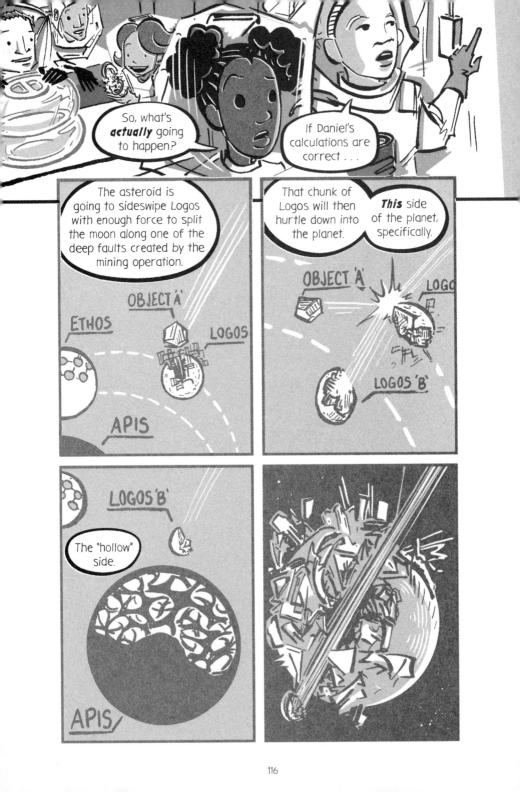

So, what's **actually** going to happen?

If Daniel's calculations are correct . . .

The asteroid is going to sideswipe Logos with enough force to split the moon along one of the deep faults created by the mining operation.

OBJECT 'A'

ETHOS

LOGOS

APIS

That chunk of Logos will then hurtle down into the planet.

**This** side of the planet, specifically.

OBJECT 'A'

LOGO

LOGOS 'B'

LOGOS 'B'

The "hollow" side.

APIS

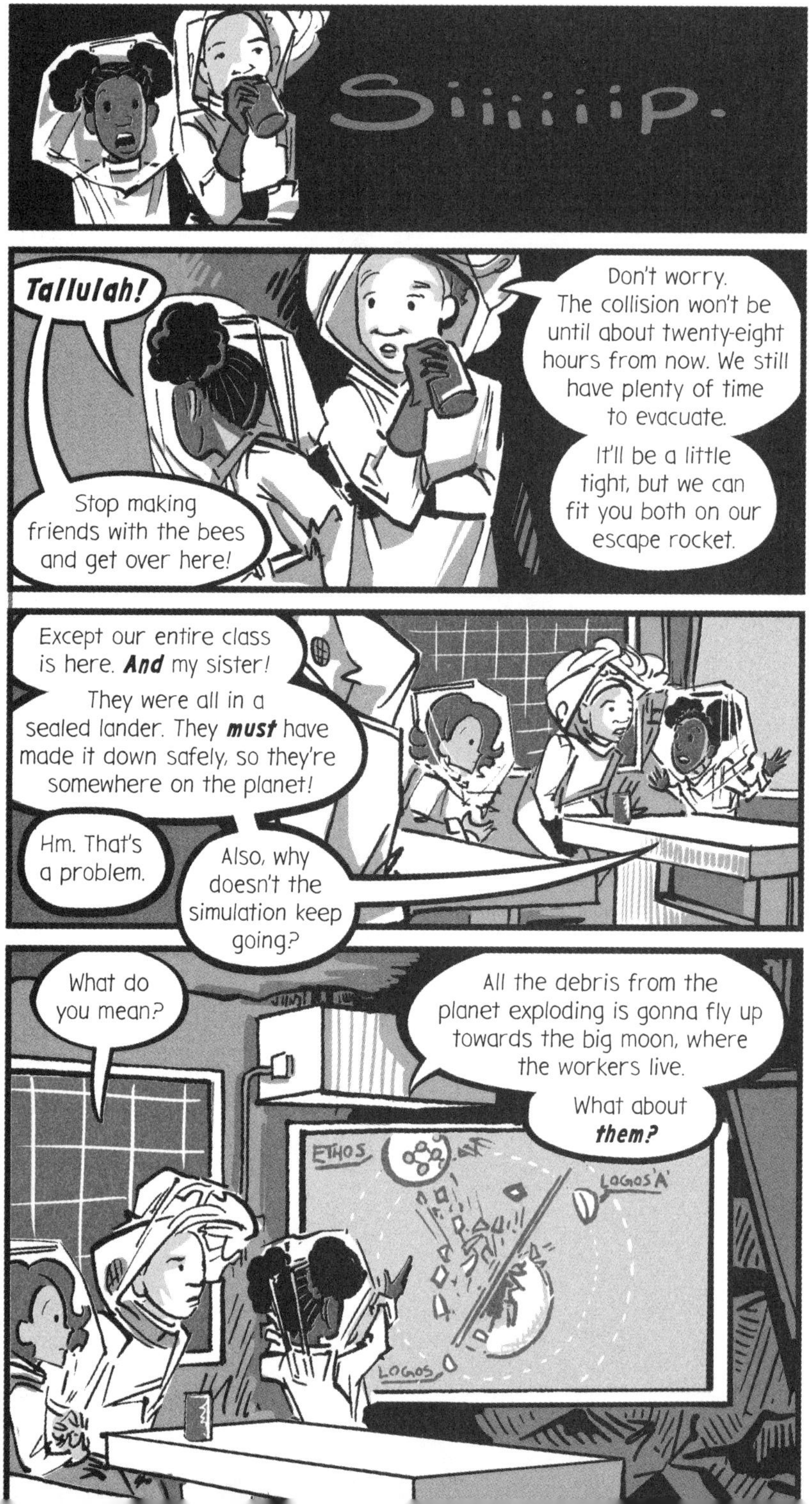
Siiiiiip.
Tallulah!
Stop making friends with the bees and get over here!
Don't worry. The collision won't be until about twenty-eight hours from now. We still have plenty of time to evacuate.
It'll be a little tight, but we can fit you both on our escape rocket.
Except our entire class is here. **And** my sister!
They were all in a sealed lander. They **must** have made it down safely, so they're somewhere on the planet!
Hm. That's a problem.
Also, why doesn't the simulation keep going?
What do you mean?
All the debris from the planet exploding is gonna fly up towards the big moon, where the workers live.
What about ***them?***
ETHOS
LOGOS 'A'
LOGOS

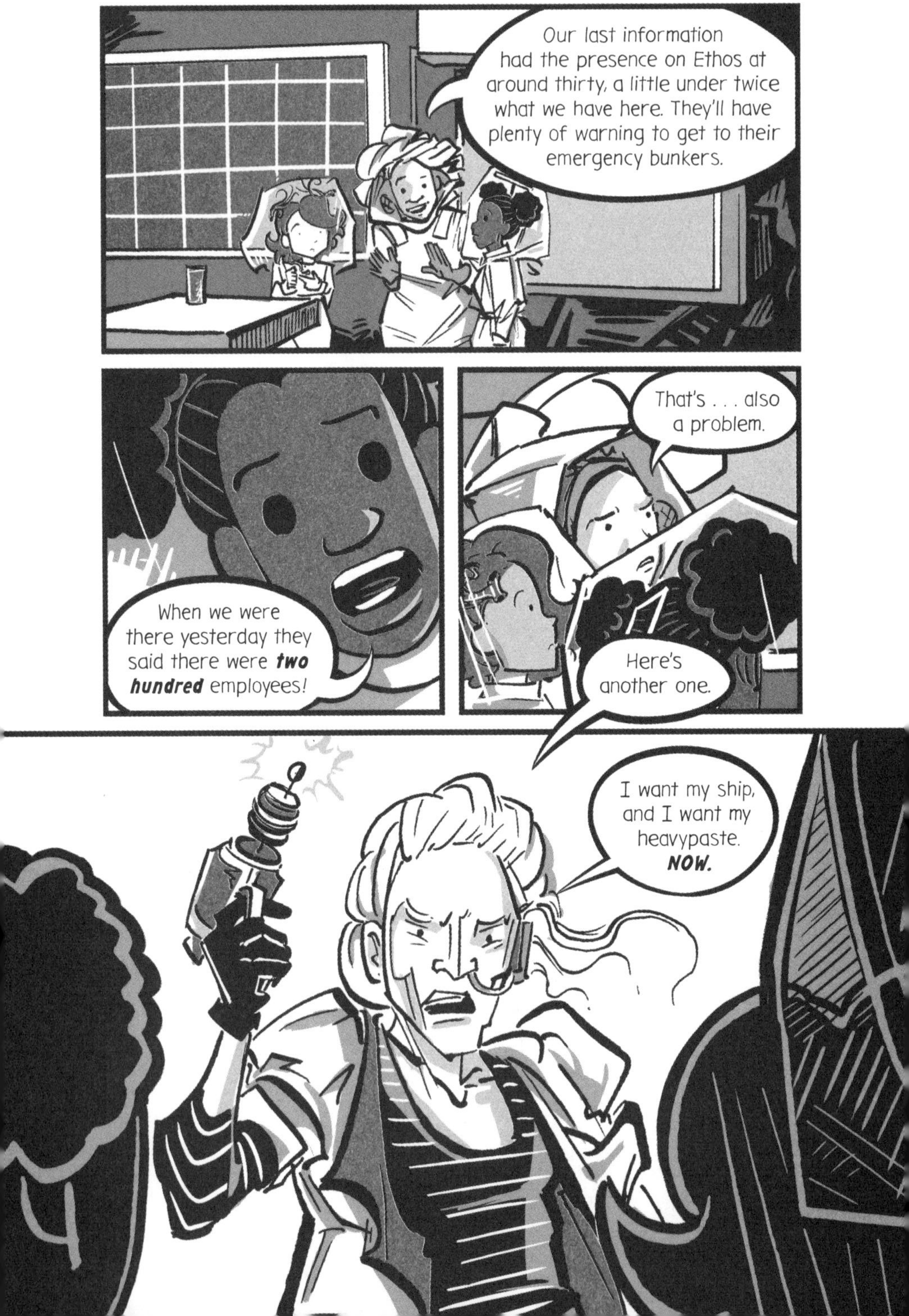
Our last information had the presence on Ethos at around thirty, a little under twice what we have here. They'll have plenty of warning to get to their emergency bunkers.
When we were there yesterday they said there were **two hundred** employees!
That's . . . also a problem.
Here's another one.
I want my ship, and I want my heavypaste. **NOW.**

(THE FOOTHOLD OUTPOST)

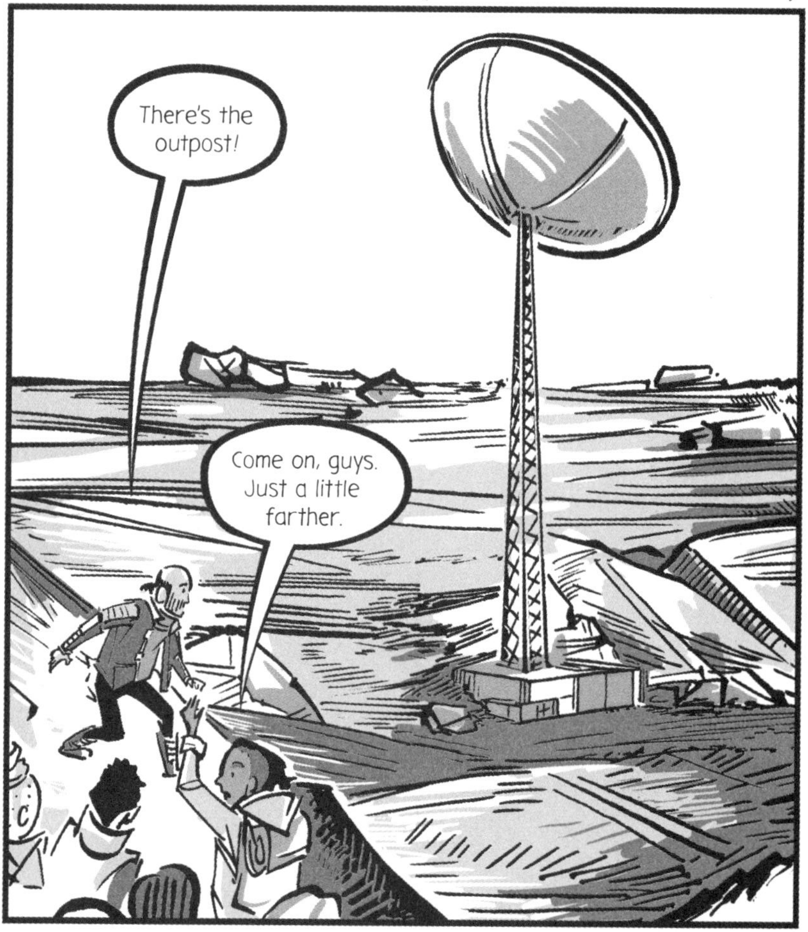
There's the outpost!
Come on, guys. Just a little farther.

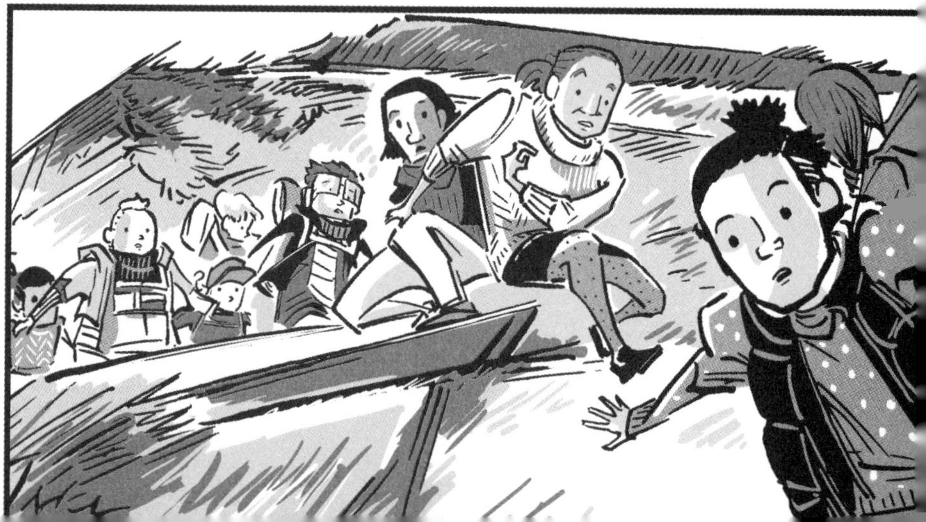

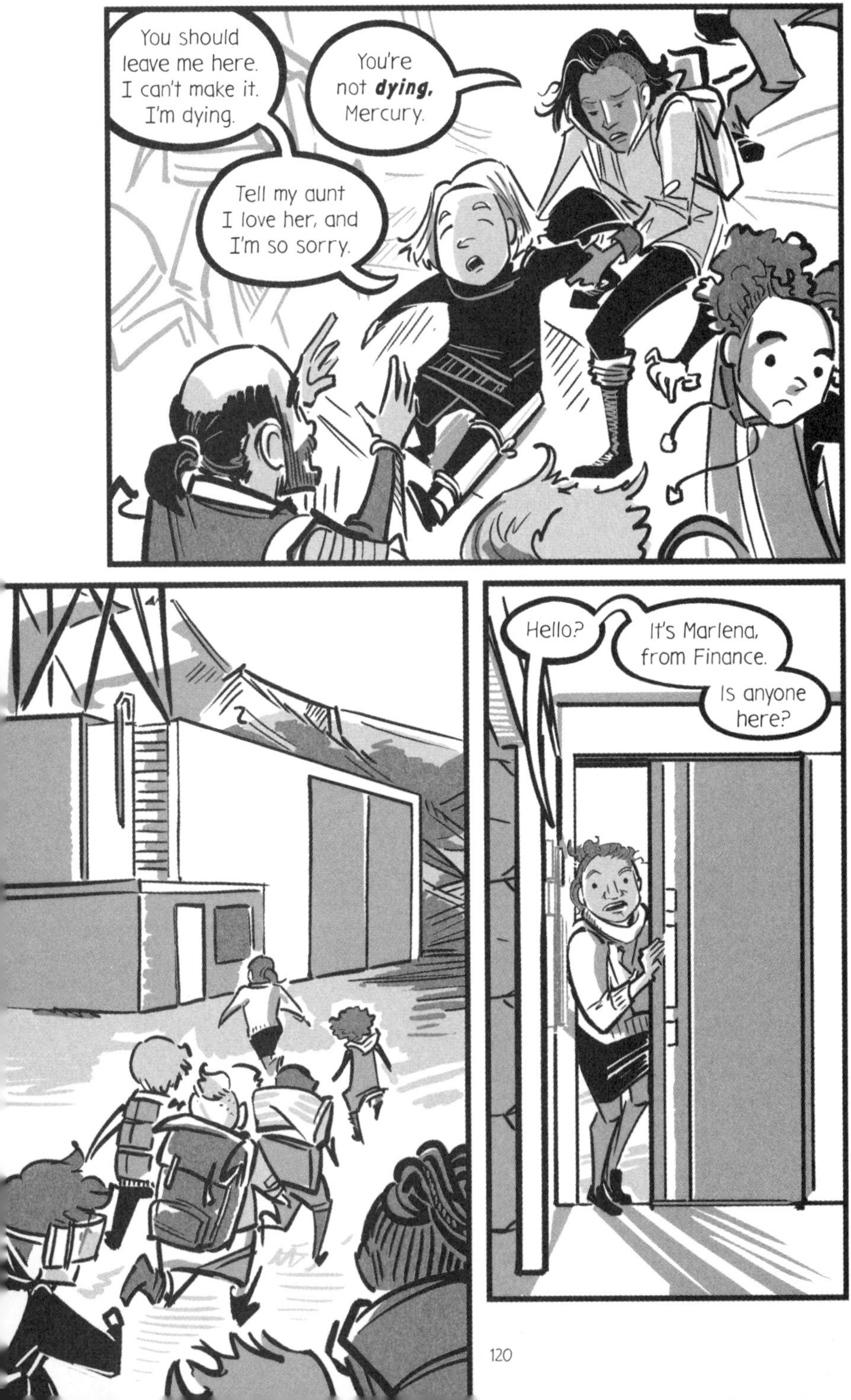
You should leave me here. I can't make it. I'm dying.
You're not **dying,** Mercury.
Tell my aunt I love her, and I'm so sorry.
Hello?
It's Marlena, from Finance.
Is anyone here?

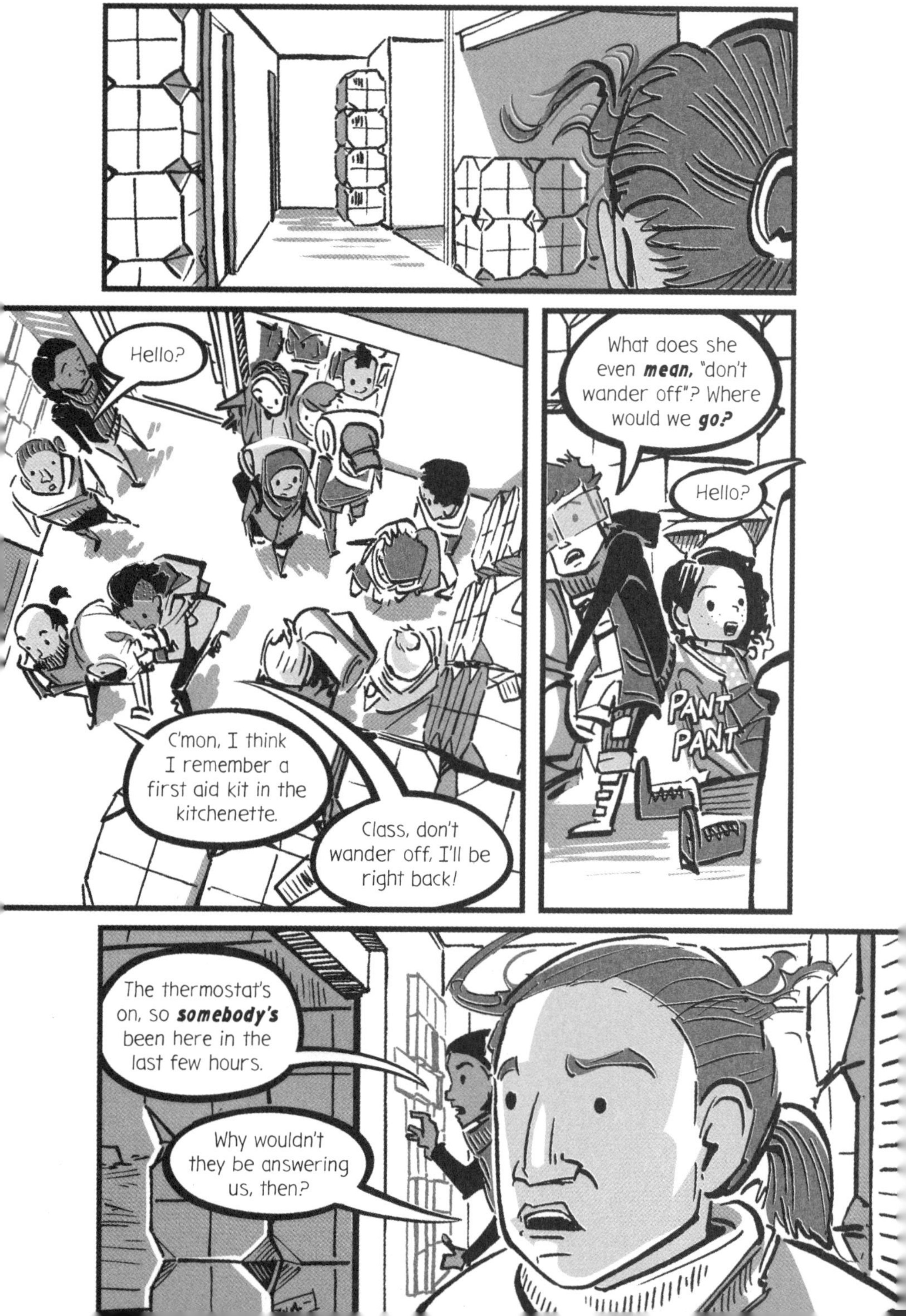
Hello?
C'mon, I think I remember a first aid kit in the kitchenette.
Class, don't wander off, I'll be right back!
What does she even **mean,** "don't wander off"? Where would we **go?**
Hello?
PANT PANT
The thermostat's on, so **somebody's** been here in the last few hours.
Why wouldn't they be answering us, then?

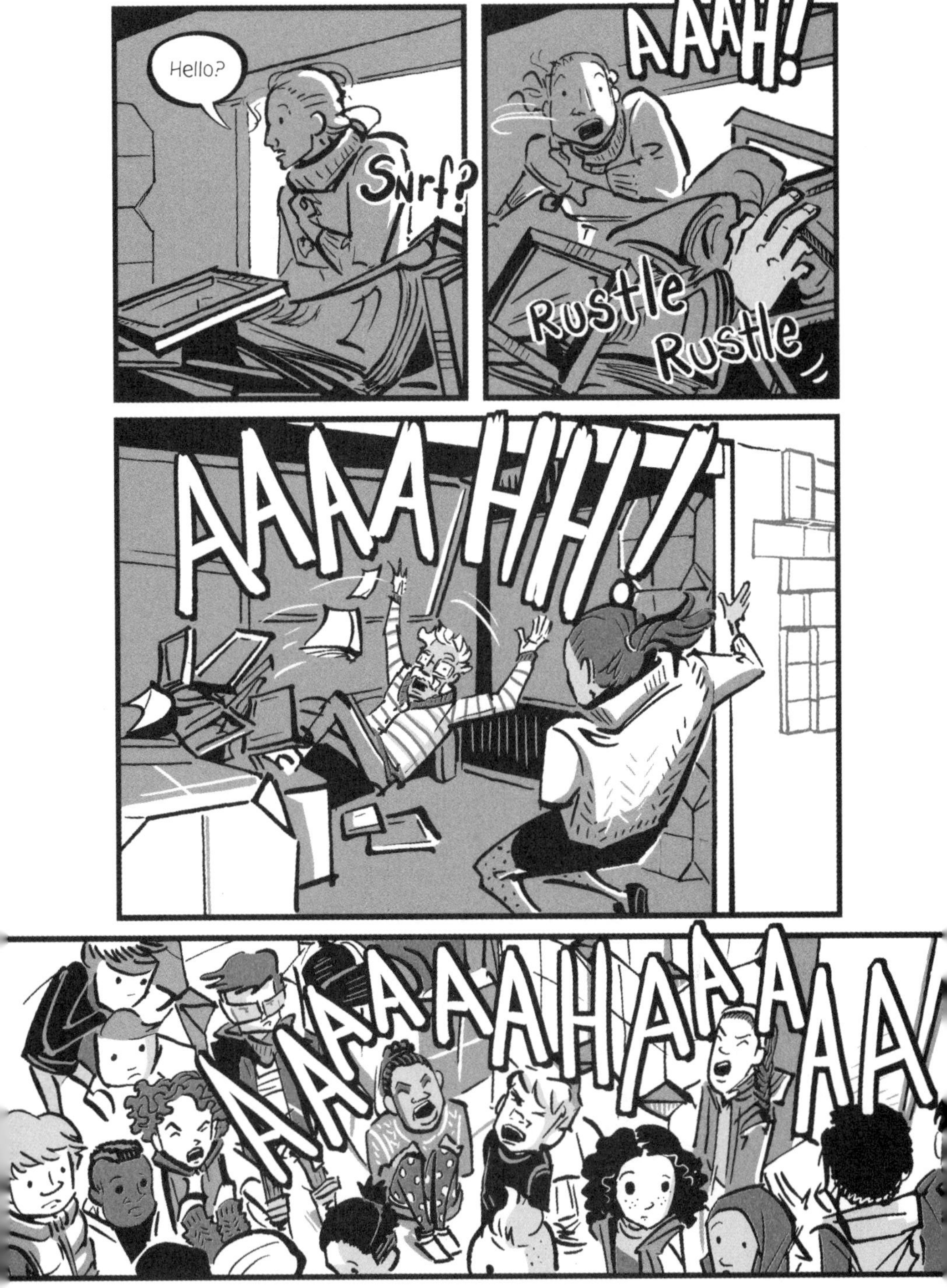
Hello?
Snrf?
AAAH!
Rustle
Rustle
AAAAHH!
AAAAAAHAAAAAA

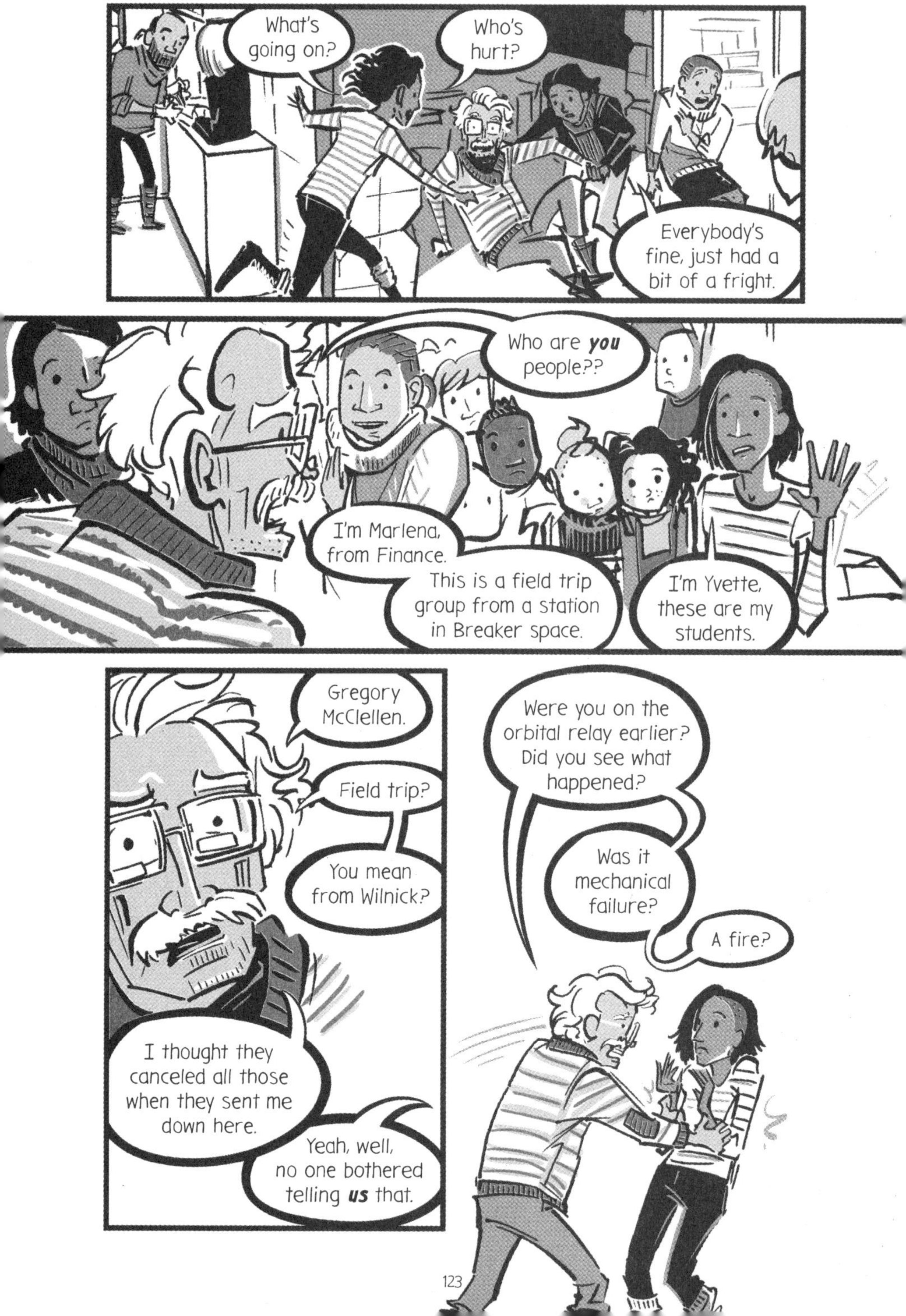
What's going on?
Who's hurt?
Everybody's fine, just had a bit of a fright.
Who are **you** people??
I'm Marlena, from Finance.
This is a field trip group from a station in Breaker space.
I'm Yvette, these are my students.
Gregory McClellen.
Field trip?
You mean from Wilnick?
I thought they canceled all those when they sent me down here.
Yeah, well, no one bothered telling **us** that.
Were you on the orbital relay earlier? Did you see what happened?
Was it mechanical failure?
A fire?

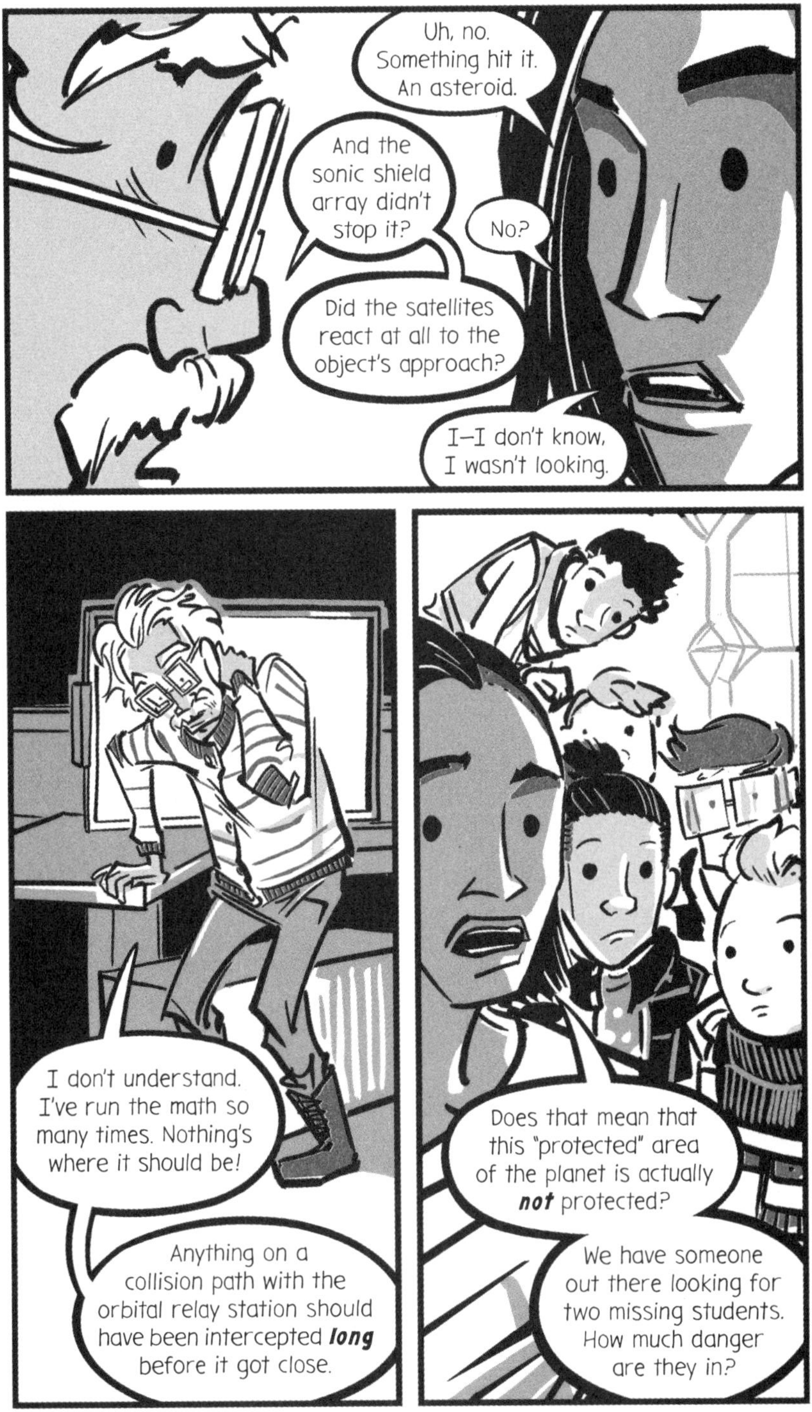

Uh, no. Something hit it. An asteroid.
And the sonic shield array didn't stop it?
No?
Did the satellites react at all to the object's approach?
I—I don't know, I wasn't looking.
I don't understand. I've run the math so many times. Nothing's where it should be!
Anything on a collision path with the orbital relay station should have been intercepted **long** before it got close.
Does that mean that this "protected" area of the planet is actually **not** protected?
We have someone out there looking for two missing students. How much danger are they in?

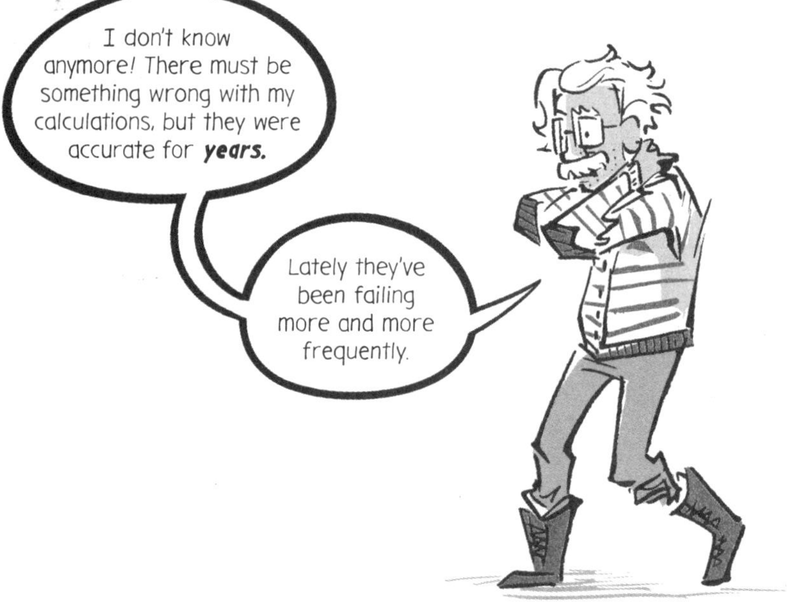
I don't know anymore! There must be something wrong with my calculations, but they were accurate for ***years.***
Lately they've been failing more and more frequently.

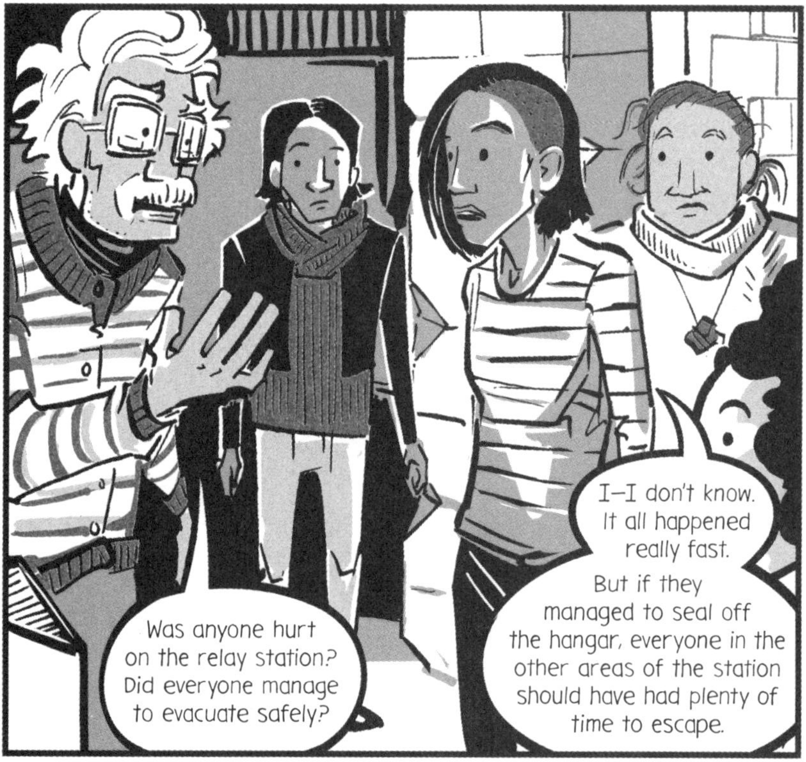
Was anyone hurt on the relay station? Did everyone manage to evacuate safely?
I–I don't know. It all happened really fast.
But if they managed to seal off the hangar, everyone in the other areas of the station should have had plenty of time to escape.

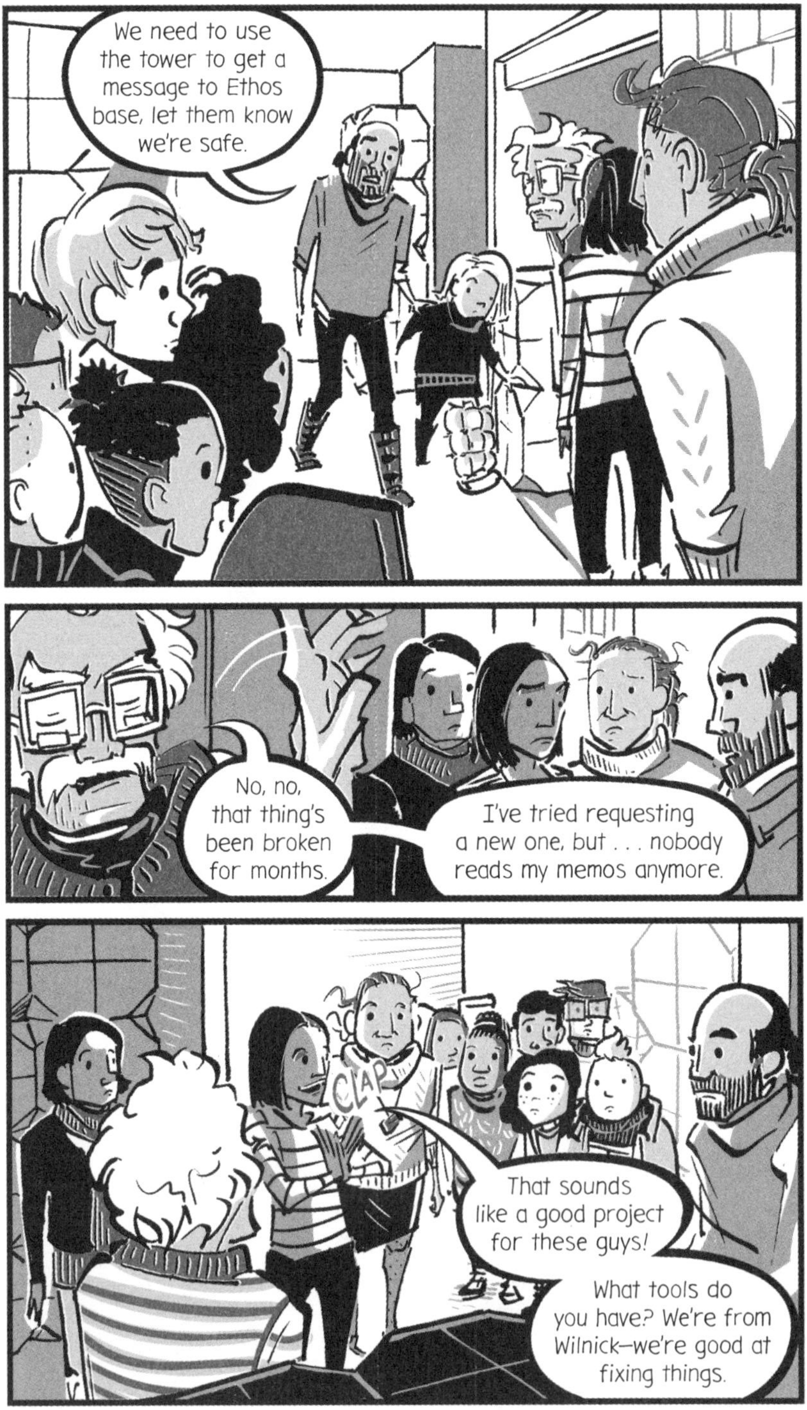
We need to use the tower to get a message to Ethos base, let them know we're safe.
No, no, that thing's been broken for months.
I've tried requesting a new one, but . . . nobody reads my memos anymore.
CLAP
That sounds like a good project for these guys!
What tools do you have? We're from Wilnick—we're good at fixing things.

(MEANWHILE)

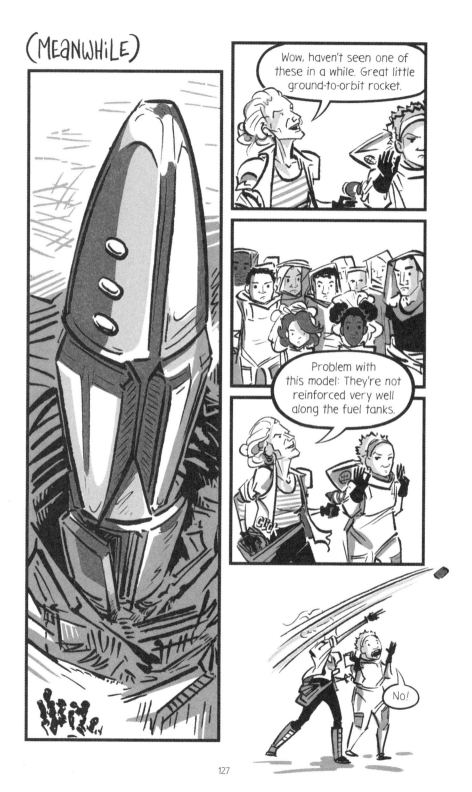

Wow, haven't seen one of these in a while. Great little ground-to-orbit rocket.

Problem with this model: They're not reinforced very well along the fuel tanks.

No!

127

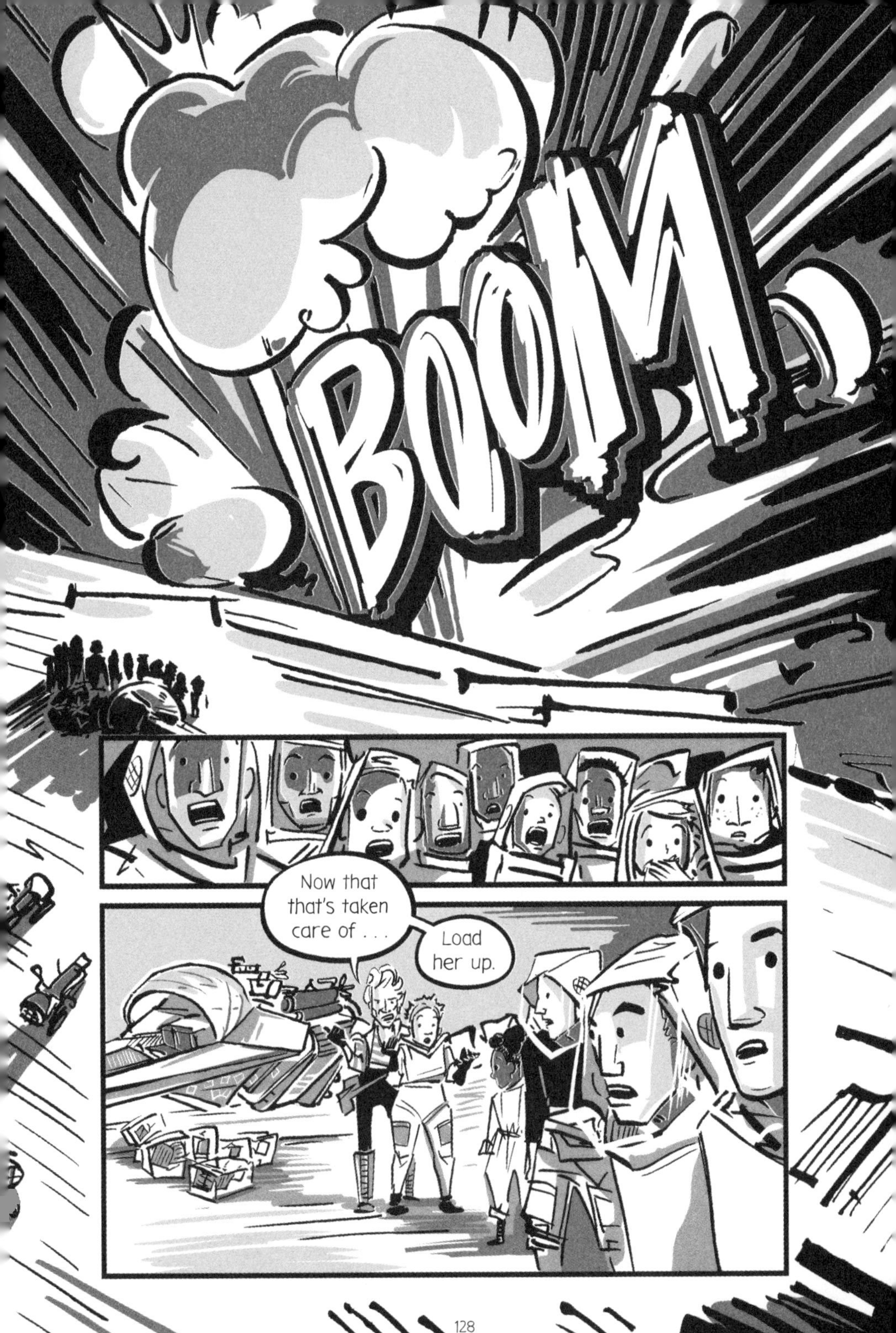
BOOM
Now that that's taken care of . . .
Load her up.

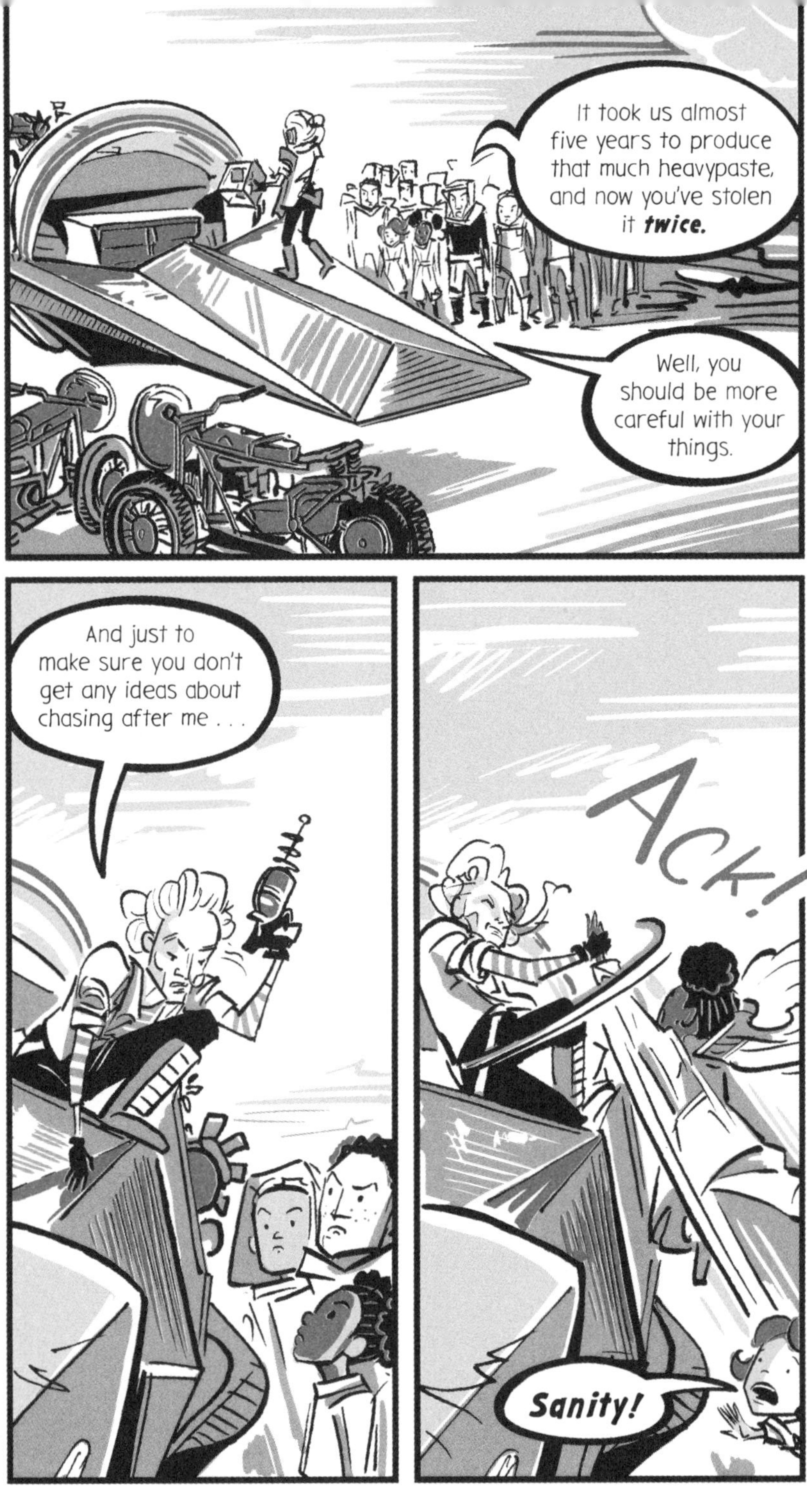
It took us almost five years to produce that much heavypaste, and now you've stolen it ***twice.***
Well, you should be more careful with your things.
And just to make sure you don't get any ideas about chasing after me . . .
ACK!
***Sanity!***

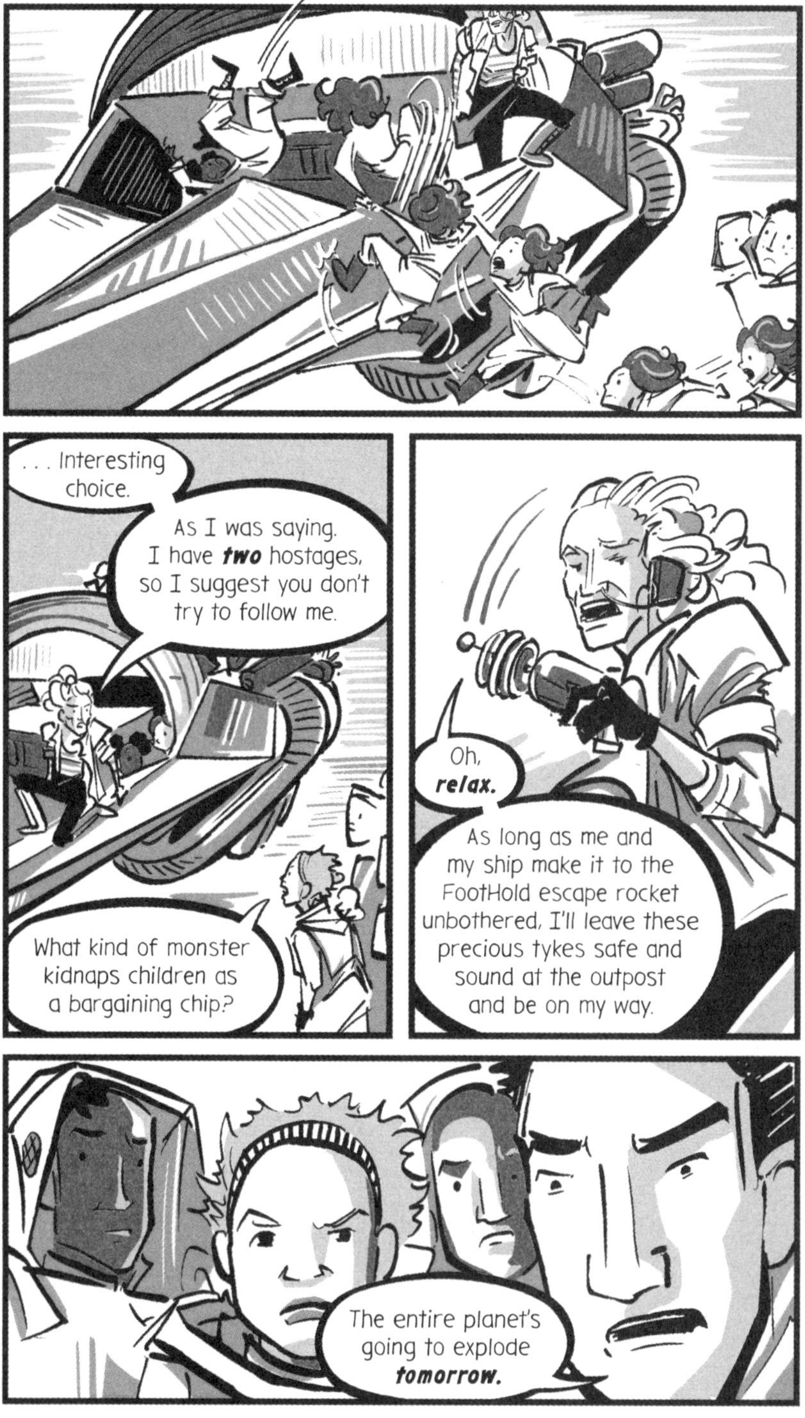
. . . Interesting choice.
As I was saying. I have **two** hostages, so I suggest you don't try to follow me.
What kind of monster kidnaps children as a bargaining chip?
Oh, **relax.**
As long as me and my ship make it to the FootHold escape rocket unbothered, I'll leave these precious tykes safe and sound at the outpost and be on my way.
The entire planet's going to explode **tomorrow.**

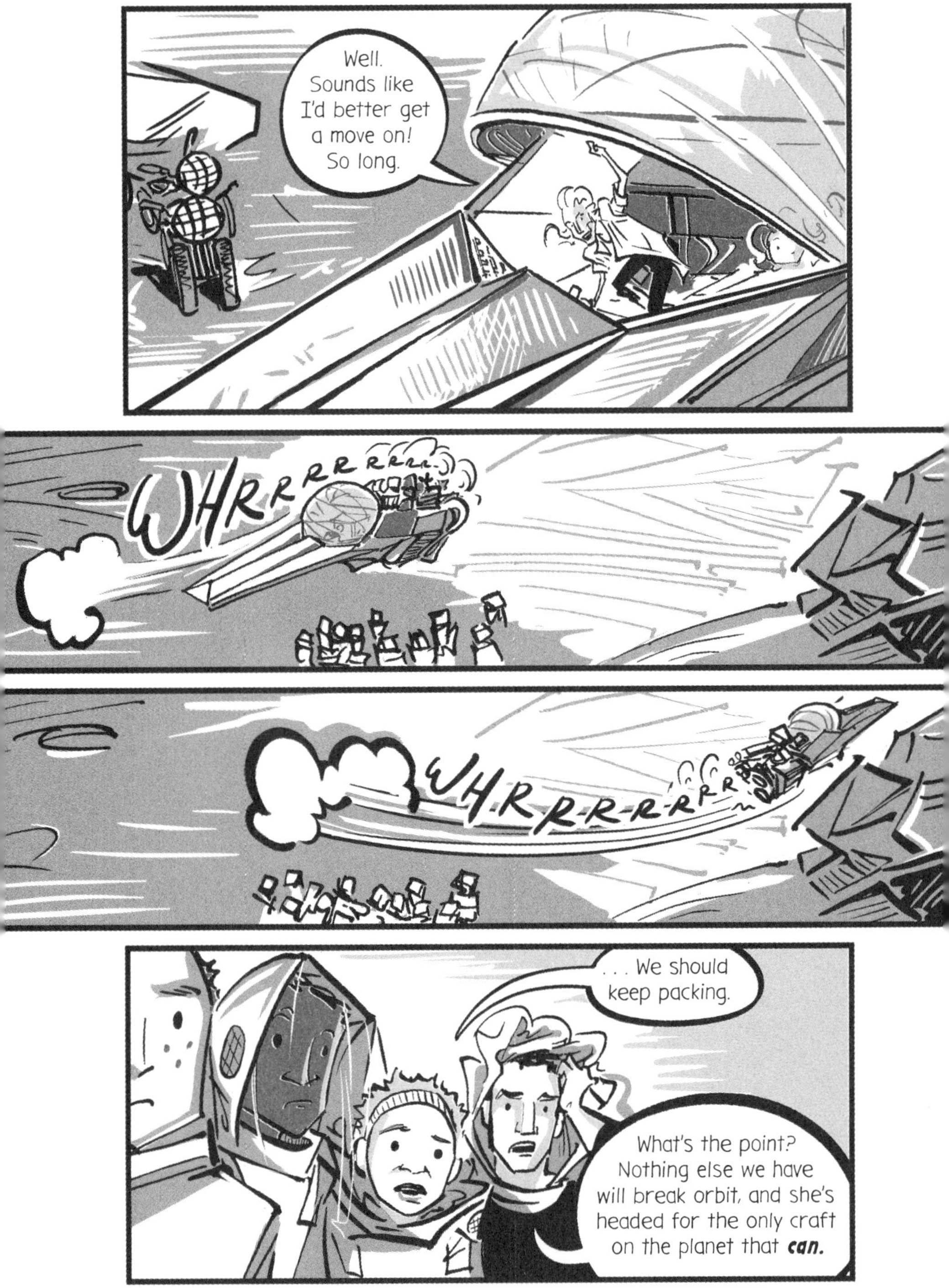
Well. Sounds like I'd better get a move on! So long.
WHRRRRRRRRR
WHRRRRRRRRRRR
. . . We should keep packing.
What's the point? Nothing else we have will break orbit, and she's headed for the only craft on the planet that **can.**

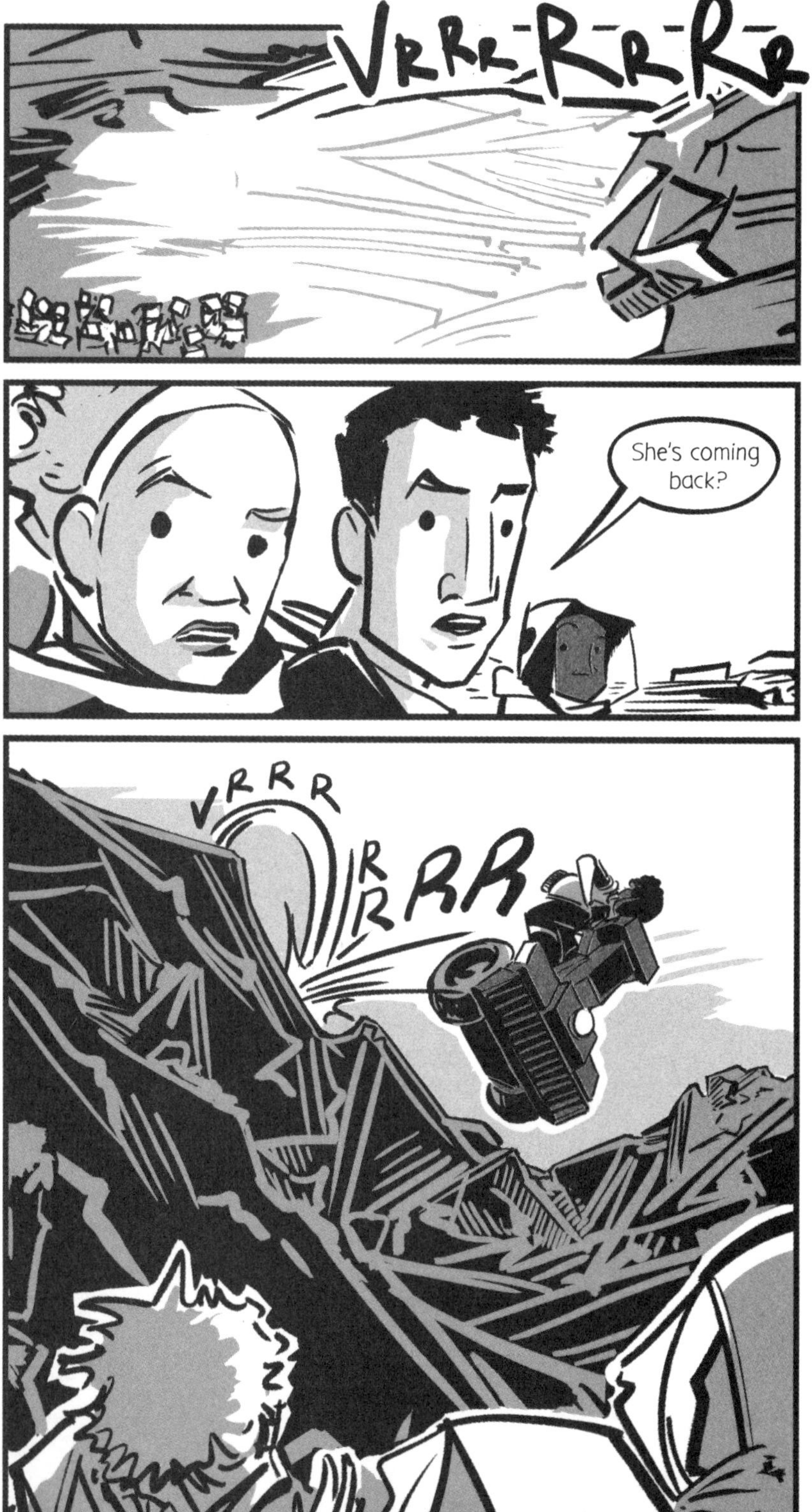
VRRRRRRRRR
She's coming back?
VRRR
RRRR

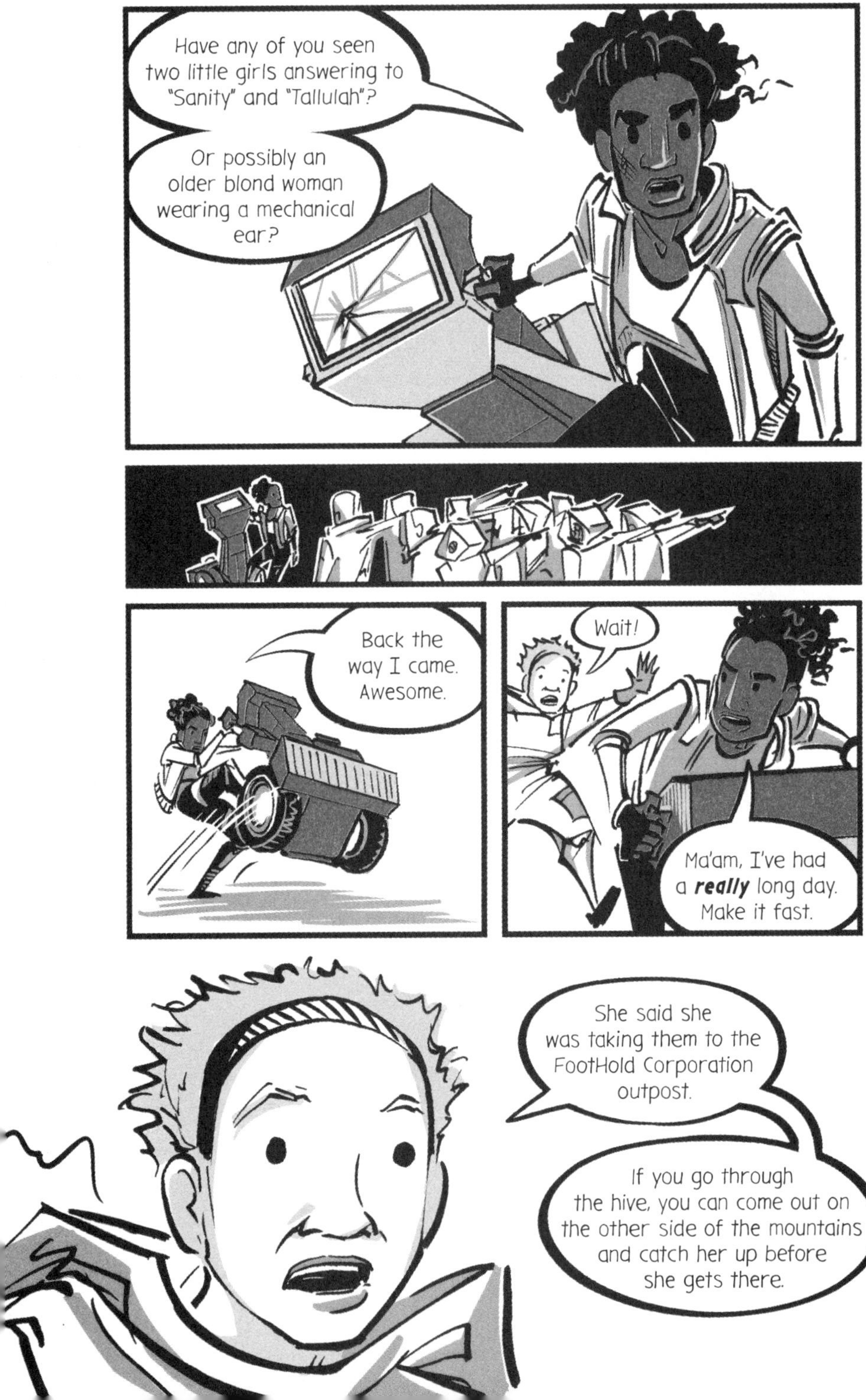
Have any of you seen two little girls answering to "Sanity" and "Tallulah"?
Or possibly an older blond woman wearing a mechanical ear?
Back the way I came. Awesome.
Wait!
Ma'am, I've had a ***really*** long day. Make it fast.
She said she was taking them to the FootHold Corporation outpost.
If you go through the hive, you can come out on the other side of the mountains and catch her up before she gets there.

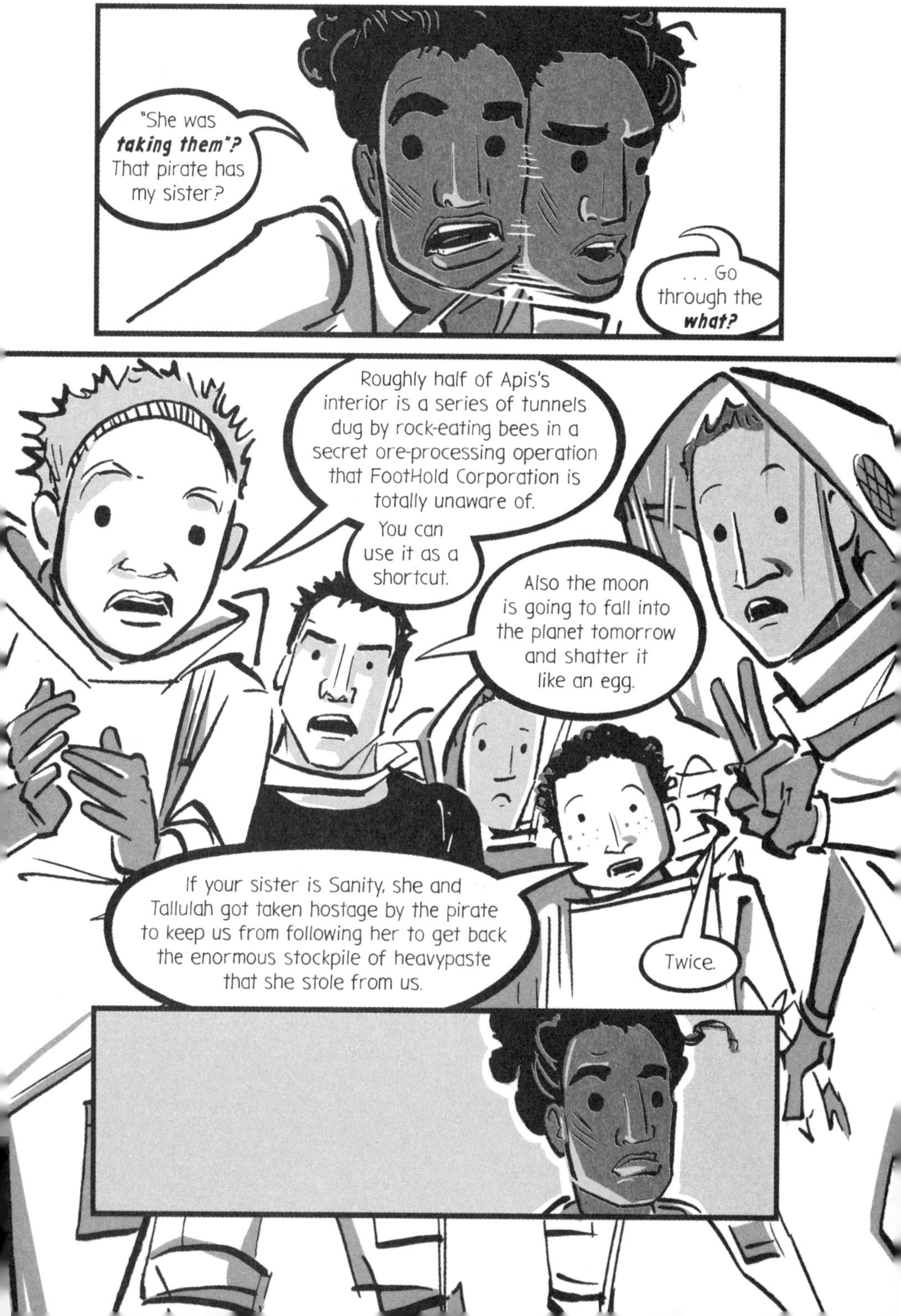
"She was ***taking them*"?** That pirate has my sister?
. . . Go through the ***what?***
Roughly half of Apis's interior is a series of tunnels dug by rock-eating bees in a secret ore-processing operation that FootHold Corporation is totally unaware of.
You can use it as a shortcut.
Also the moon is going to fall into the planet tomorrow and shatter it like an egg.
If your sister is Sanity, she and Tallulah got taken hostage by the pirate to keep us from following her to get back the enormous stockpile of heavypaste that she stole from us.
Twice.

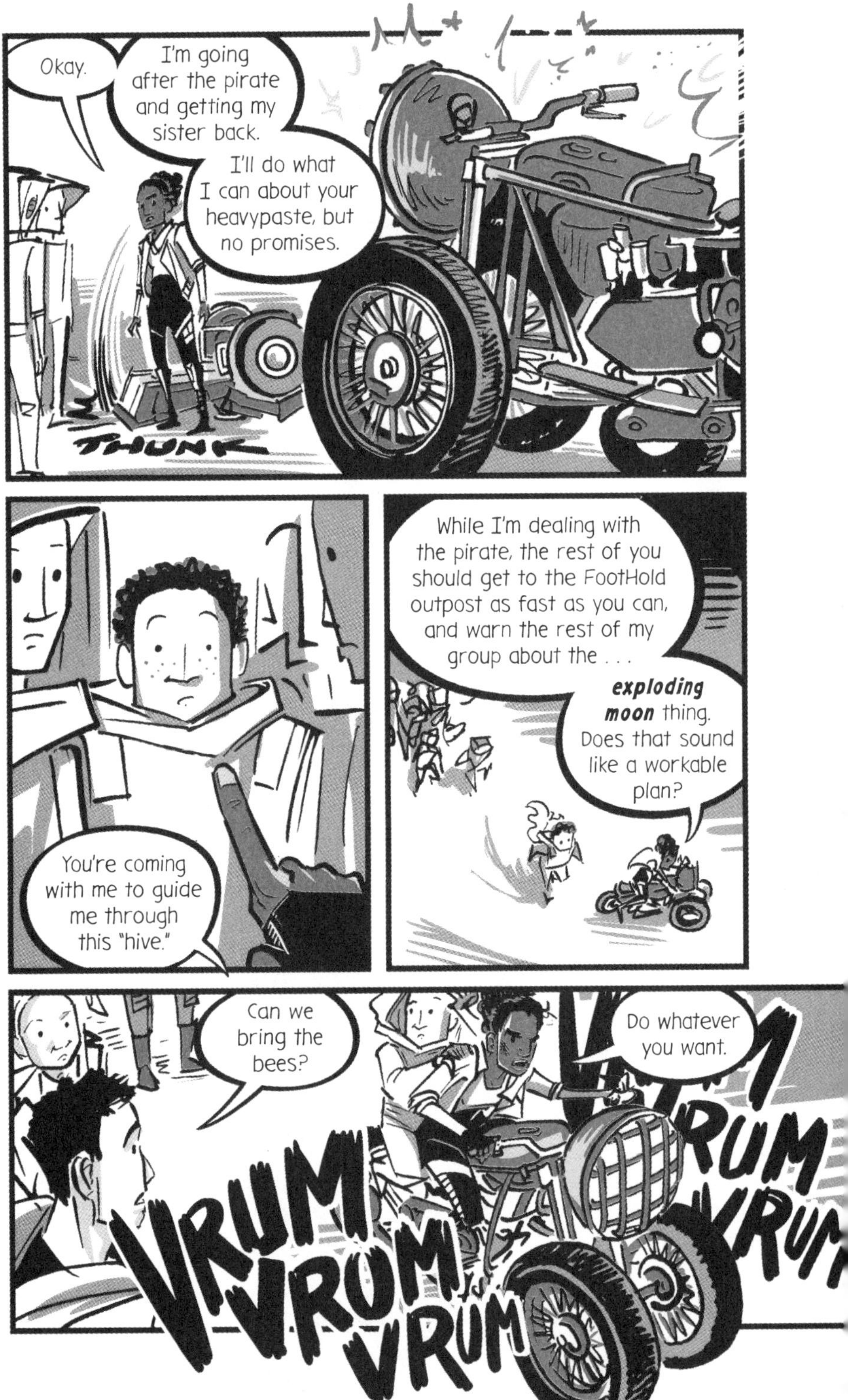
Okay.
I'm going after the pirate and getting my sister back.
I'll do what I can about your heavypaste, but no promises.
THUNK
You're coming with me to guide me through this "hive."
While I'm dealing with the pirate, the rest of you should get to the FootHold outpost as fast as you can, and warn the rest of my group about the . . .
exploding moon thing. Does that sound like a workable plan?
Can we bring the bees?
Do whatever you want.
VRUM VRUM VRUM
VRUM VRUM

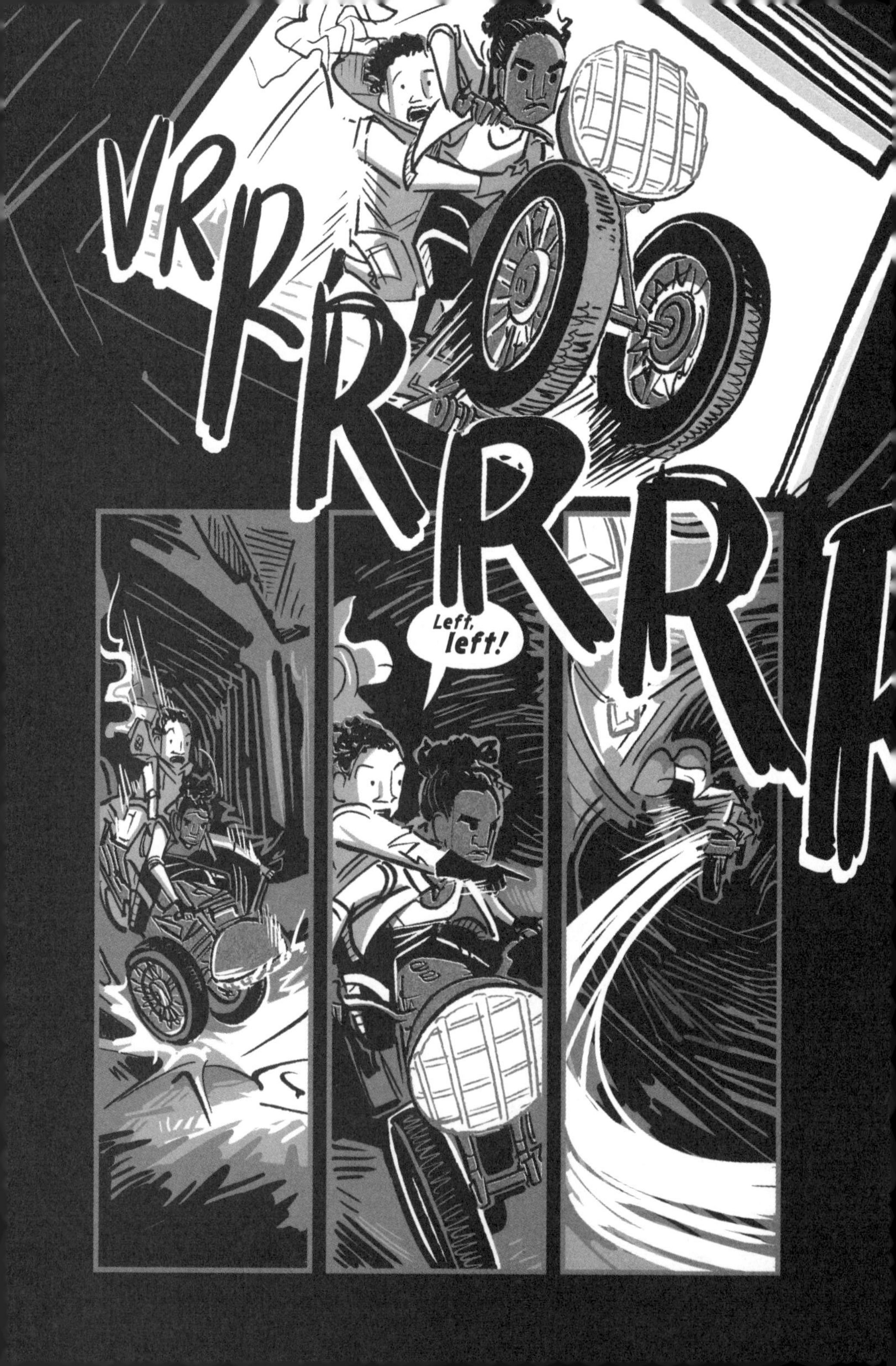
VRRRROOOOM
Left, left!

(HALFWAY TO THE OUTPOST)

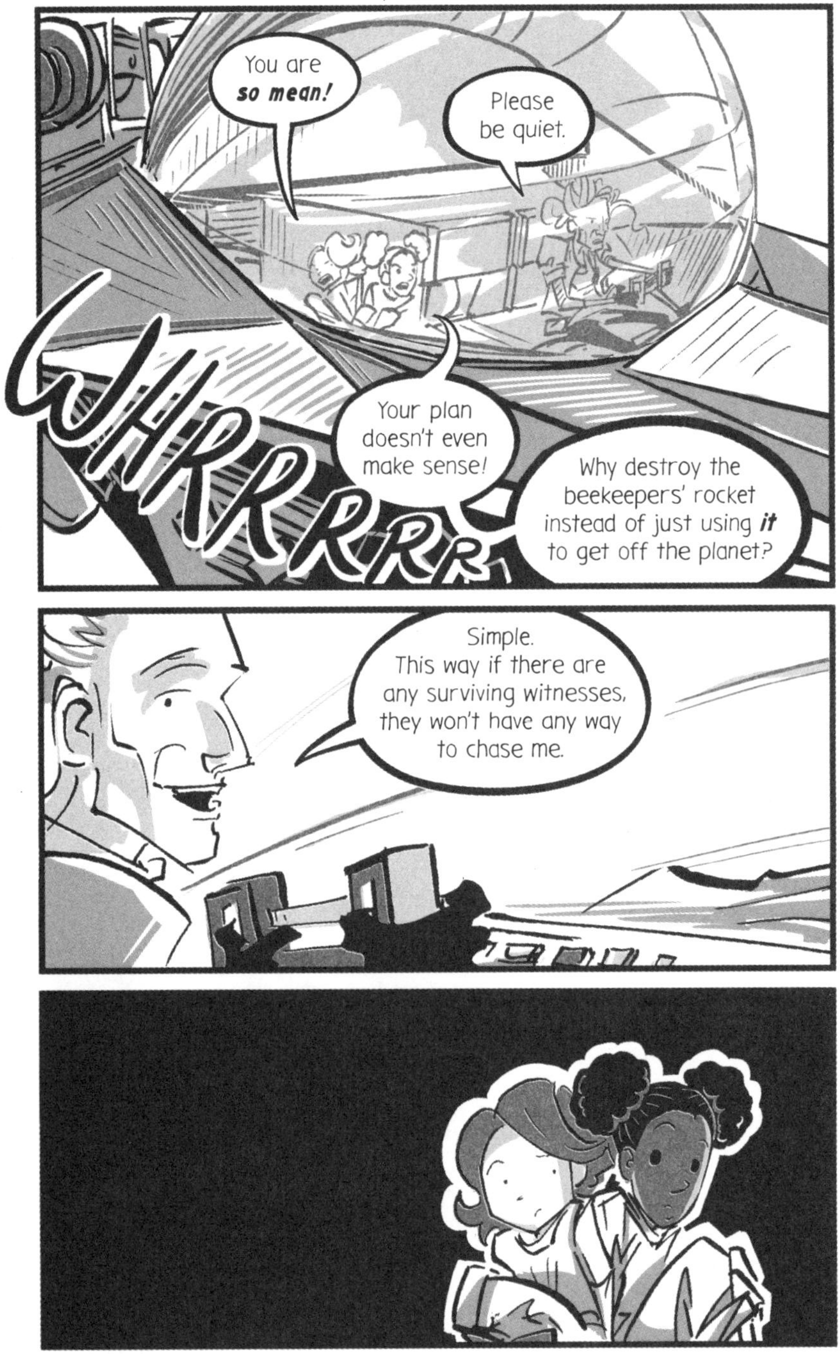
You are *so mean!*
Please be quiet.
WHRRRRR
Your plan doesn't even make sense!
Why destroy the beekeepers' rocket instead of just using *it* to get off the planet?
Simple. This way if there are any surviving witnesses, they won't have any way to chase me.

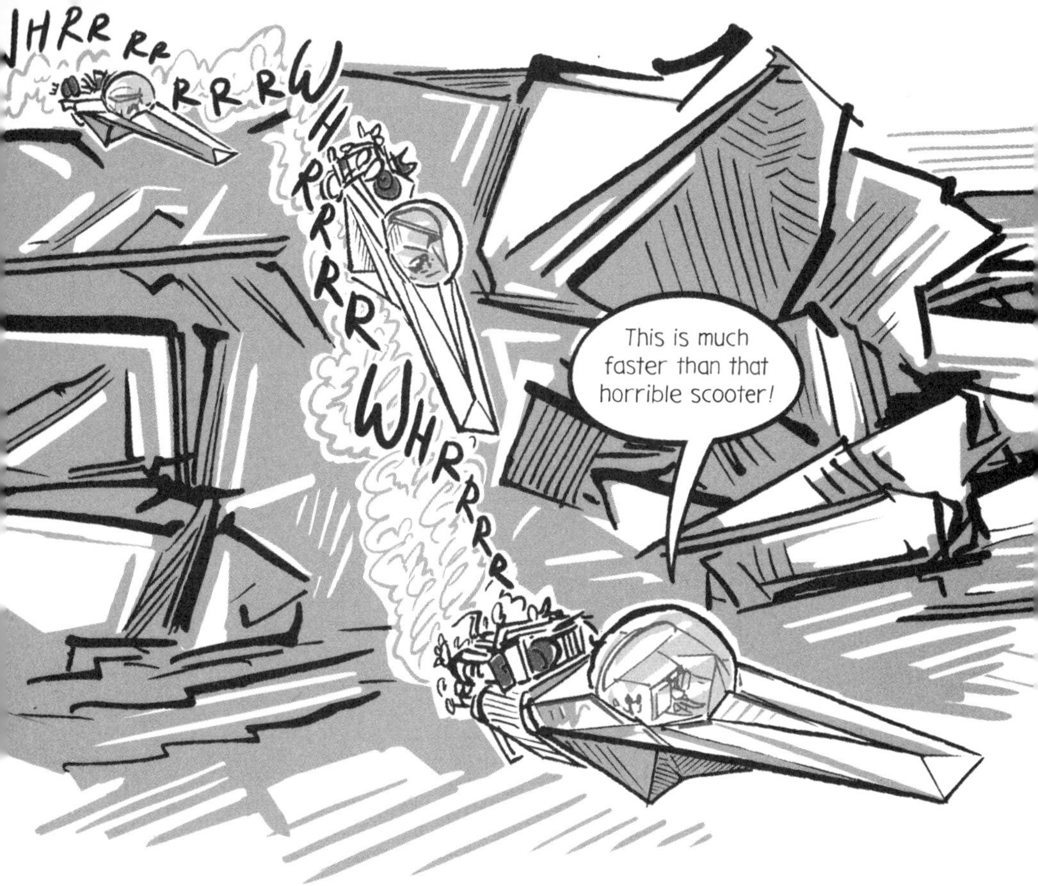
HRR RR RRRW
HRRRRRR
WHRRRRR
This is much faster than that horrible scooter!

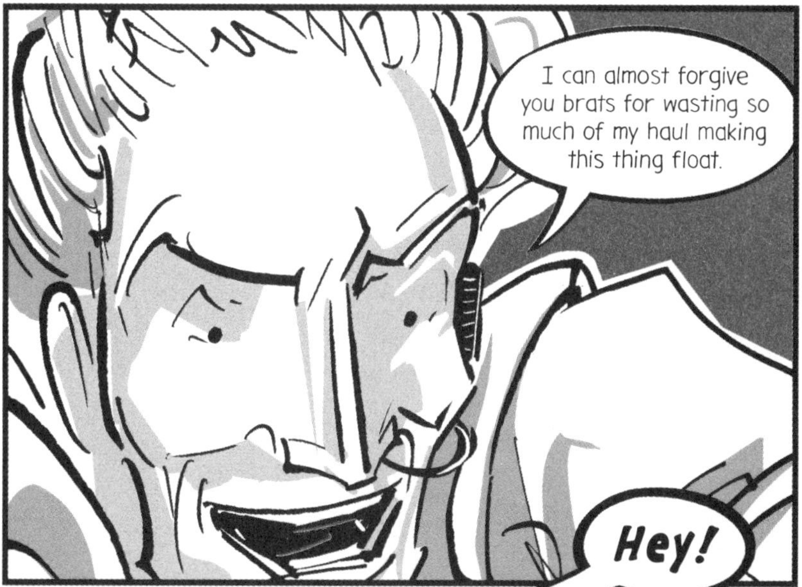
I can almost forgive you brats for wasting so much of my haul making this thing float.
Hey!

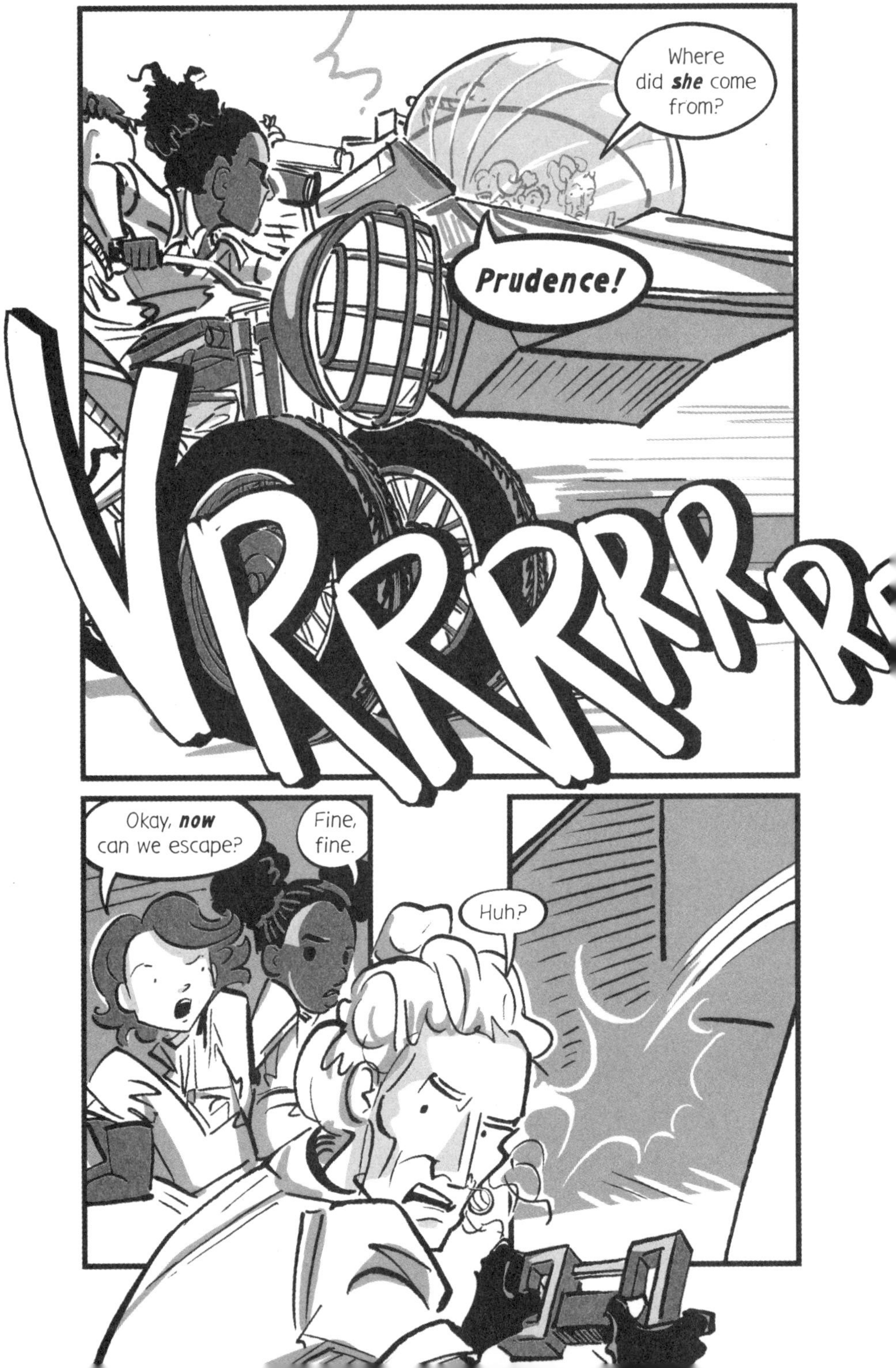
Where did *she* come from?
*Prudence!*
VRRRRRR
Okay, *now* can we escape?
Fine, fine.
Huh?

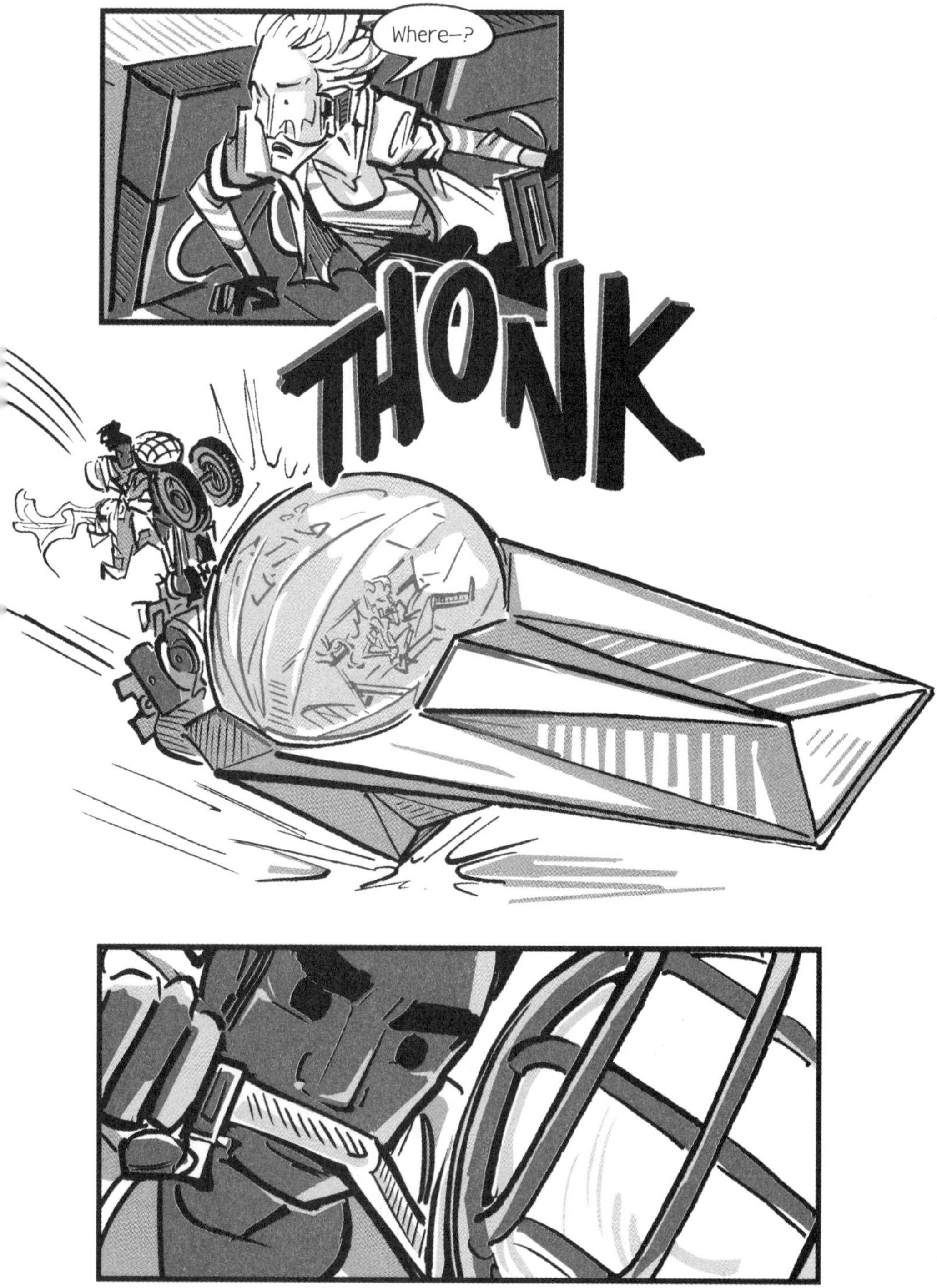
Where–?
THONK

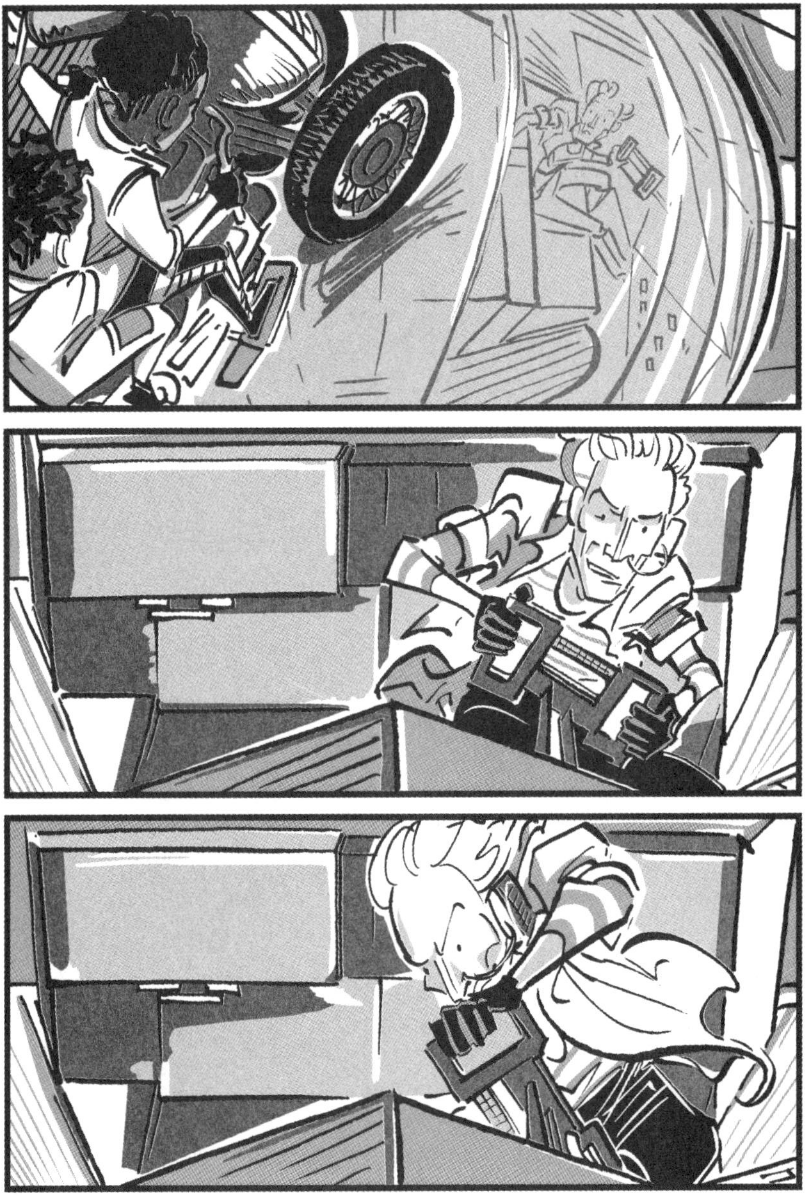

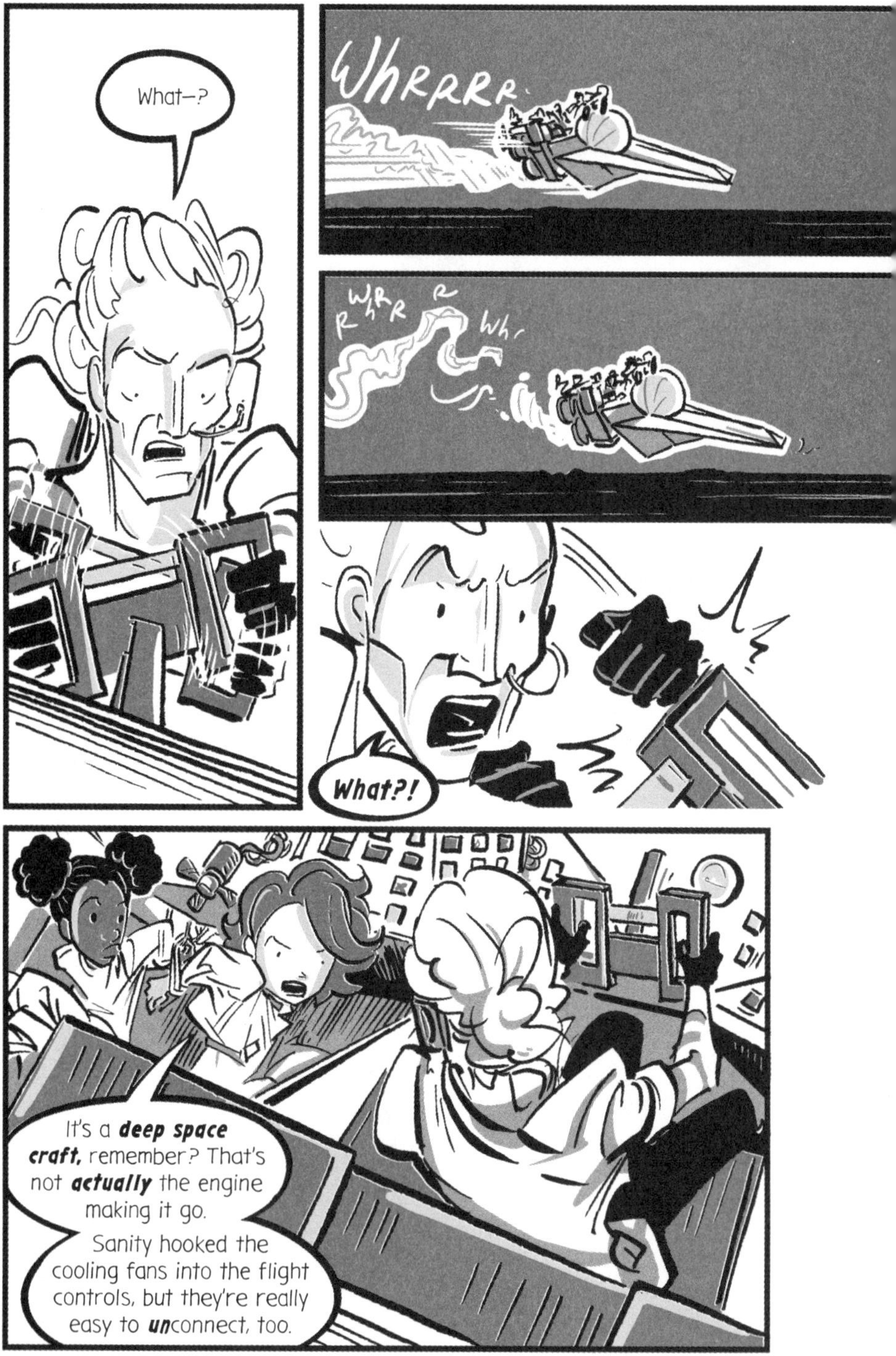
What—?
Whrrrrr
Whrrr r
Whr
What?!
It's a **deep space craft,** remember? That's not **actually** the engine making it go.
Sanity hooked the cooling fans into the flight controls, but they're really easy to **un**connect, too.

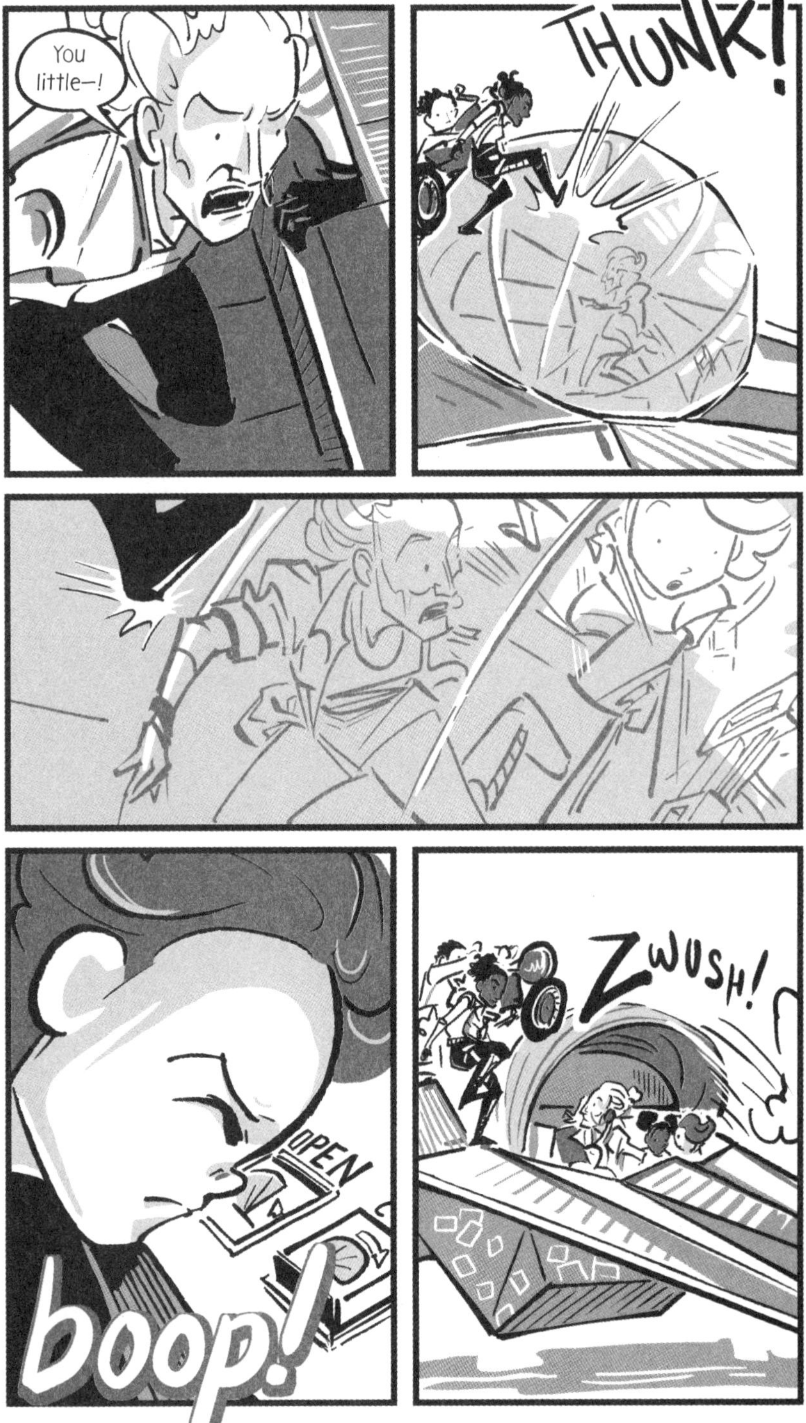
You little–!
THUNK!
OPEN
boop!
ZWUSH!

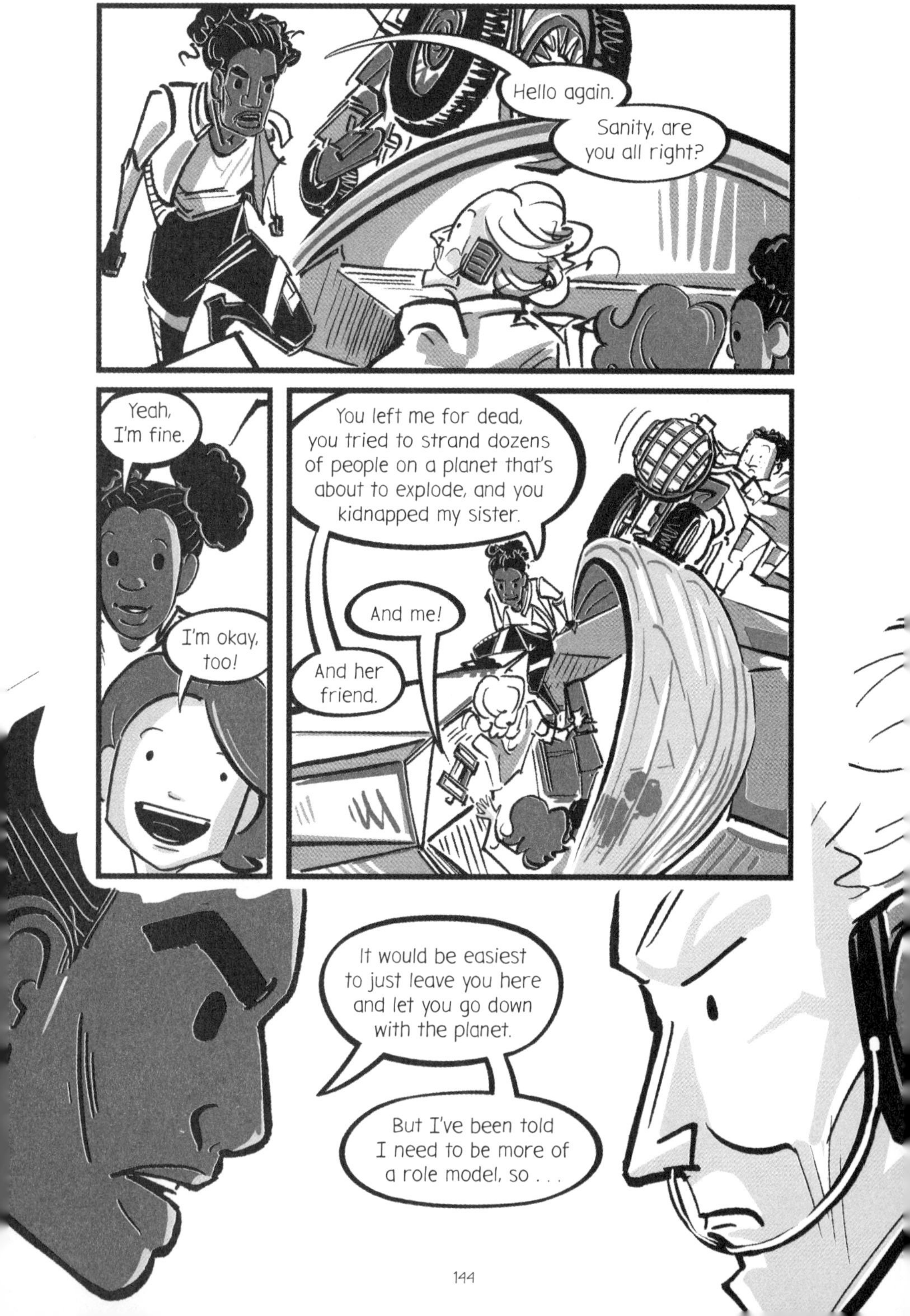
Hello again.
Sanity, are you all right?
Yeah, I'm fine.
I'm okay, too!
You left me for dead, you tried to strand dozens of people on a planet that's about to explode, and you kidnapped my sister.
And her friend.
And me!
It would be easiest to just leave you here and let you go down with the planet.
But I've been told I need to be more of a role model, so . . .

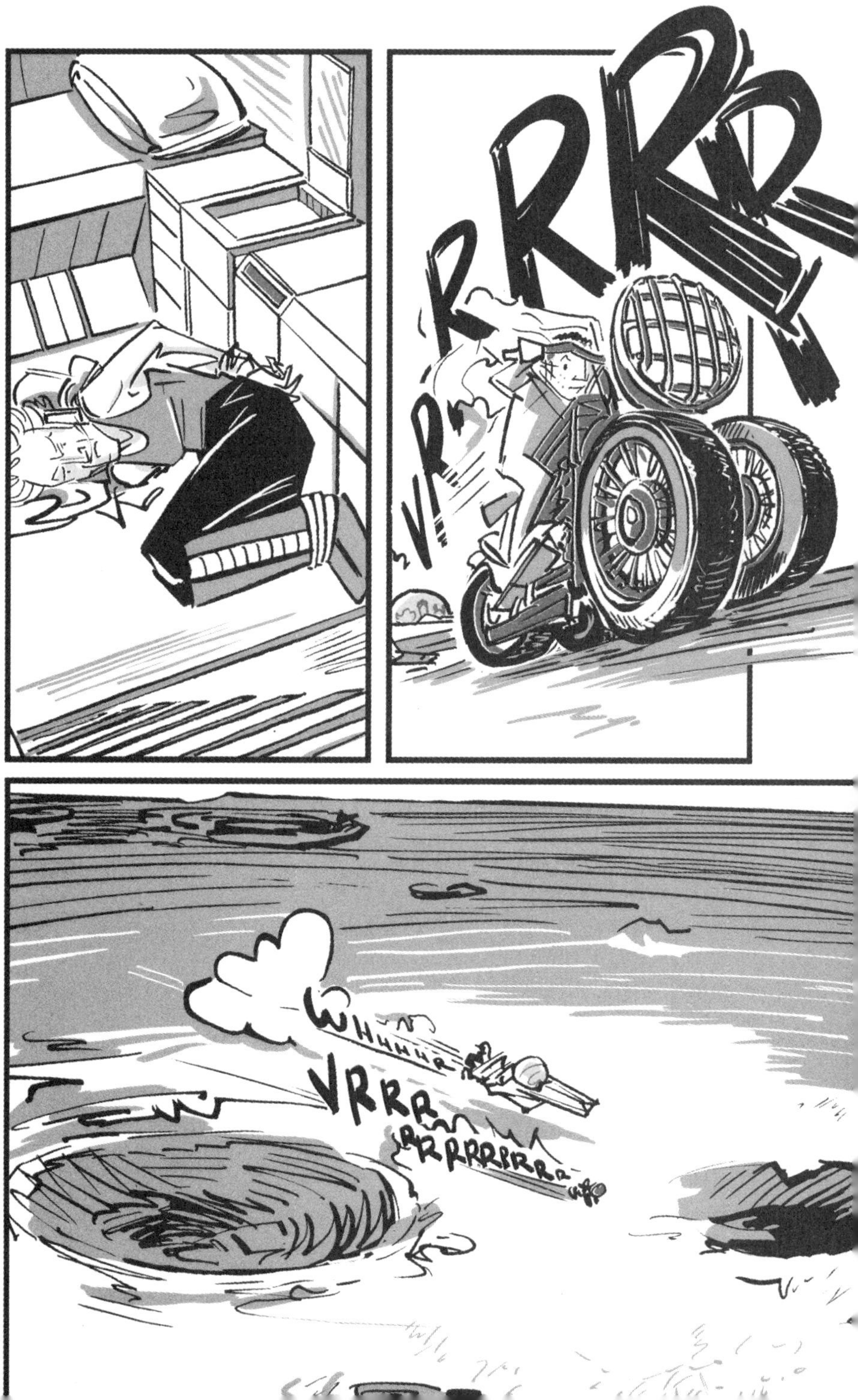
VRRRRRR
WHHHHHR
VRRR
RRRRRRRRRR

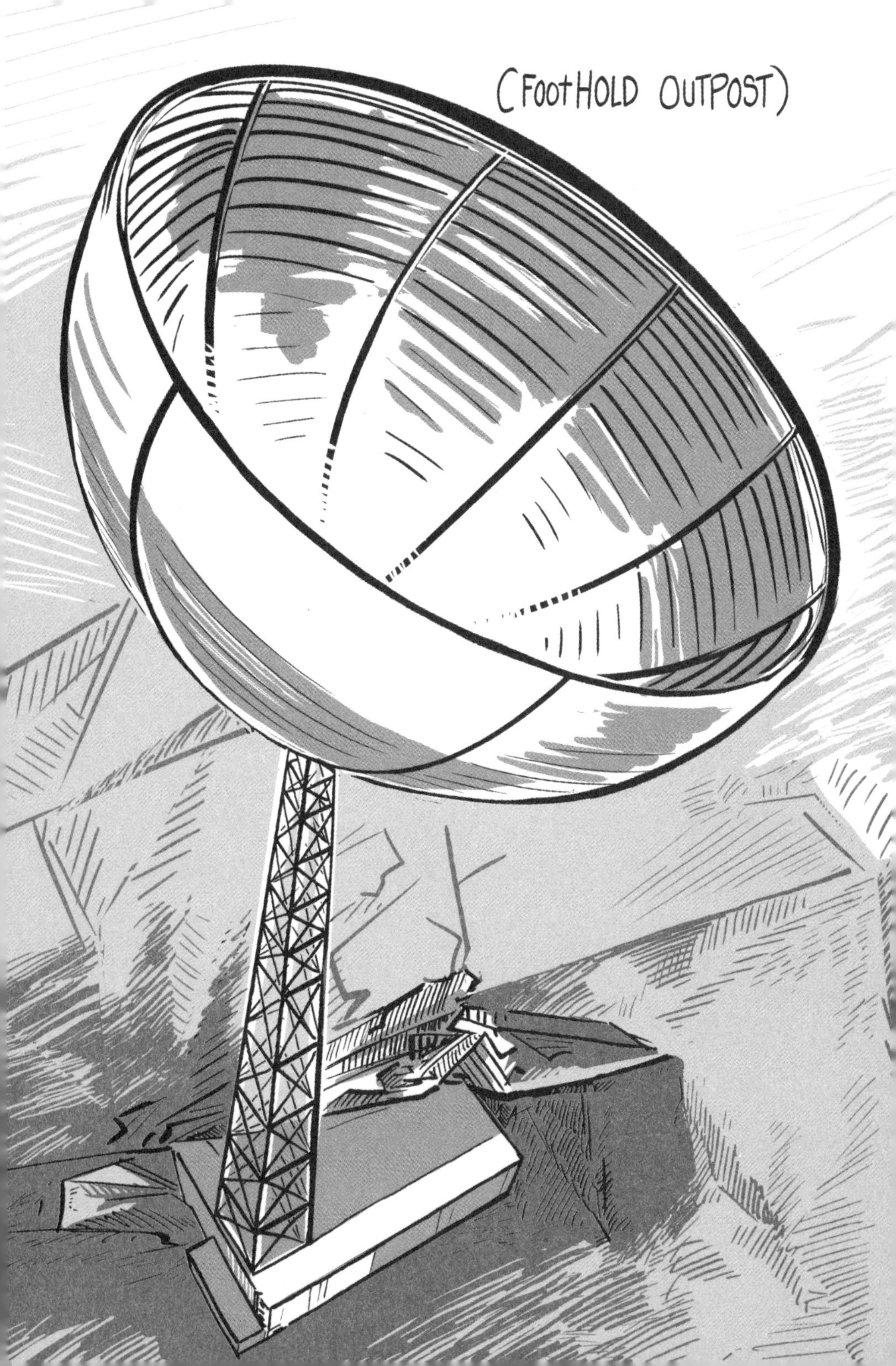
(FOOTHOLD OUTPOST)

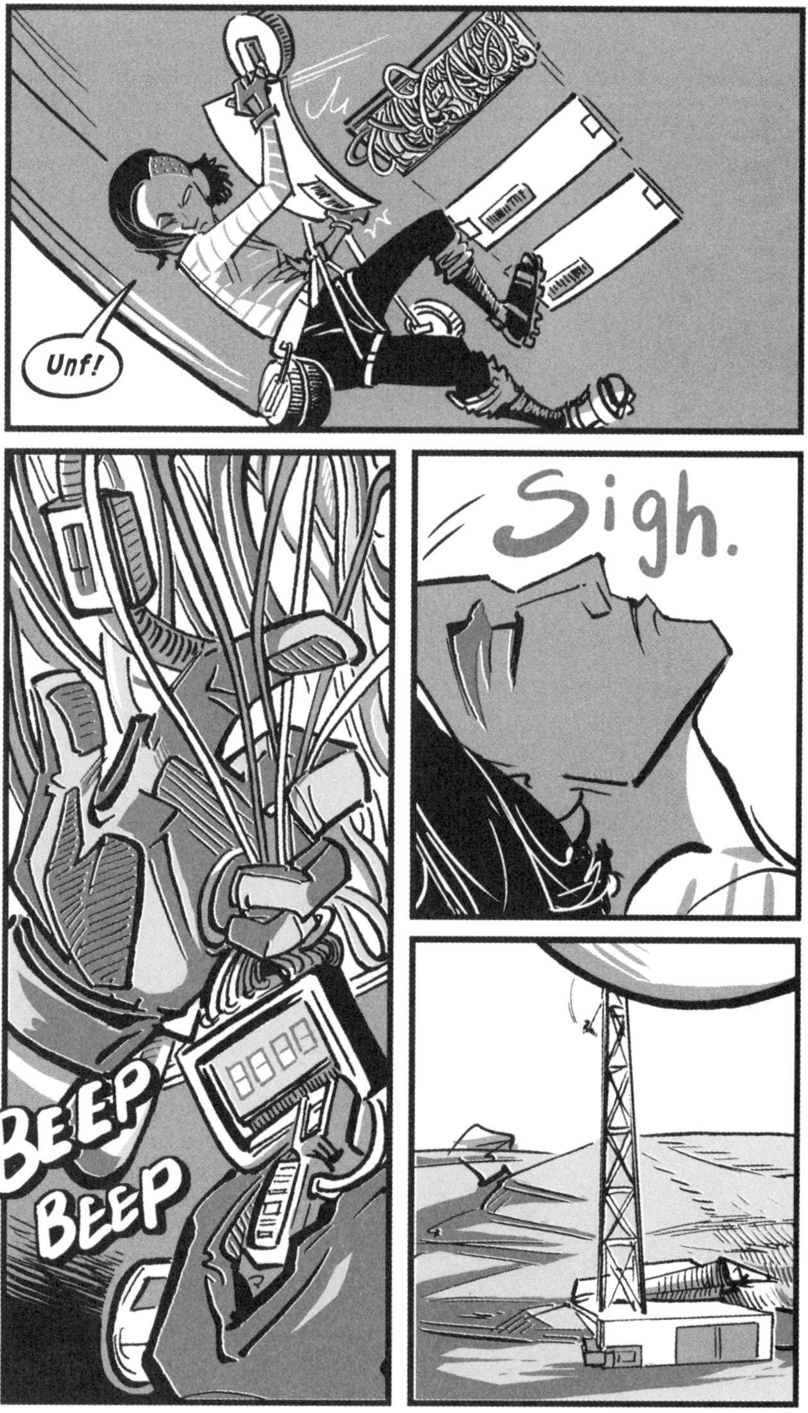
Unf!
Sigh.
BEEP
BEEP

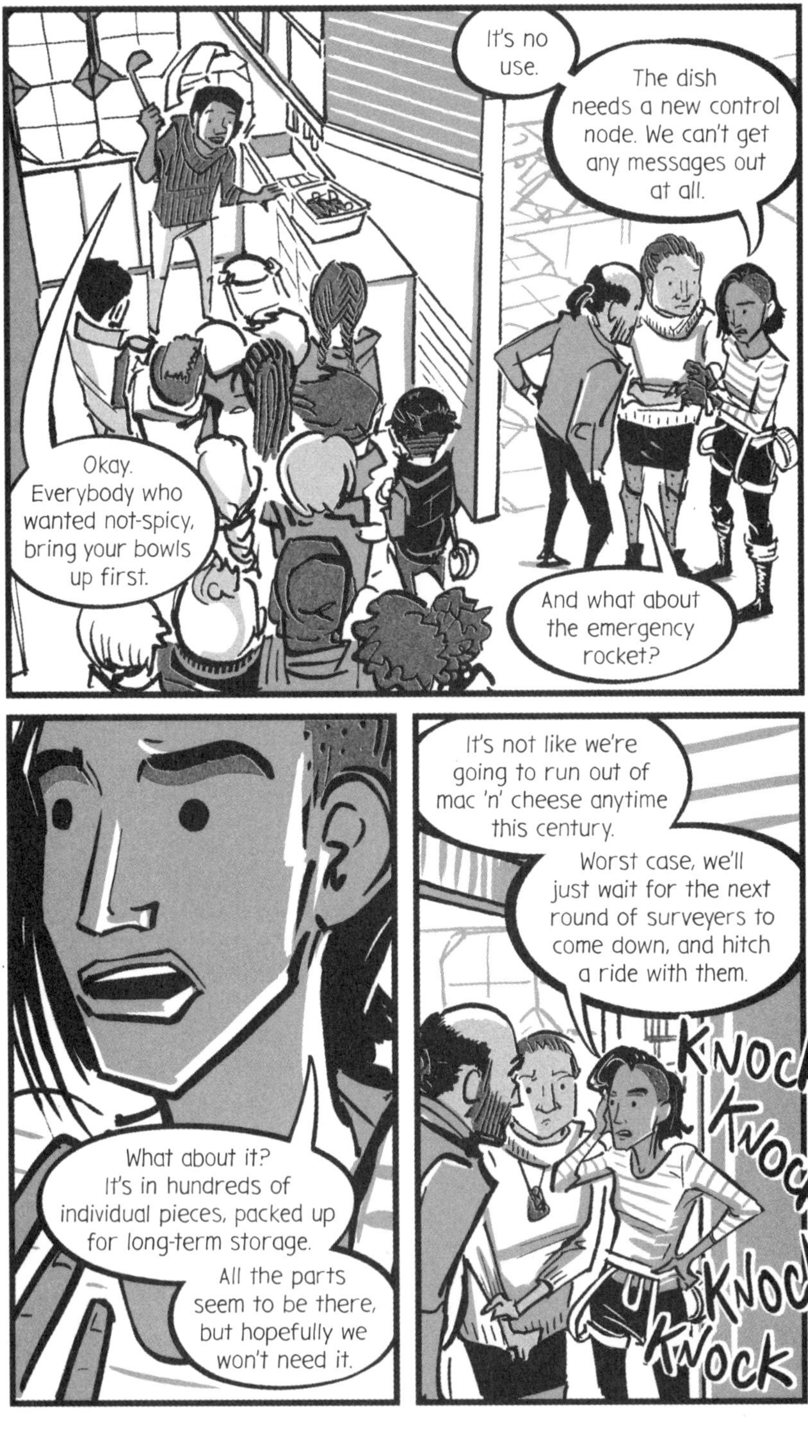
It's no use.
The dish needs a new control node. We can't get any messages out at all.
Okay. Everybody who wanted not-spicy, bring your bowls up first.
And what about the emergency rocket?
What about it? It's in hundreds of individual pieces, packed up for long-term storage.
All the parts seem to be there, but hopefully we won't need it.
It's not like we're going to run out of mac 'n' cheese anytime this century.
Worst case, we'll just wait for the next round of surveyers to come down, and hitch a ride with them.
KNOCK
KNOCK
KNOCK
KNOCK
KNOCK

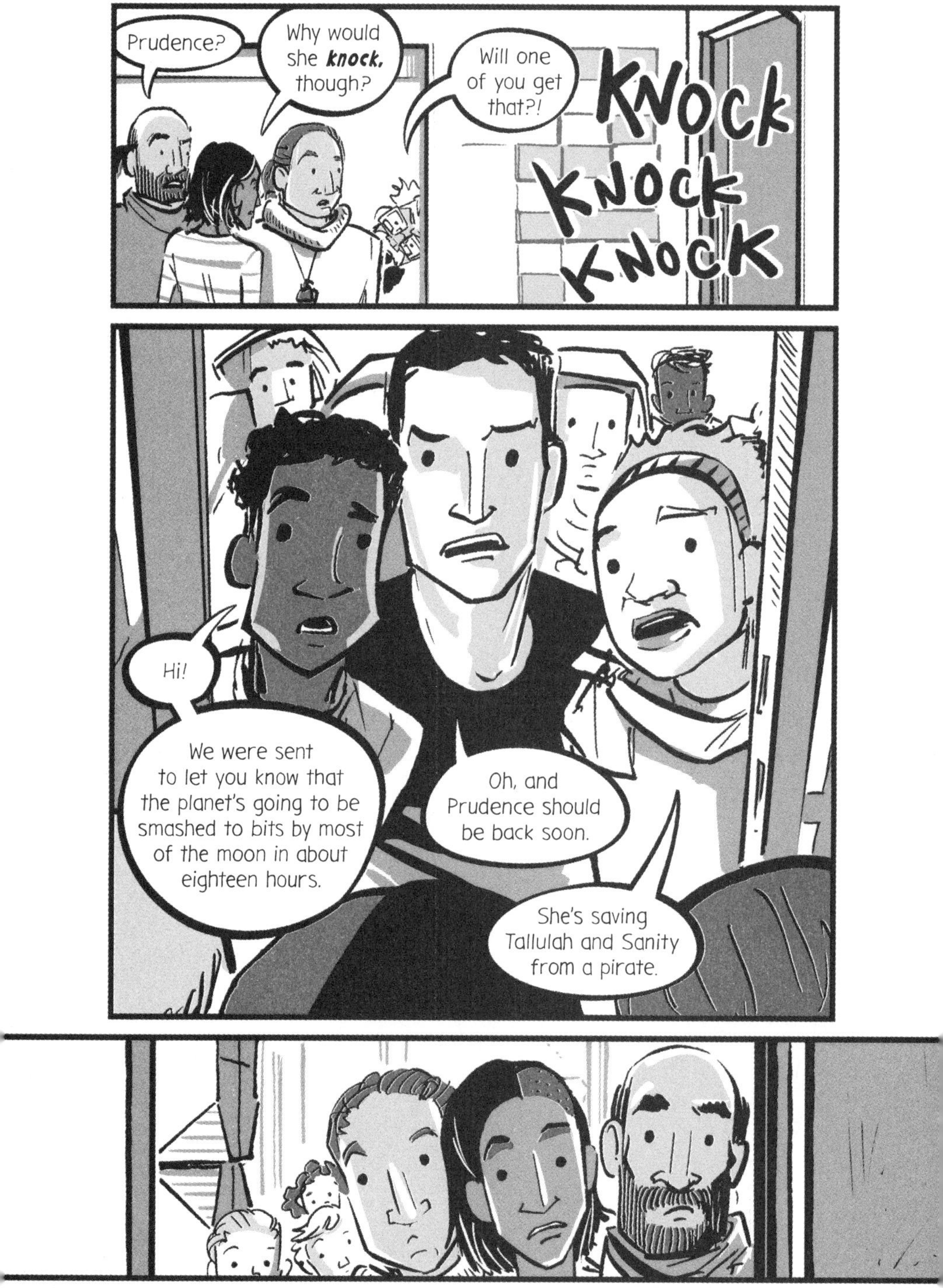
Prudence?
Why would she **knock,** though?
Will one of you get that?!
KNOCK
KNOCK
KNOCK
Hi!
We were sent to let you know that the planet's going to be smashed to bits by most of the moon in about eighteen hours.
Oh, and Prudence should be back soon.
She's saving Tallulah and Sanity from a pirate.

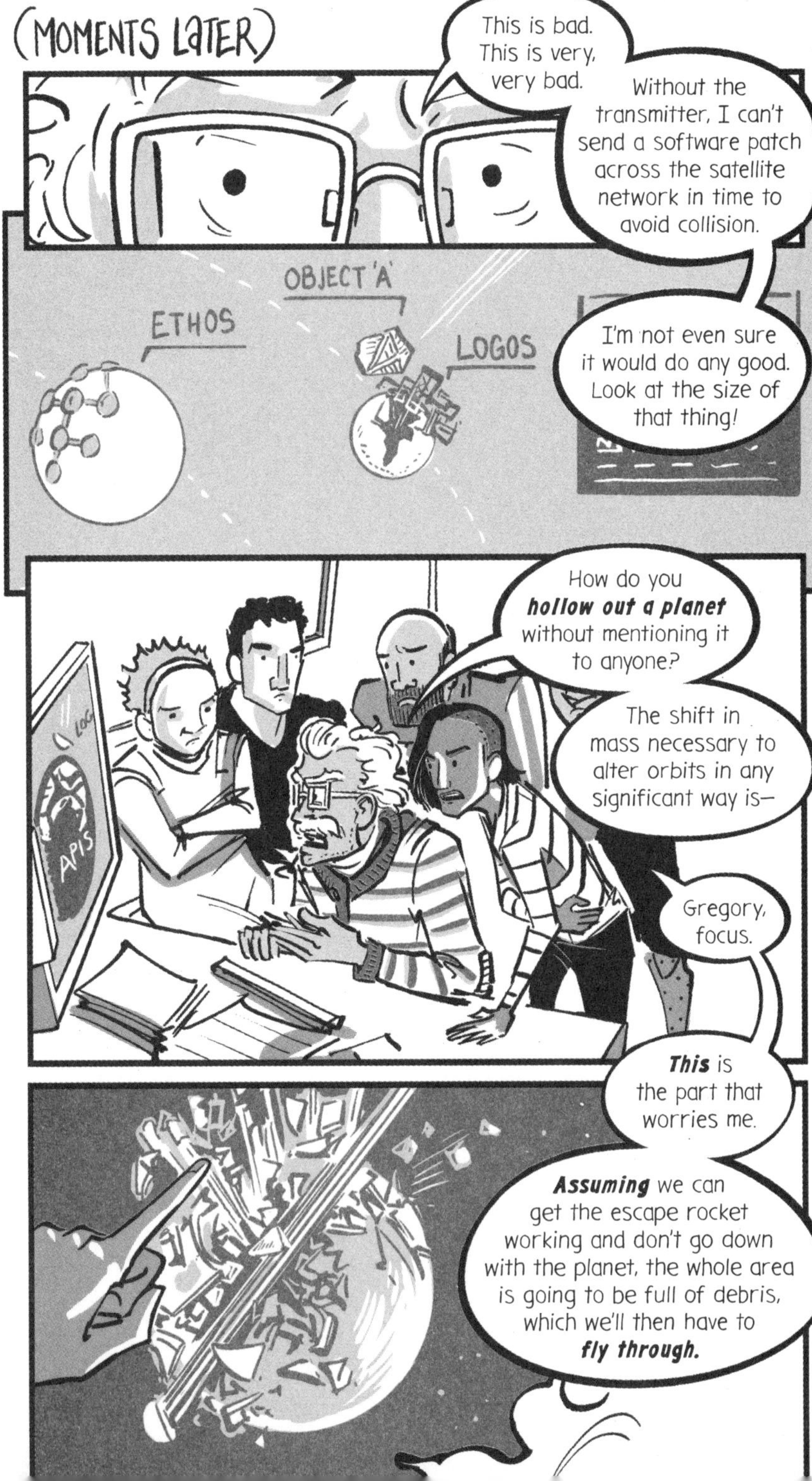
(MOMENTS LATER)
This is bad. This is very, very bad.
Without the transmitter, I can't send a software patch across the satellite network in time to avoid collision.
OBJECT 'A'
ETHOS
LOGOS
I'm not even sure it would do any good. Look at the size of that thing!
How do you **hollow out a planet** without mentioning it to anyone?
The shift in mass necessary to alter orbits in any significant way is—
Gregory, focus.
APIS
**This** is the part that worries me.
**Assuming** we can get the escape rocket working and don't go down with the planet, the whole area is going to be full of debris, which we'll then have to **fly through.**

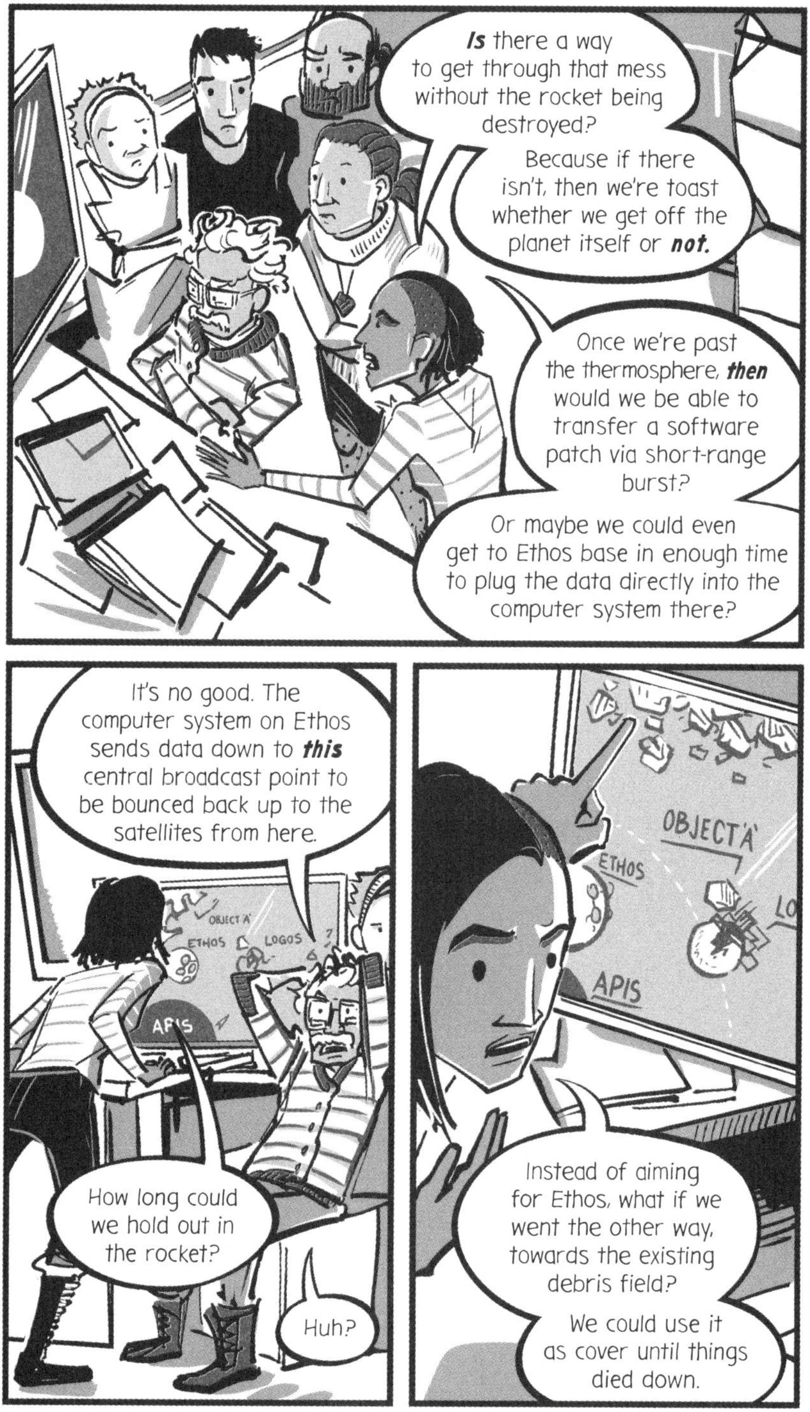

*Is* there a way to get through that mess without the rocket being destroyed?
Because if there isn't, then we're toast whether we get off the planet itself or ***not.***
Once we're past the thermosphere, ***then*** would we be able to transfer a software patch via short-range burst?
Or maybe we could even get to Ethos base in enough time to plug the data directly into the computer system there?
It's no good. The computer system on Ethos sends data down to ***this*** central broadcast point to be bounced back up to the satellites from here.
OBJECT 'A'
ETHOS
LOGOS
APIS
How long could we hold out in the rocket?
Huh?
OBJECT 'A'
ETHOS
APIS
Instead of aiming for Ethos, what if we went the other way, towards the existing debris field?
We could use it as cover until things died down.

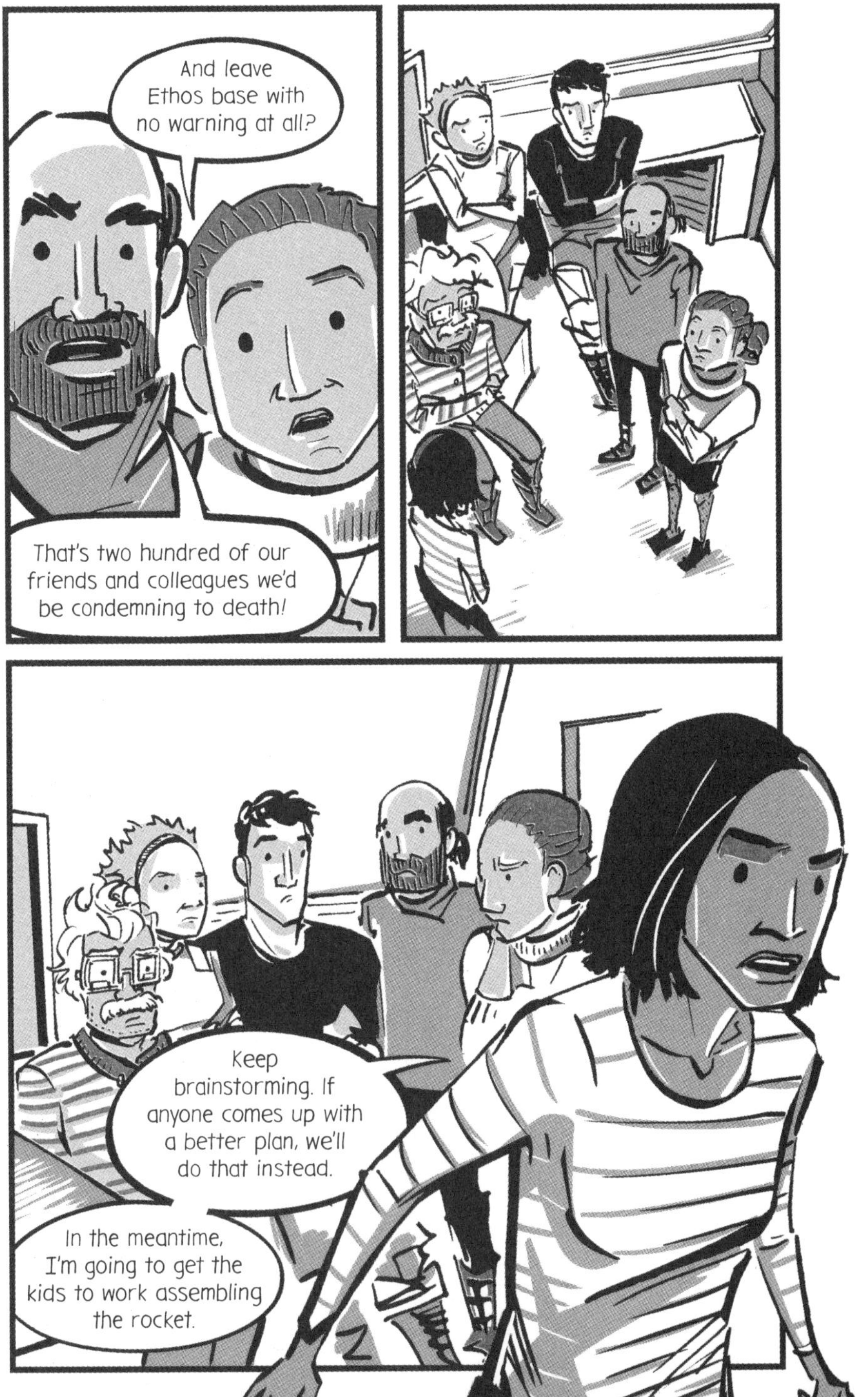

And leave Ethos base with no warning at all?
That's two hundred of our friends and colleagues we'd be condemning to death!
Keep brainstorming. If anyone comes up with a better plan, we'll do that instead.
In the meantime, I'm going to get the kids to work assembling the rocket.

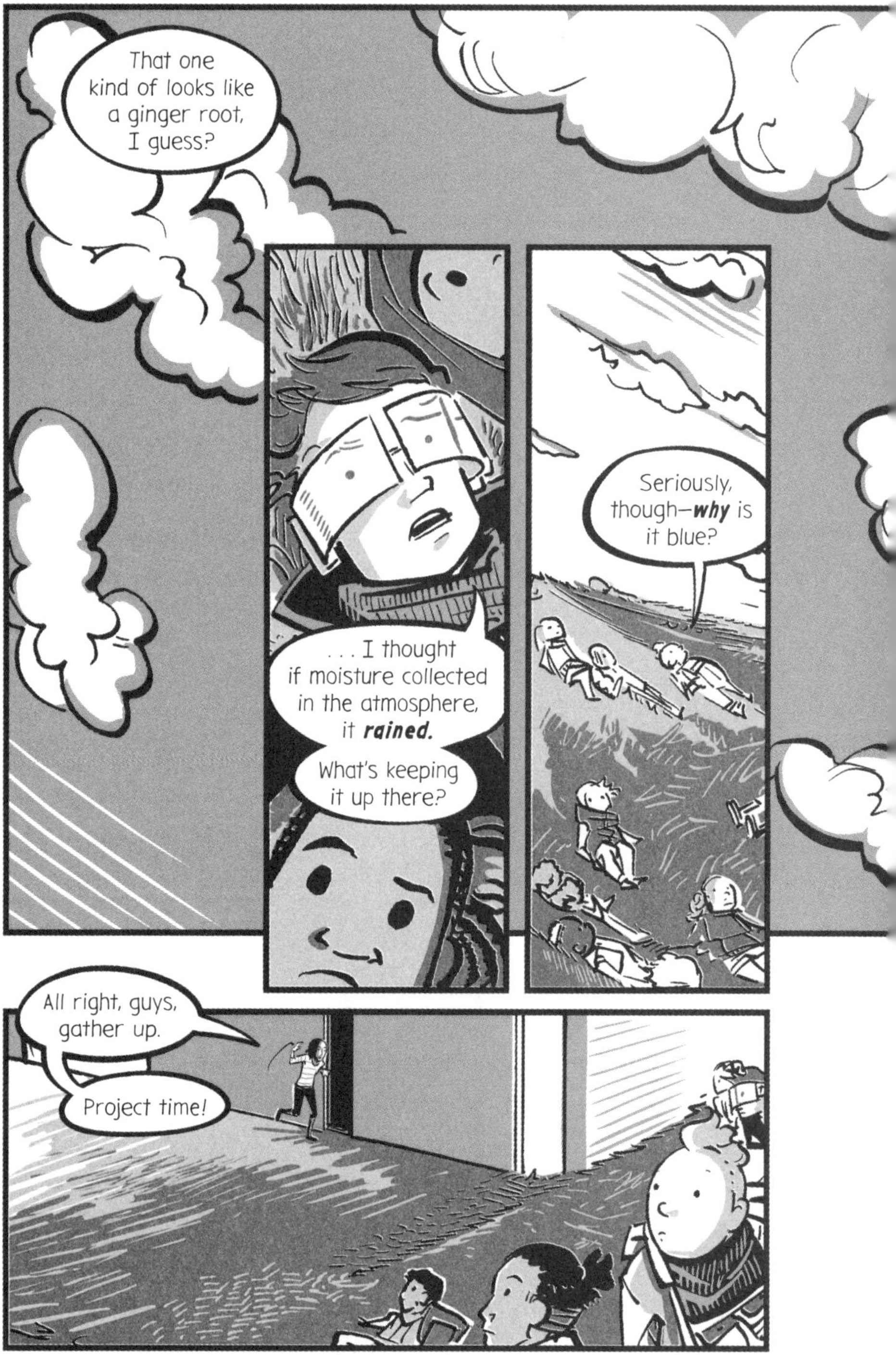
That one kind of looks like a ginger root, I guess?
. . . I thought if moisture collected in the atmosphere, it **rained.**
What's keeping it up there?
Seriously, though—**why** is it blue?
All right, guys, gather up.
Project time!

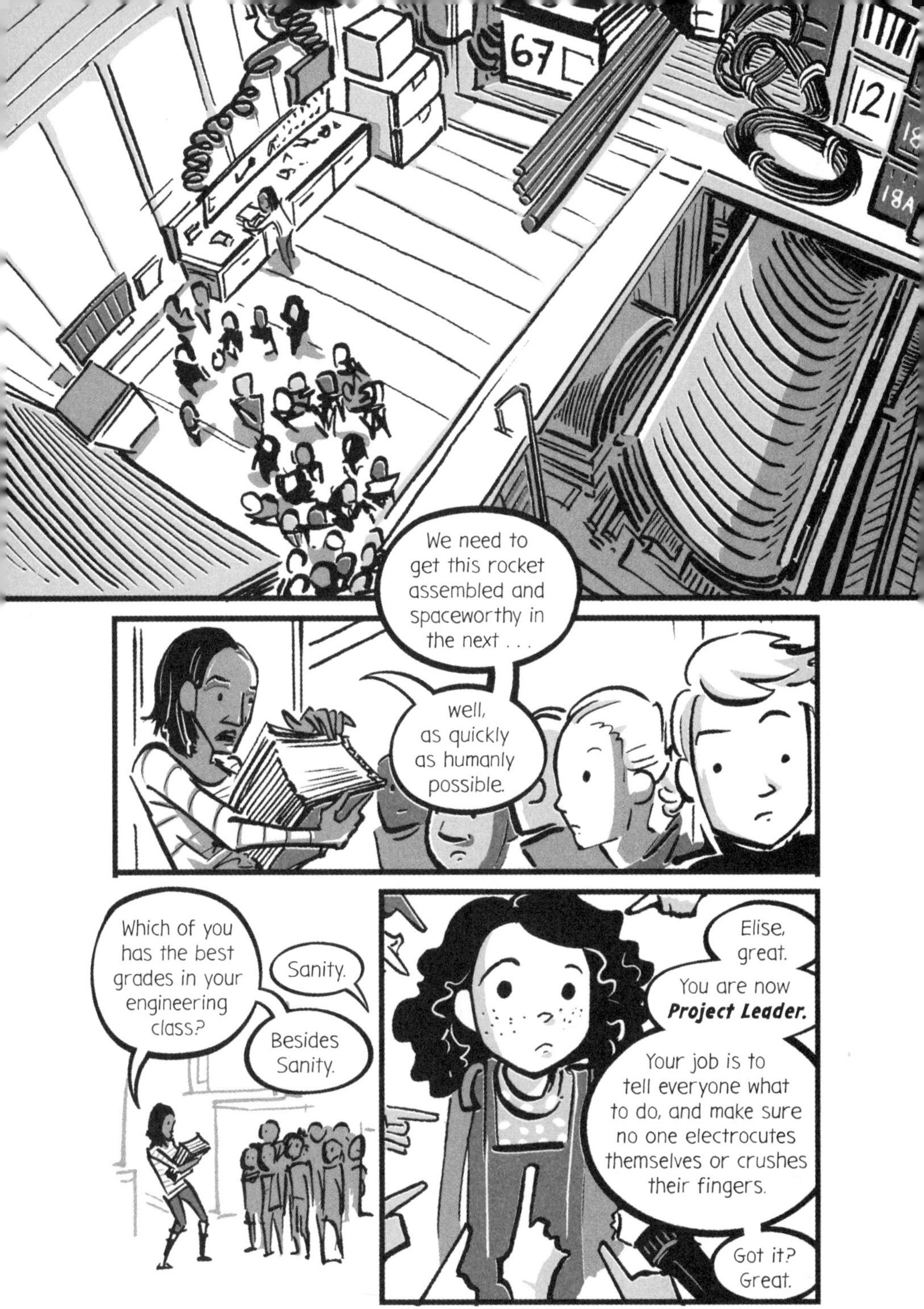
67
121
18A
We need to get this rocket assembled and spaceworthy in the next . . .
well, as quickly as humanly possible.
Which of you has the best grades in your engineering class?
Sanity.
Besides Sanity.
Elise, great.
You are now **Project Leader.**
Your job is to tell everyone what to do, and make sure no one electrocutes themselves or crushes their fingers.
Got it? Great.

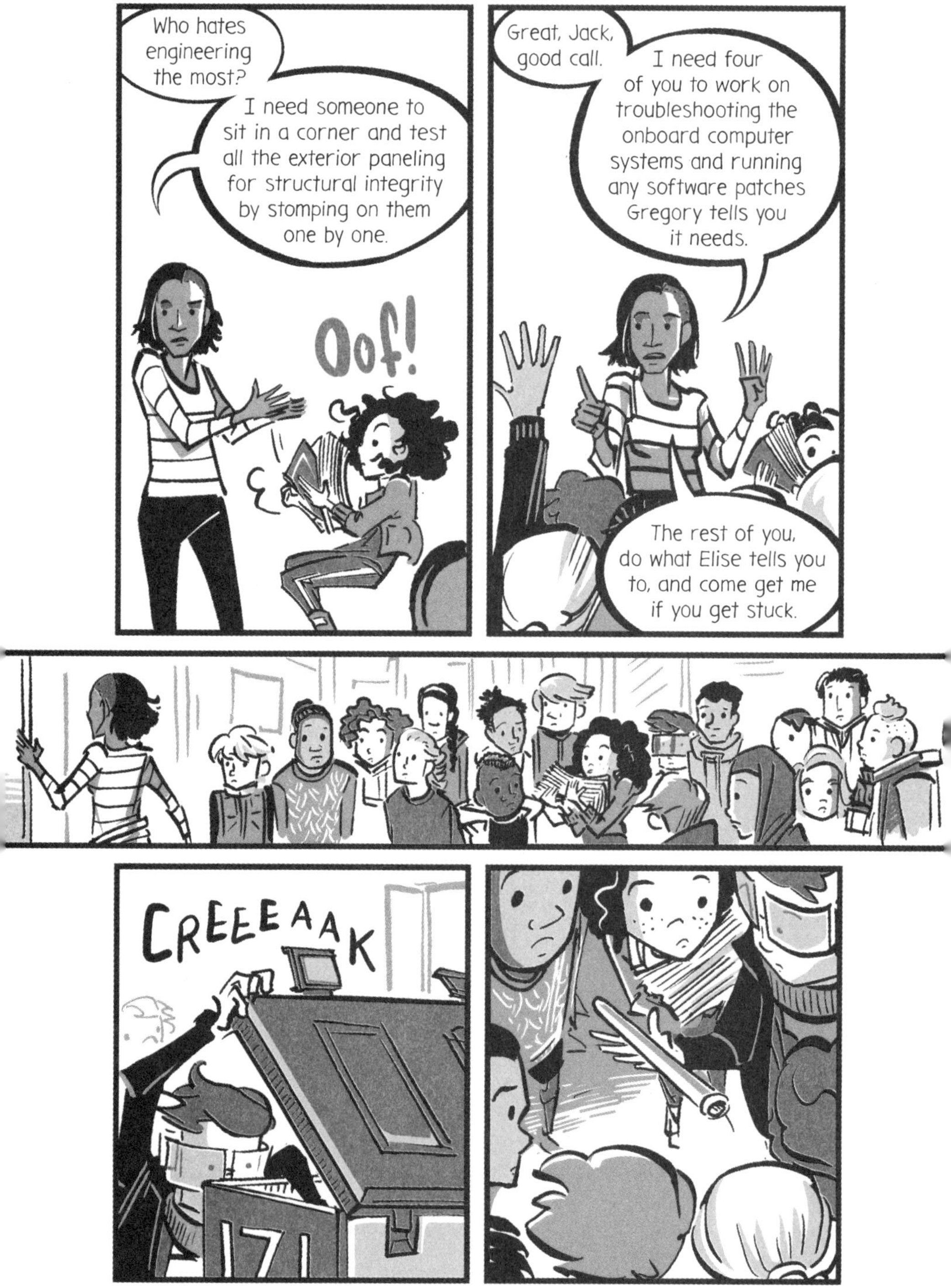
Who hates engineering the most?
I need someone to sit in a corner and test all the exterior paneling for structural integrity by stomping on them one by one.
Oof!
Great, Jack, good call.
I need four of you to work on troubleshooting the onboard computer systems and running any software patches Gregory tells you it needs.
The rest of you, do what Elise tells you to, and come get me if you get stuck.
CREEEAAK

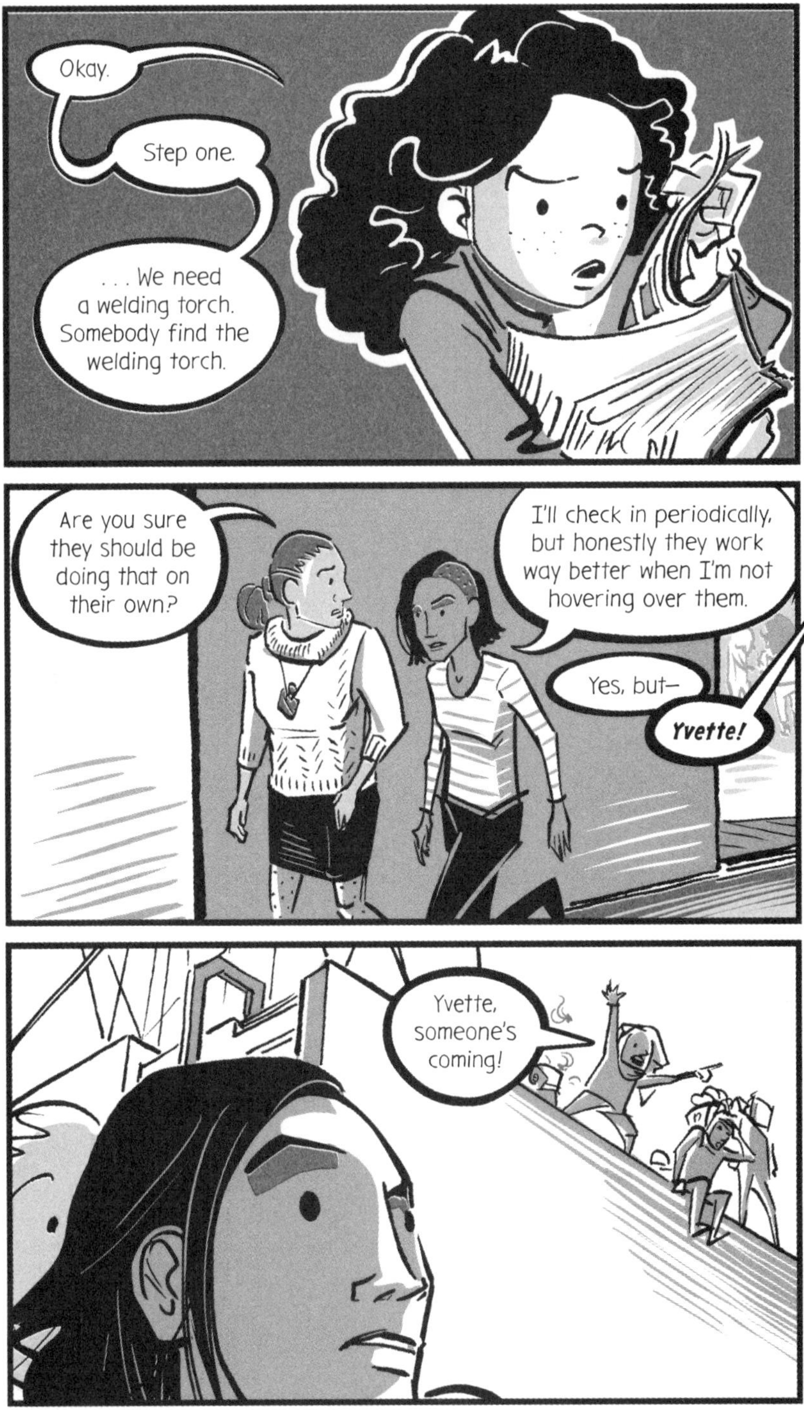
Okay.
Step one.
. . . We need a welding torch. Somebody find the welding torch.
Are you sure they should be doing that on their own?
I'll check in periodically, but honestly they work way better when I'm not hovering over them.
Yes, but—
Yvette!
Yvette, someone's coming!

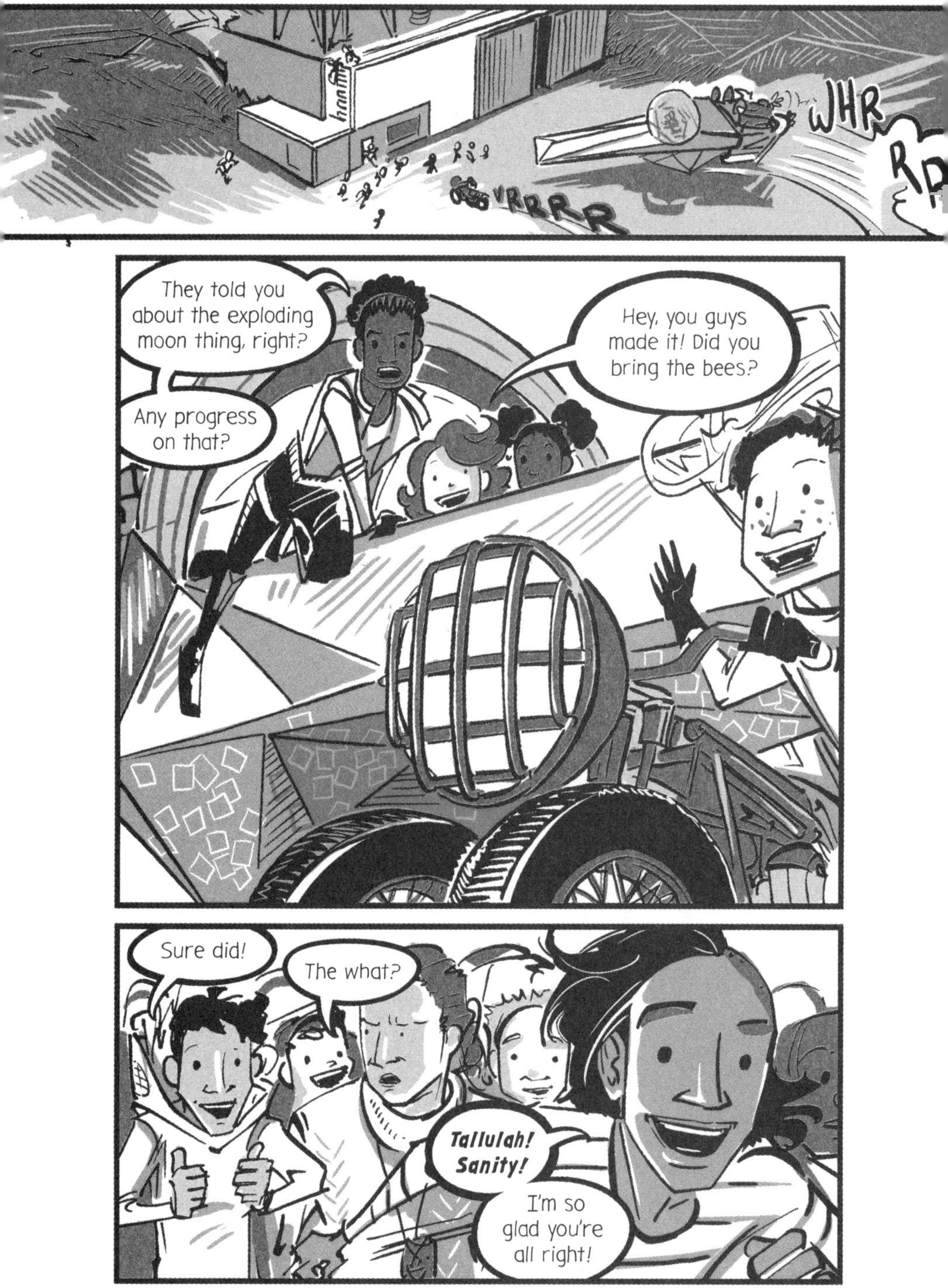
VRRRR
WHR
They told you about the exploding moon thing, right?
Any progress on that?
Hey, you guys made it! Did you bring the bees?
Sure did!
The what?
Tallulah! Sanity!
I'm so glad you're all right!

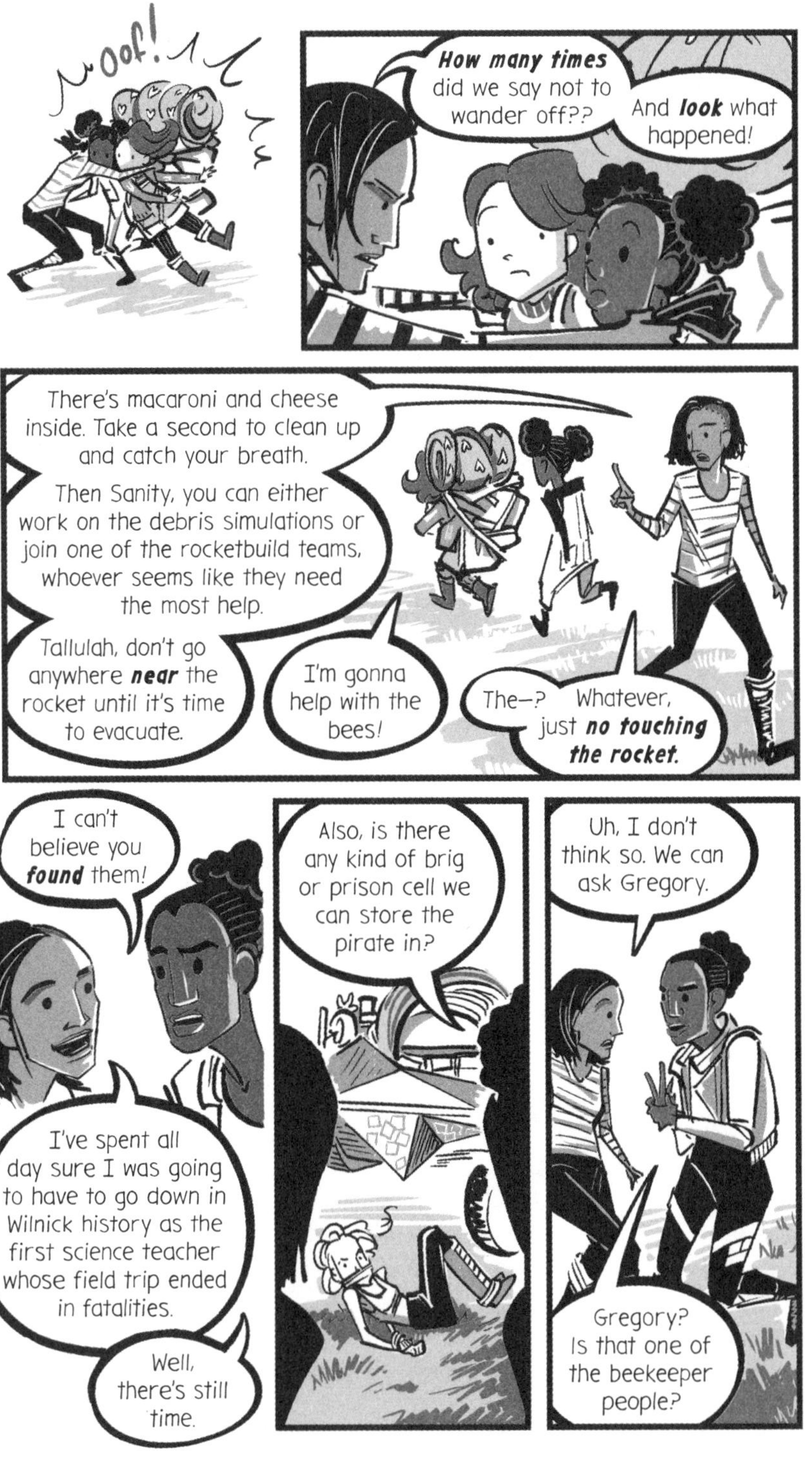
Oof!
**How many times** did we say not to wander off??
And **look** what happened!
There's macaroni and cheese inside. Take a second to clean up and catch your breath.
Then Sanity, you can either work on the debris simulations or join one of the rocketbuild teams, whoever seems like they need the most help.
Tallulah, don't go anywhere **near** the rocket until it's time to evacuate.
I'm gonna help with the bees!
The—? Whatever, just **no touching the rocket.**
I can't believe you **found** them!
I've spent all day sure I was going to have to go down in Wilnick history as the first science teacher whose field trip ended in fatalities.
Well, there's still time.
Also, is there any kind of brig or prison cell we can store the pirate in?
Uh, I don't think so. We can ask Gregory.
Gregory? Is that one of the beekeeper people?

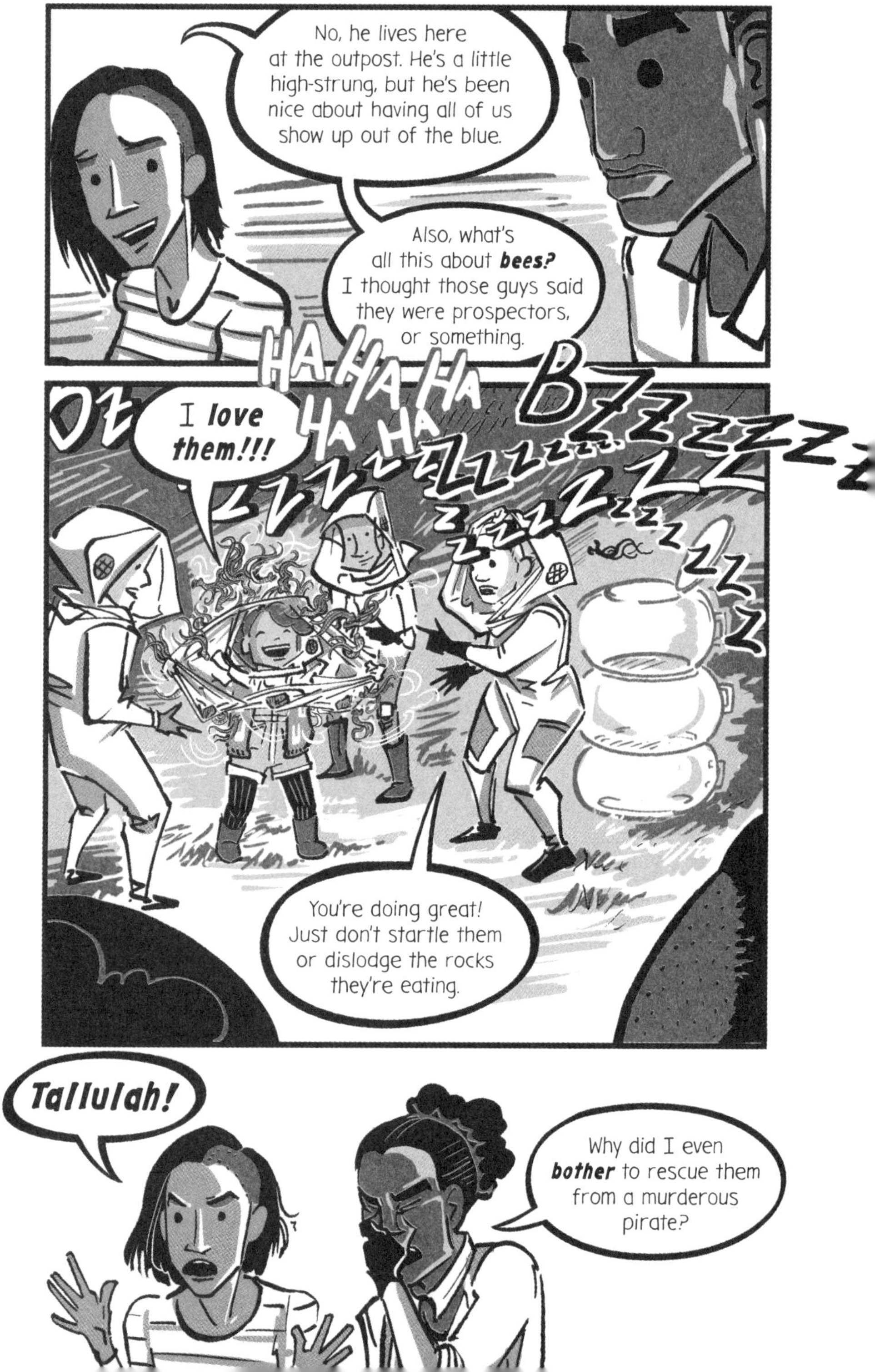

No, he lives here at the outpost. He's a little high-strung, but he's been nice about having all of us show up out of the blue.
Also, what's all this about **bees?** I thought those guys said they were prospectors, or something.
I **love them!!!**
HA HA HA HA HA HA
BZZZZZZZZ
You're doing great! Just don't startle them or dislodge the rocks they're eating.
**Tallulah!**
Why did I even **bother** to rescue them from a murderous pirate?

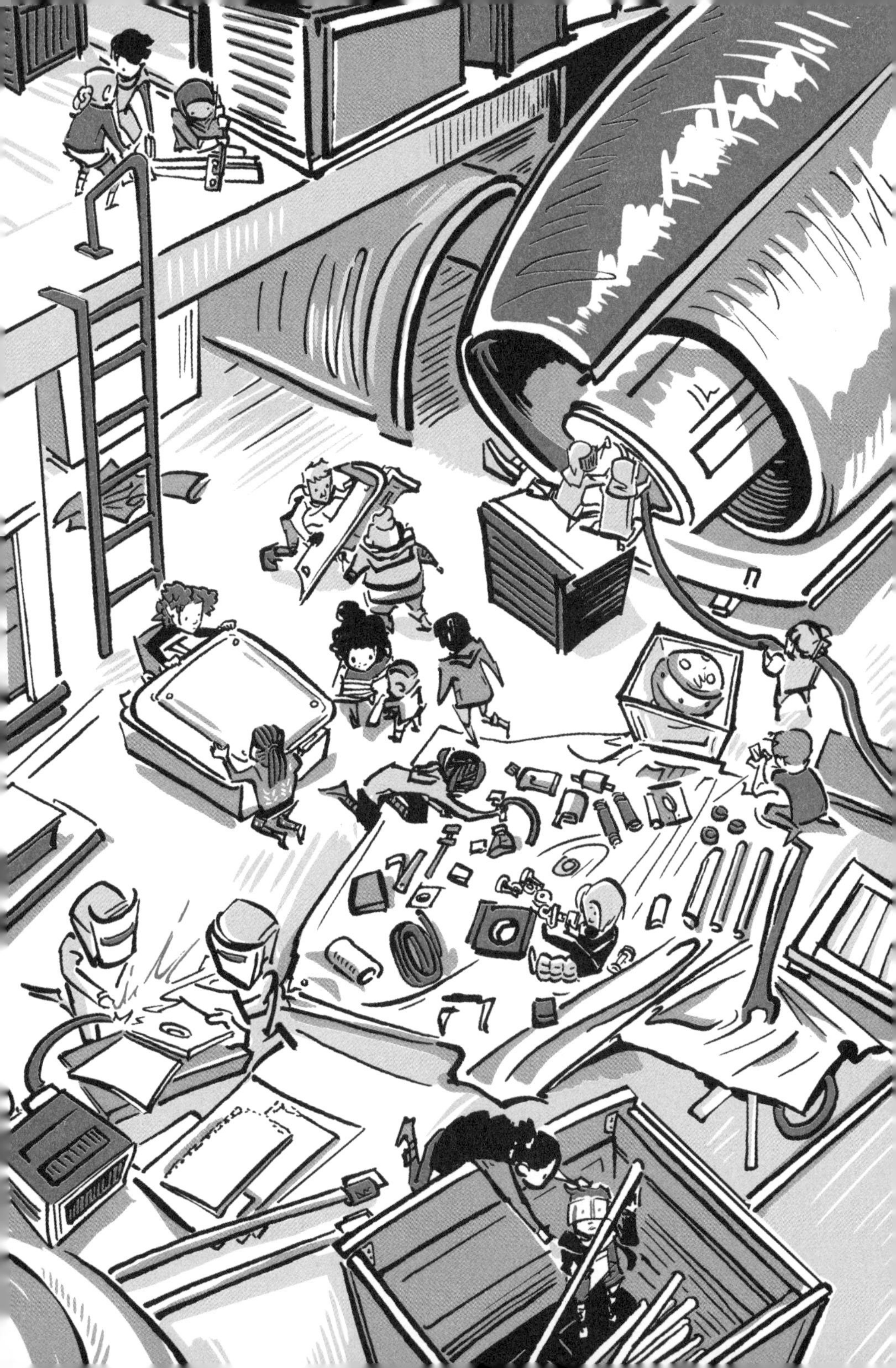

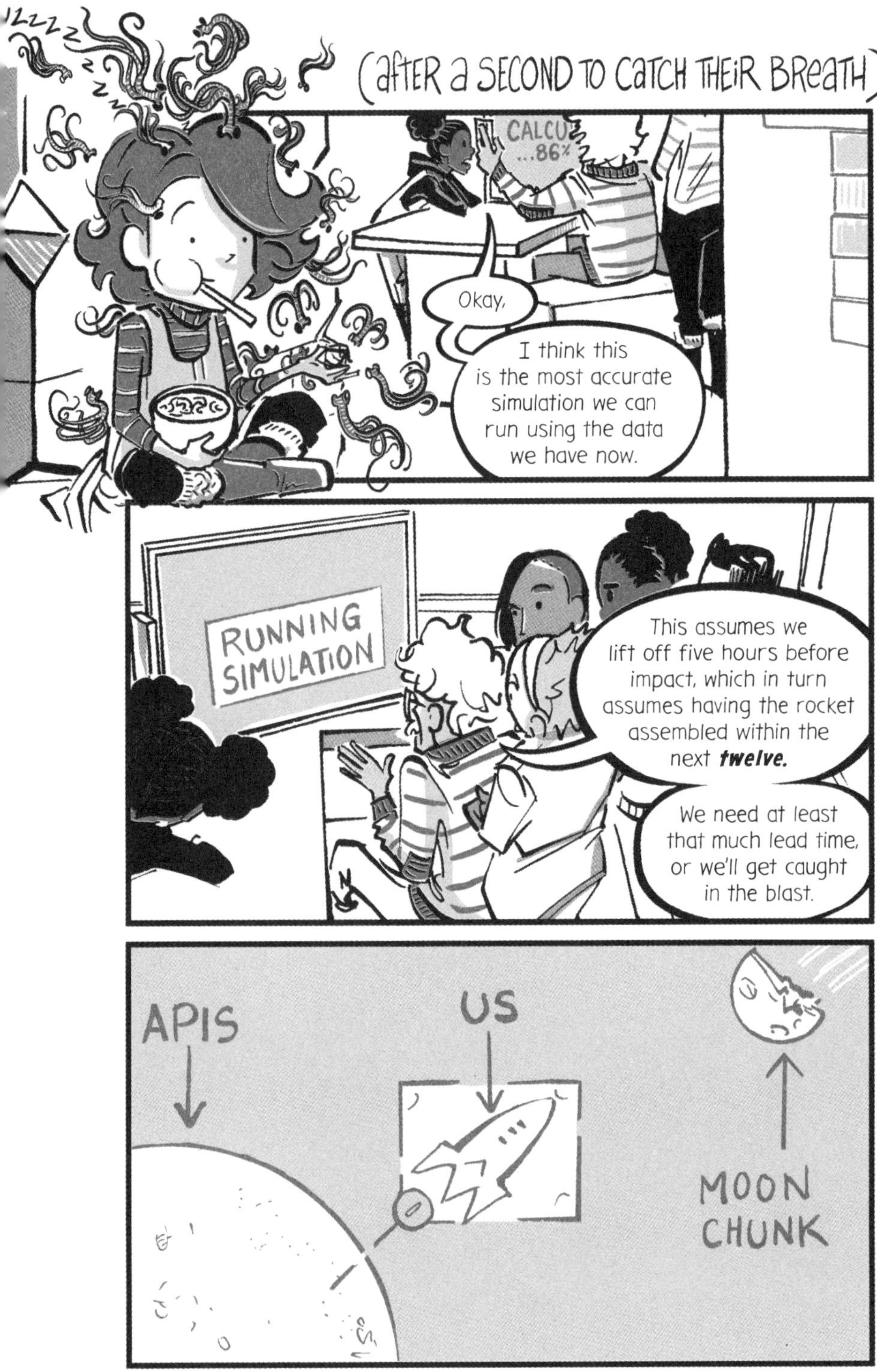
ZZZZZ
(after a SECOND TO CATCH THEIR BREATH)
CALCU...86%
Okay,
I think this is the most accurate simulation we can run using the data we have now.
RUNNING SIMULATION
This assumes we lift off five hours before impact, which in turn assumes having the rocket assembled within the next ***twelve.***
We need at least that much lead time, or we'll get caught in the blast.
APIS
US
MOON CHUNK

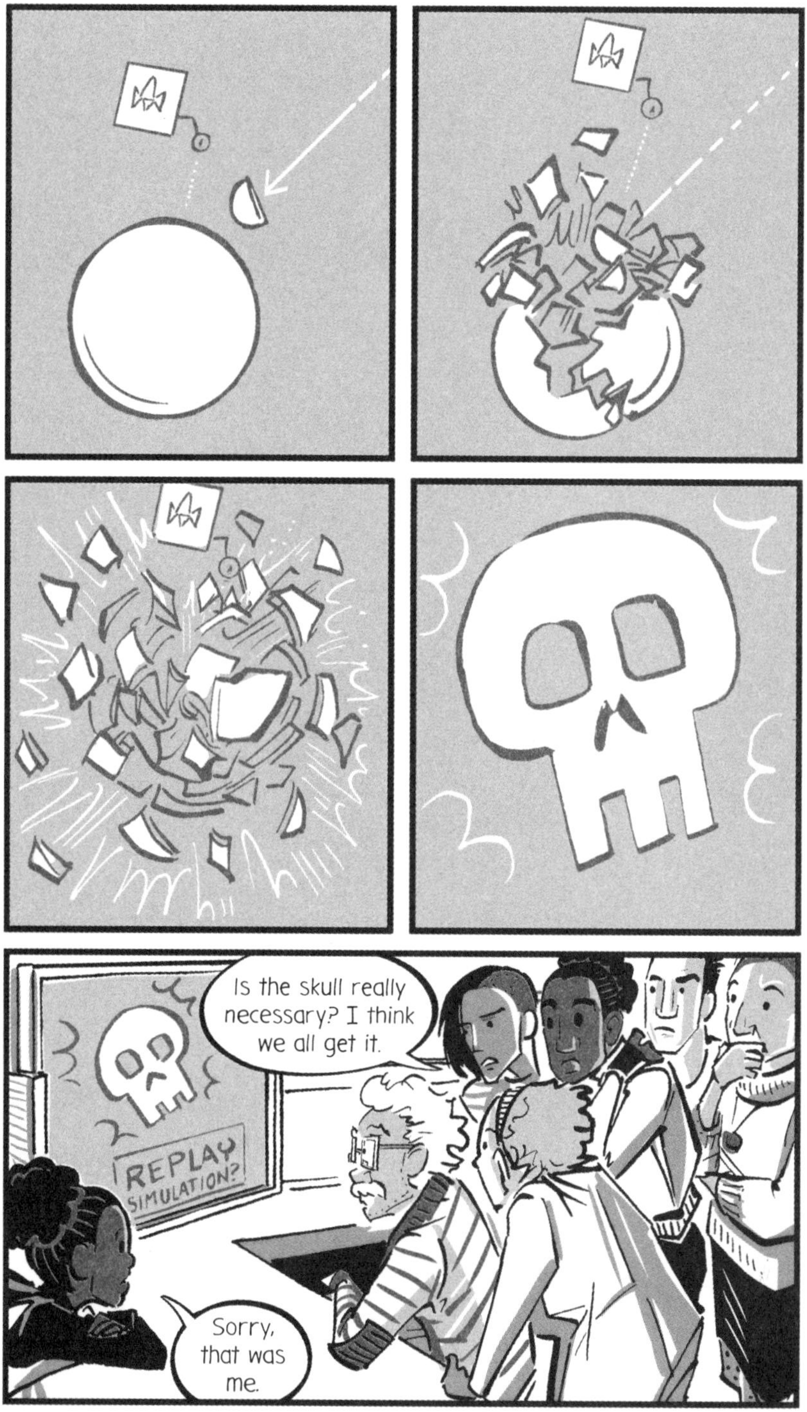
Is the skull really necessary? I think we all get it.
REPLAY SIMULATION?
Sorry, that was me.

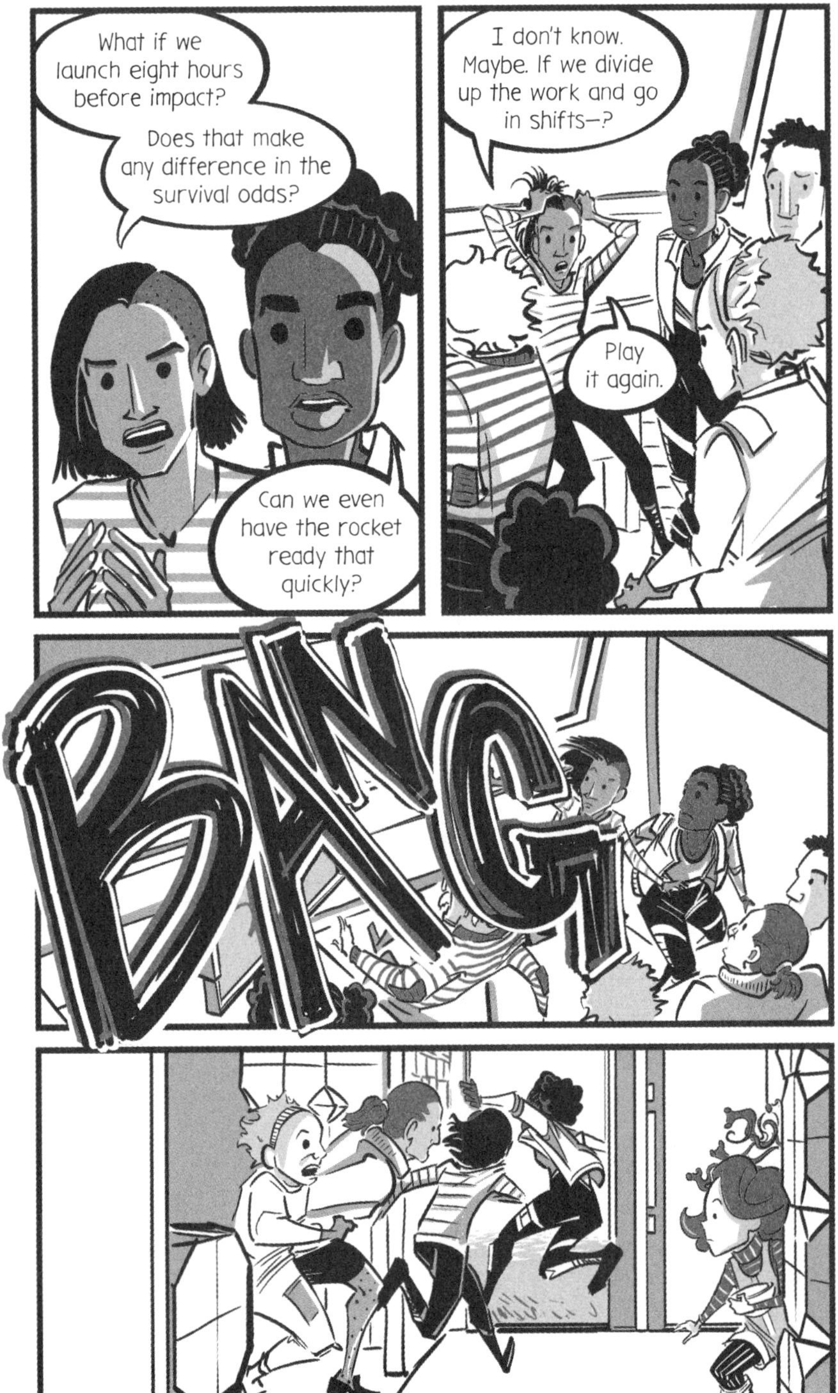
What if we launch eight hours before impact?
Does that make any difference in the survival odds?
Can we even have the rocket ready that quickly?
I don't know. Maybe. If we divide up the work and go in shifts—?
Play it again.
BANG

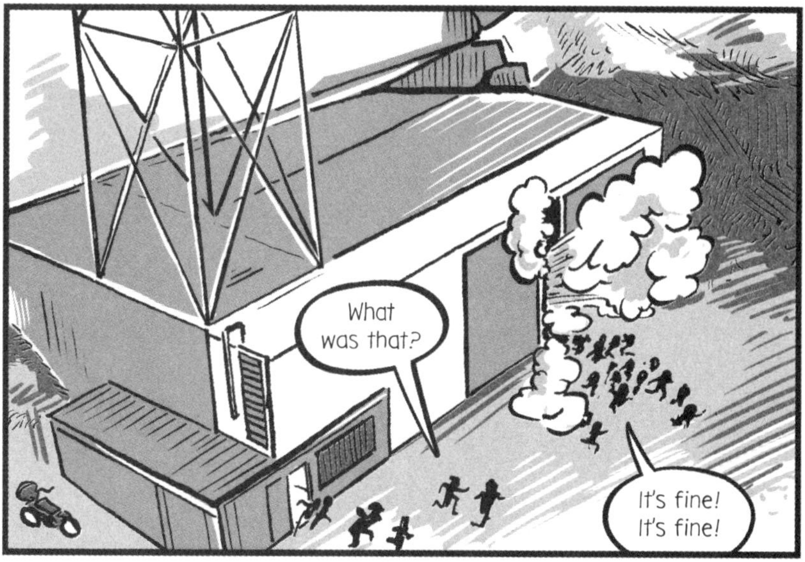
What was that?
It's fine! It's fine!

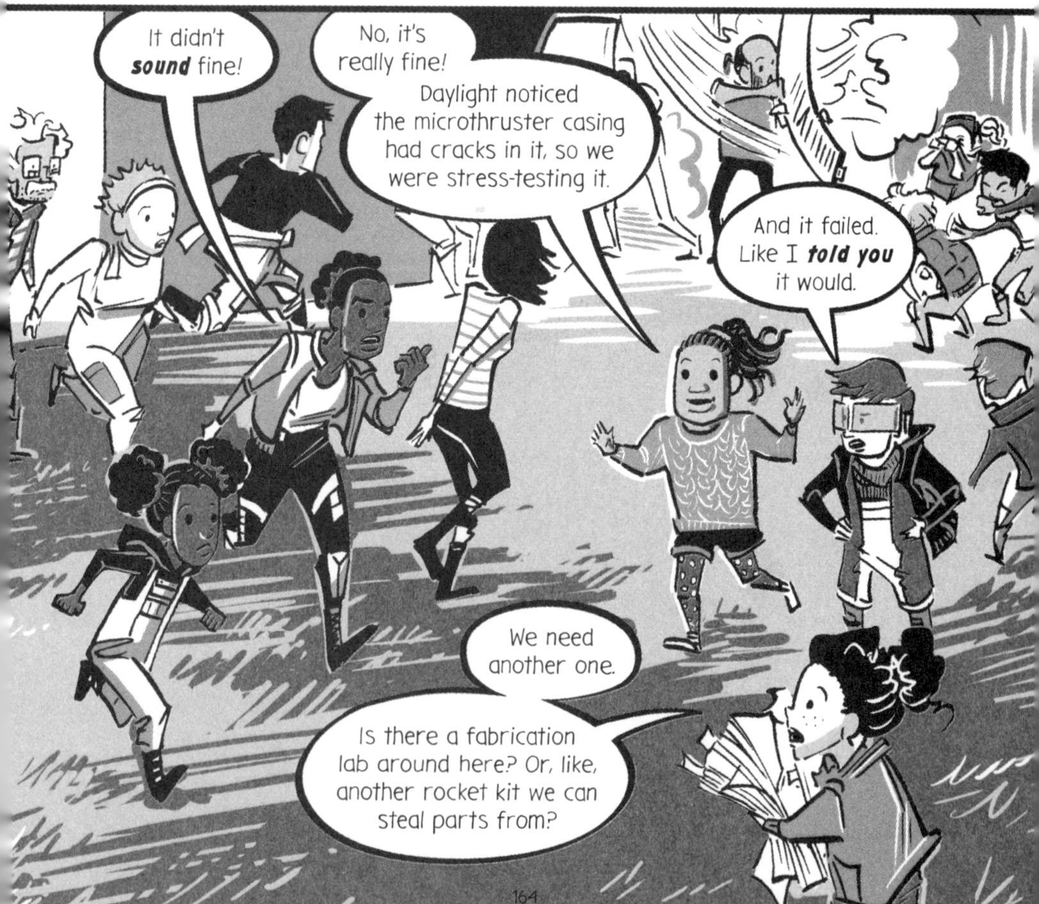
It didn't **sound** fine!
No, it's really fine!
Daylight noticed the microthruster casing had cracks in it, so we were stress-testing it.
And it failed. Like I ***told you*** it would.
We need another one.
Is there a fabrication lab around here? Or, like, another rocket kit we can steal parts from?

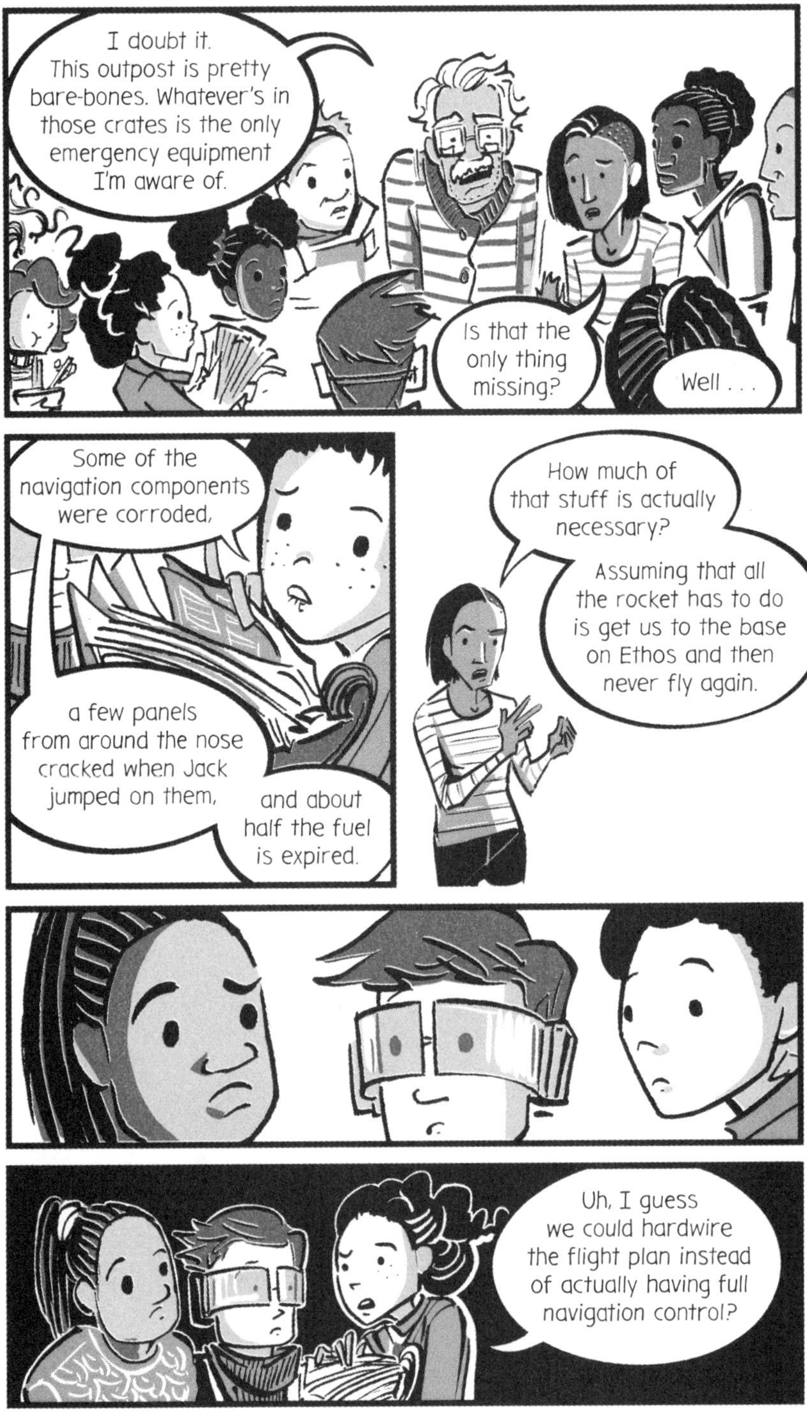
I doubt it. This outpost is pretty bare-bones. Whatever's in those crates is the only emergency equipment I'm aware of.
Is that the only thing missing?
Well . . .
Some of the navigation components were corroded,
a few panels from around the nose cracked when Jack jumped on them,
and about half the fuel is expired.
How much of that stuff is actually necessary?
Assuming that all the rocket has to do is get us to the base on Ethos and then never fly again.
Uh, I guess we could hardwire the flight plan instead of actually having full navigation control?

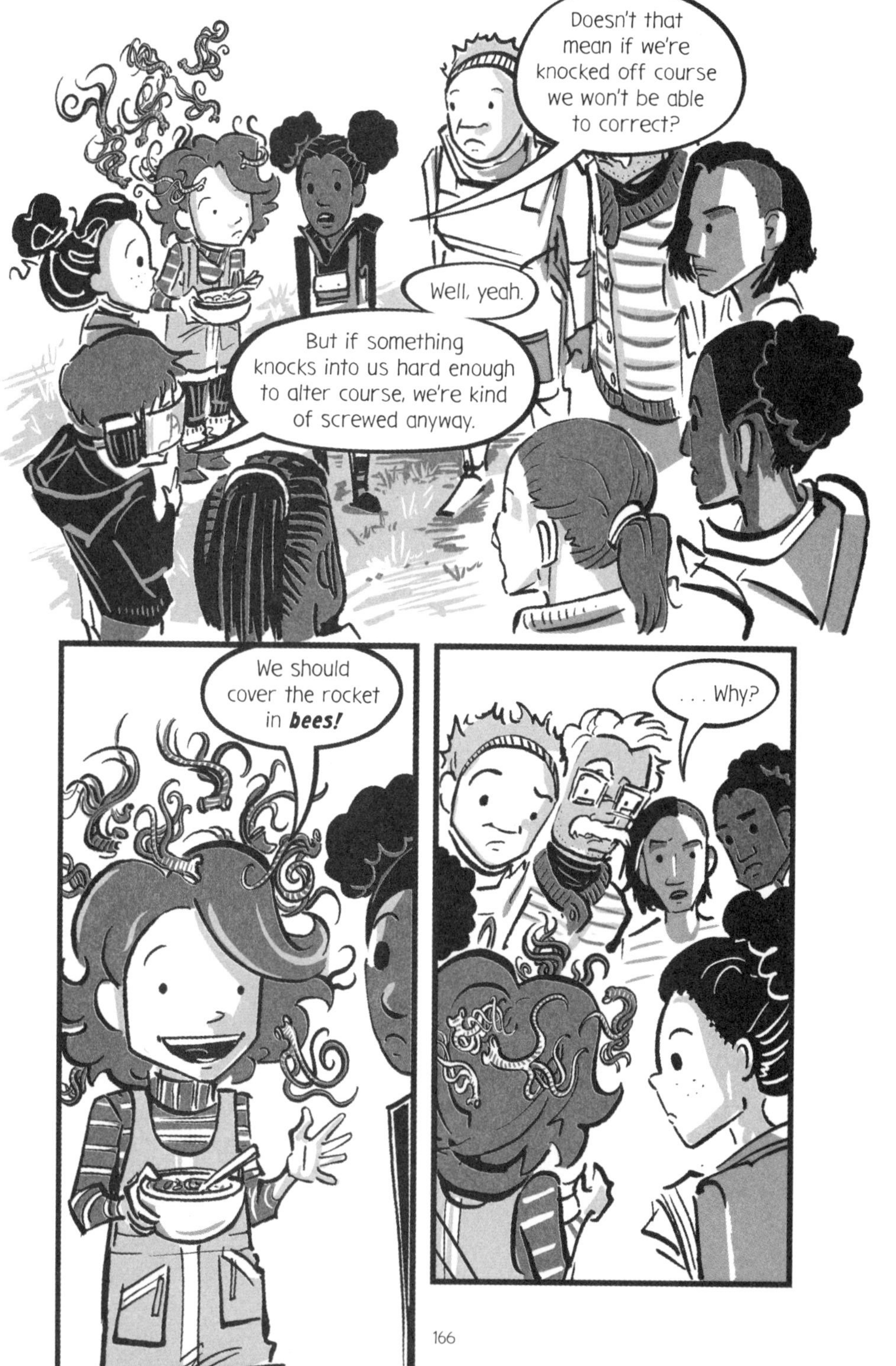
Doesn't that mean if we're knocked off course we won't be able to correct?
Well, yeah.
But if something knocks into us hard enough to alter course, we're kind of screwed anyway.
We should cover the rocket in ***bees!***
. . . Why?

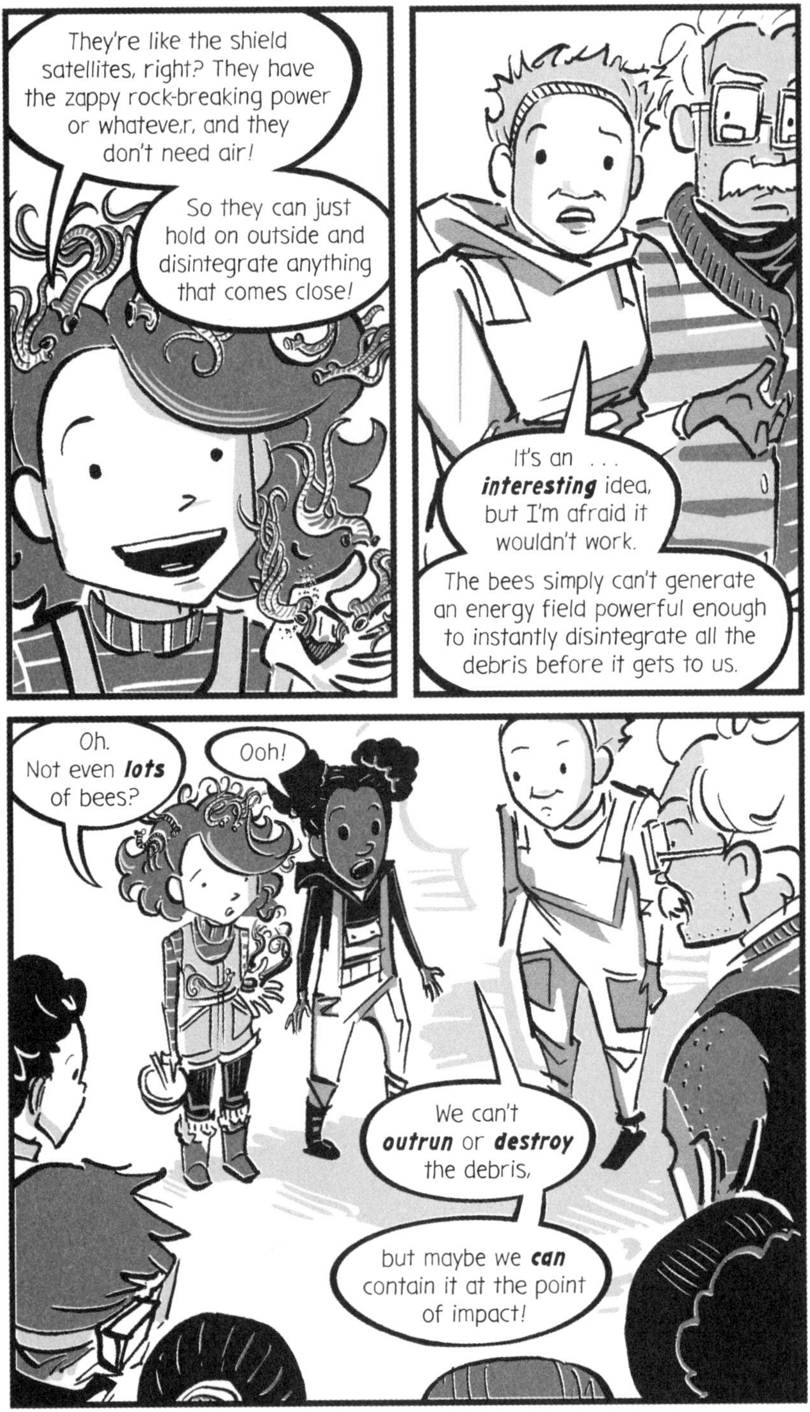
They're like the shield satellites, right? They have the zappy rock-breaking power or whateve,r, and they don't need air!
So they can just hold on outside and disintegrate anything that comes close!
It's an . . . **interesting** idea, but I'm afraid it wouldn't work.
The bees simply can't generate an energy field powerful enough to instantly disintegrate all the debris before it gets to us.
Oh. Not even **lots** of bees?
Ooh!
We can't **outrun** or **destroy** the debris,
but maybe we **can** contain it at the point of impact!

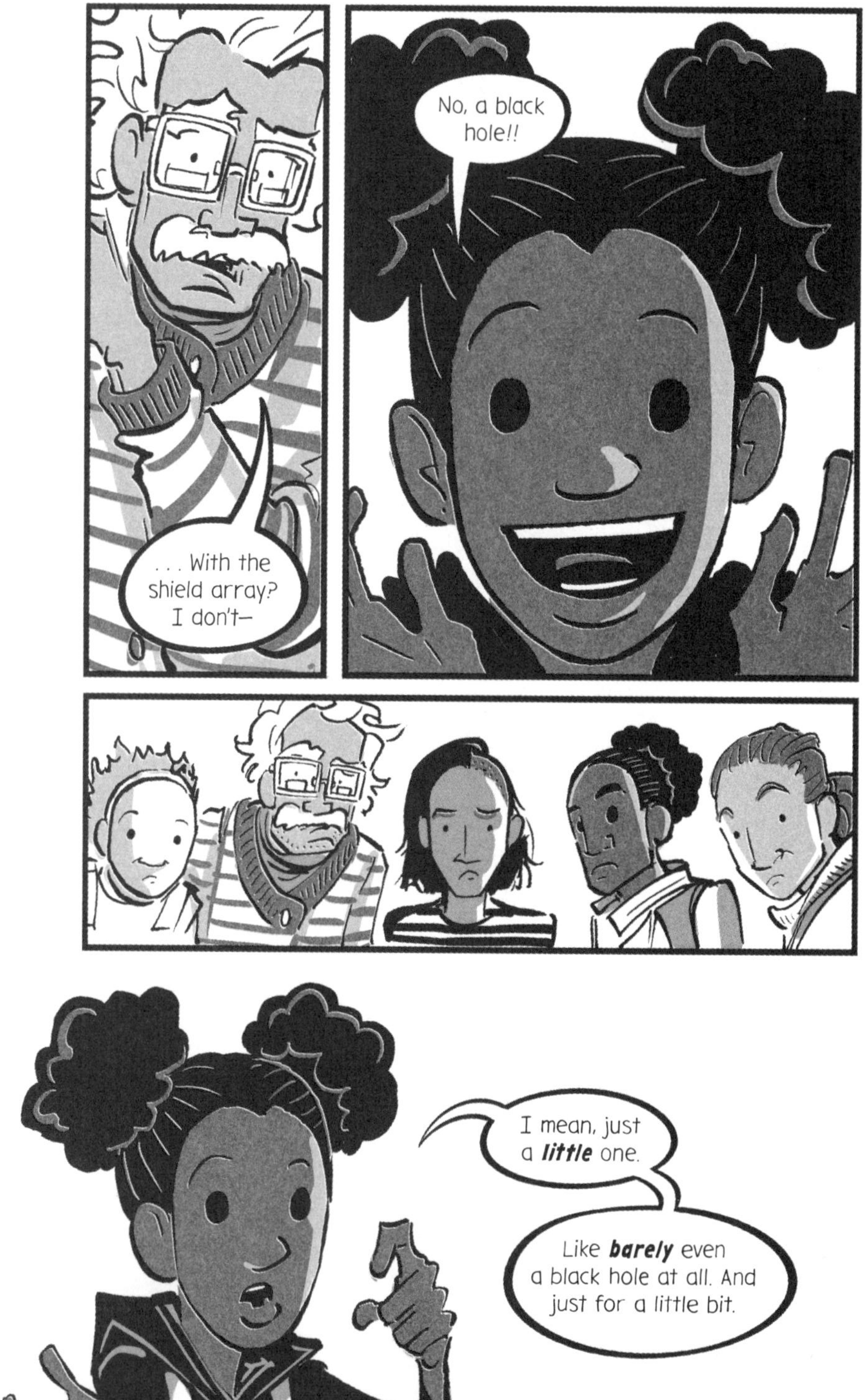
. . . With the shield array? I don't—
No, a black hole!!
I mean, just a **little** one.
Like **barely** even a black hole at all. And just for a little bit.

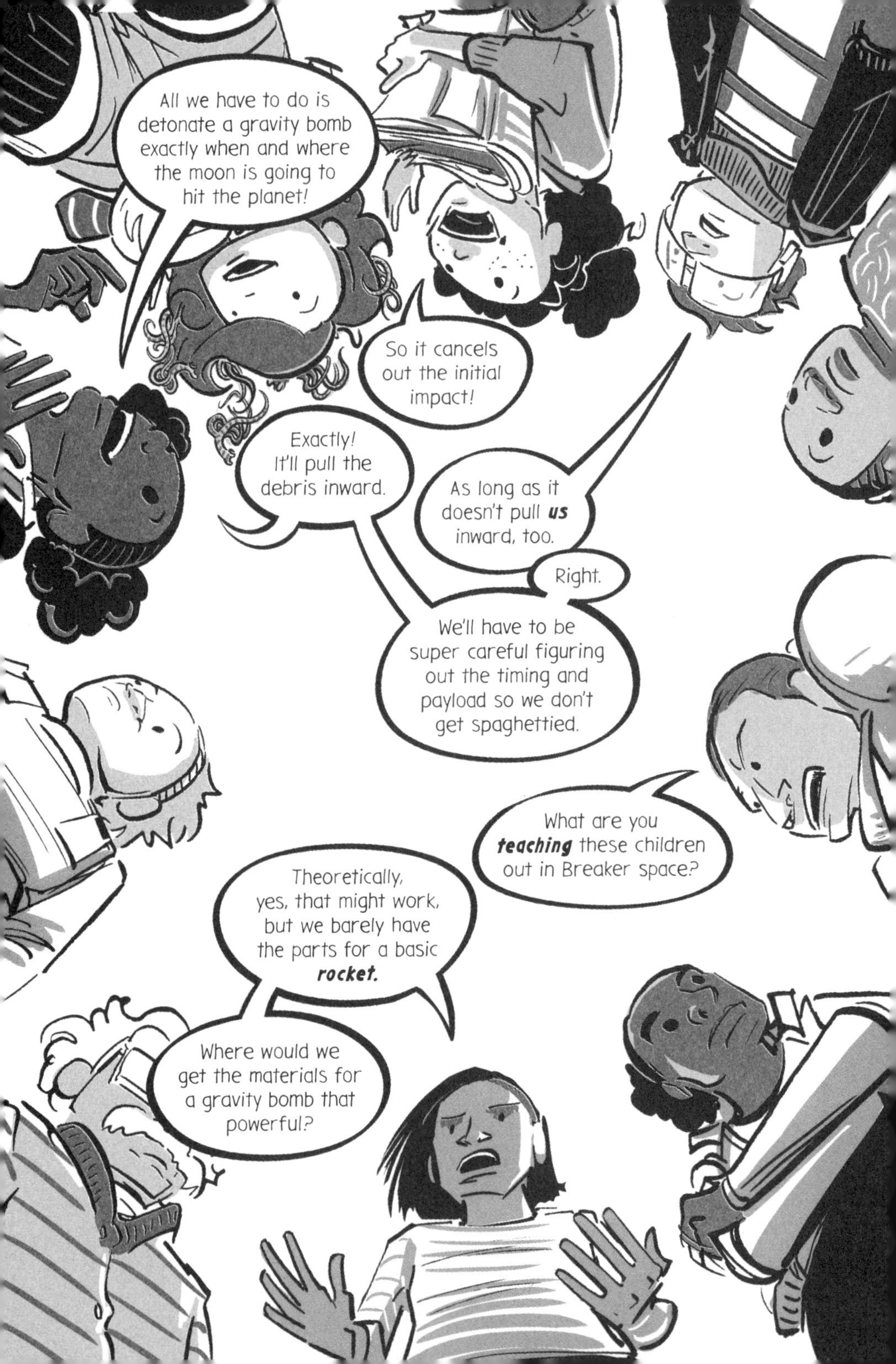
All we have to do is detonate a gravity bomb exactly when and where the moon is going to hit the planet!
So it cancels out the initial impact!
Exactly! It'll pull the debris inward.
As long as it doesn't pull **us** inward, too.
Right.
We'll have to be super careful figuring out the timing and payload so we don't get spaghettied.
What are you **teaching** these children out in Breaker space?
Theoretically, yes, that might work, but we barely have the parts for a basic **rocket.**
Where would we get the materials for a gravity bomb that powerful?

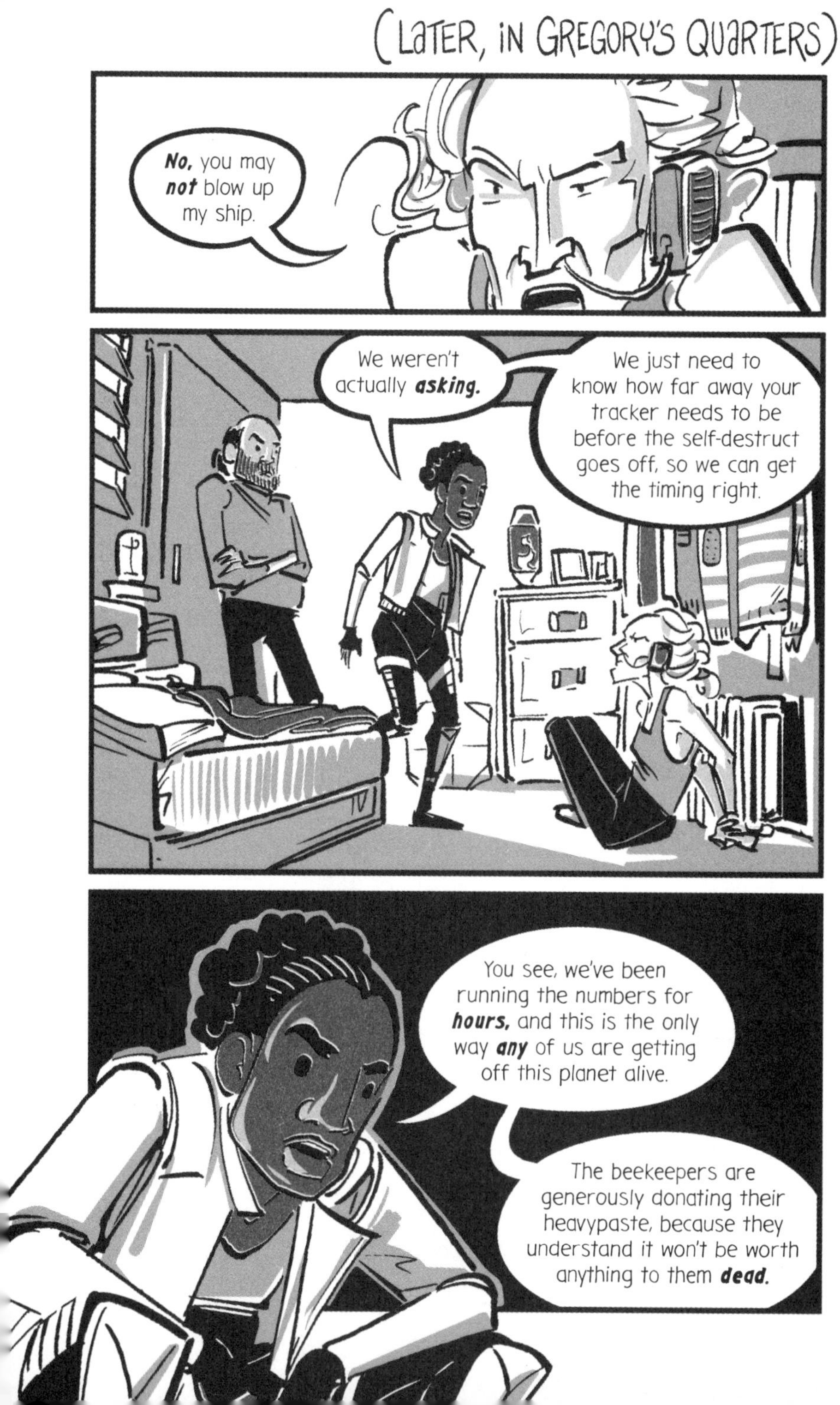
(LATER, IN GREGORY'S QUARTERS)
**No,** you may **not** blow up my ship.
We weren't actually **asking.**
We just need to know how far away your tracker needs to be before the self-destruct goes off, so we can get the timing right.
You see, we've been running the numbers for **hours,** and this is the only way **any** of us are getting off this planet alive.
The beekeepers are generously donating their heavypaste, because they understand it won't be worth anything to them **dead.**

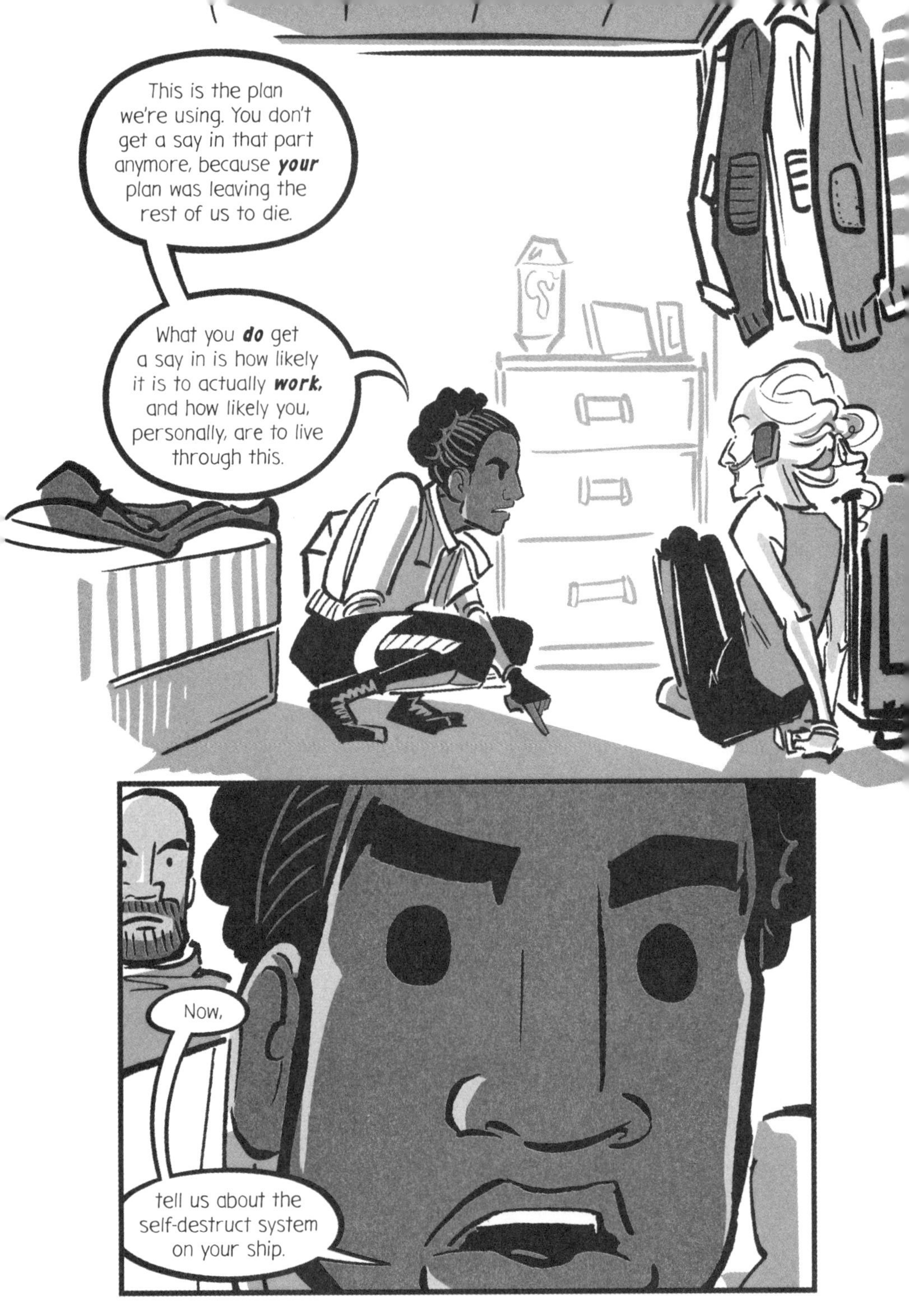
This is the plan we're using. You don't get a say in that part anymore, because ***your*** plan was leaving the rest of us to die.
What you ***do*** get a say in is how likely it is to actually ***work,*** and how likely you, personally, are to live through this.
Now,
tell us about the self-destruct system on your ship.

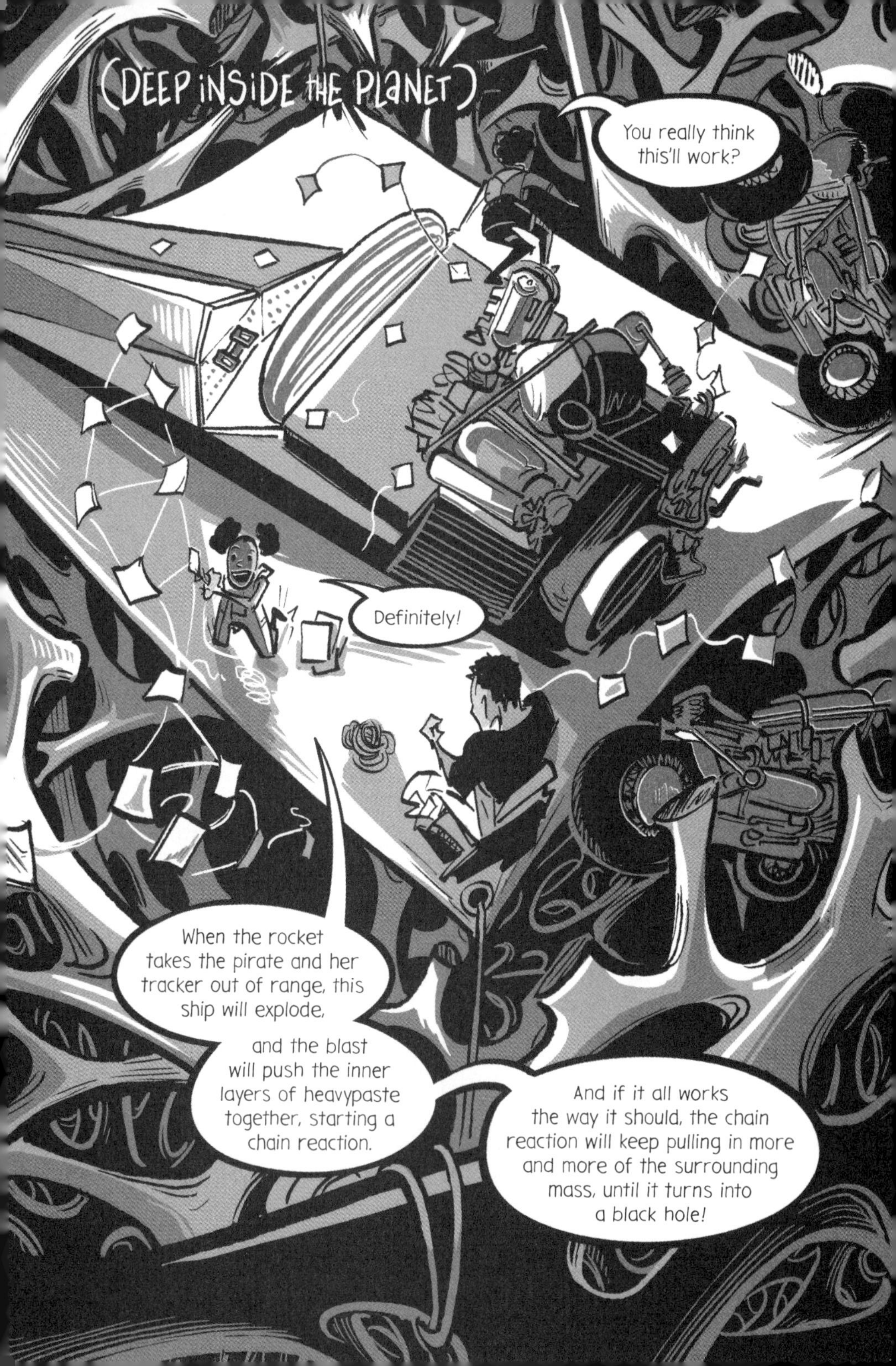
(DEEP INSIDE THE PLANET)
You really think this'll work?
Definitely!
When the rocket takes the pirate and her tracker out of range, this ship will explode,
and the blast will push the inner layers of heavypaste together, starting a chain reaction.
And if it all works the way it should, the chain reaction will keep pulling in more and more of the surrounding mass, until it turns into a black hole!

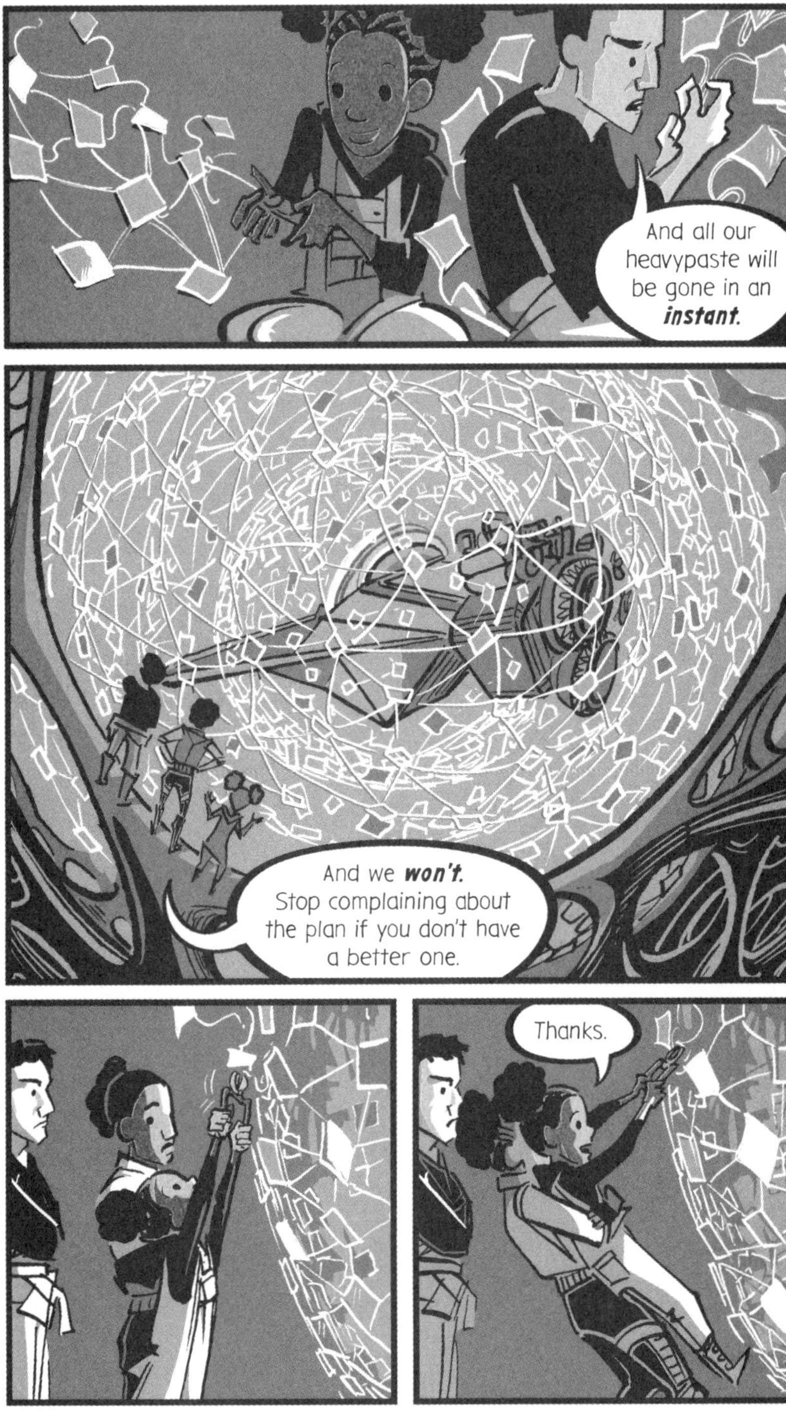
And all our heavypaste will be gone in an **instant**.
And we **won't**. Stop complaining about the plan if you don't have a better one.
Thanks.

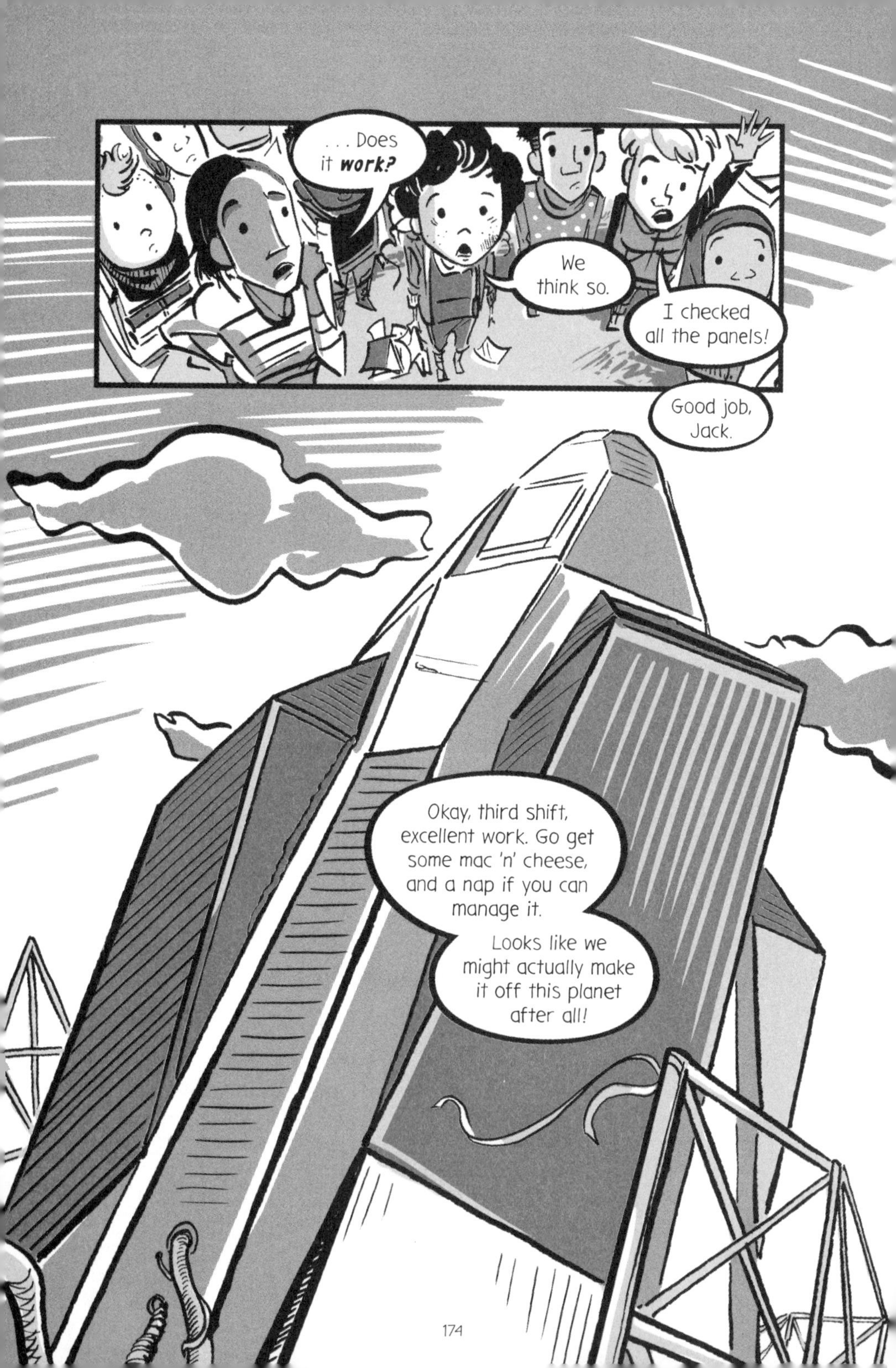

. . . Does it **work?**
We think so.
I checked all the panels!
Good job, Jack.
Okay, third shift, excellent work. Go get some mac 'n' cheese, and a nap if you can manage it.
Looks like we might actually make it off this planet after all!

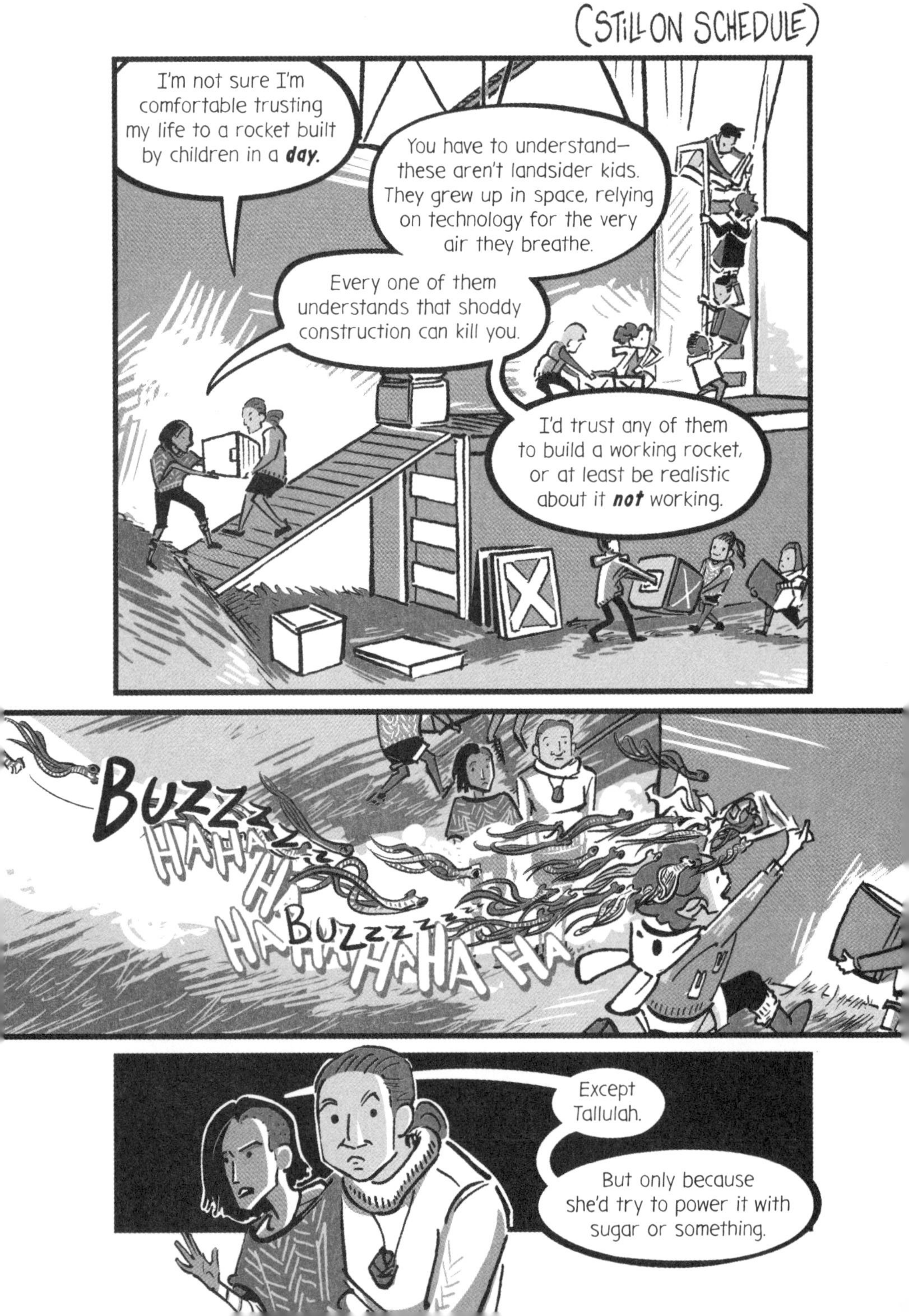
(STILL ON SCHEDULE)
I'm not sure I'm comfortable trusting my life to a rocket built by children in a **day.**
You have to understand— these aren't landsider kids. They grew up in space, relying on technology for the very air they breathe.
Every one of them understands that shoddy construction can kill you.
I'd trust any of them to build a working rocket, or at least be realistic about it **not** working.
BUZZZZ
HAHAH
BUZZZZZZ
HAHAHAHAHA HA
Except Tallulah.
But only because she'd try to power it with sugar or something.

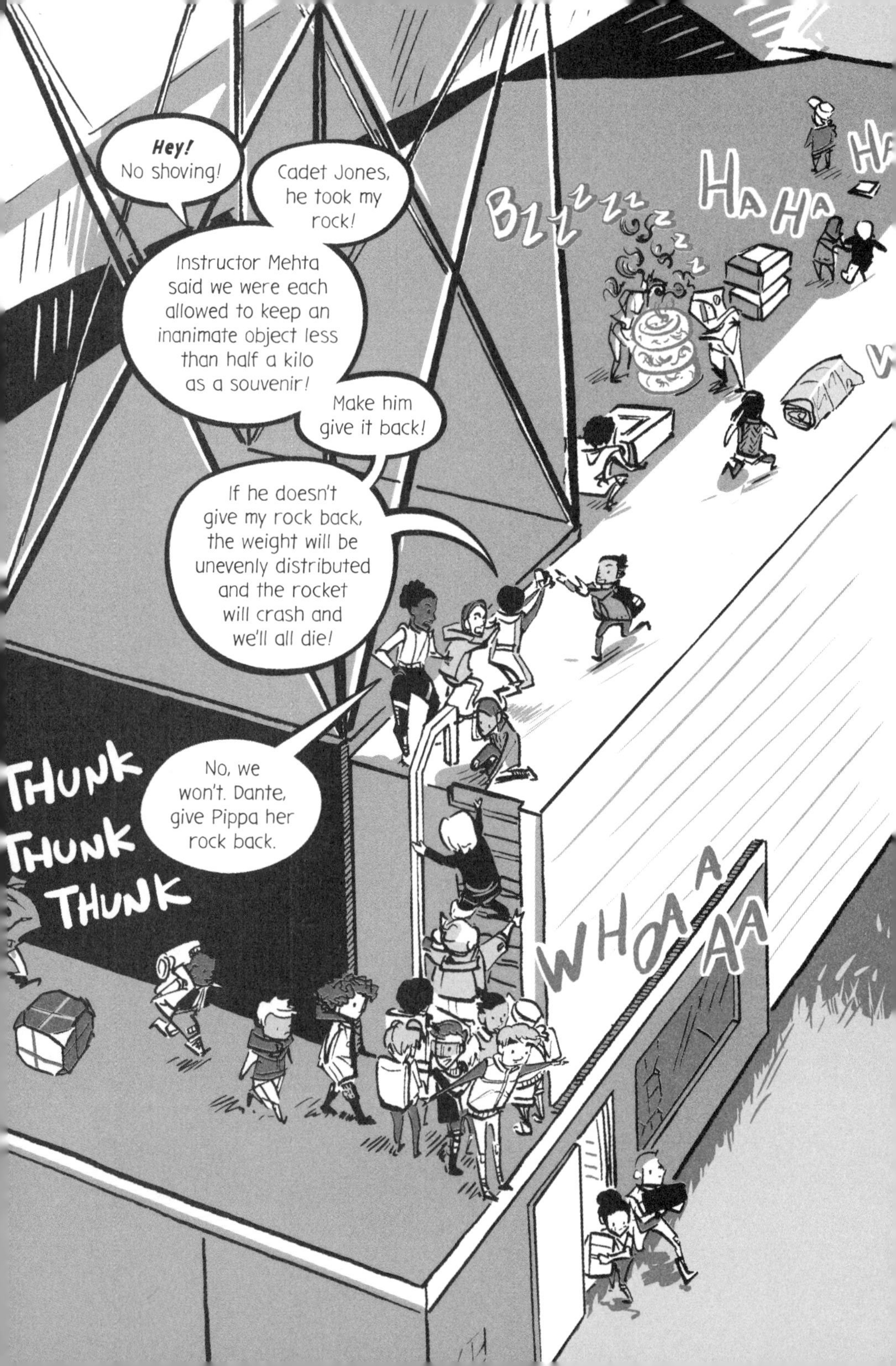

**Hey!** No shoving!
Cadet Jones, he took my rock!
Instructor Mehta said we were each allowed to keep an inanimate object less than half a kilo as a souvenir!
Make him give it back!
If he doesn't give my rock back, the weight will be unevenly distributed and the rocket will crash and we'll all die!
No, we won't. Dante, give Pippa her rock back.
BZZZZZZZZ
HA HA HA
THUNK THUNK THUNK
WHOAAAA

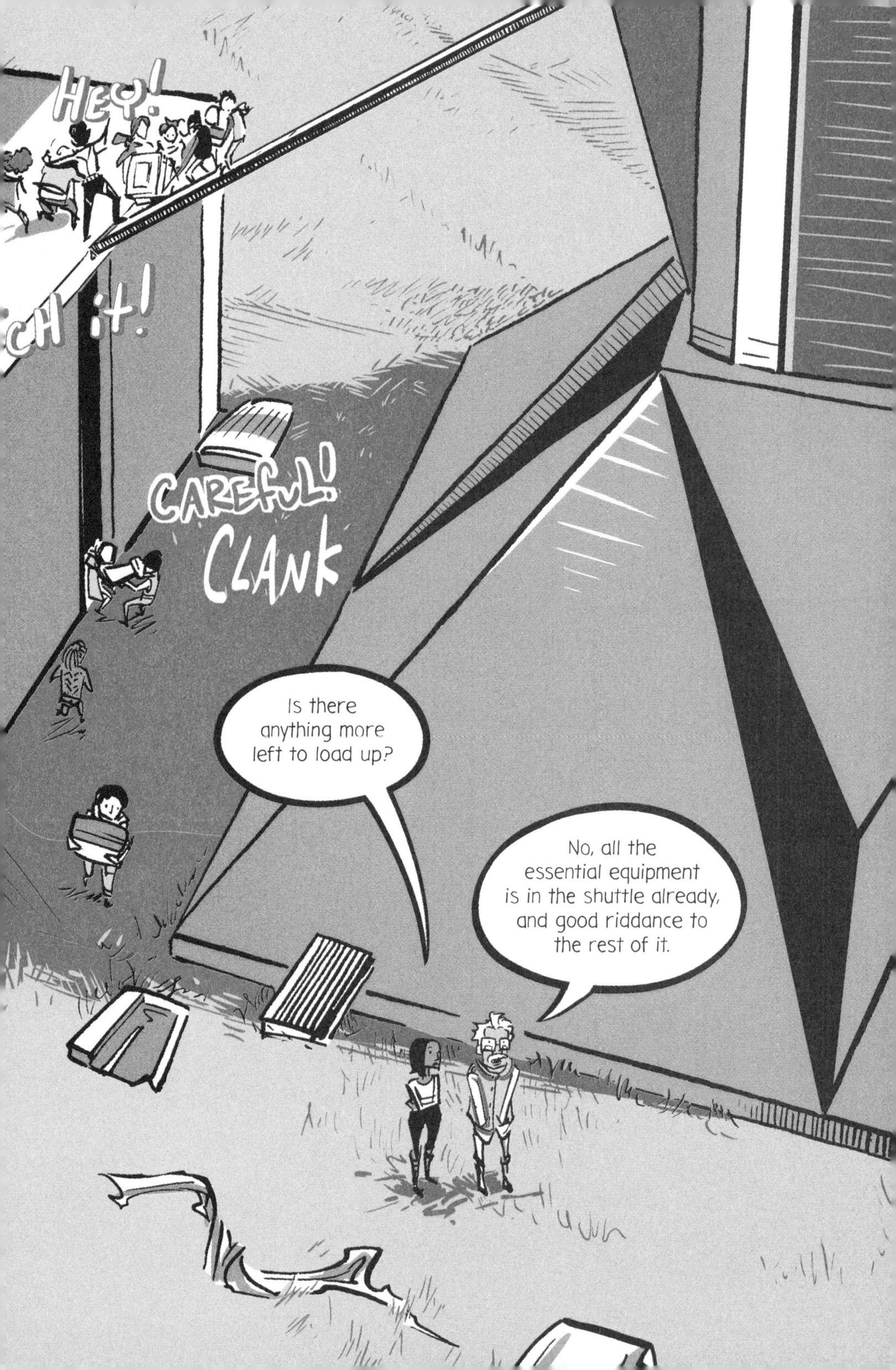
HEY!
CH it!
CAREFUL!
CLANK
Is there anything more left to load up?
No, all the essential equipment is in the shuttle already, and good riddance to the rest of it.

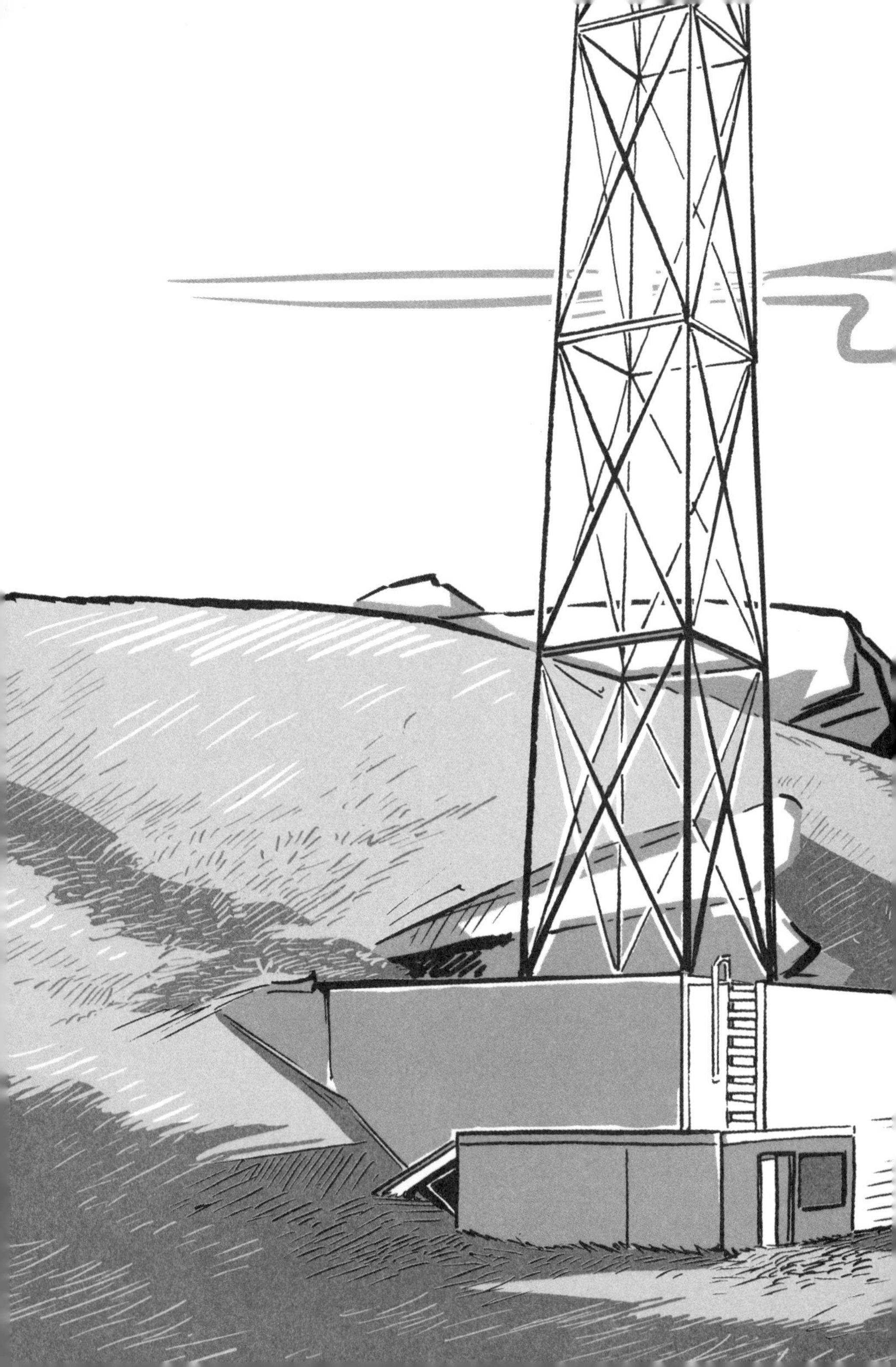

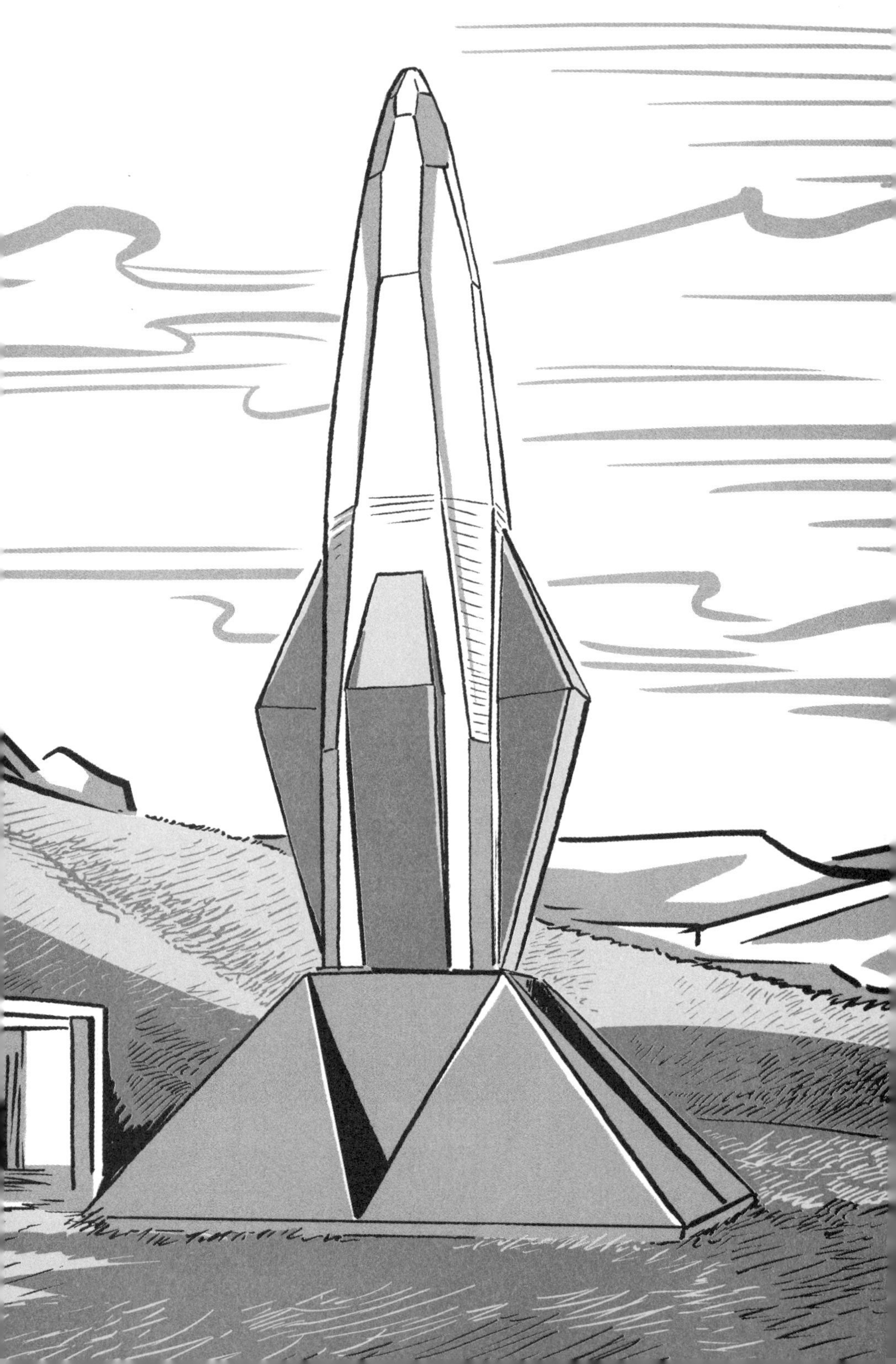

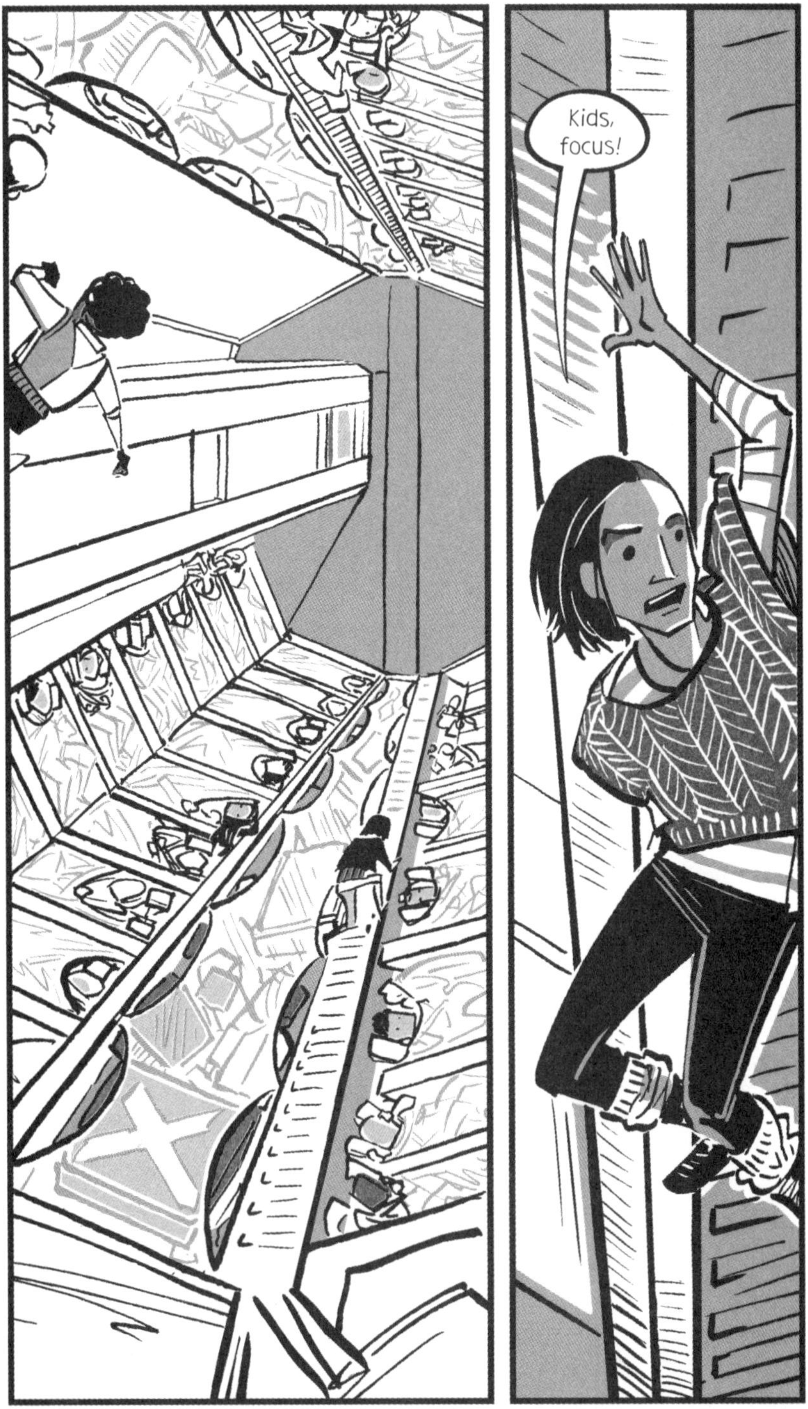
Kids,
focus!

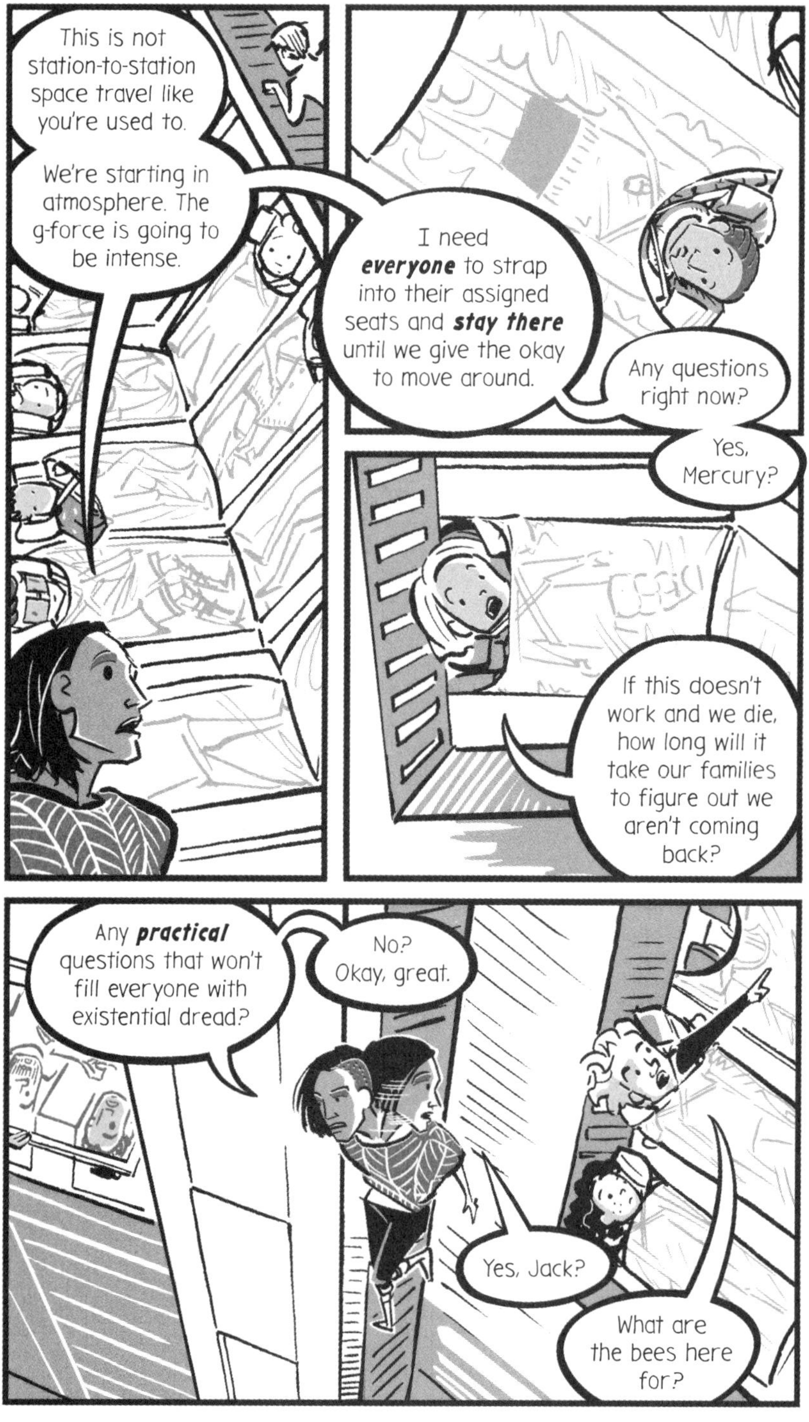

This is not station-to-station space travel like you're used to.
We're starting in atmosphere. The g-force is going to be intense.
I need **everyone** to strap into their assigned seats and **stay there** until we give the okay to move around.
Any questions right now?
Yes, Mercury?
If this doesn't work and we die, how long will it take our families to figure out we aren't coming back?
Any **practical** questions that won't fill everyone with existential dread?
No? Okay, great.
Yes, Jack?
What are the bees here for?

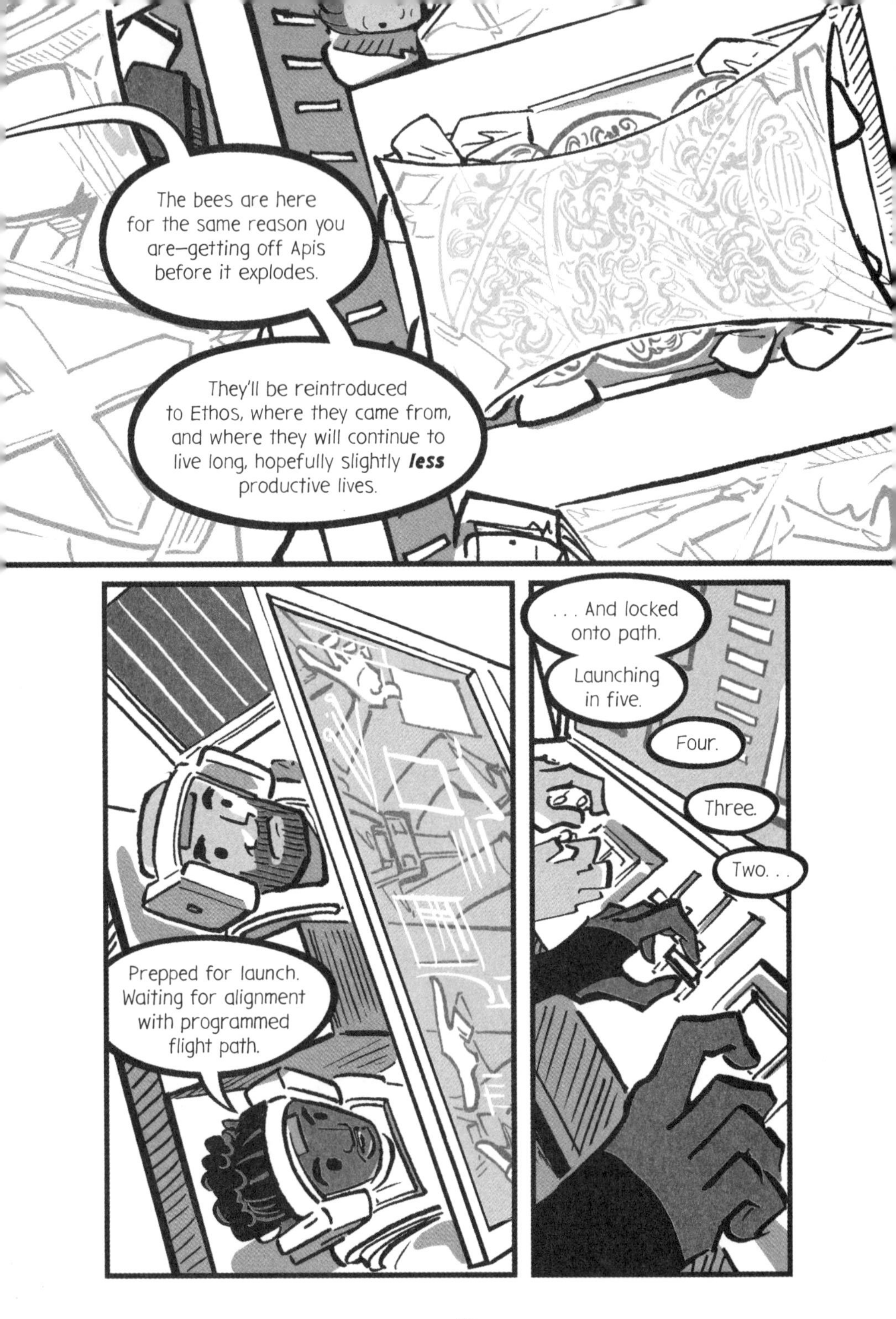
The bees are here for the same reason you are—getting off Apis before it explodes.
They'll be reintroduced to Ethos, where they came from, and where they will continue to live long, hopefully slightly ***less*** productive lives.
Prepped for launch. Waiting for alignment with programmed flight path.
. . . And locked onto path.
Launching in five.
Four.
Three.
Two. . .

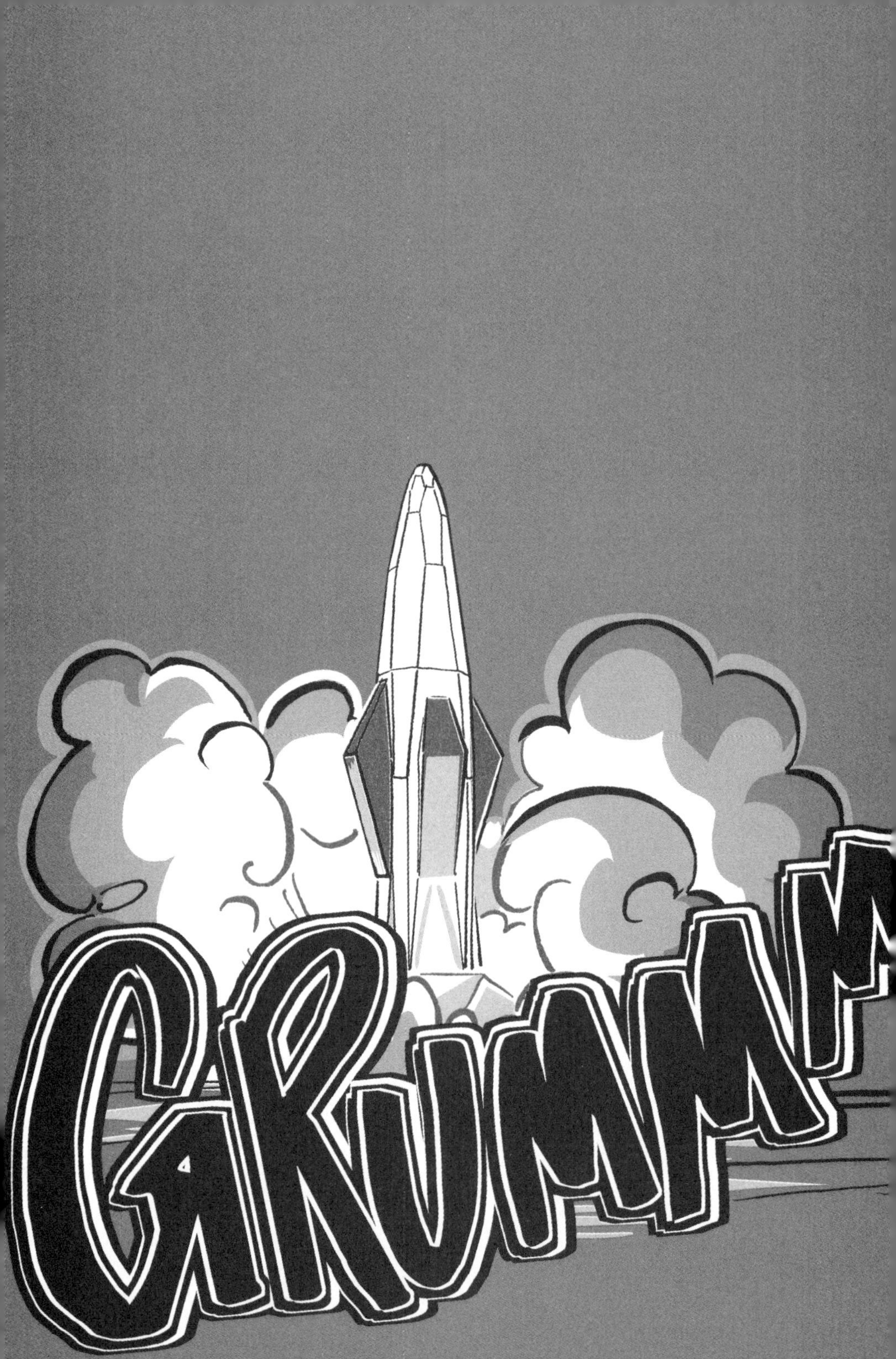
GaRUMMMM

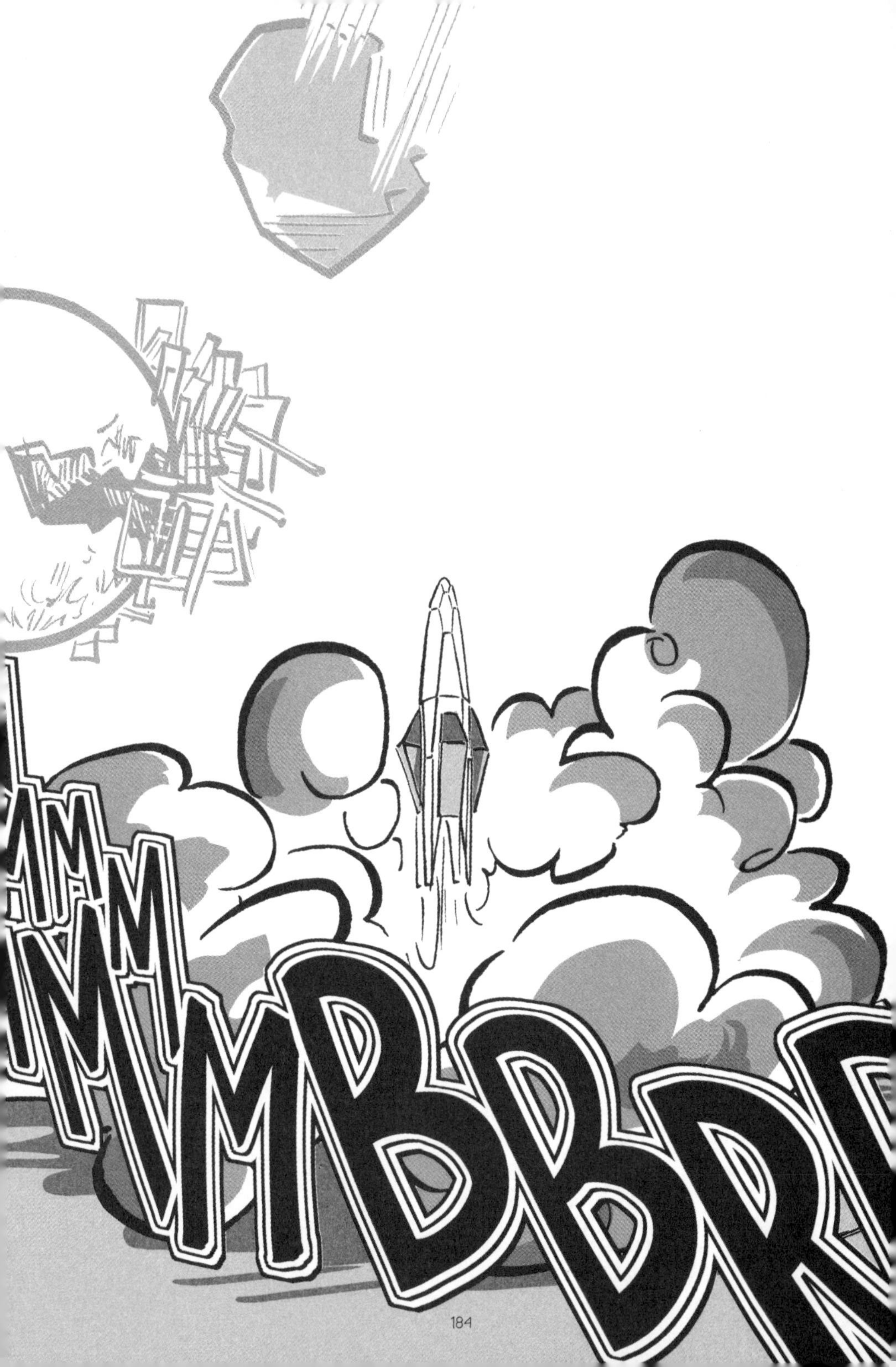

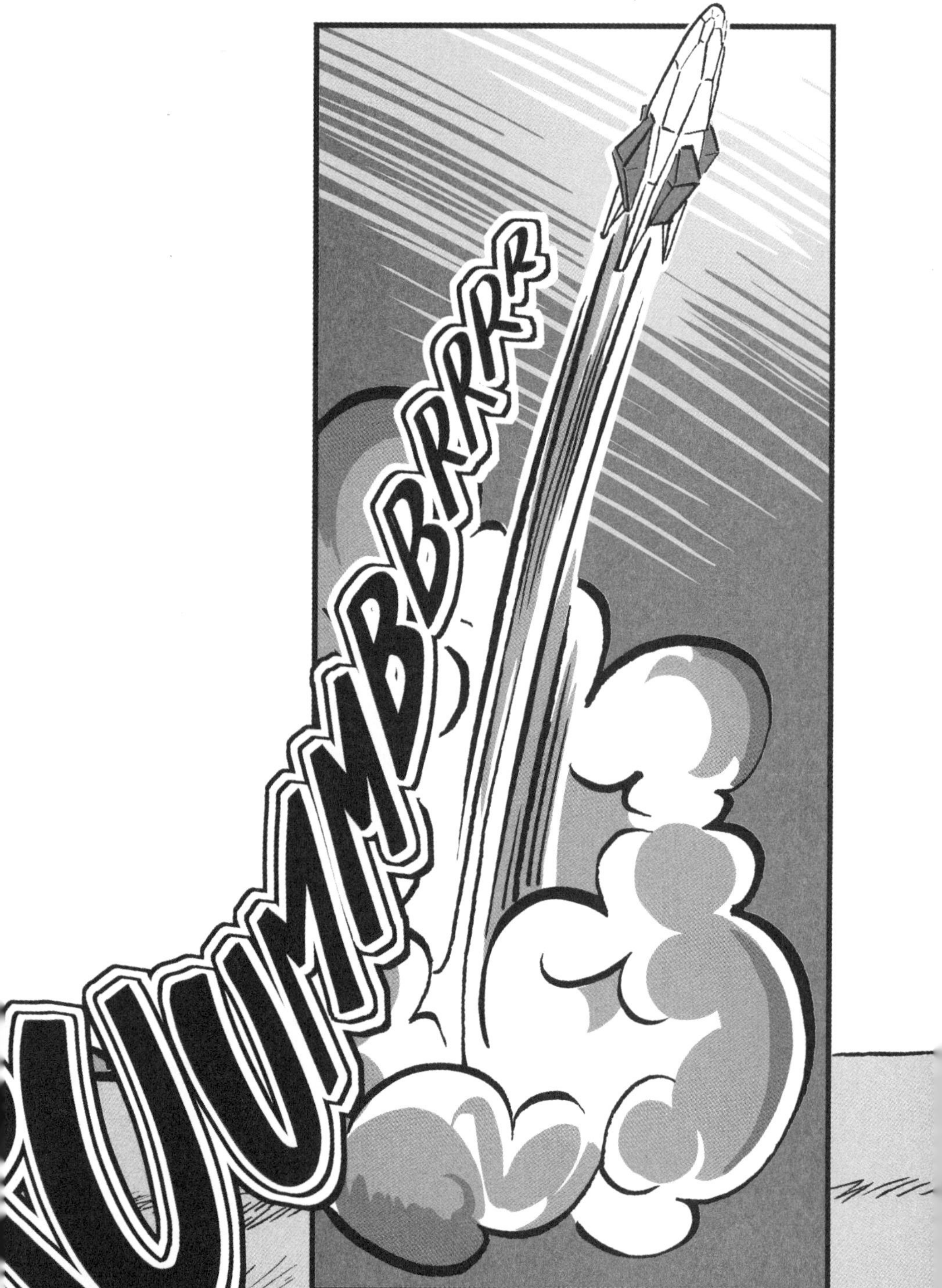
UUMMBBRRRR

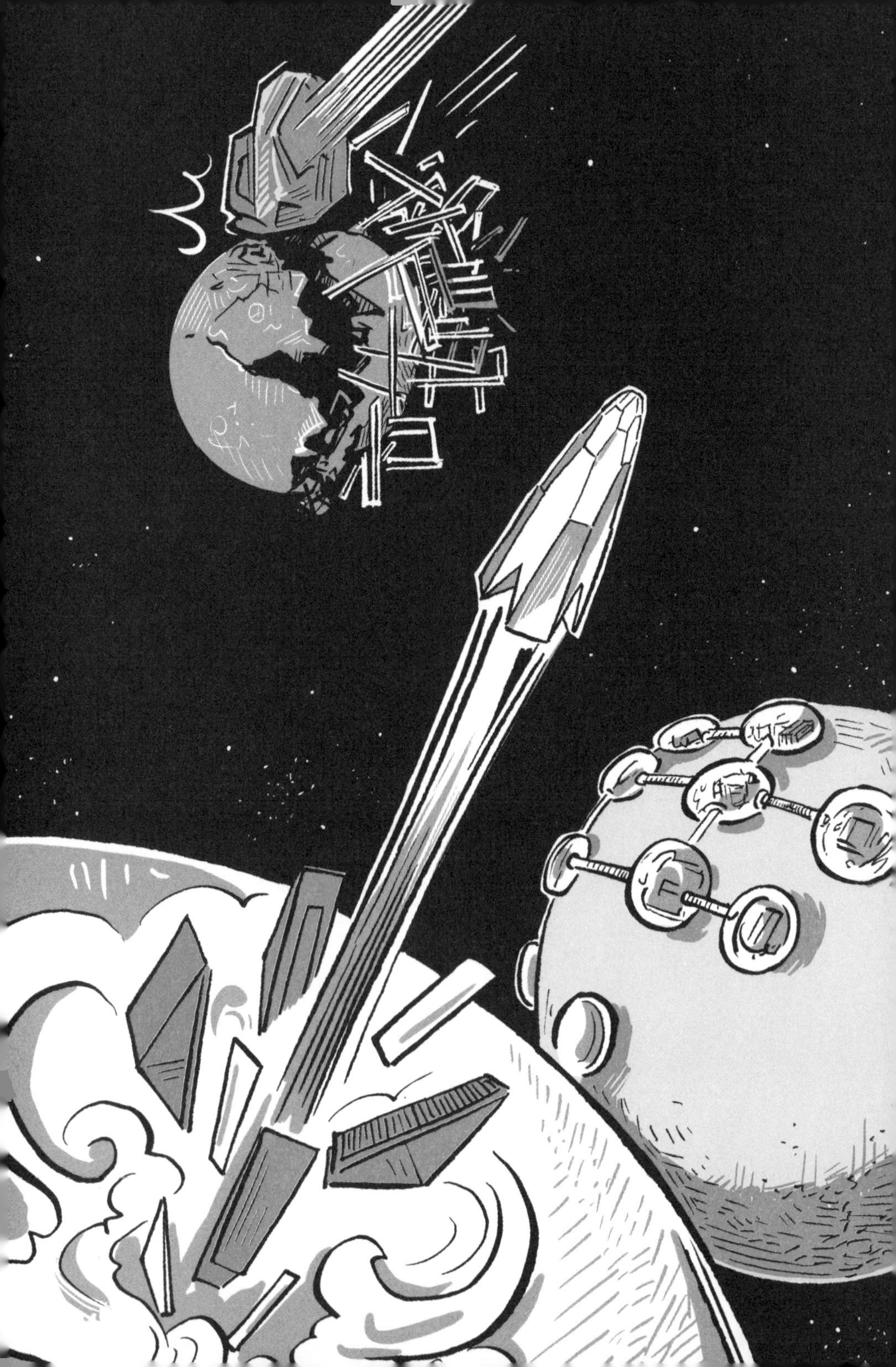

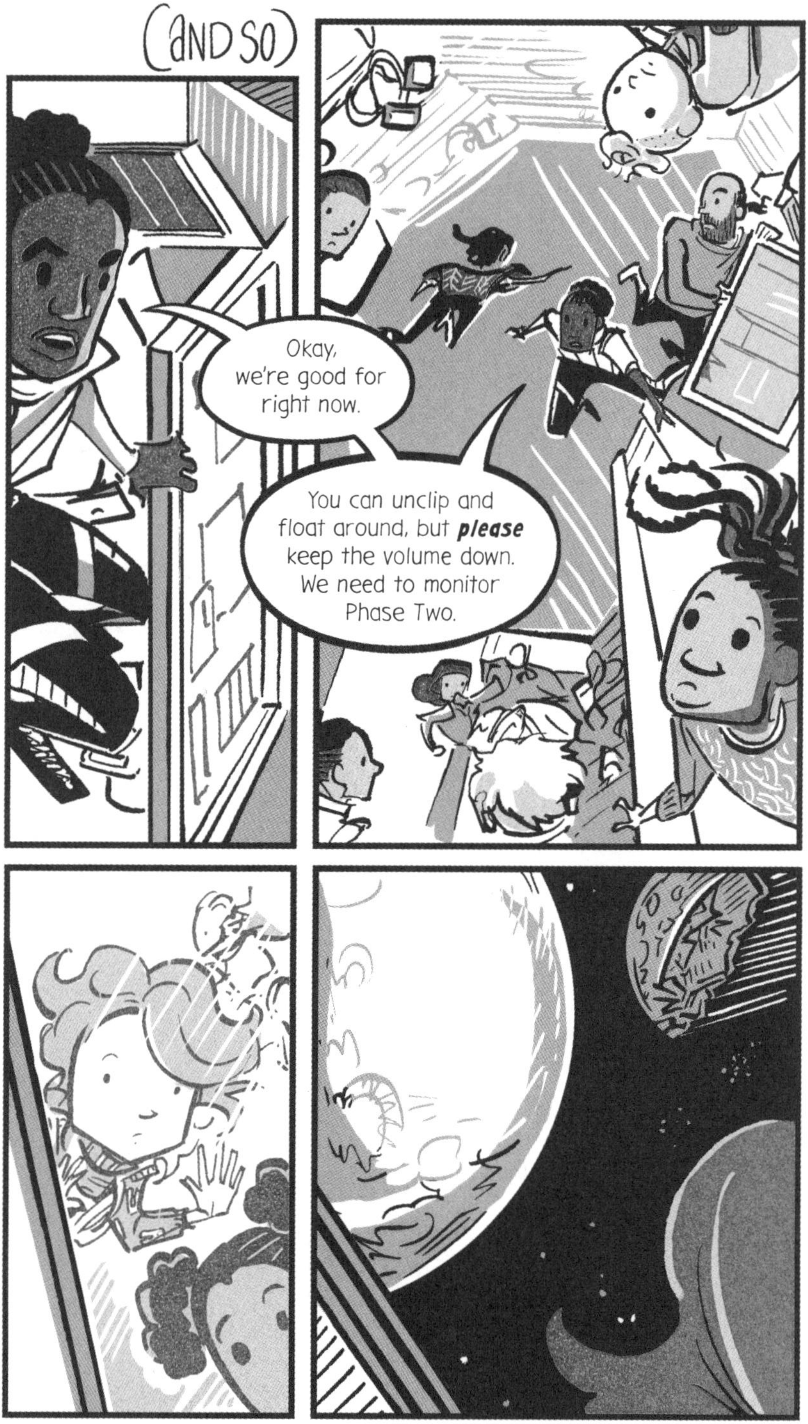
(and so)
Okay, we're good for right now.
You can unclip and float around, but ***please*** keep the volume down. We need to monitor Phase Two.

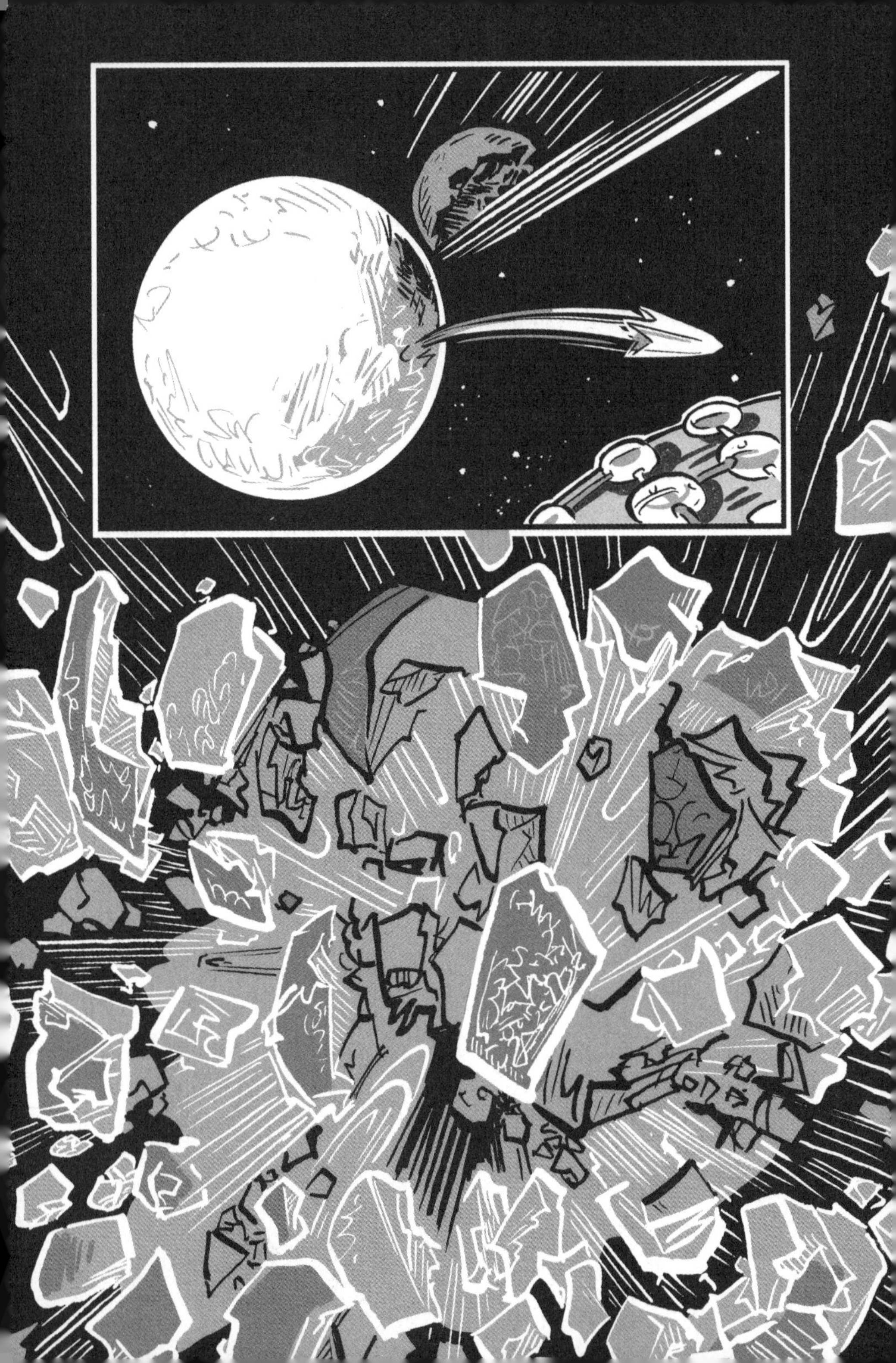

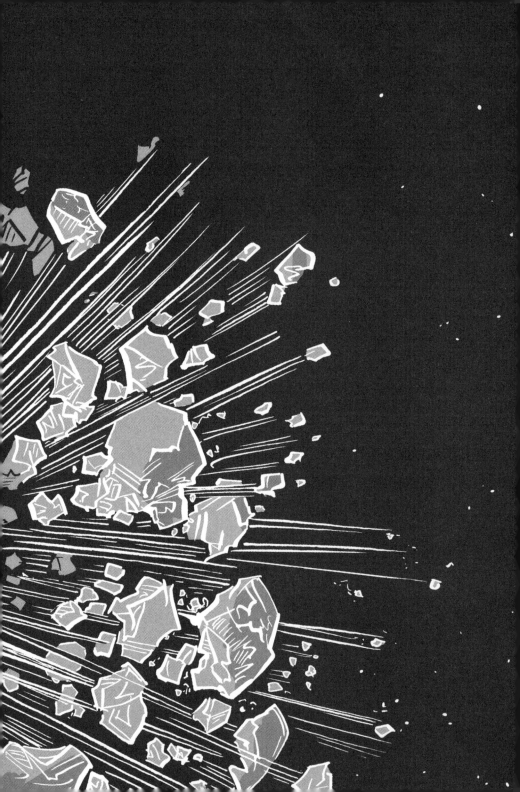

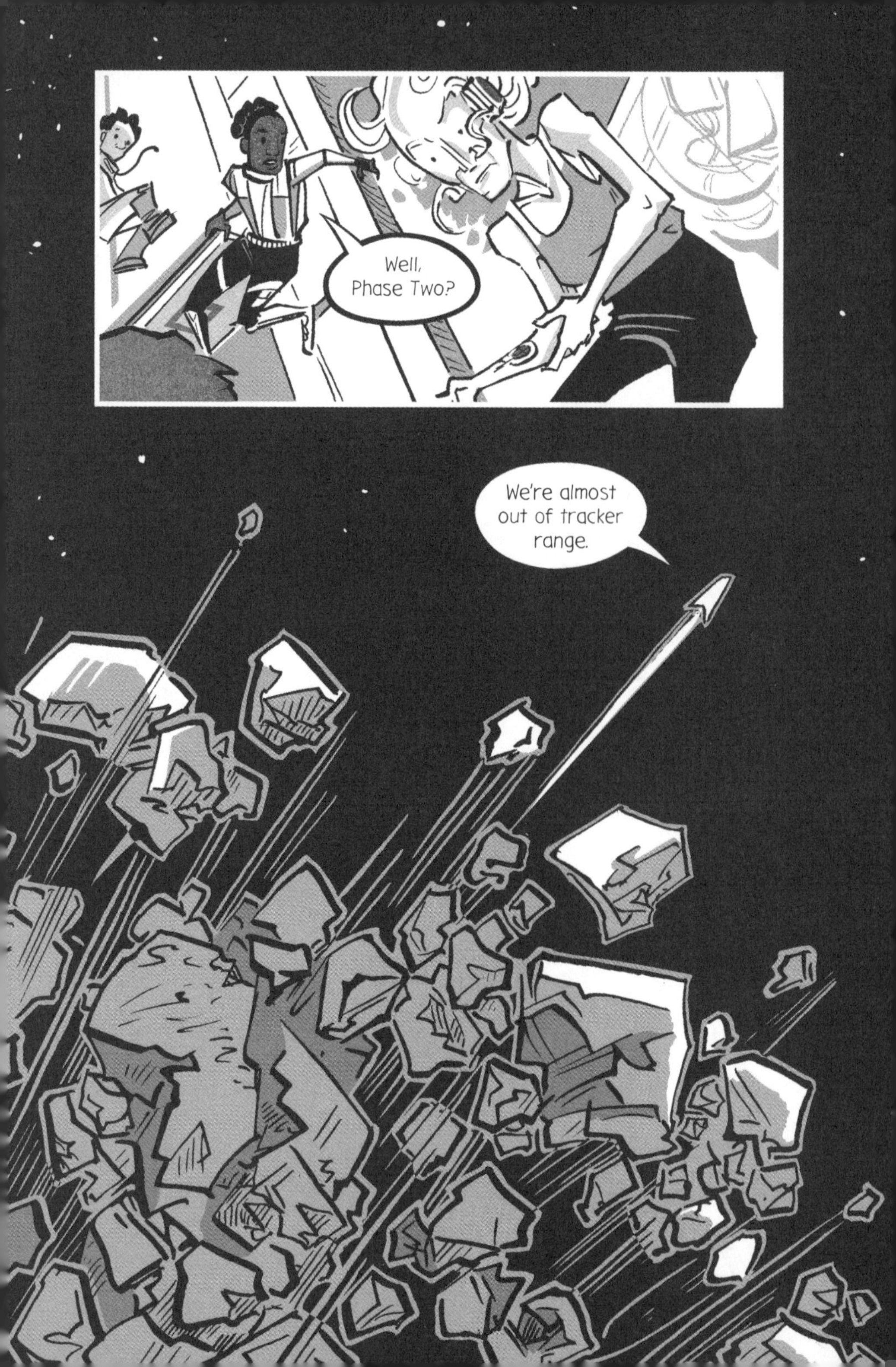
Well, Phase Two?
We're almost out of tracker range.

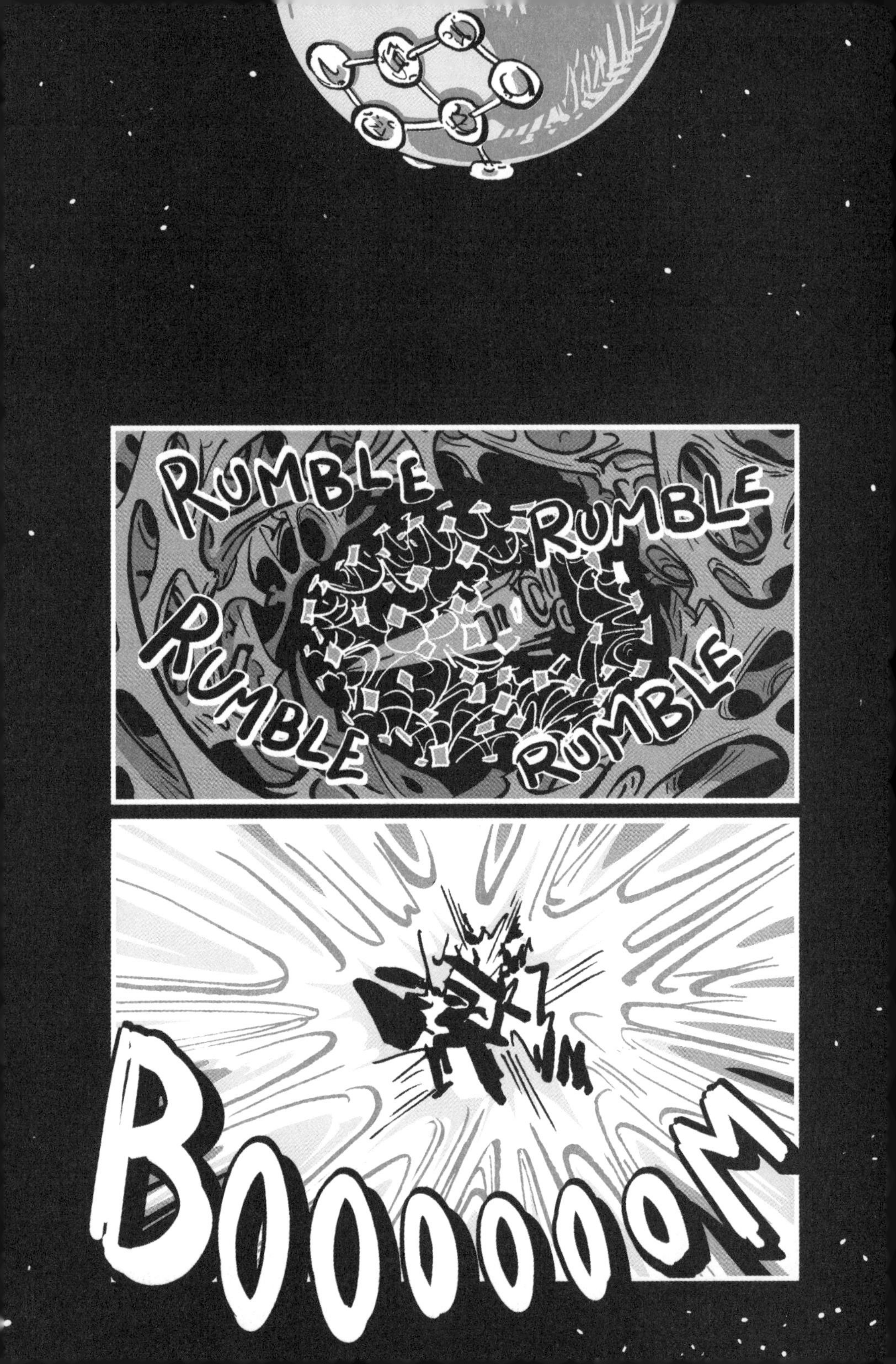
RUMBLE
RUMBLE
RUMBLE
RUMBLE
RUMBLE
BOOOOOOM

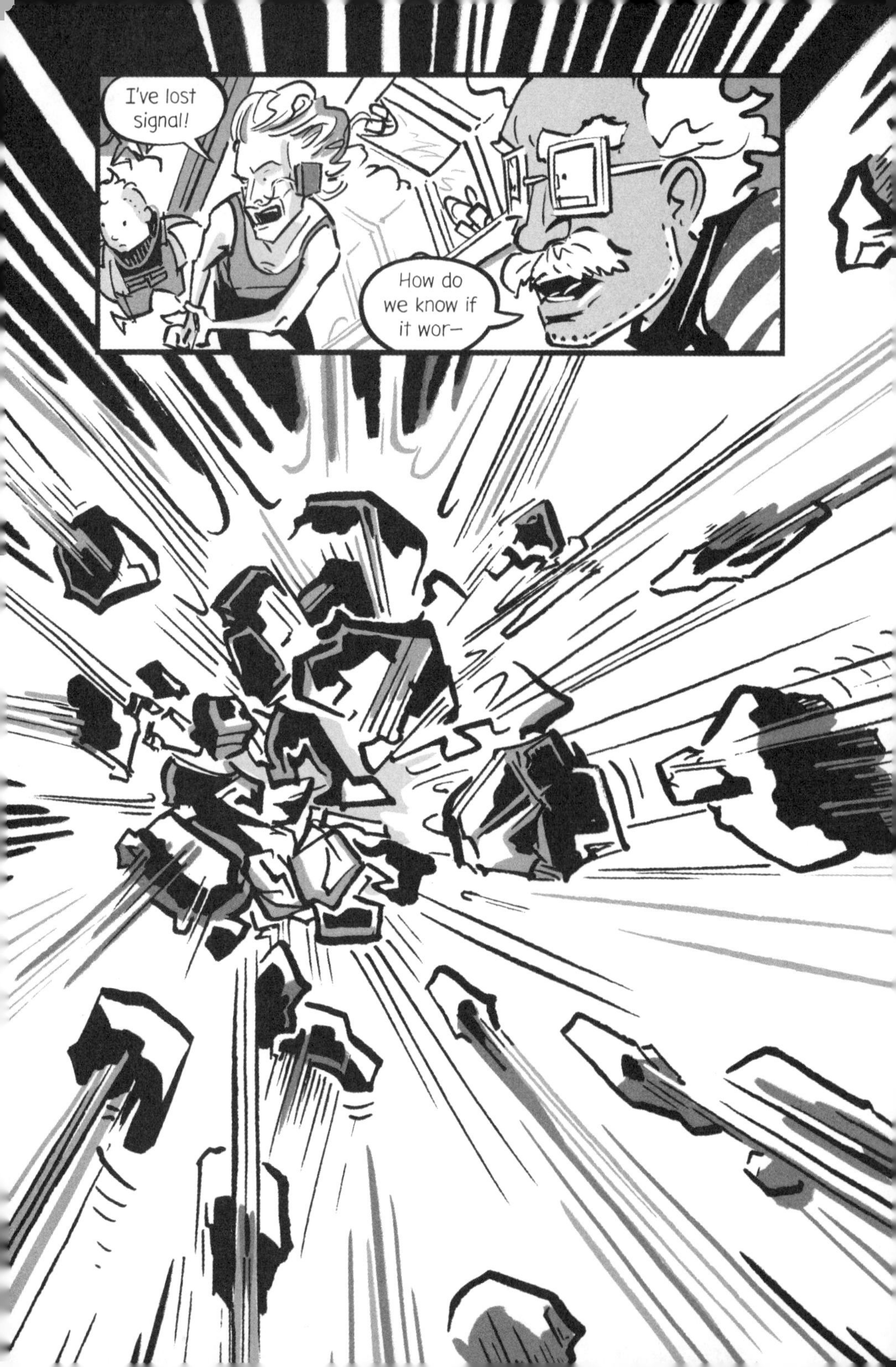
I've lost signal!
How do we know if it wor—

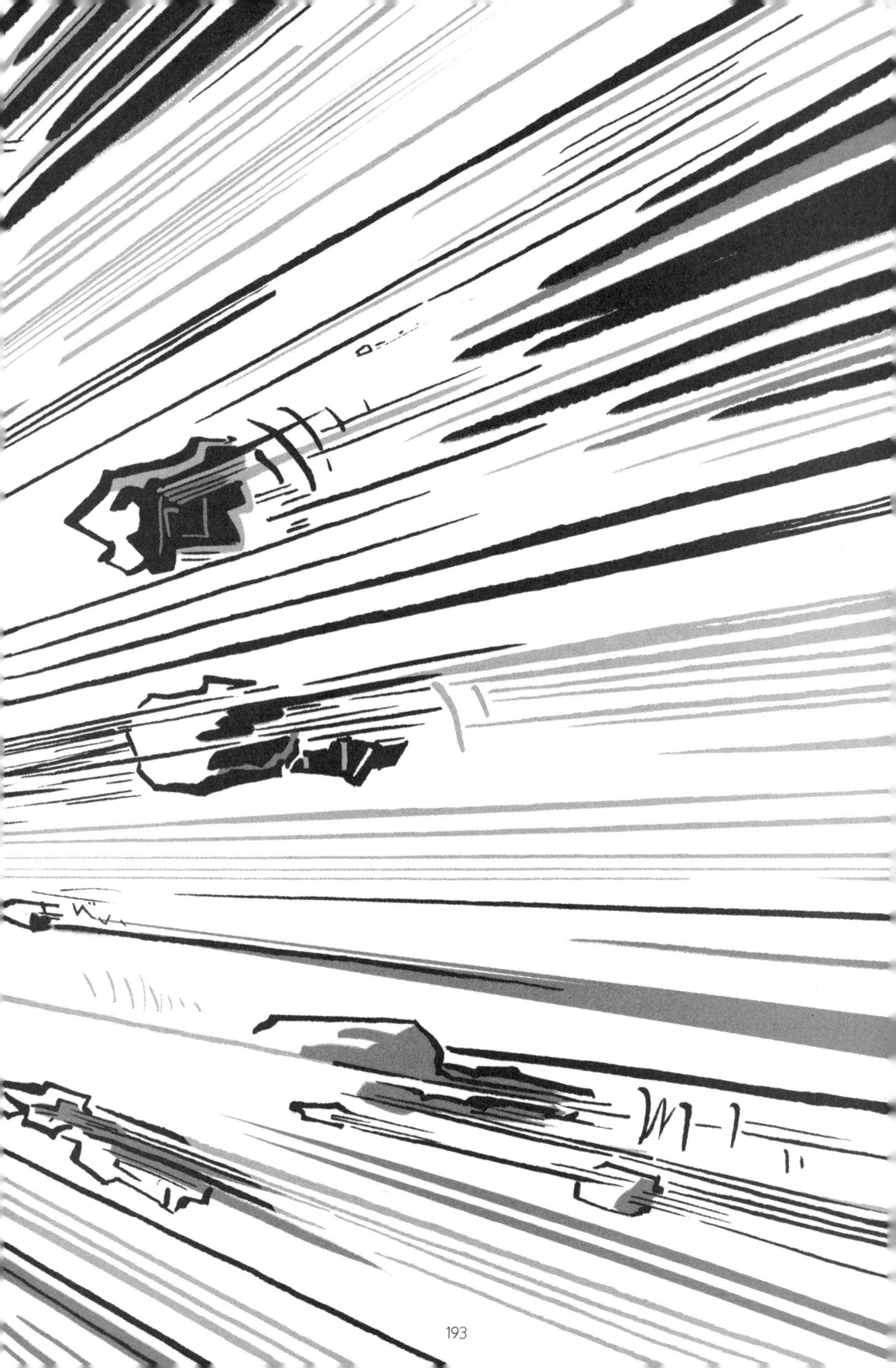

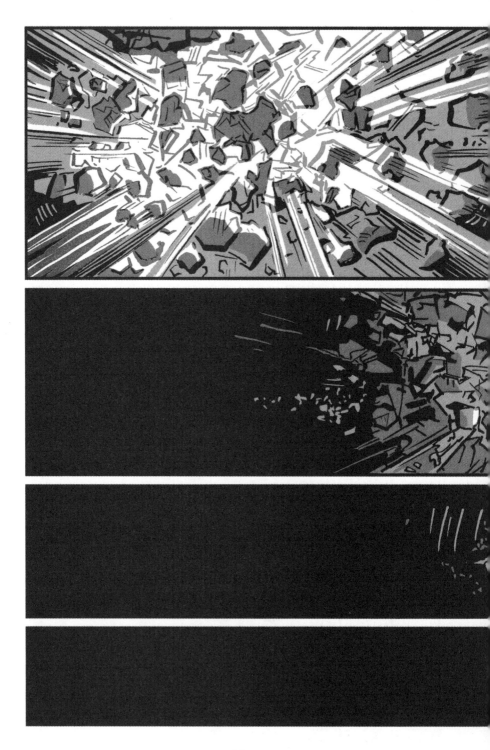

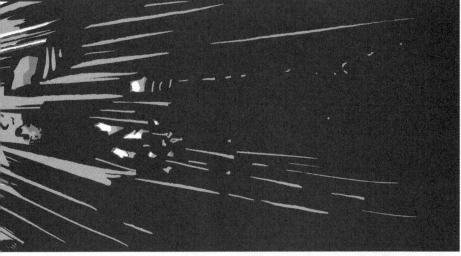

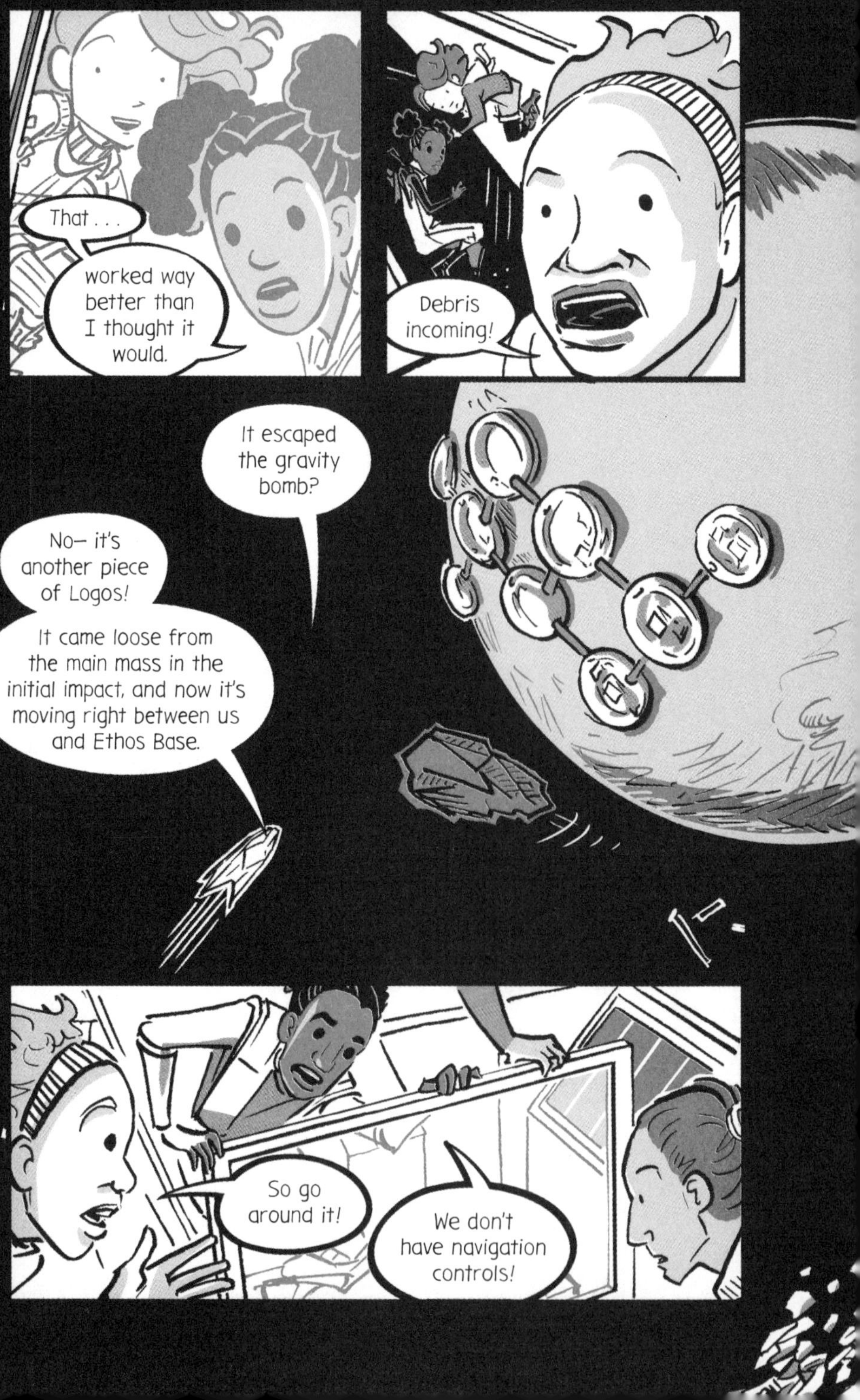

That . . .
worked way better than I thought it would.
Debris incoming!
It escaped the gravity bomb?
No— it's another piece of Logos!
It came loose from the main mass in the initial impact, and now it's moving right between us and Ethos Base.
So go around it!
We don't have navigation controls!

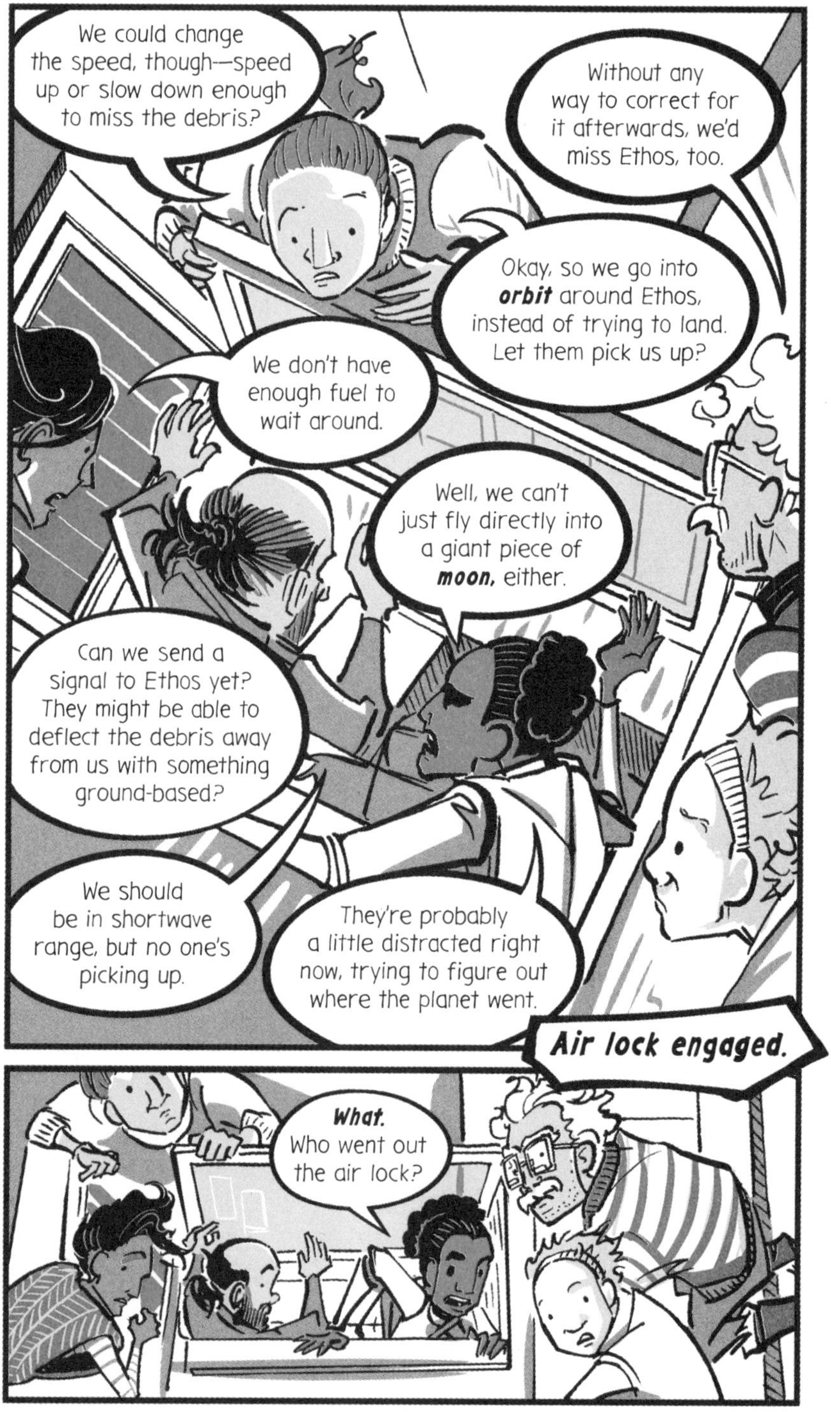
We could change the speed, though—speed up or slow down enough to miss the debris?
Without any way to correct for it afterwards, we'd miss Ethos, too.
Okay, so we go into **orbit** around Ethos, instead of trying to land. Let them pick us up?
We don't have enough fuel to wait around.
Well, we can't just fly directly into a giant piece of **moon,** either.
Can we send a signal to Ethos yet? They might be able to deflect the debris away from us with something ground-based?
We should be in shortwave range, but no one's picking up.
They're probably a little distracted right now, trying to figure out where the planet went.
Air lock engaged.
**What.** Who went out the air lock?

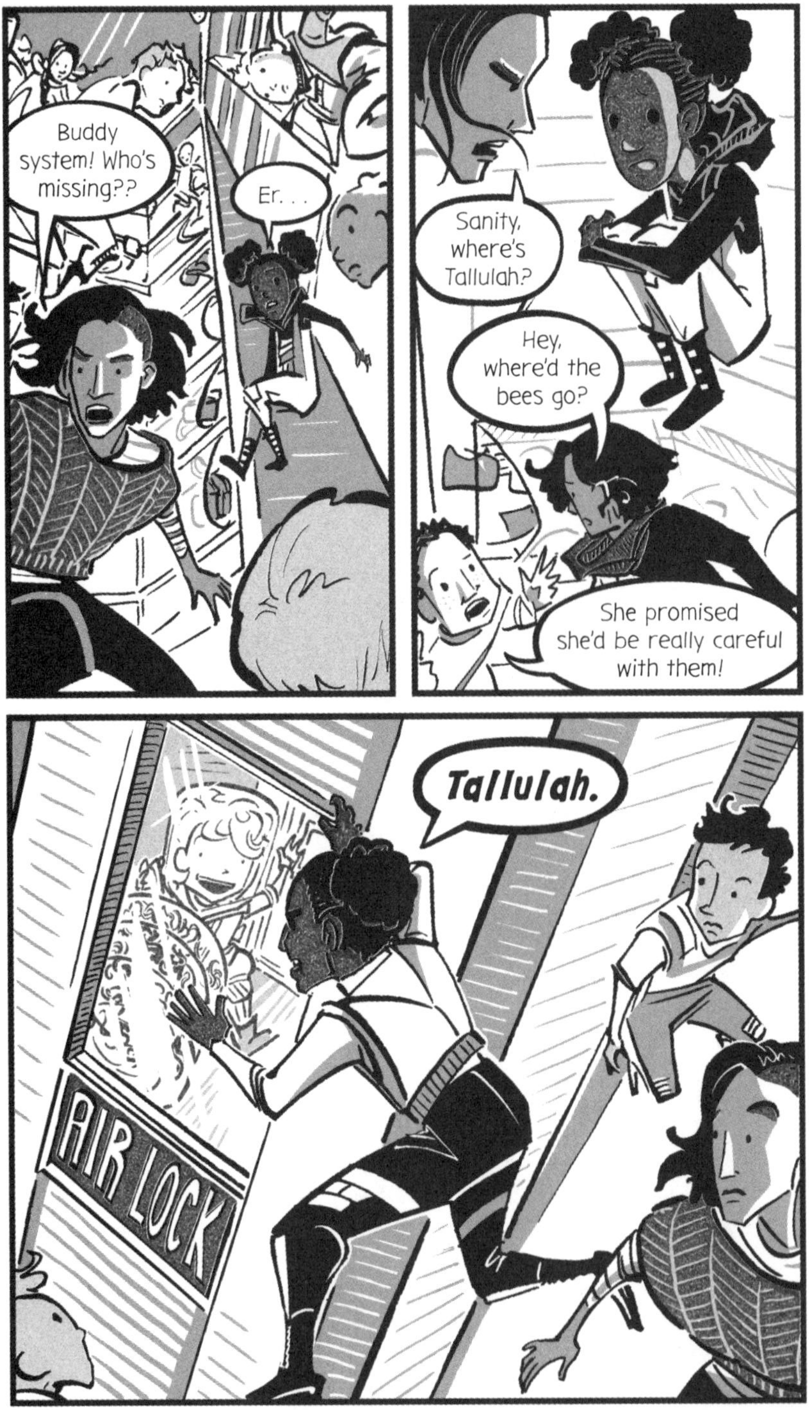

Buddy system! Who's missing??
Er. . .
Sanity, where's Tallulah?
Hey, where'd the bees go?
She promised she'd be really careful with them!
Tallulah.
AIR LOCK

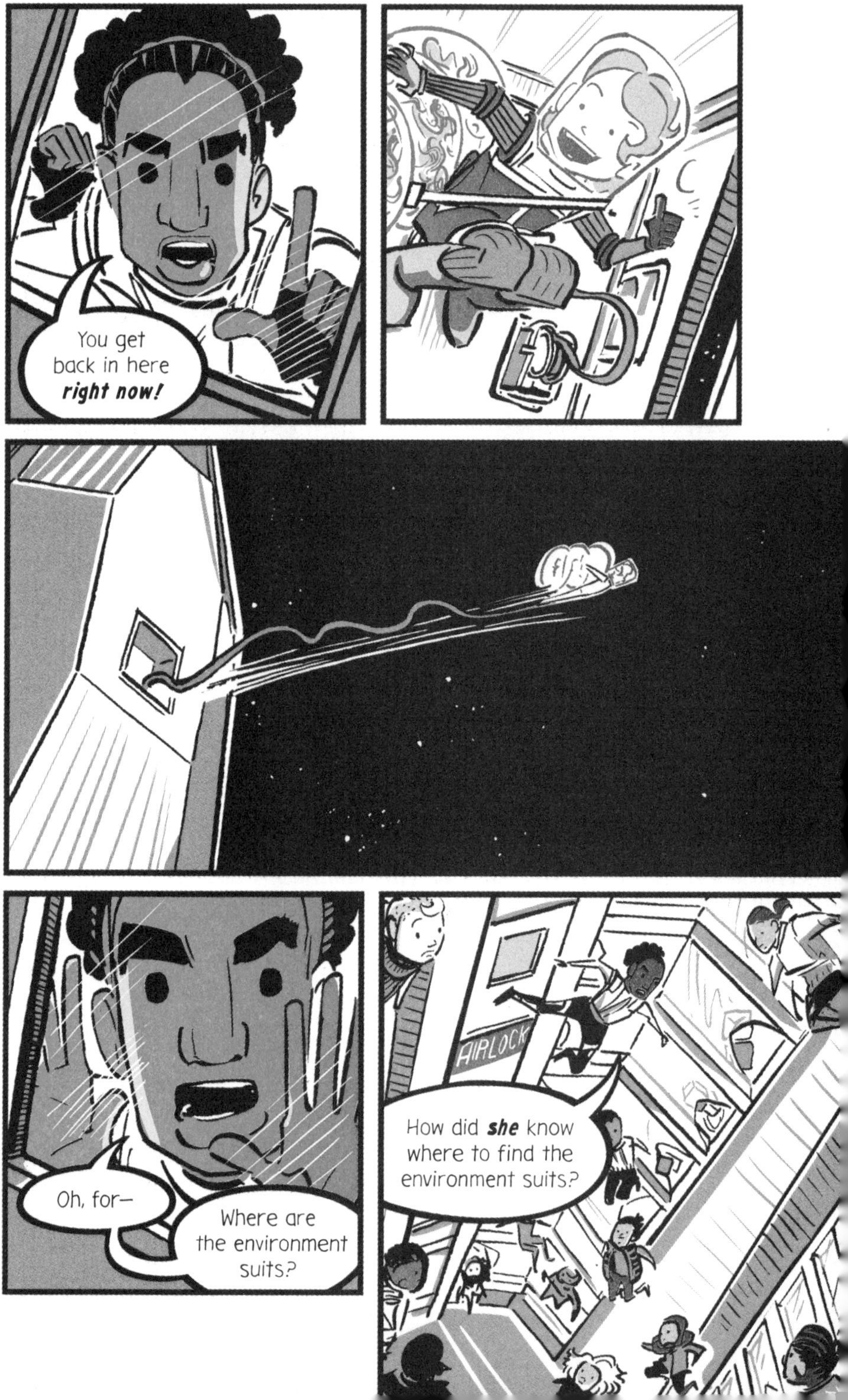
You get back in here **right now!**
AIRLOCK
Oh, for—
Where are the environment suits?
How did **she** know where to find the environment suits?

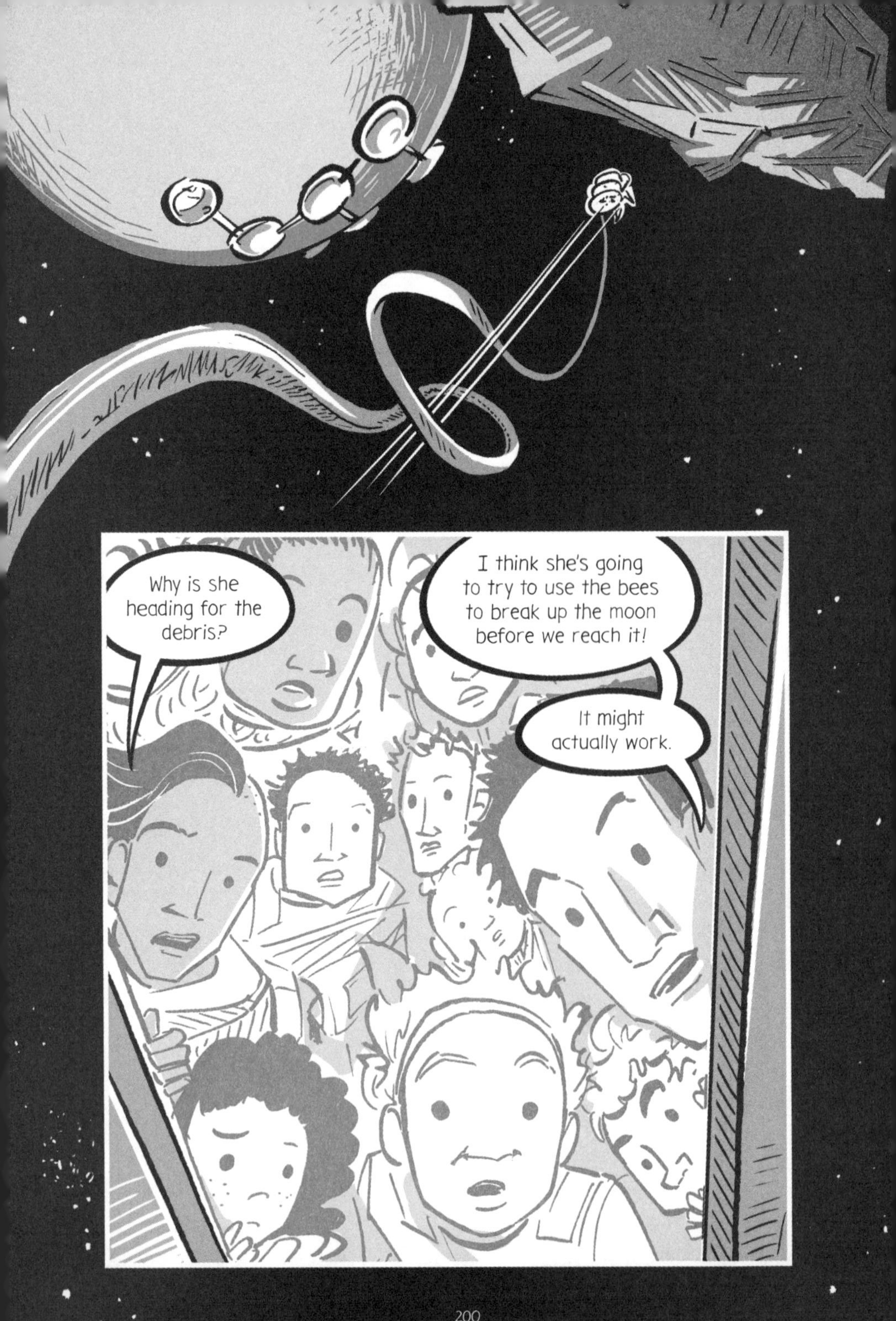
Why is she heading for the debris?
I think she's going to try to use the bees to break up the moon before we reach it!
It might actually work.

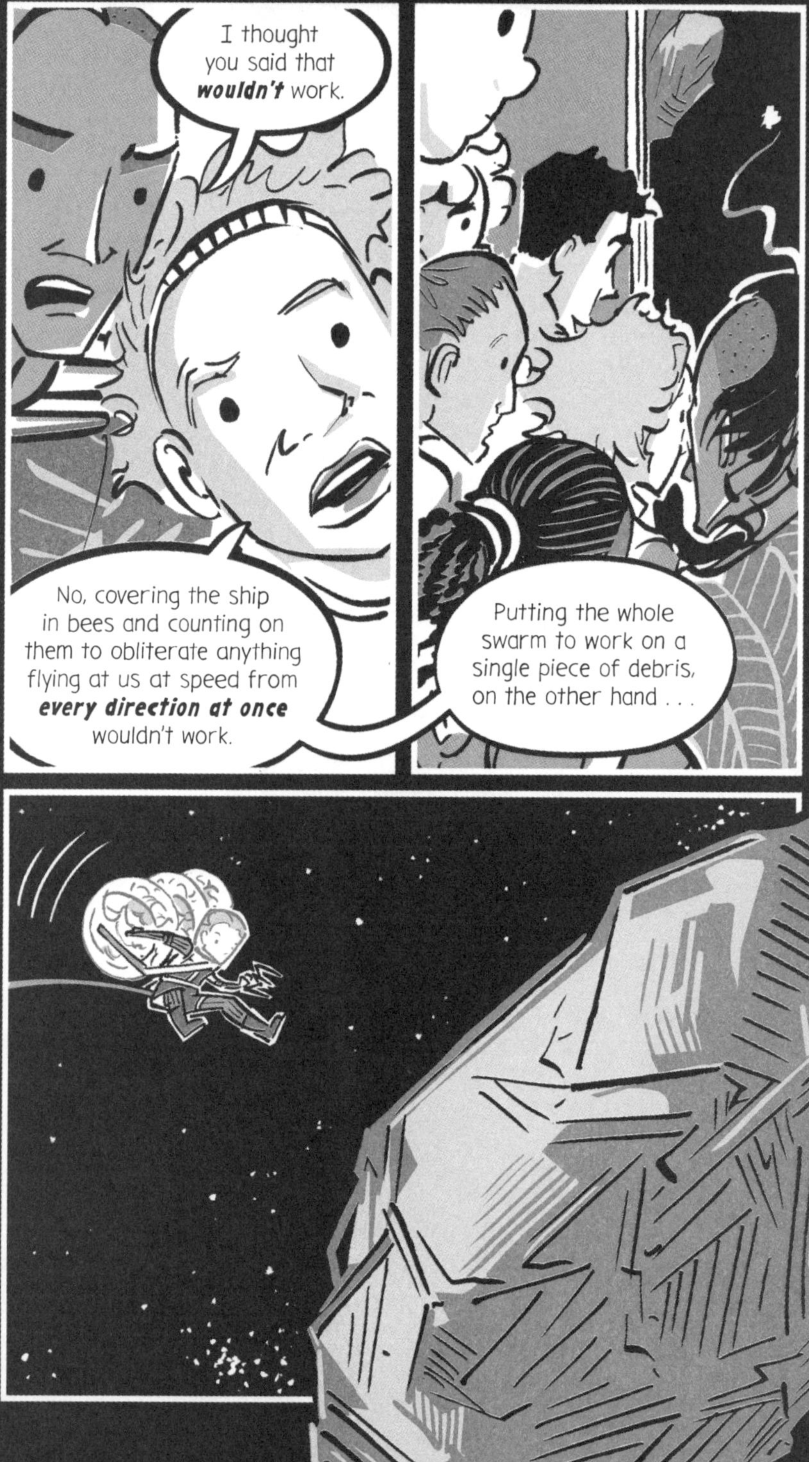
I thought you said that ***wouldn't*** work.
No, covering the ship in bees and counting on them to obliterate anything flying at us at speed from ***every direction at once*** wouldn't work.
Putting the whole swarm to work on a single piece of debris, on the other hand . . .

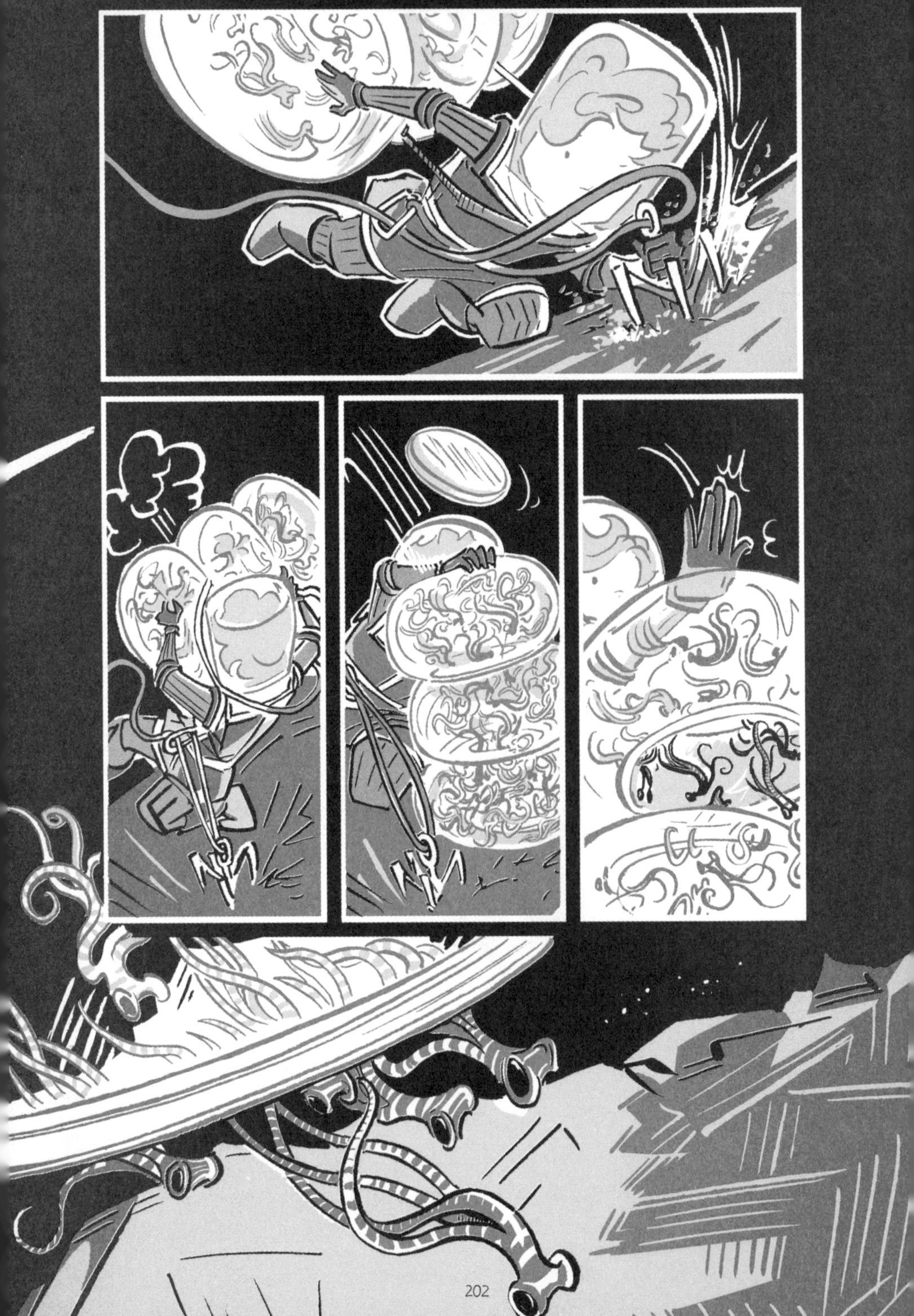

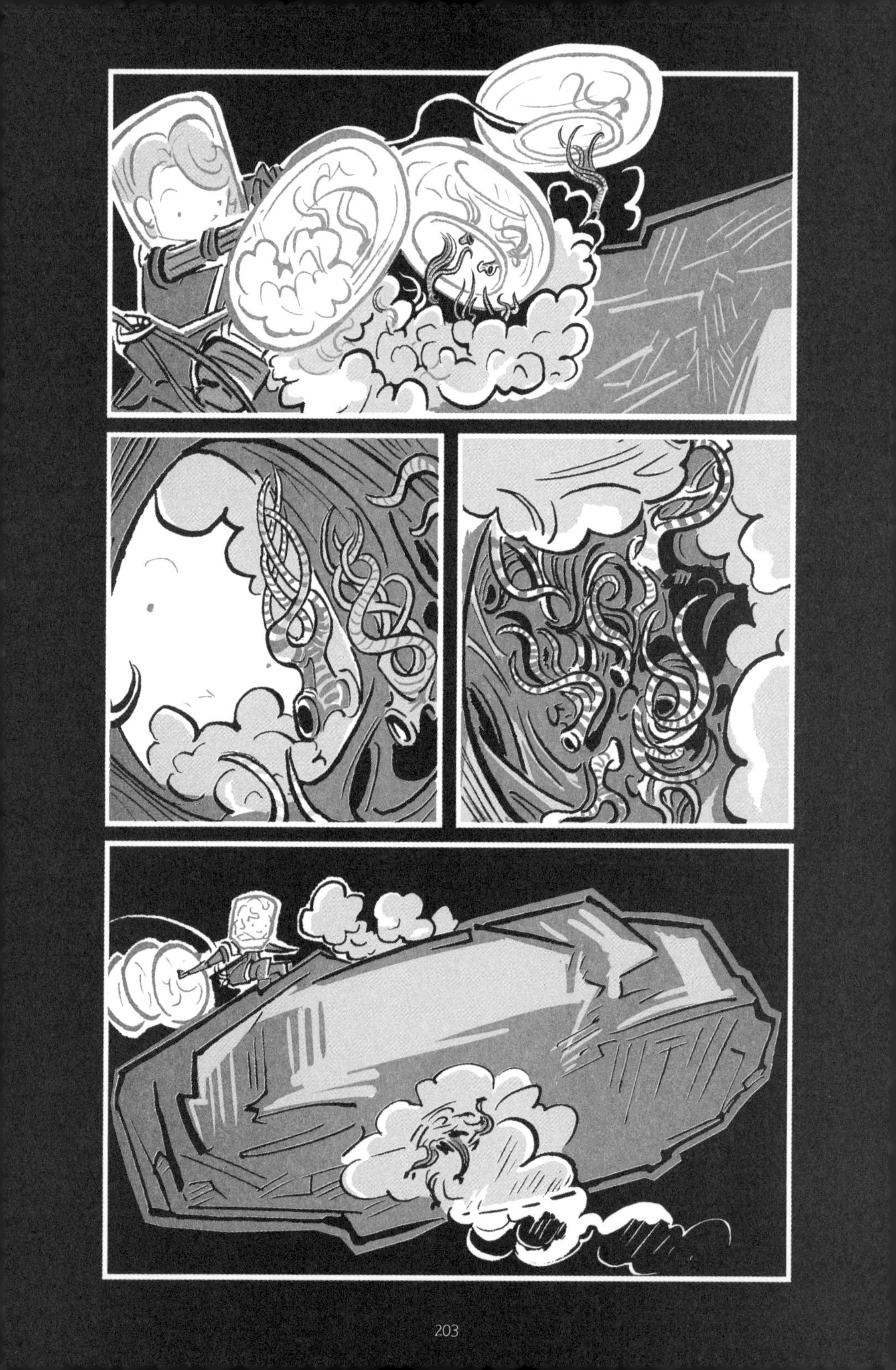

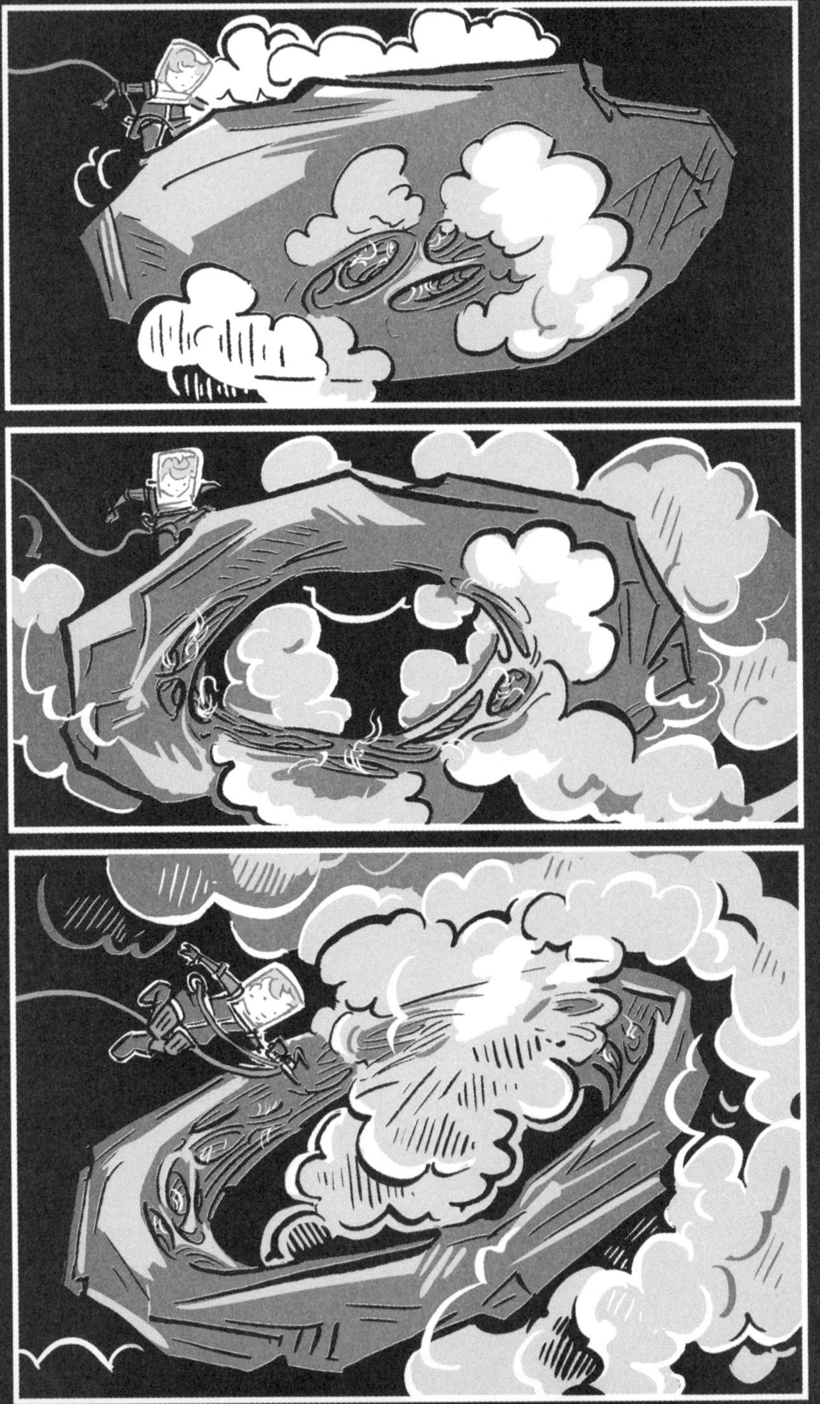

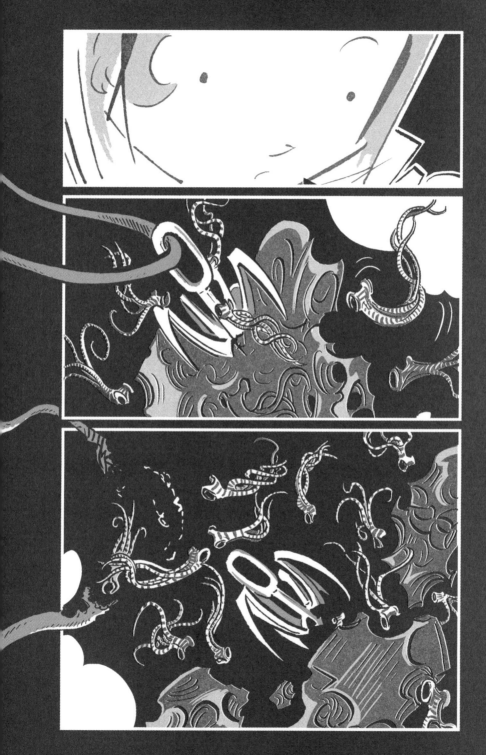

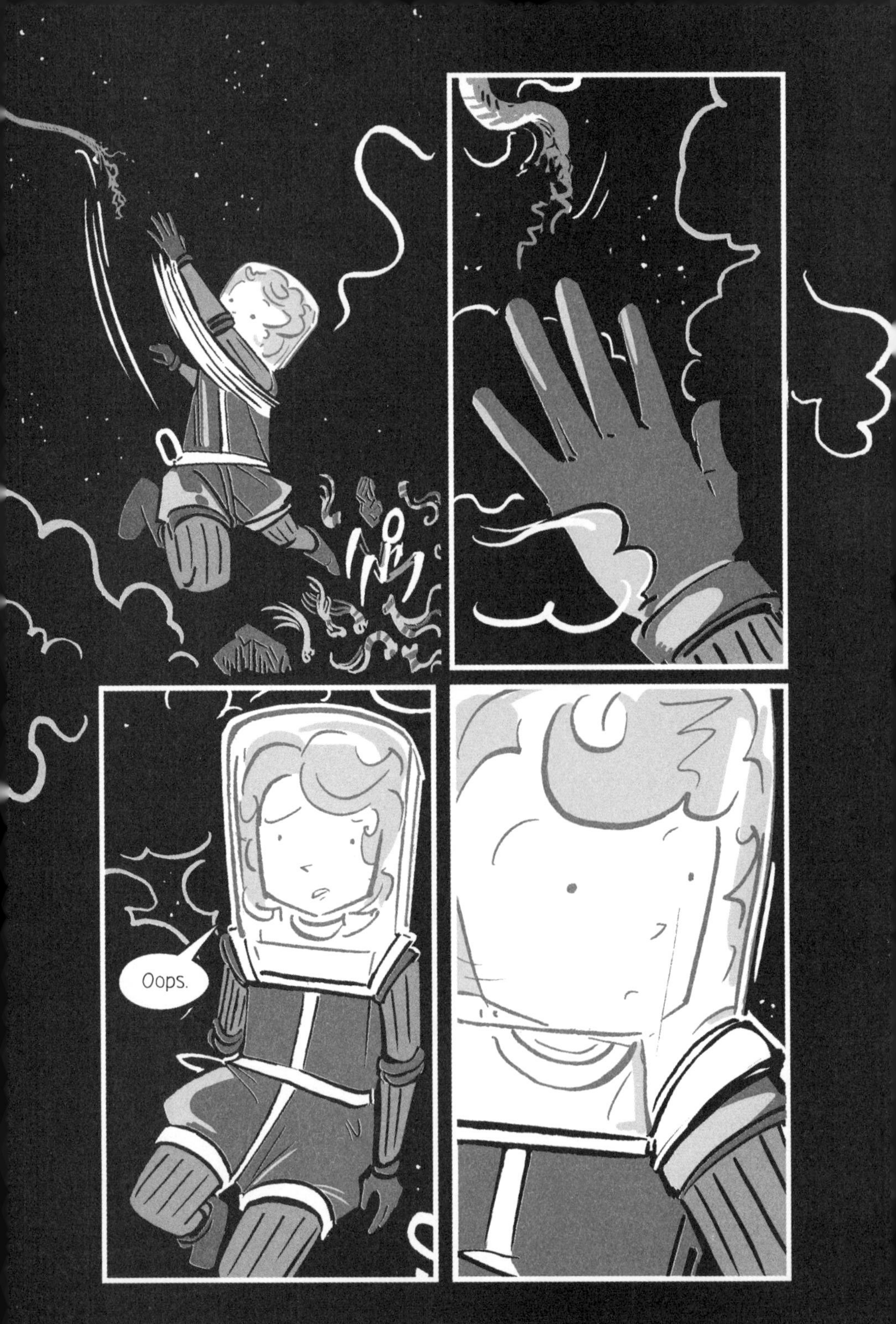
Oops.

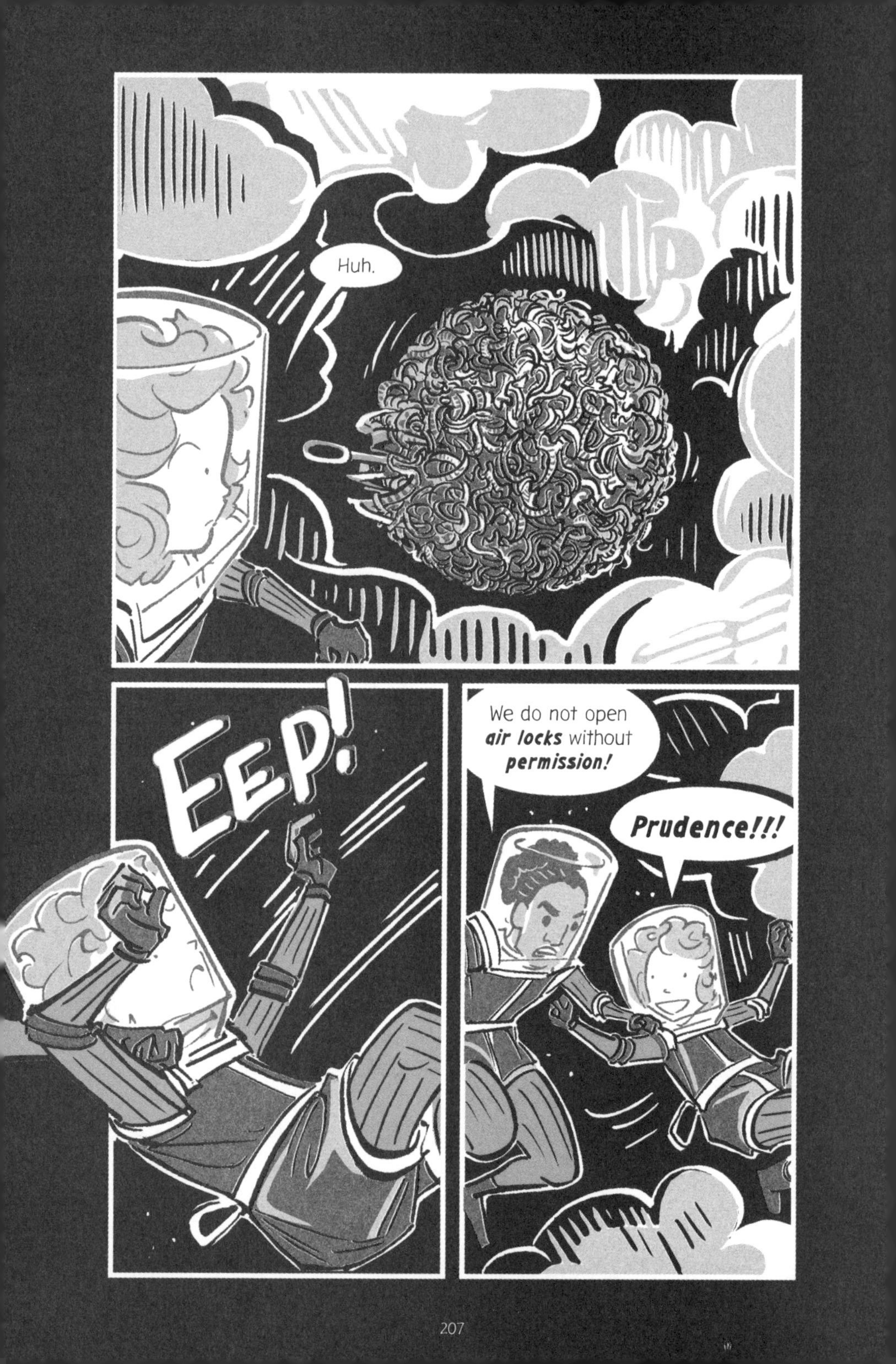
Huh.
EEP!
We do not open air locks without permission!
Prudence!!!

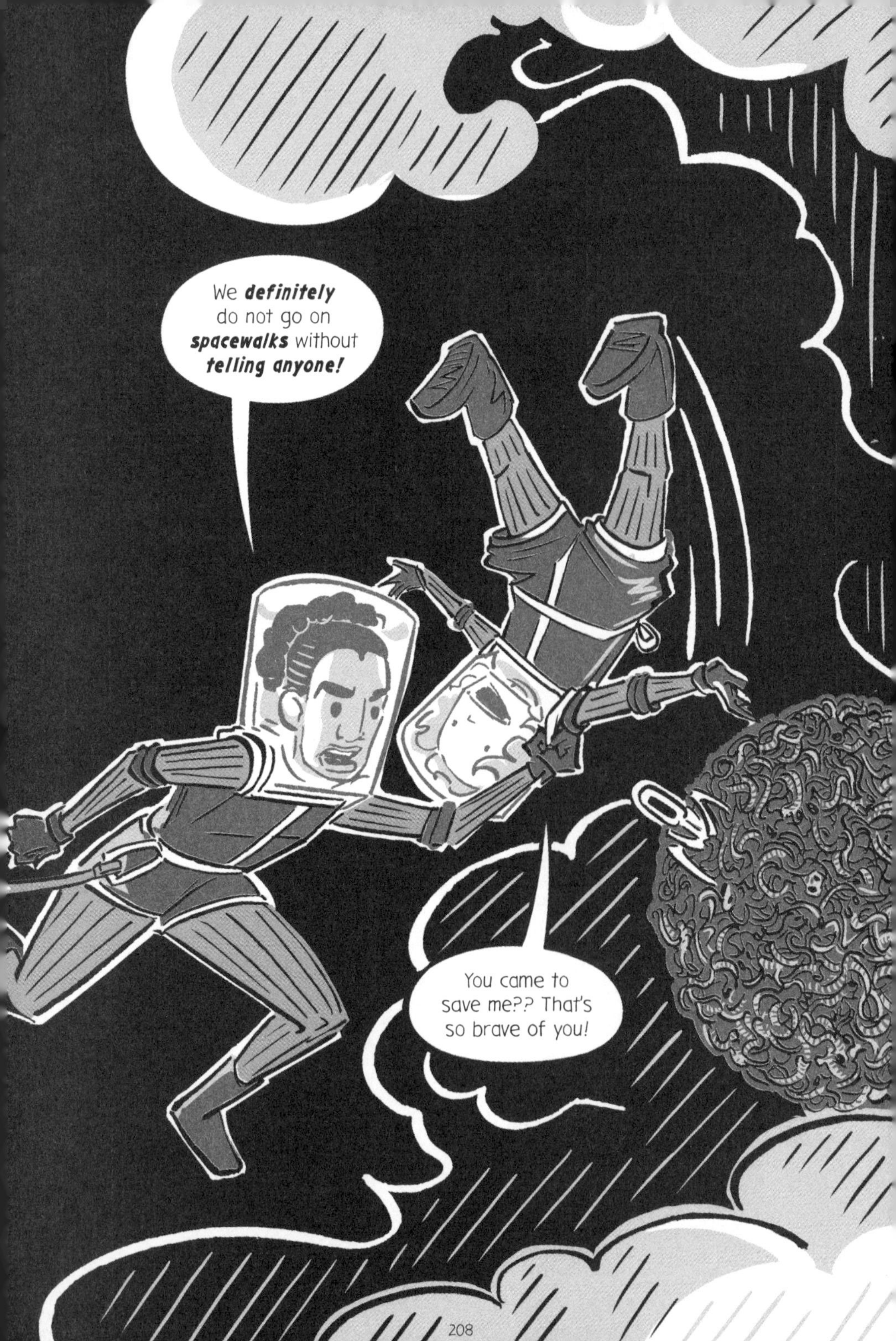
We **definitely** do not go on **spacewalks** without **telling anyone!**
You came to save me?? That's so brave of you!

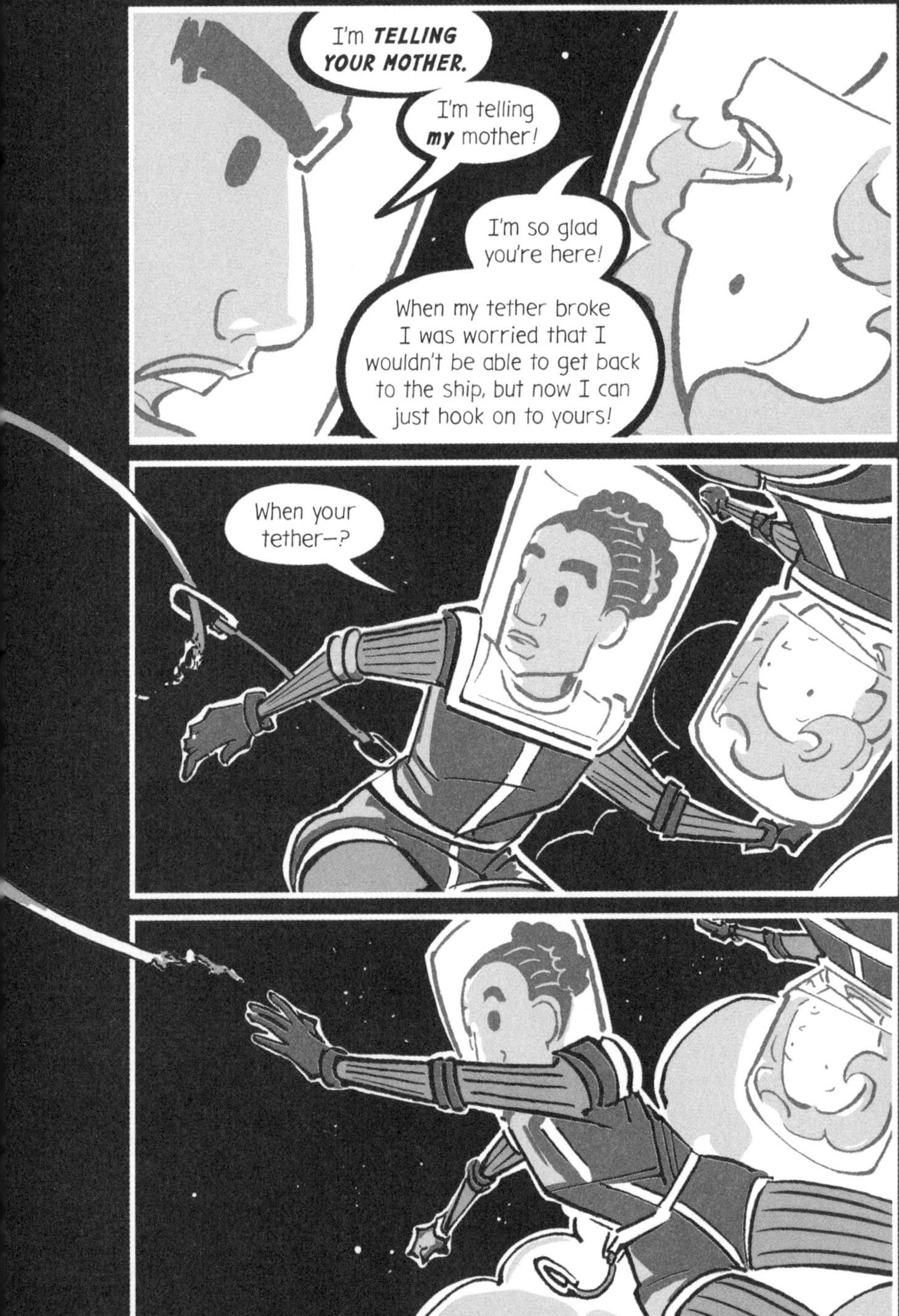
I'm **TELLING YOUR MOTHER.**
I'm telling ***my*** mother!
I'm so glad you're here!
When my tether broke I was worried that I wouldn't be able to get back to the ship, but now I can just hook on to yours!
When your tether—?

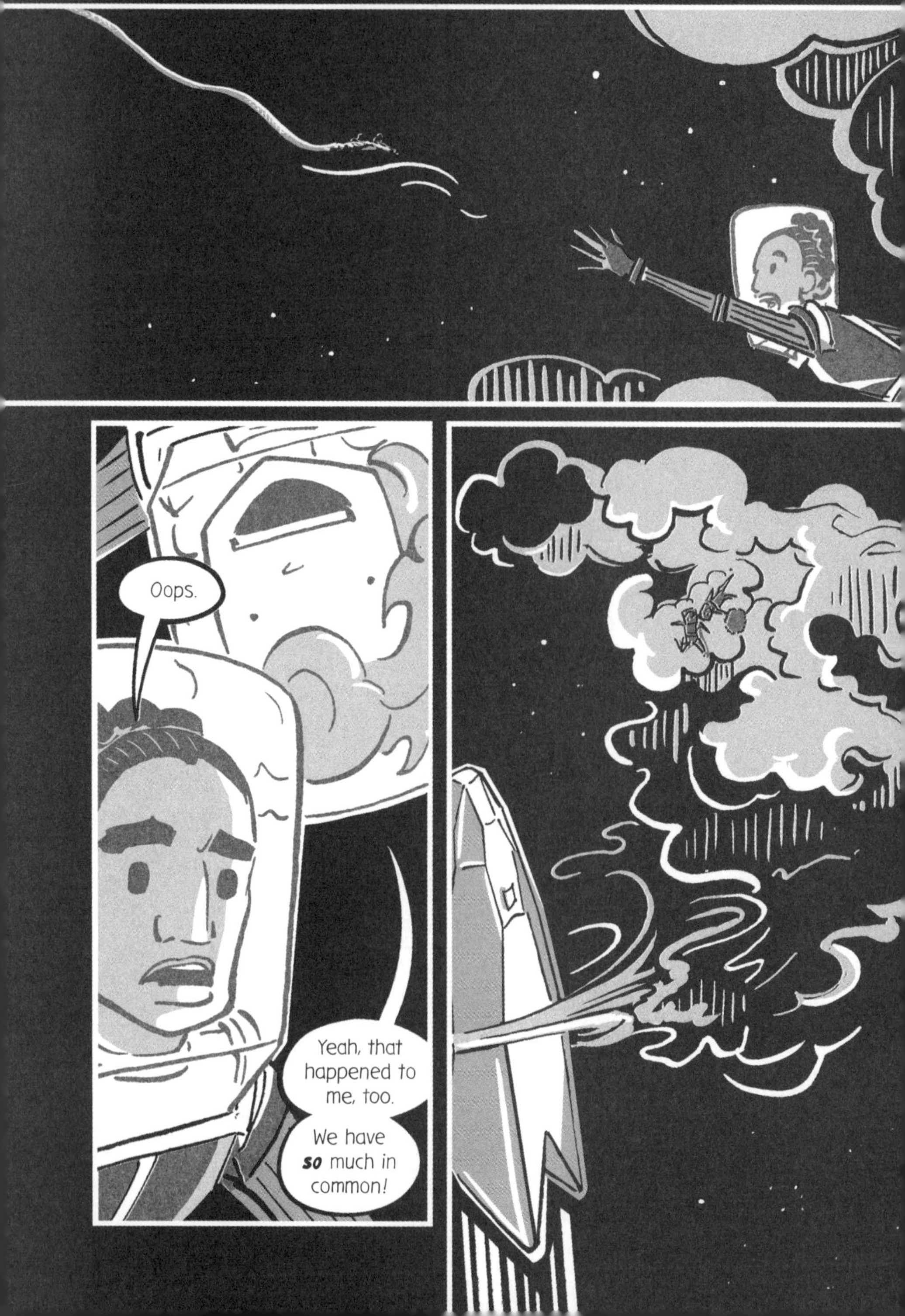
Oops.
Yeah, that happened to me, too.
We have **so** much in common!

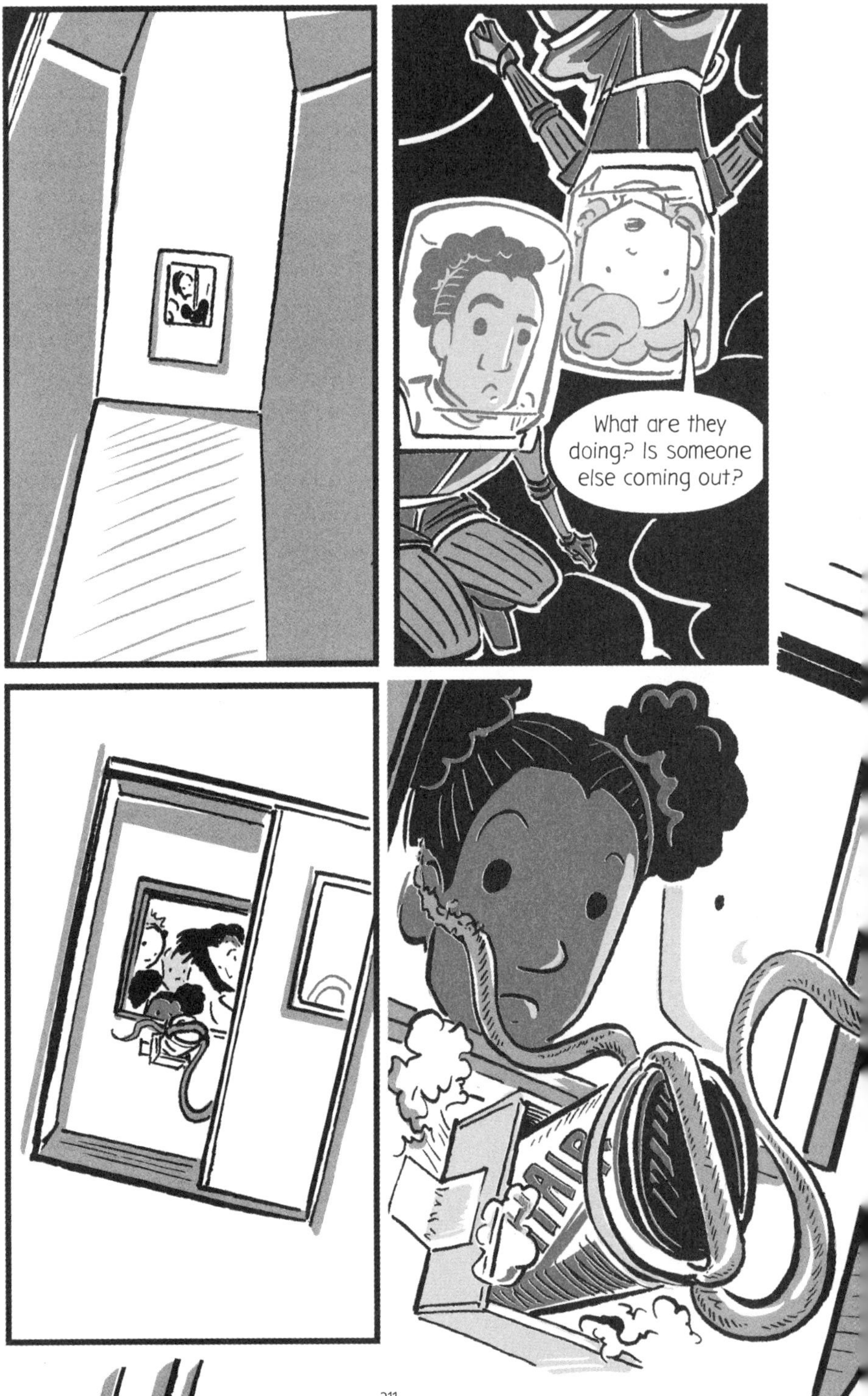
What are they doing? Is someone else coming out?

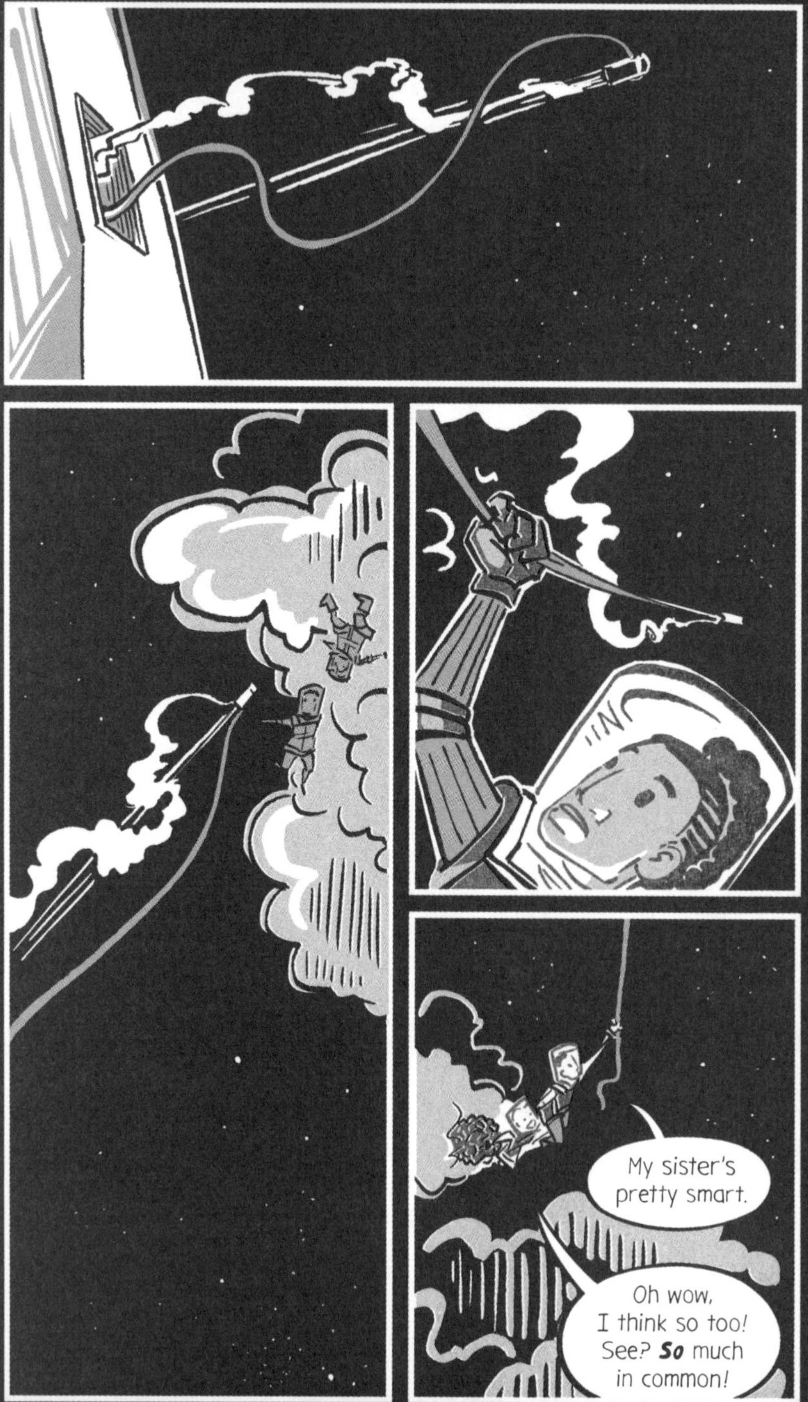
My sister's pretty smart.
Oh wow, I think so too! See? **So** much in common!

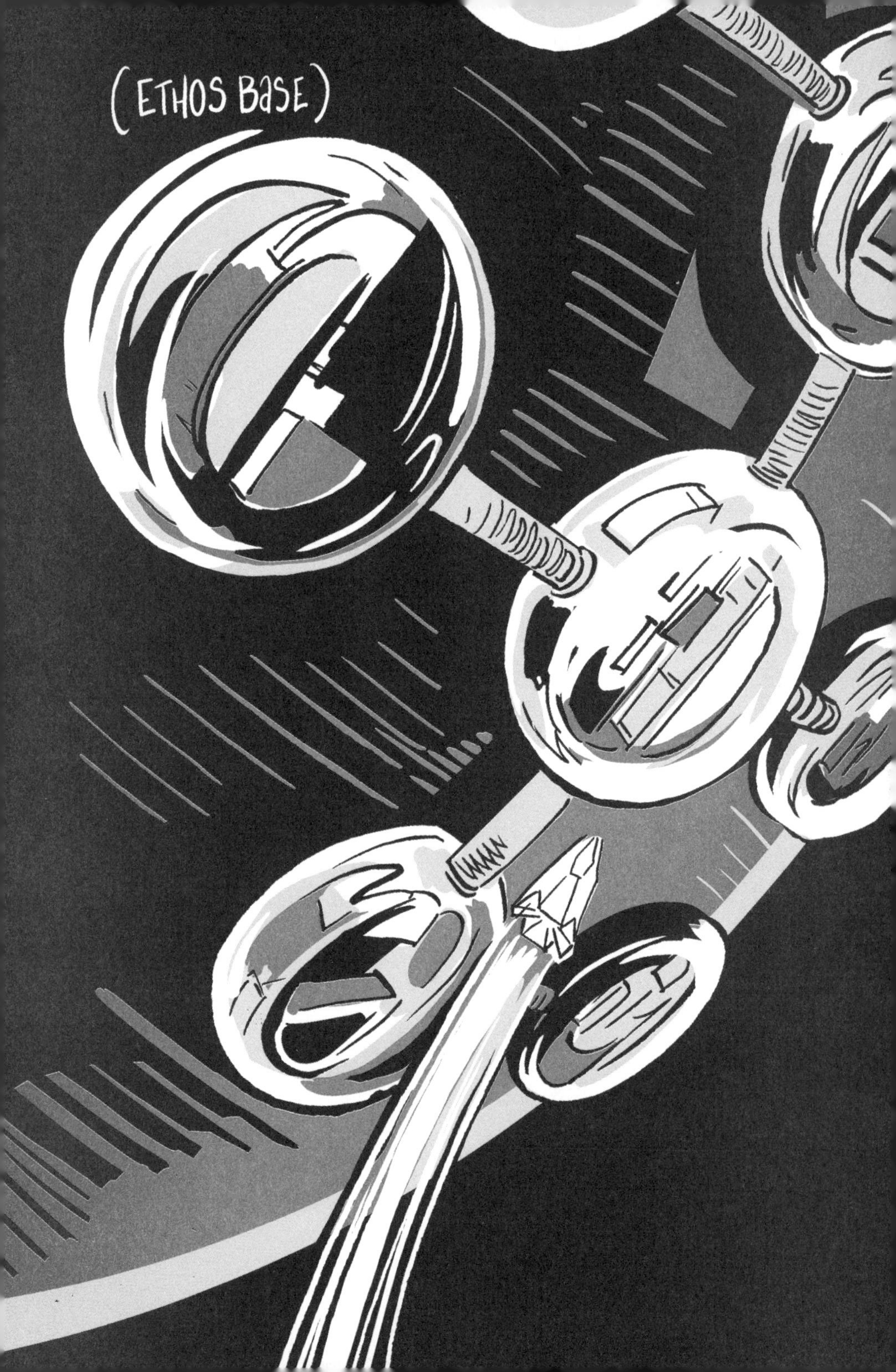
( ETHOS BASE )

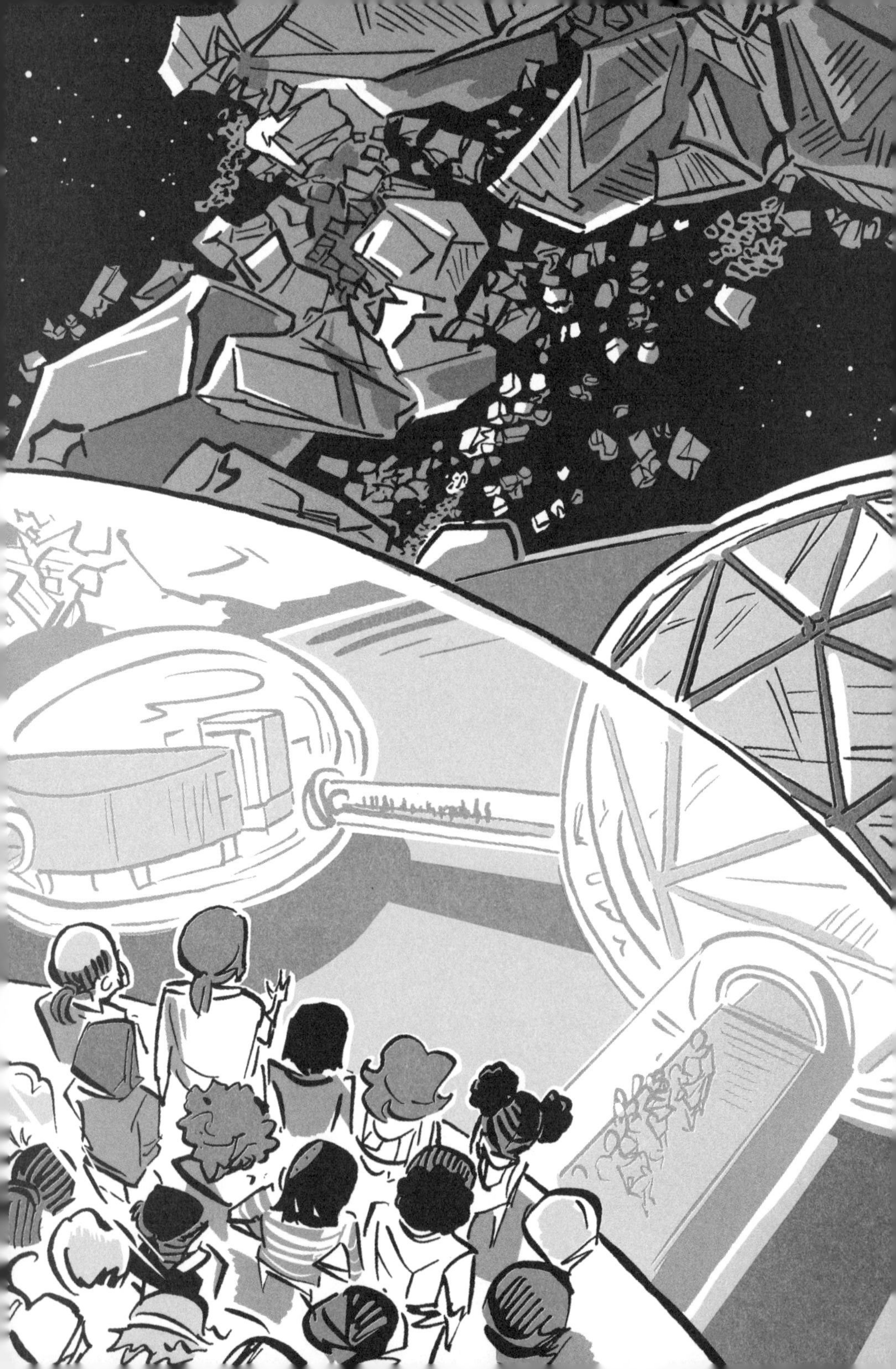

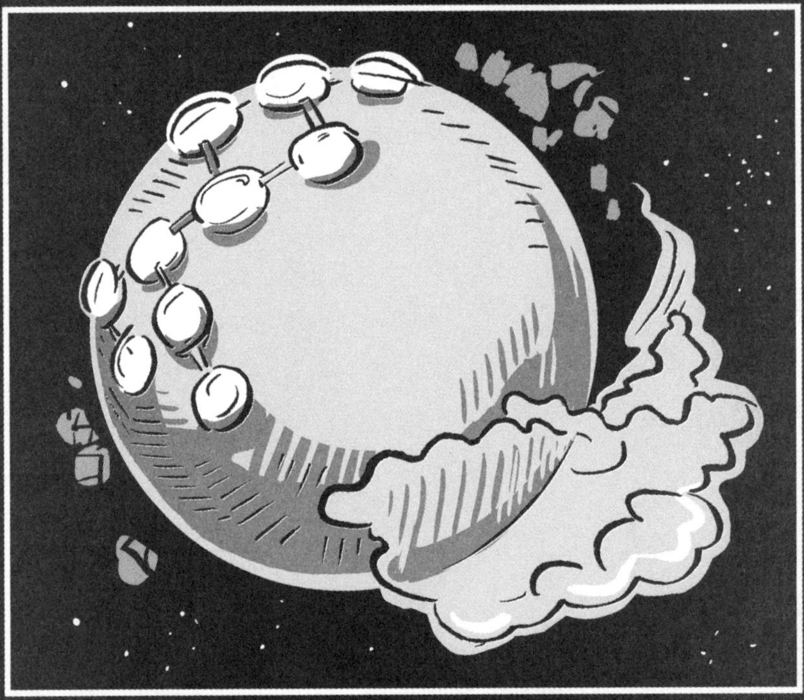
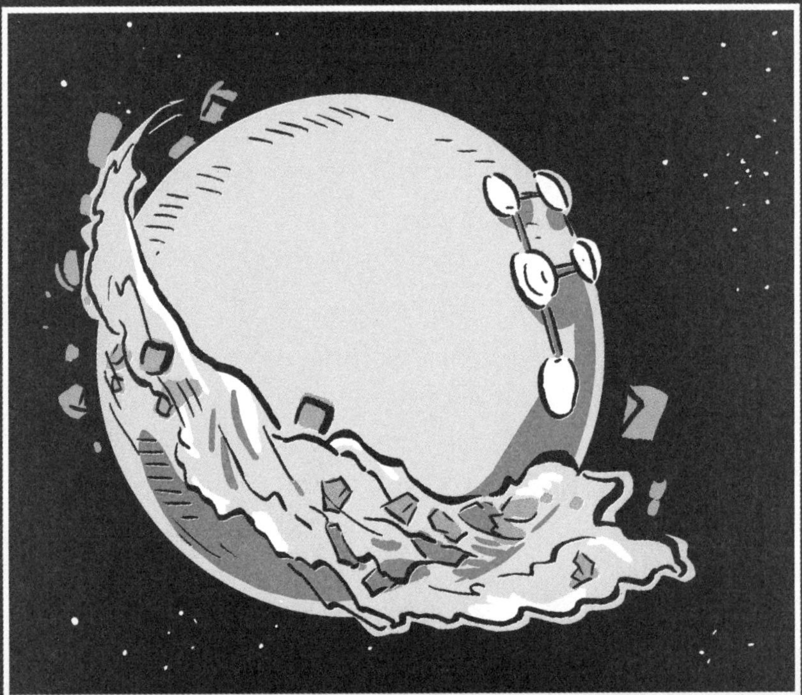

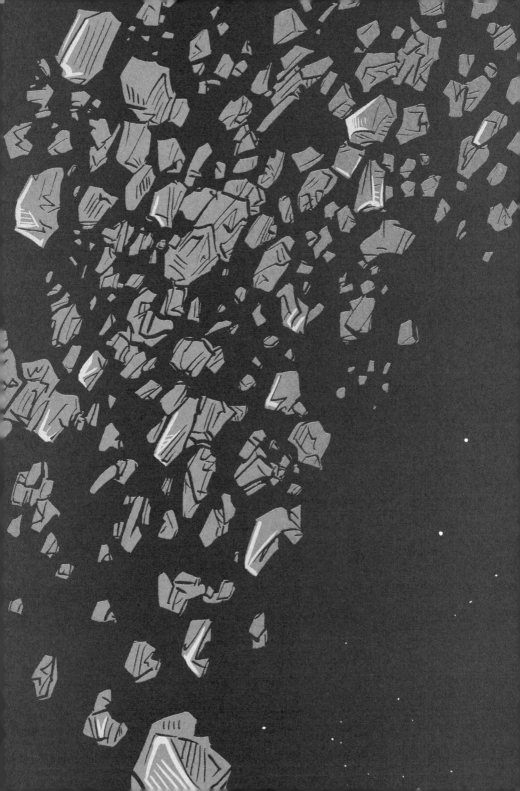

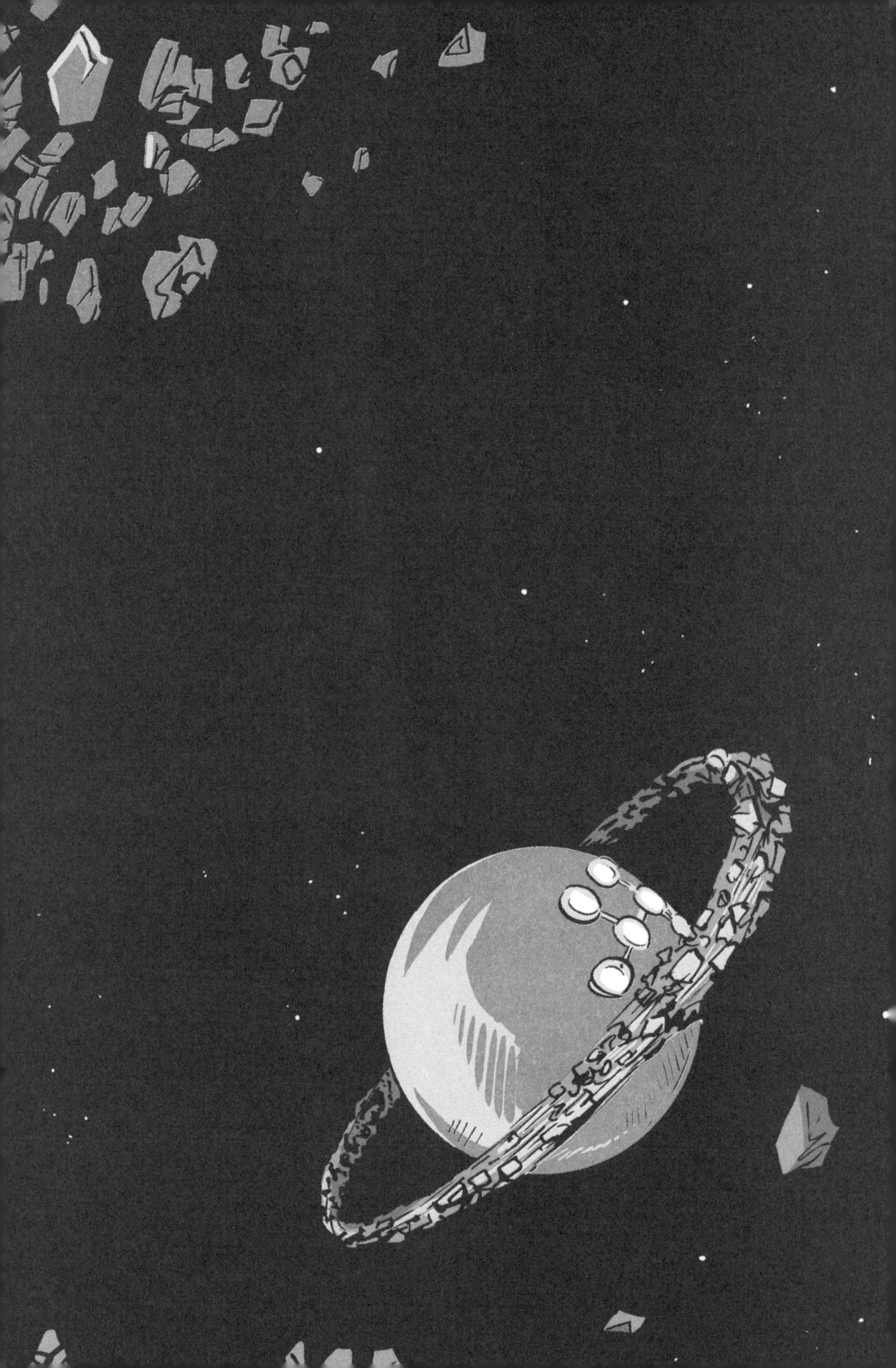

(BACK ON WILNICK)

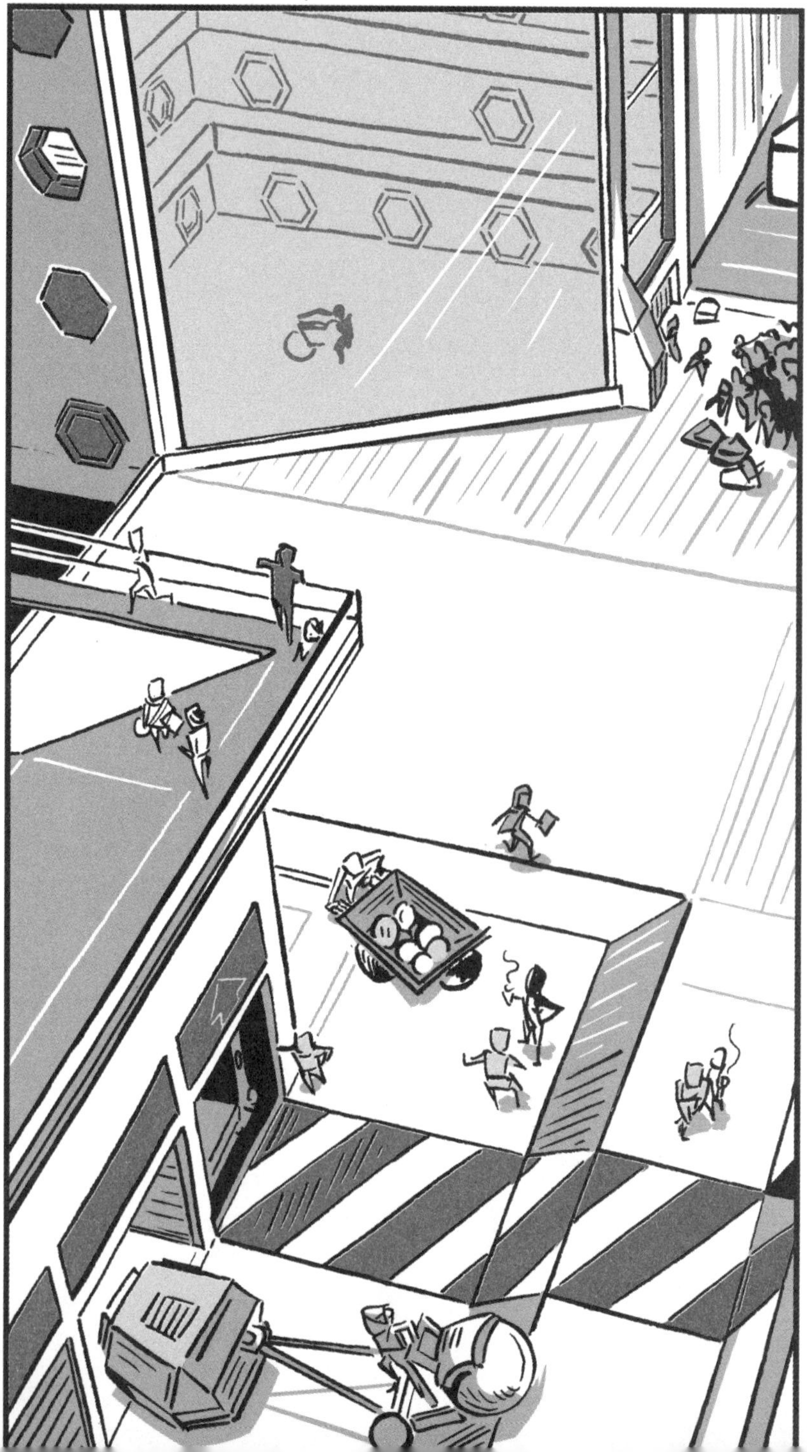

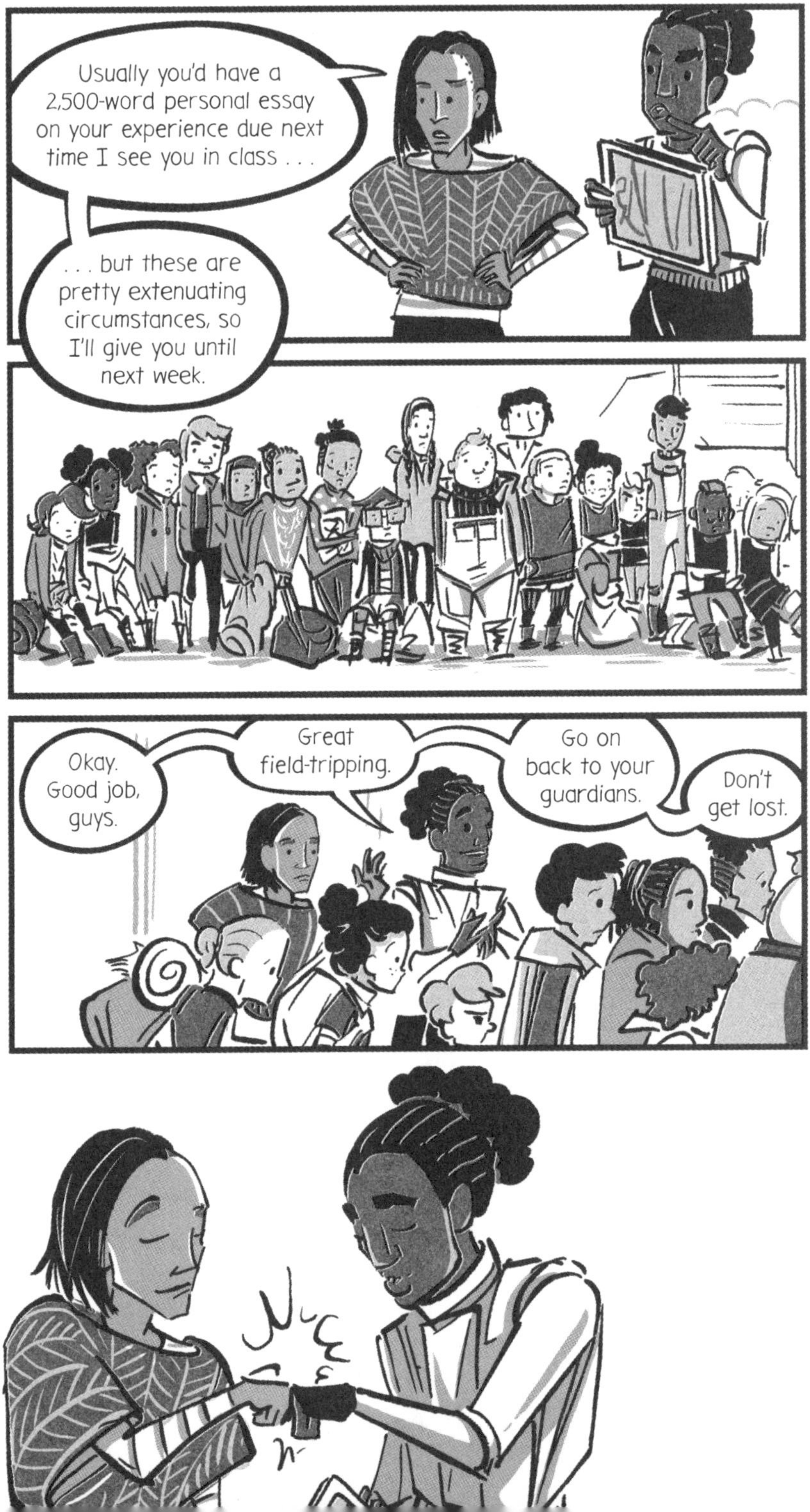
Usually you'd have a 2,500-word personal essay on your experience due next time I see you in class . . .
. . . but these are pretty extenuating circumstances, so I'll give you until next week.
Okay. Good job, guys.
Great field-tripping.
Go on back to your guardians.
Don't get lost.

(STATION ADMINISTRATION)

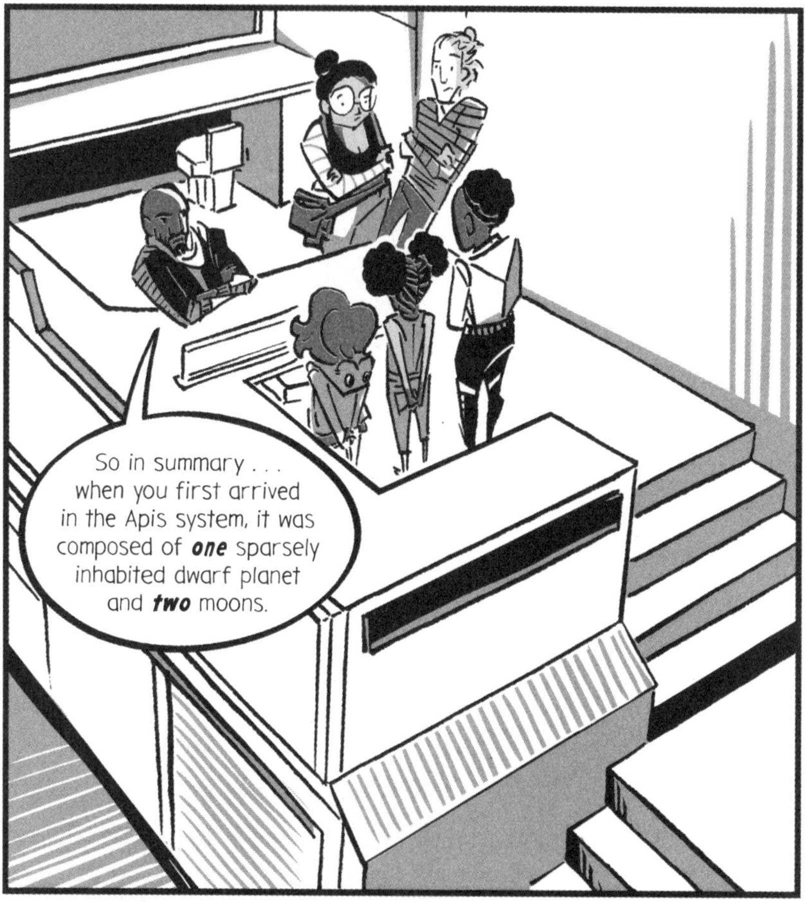
So in summary . . . when you first arrived in the Apis system, it was composed of ***one*** sparsely inhabited dwarf planet and ***two*** moons.

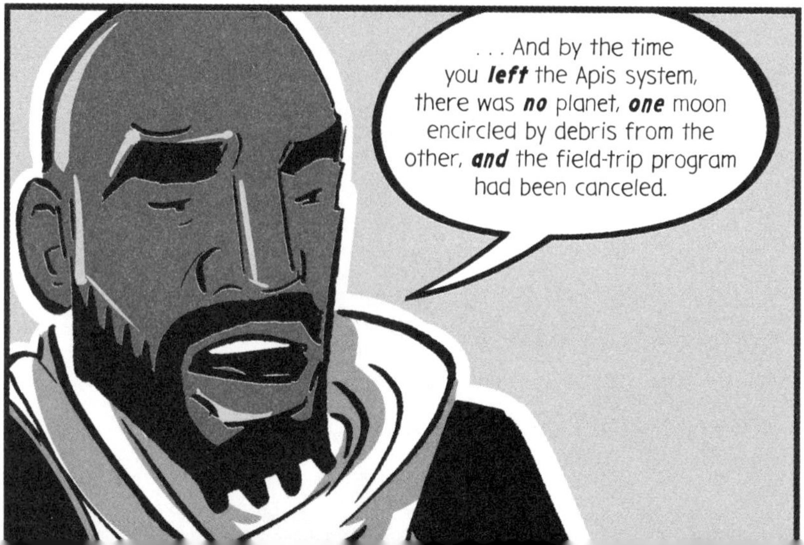
. . . And by the time you ***left*** the Apis system, there was ***no*** planet, ***one*** moon encircled by debris from the other, ***and*** the field-trip program had been canceled.

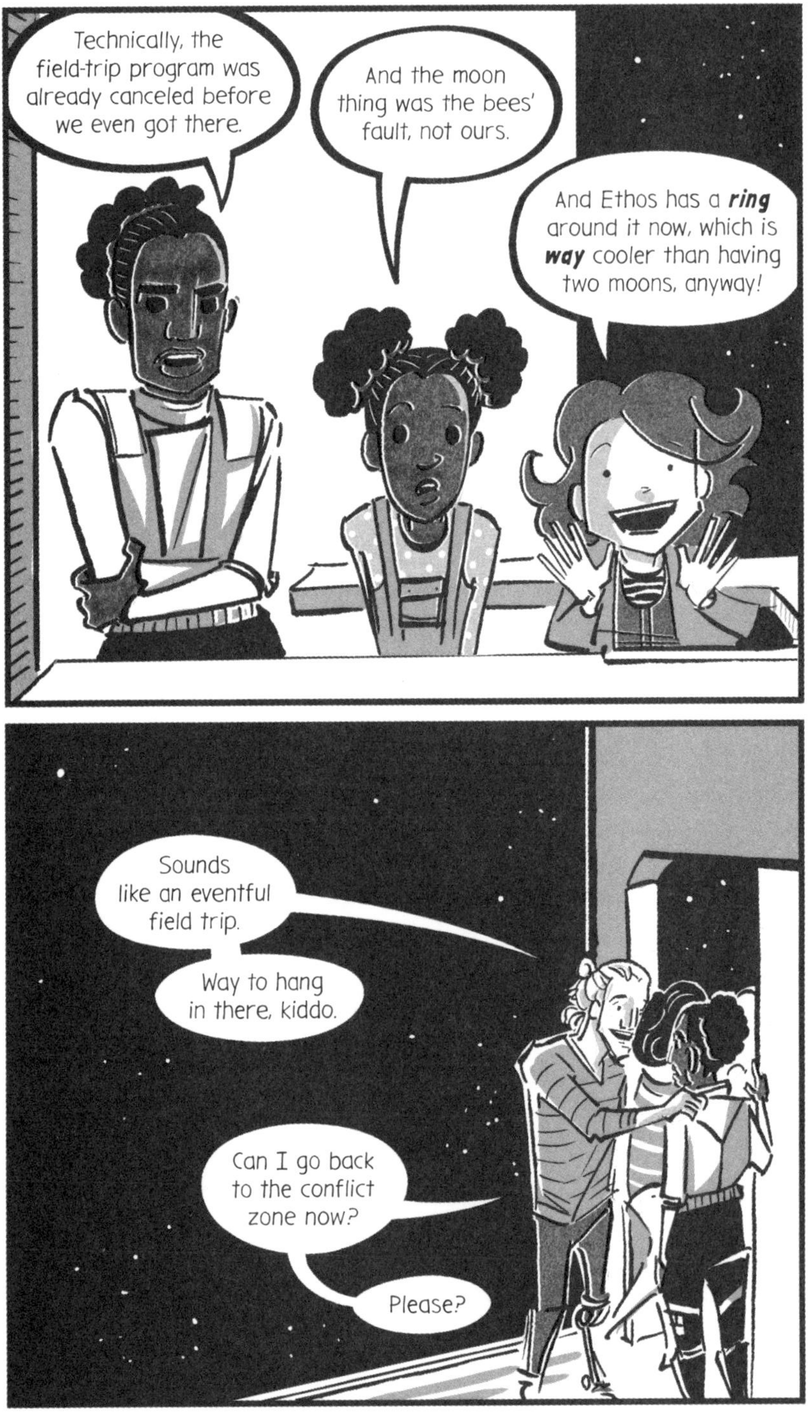
Technically, the field-trip program was already canceled before we even got there.
And the moon thing was the bees' fault, not ours.
And Ethos has a **ring** around it now, which is **way** cooler than having two moons, anyway!
Sounds like an eventful field trip.
Way to hang in there, kiddo.
Can I go back to the conflict zone now?
Please?

(VEGA-DAVISSON RESIDENCE)

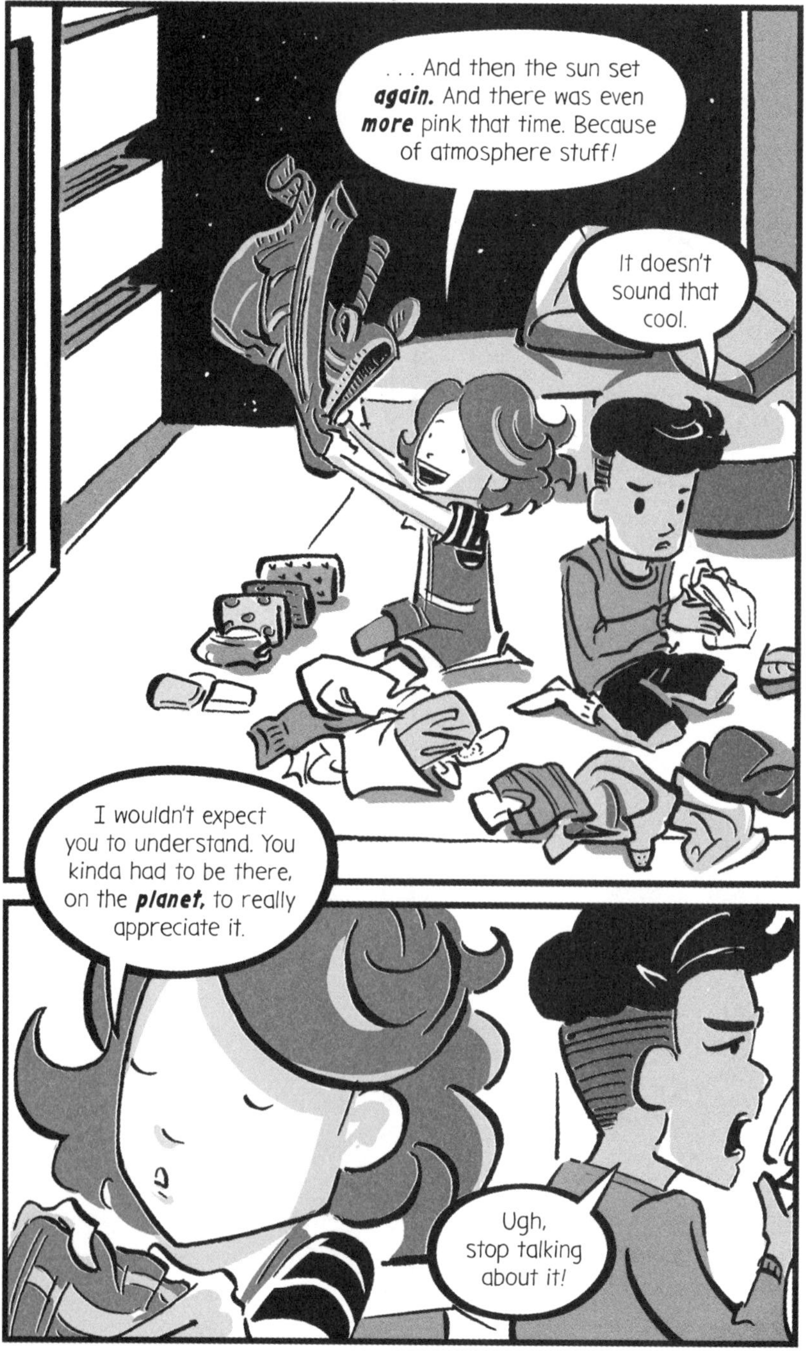
. . . And then the sun set **again.** And there was even **more** pink that time. Because of atmosphere stuff!
It doesn't sound that cool.
I wouldn't expect you to understand. You kinda had to be there, on the **planet,** to really appreciate it.
Ugh, stop talking about it!

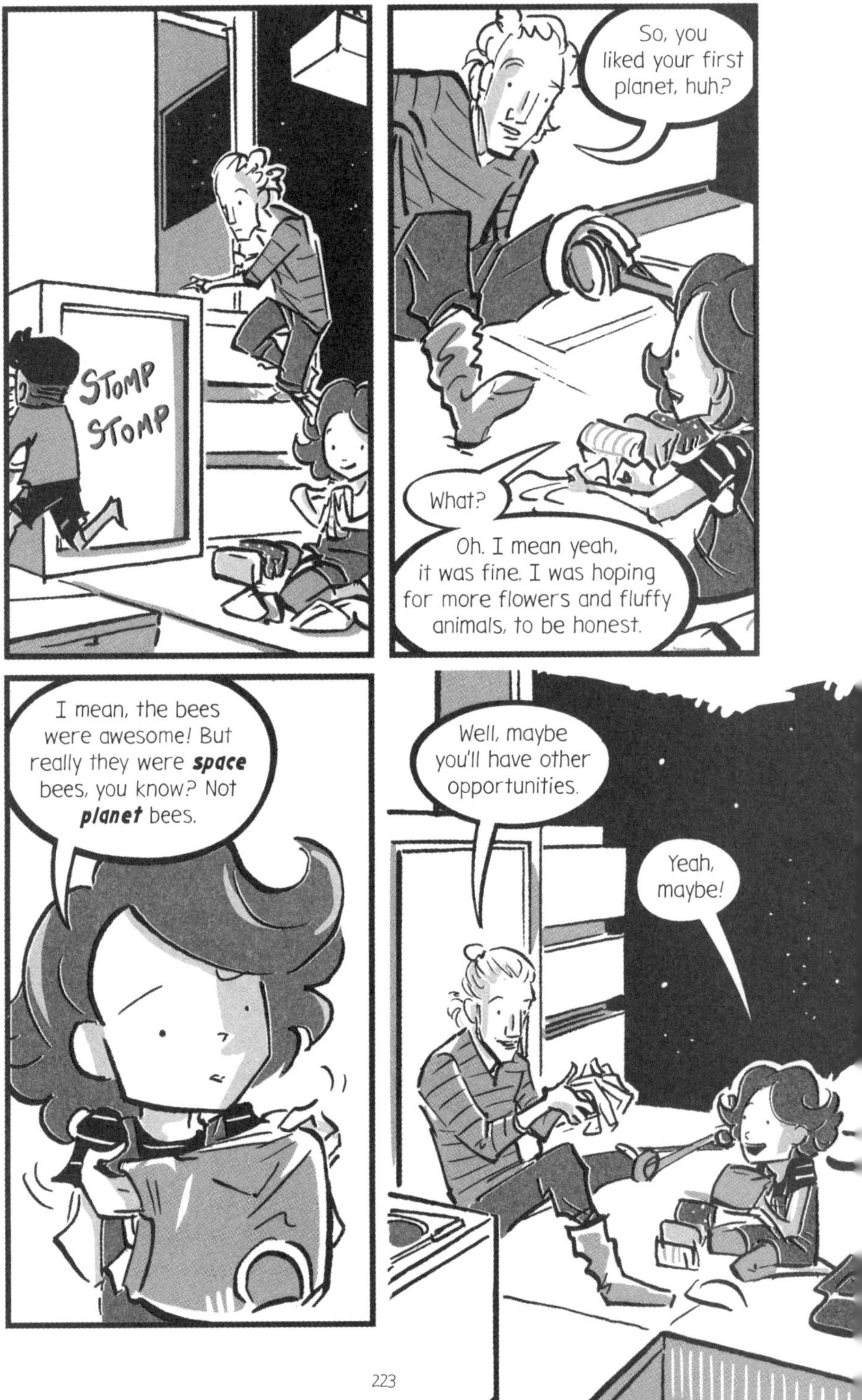
STOMP
STOMP
So, you liked your first planet, huh?
What?
Oh. I mean yeah, it was fine. I was hoping for more flowers and fluffy animals, to be honest.
I mean, the bees were awesome! But really they were **space** bees, you know? Not **planet** bees.
Well, maybe you'll have other opportunities.
Yeah, maybe!

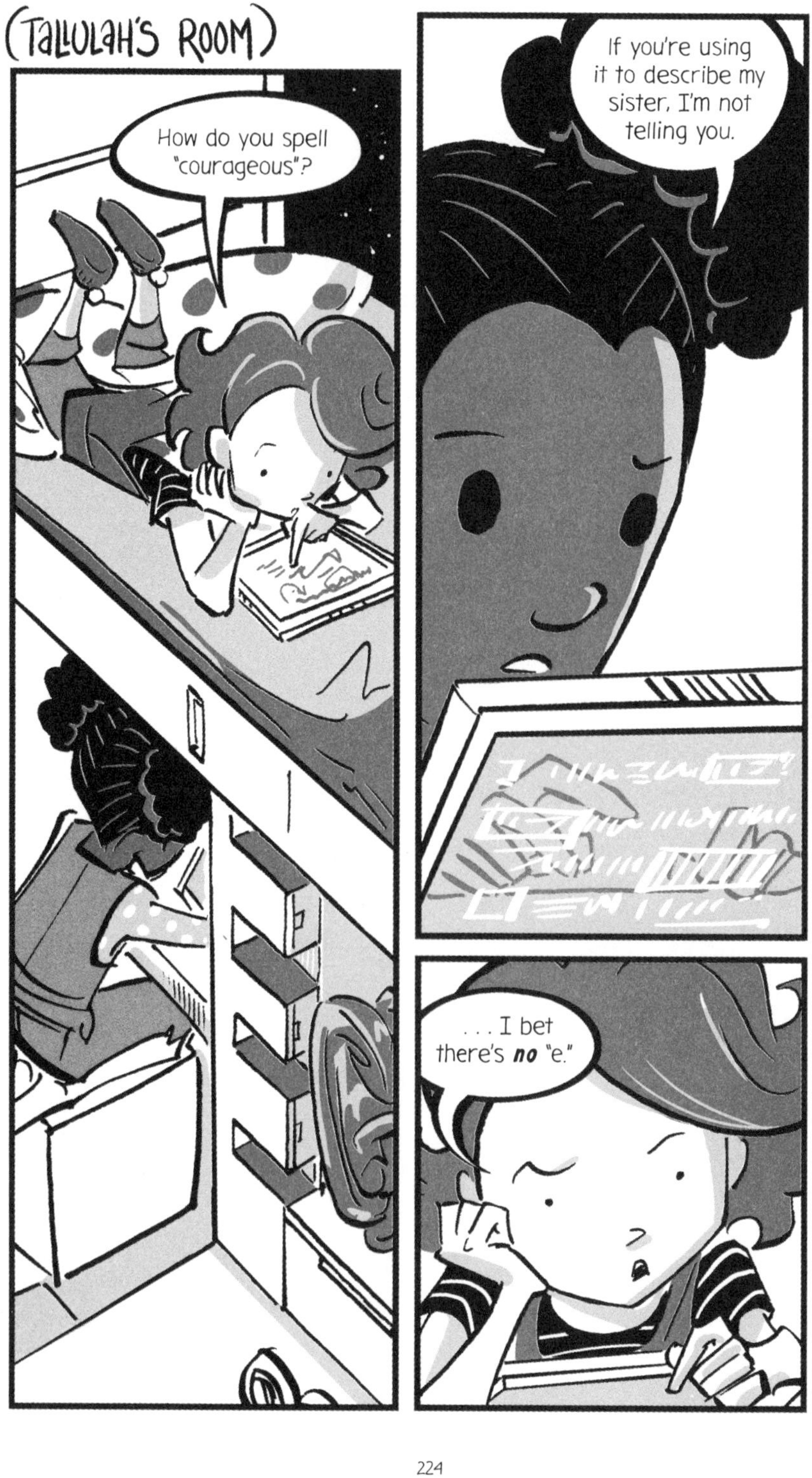
(Tallulah's Room)
How do you spell "courageous"?
If you're using it to describe my sister, I'm not telling you.
. . . I bet there's ***no*** "e."

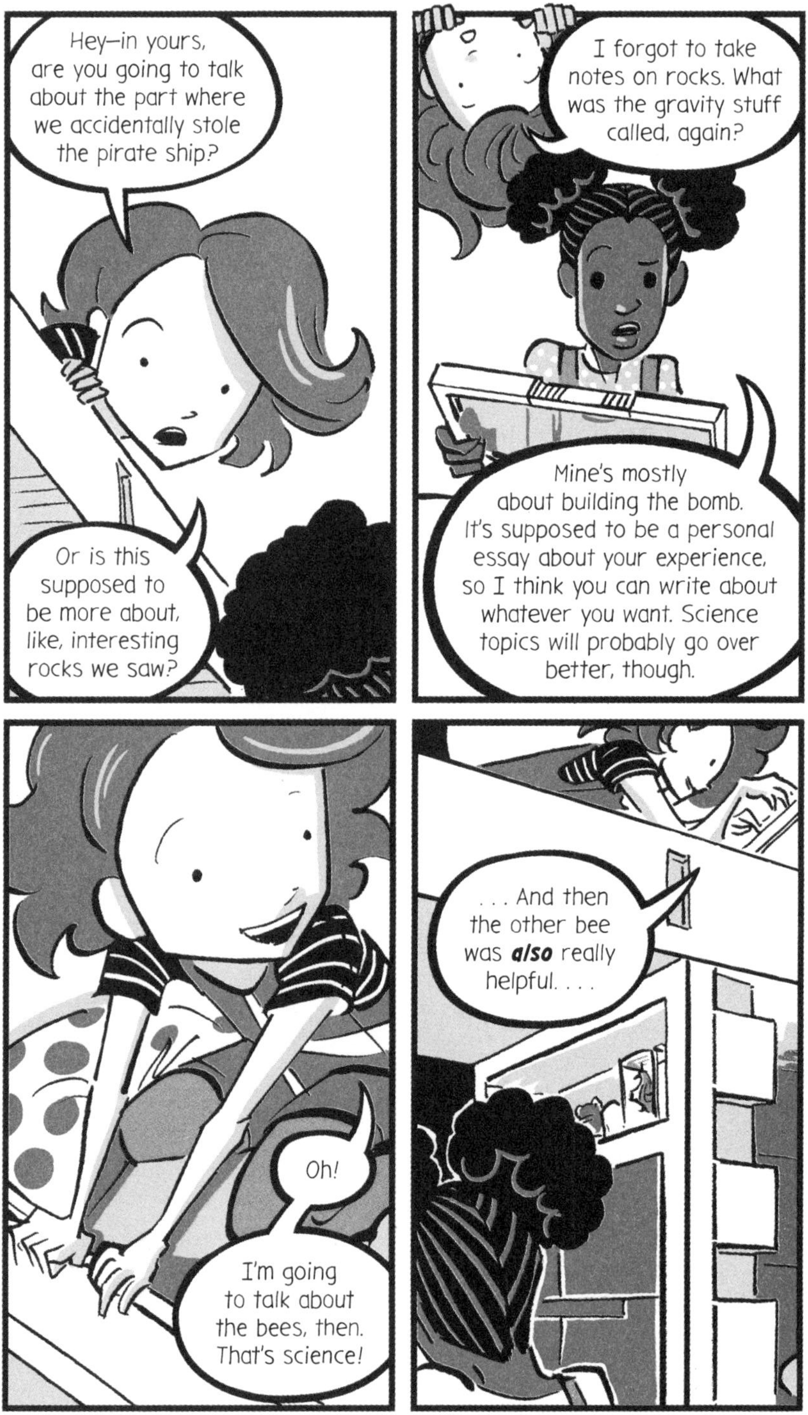
Hey—in yours, are you going to talk about the part where we accidentally stole the pirate ship?
Or is this supposed to be more about, like, interesting rocks we saw?
I forgot to take notes on rocks. What was the gravity stuff called, again?
Mine's mostly about building the bomb. It's supposed to be a personal essay about your experience, so I think you can write about whatever you want. Science topics will probably go over better, though.
Oh!
I'm going to talk about the bees, then. That's science!
. . . And then the other bee was *also* really helpful. . . .

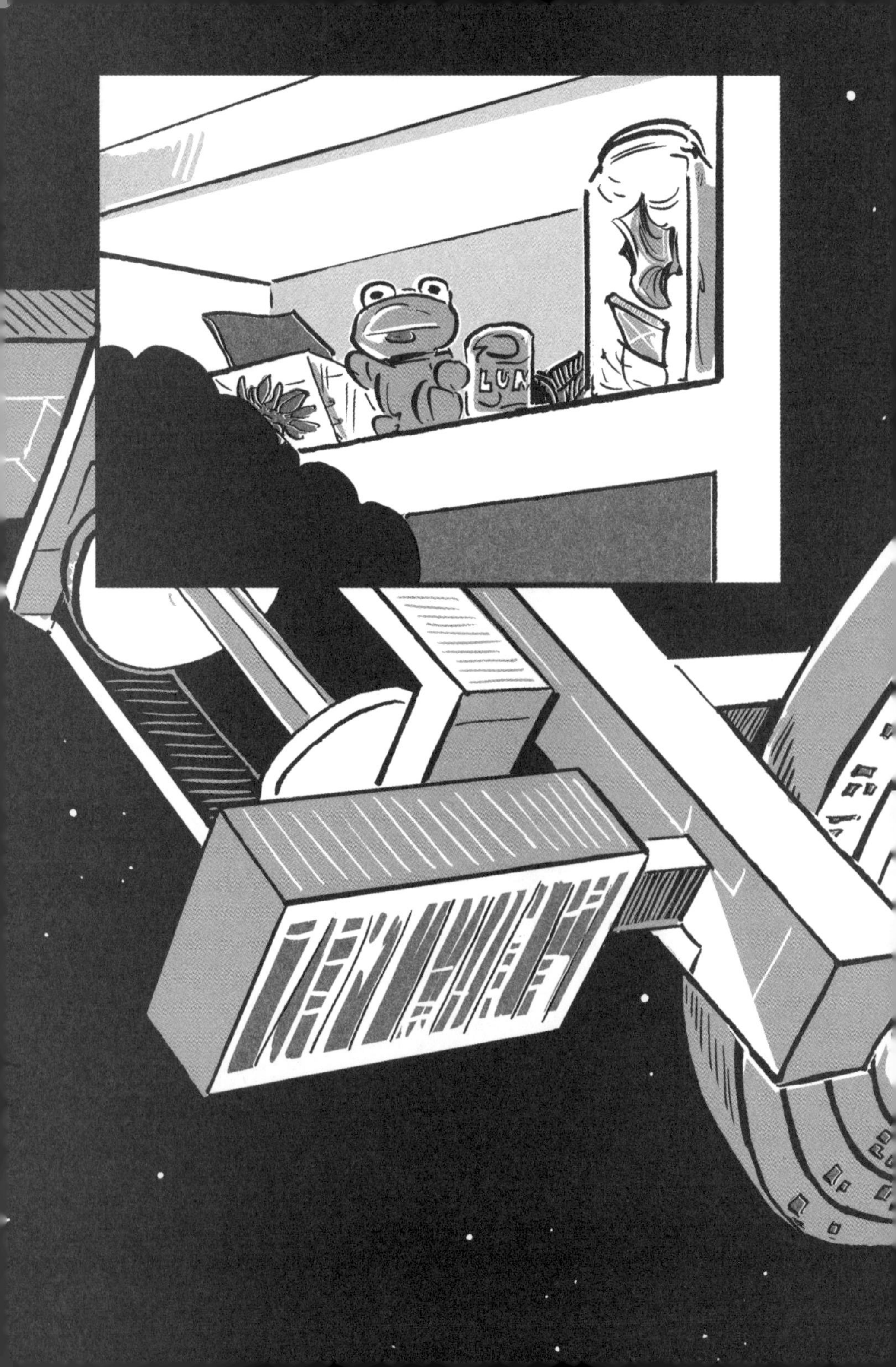

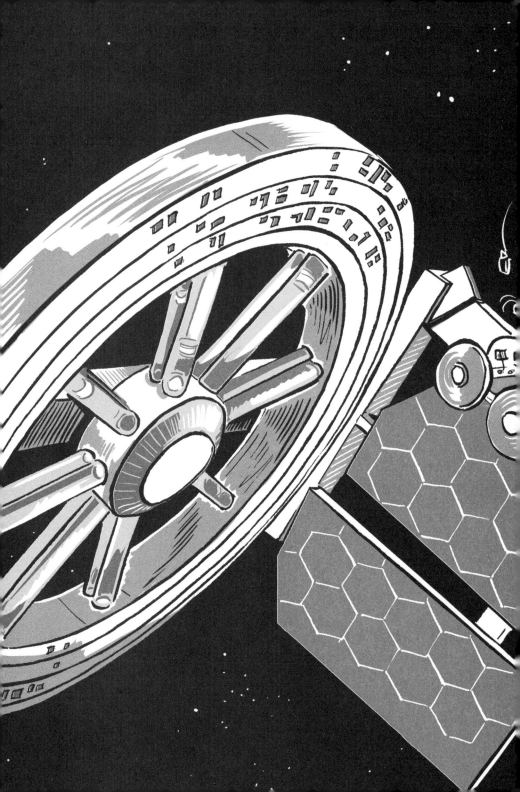

**MOLLY BROOKS** wrote and illustrated
*Sanity & Tallulah,* and is the illustrator of *Flying Machines:*
*How the Wright Brothers Soared* by Alison Wilgus, as
well as many short comics. Her work has appeared in
the *Guardian,* the *Boston Globe,* the *Nashville Scene,*
*BUST* magazine, ESPN social, *Sports Illustrated* online,
and others. Molly lives and works in Brooklyn, where she
spends her spare time watching vintage buddy-cop shows
and documenting her cats.

**mollybrooks.com**

Stay tuned for
more adventures with

# Sanity &

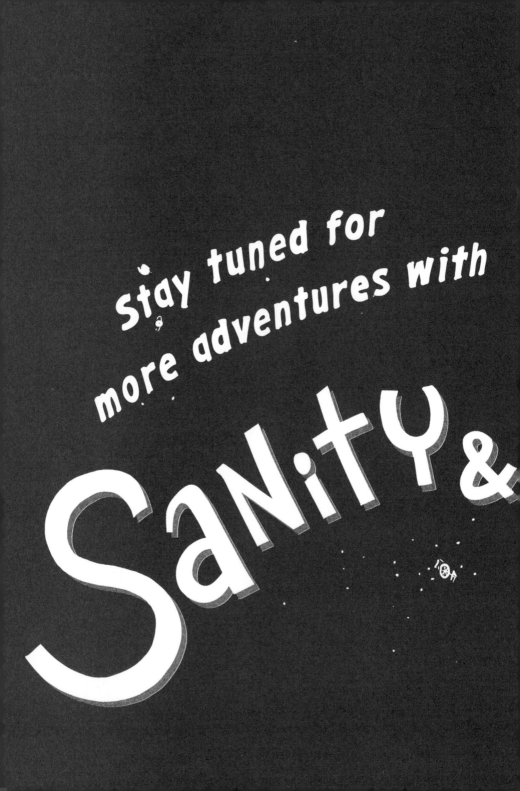

# TALLULAH

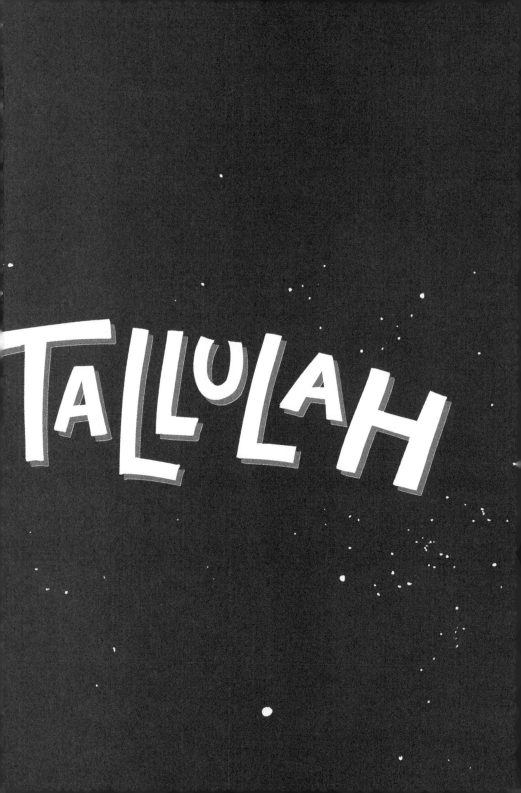

# Don't Miss

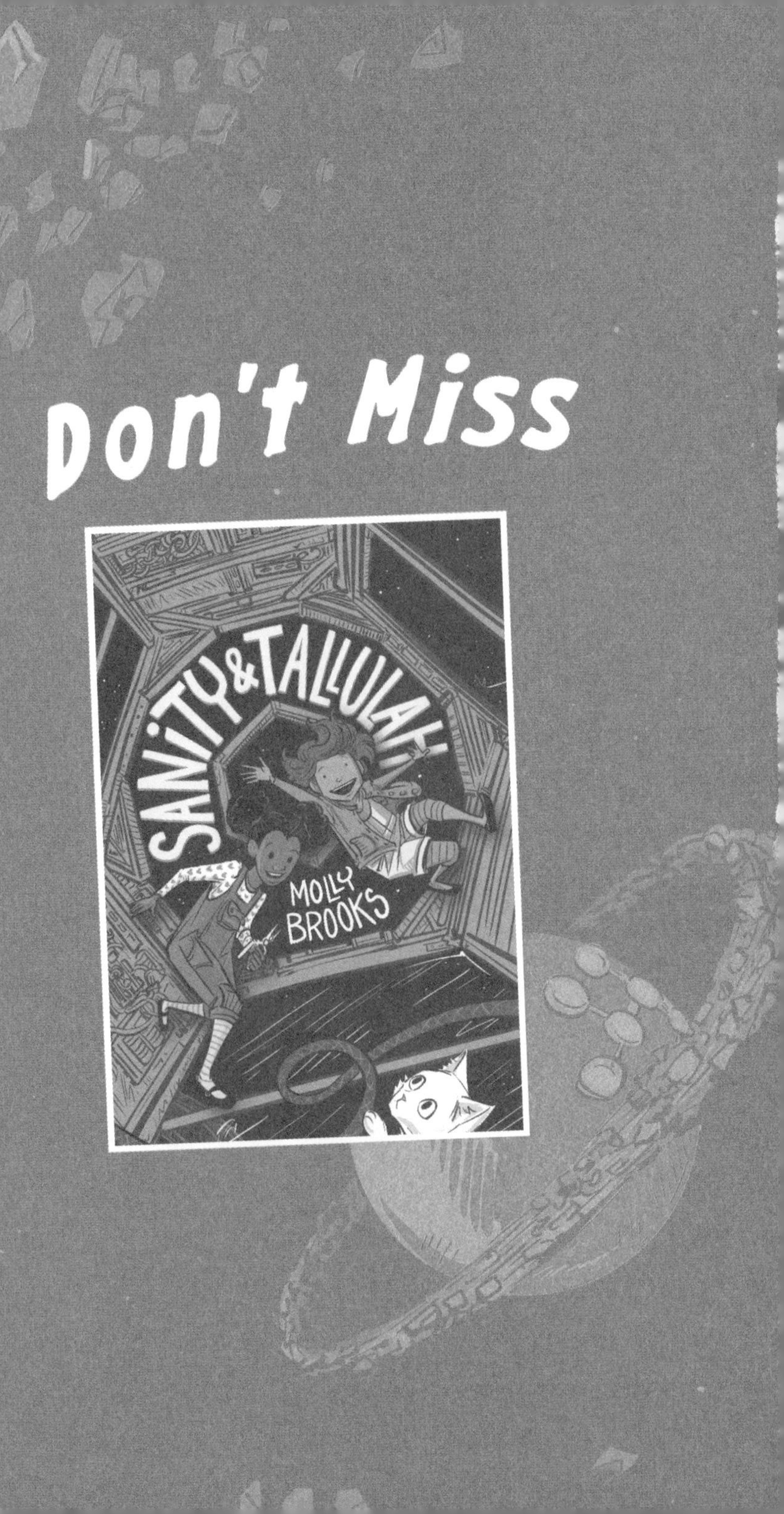
SANITY & TALLULAH
MOLLY BROOKS